T0365713

"NO WAY OUT"

"THE GAME NEVER CHANGES"

Stanley McCray

Order this book online at www.trafford.com
or email orders@trafford.com

Most Trafford titles are also available at major online book retailers.

Printed in the United States of America.

ISBN: 978-1-4120-9647-8 (sc)

Trafford rev. 07/23/2012

 www.trafford.com

North America & international
toll-free: 1 888 232 4444 (USA & Canada)
phone: 250 383 6864 ♦ fax: 812 355 4082

ACKNOWLEDGEMENTS

First and foremost I would like to give all praise to Allah (God) the most high, the creator for without Him nothing could be possible.

I would also like to thank Q. Johnson, because he was the one who inspired me to be a Writer. To my family especially my mom thanks for all the love and support, I couldn't do it without you. Shout out to my brothers, Tee, who's my biggest supporter in all aspects, and Terrell keep ya head up. To my sisters Tykisha big ups and much love for graduating from college, and Monique no matter what you know I love you. Extended family Uncle Boo, Aunt Pumpkin, Moe, Lil' John and the Daniels family much love.

I definitely have to shout out all the people who have been there for me or touched my life in some ways during this hard journey behind these prison walls. Thank you Ms. Nekeyshia Hines for everything, words cannot express all the support and love you've shown a soldier. I got mad love for ya. Kayanna Smith, we go back like car seats, I must thank you for all the support you've given me, words can't even express it, and I got much love for you. To Destiny, my daughter stay focused and I love you . . . the world ain't big enough for you. Rico, I love you and I always will no matter what. Stanley, I love you as well keep your head up. Mechelle Davis a.k.a. Ms. Mee Mee stay out them go-go's, I love you and thanks for all the help when I needed it. Asia and Tiarra, Monique Brunson, Darcia-you finally got that little girl huh, Eric and Bakasia, Sharmain Lucas much love, Tamisha Lucas love you. To Ms. "Jay" hope you enjoy motherhood tell Weezy I send my Salaams. Tiarra what's up? Myeisha "5 star" JY til we die . . . To Kyia Reynolds you know what it is.

A special shout out goes to all the soldiers in the struggle, my co-defendants, Boo-Boo and Delonte y'all know the bond is inseparable.

Keep y'all heads up and I love y'all. My partner Dario a.k.a. Young Neefy, Rodney Miles and Charlene—"NY stand up", Mike Surrell and the Surrell family, love you Dee Dee. Big Russ—Trinidad finest. Fighter Lane, Eastgate Fatts, Greg Brice, B.F. and my twin Vonn, Antone White much love homie told you I would do this, keep ya head up. Lil' Donnie (MLK), Jamal, Earl Tinker, Butch Boogie (Brooklyn's Finest), Sly, Nutty, Kenneth Lampkin (Nu-Nu) best up and coming writer. Baby Daddy, Swearl love to death stay focused out there. Moochie, Big Scrap, Shorty Parks, Wee-Wee, Marvin Sanders, Fu-lay, Whitey, Mike Lucas, Joe-Joe (Valley Green), Anthony Gardner, Mink, Lawrence "L" 15th Pl., Ed Pooh, Big "O", and Murdock. Joe Bugg and Big Terry, Gee Gee, Killah Red, scared ass Tee, these are my Florida partners. L.D.P., Barry Farms, Linda Pollin, Trinidad, K.G. I ain't forgot you, I know you up Terre Haute. S.E., S.W., N.E. and N.W., DC much love. Allenwood Penitentiary, Atwater, Big Sandy, and all the other spots where they holding all the soldiers at, shout out to all y'all. Remember y'all the struggle never ends. If I forgot anyone please forgive me it was not intentional, I've been under so much pressure to get this book finished that I may have forgotten a few people.

CHAPTER 1

"Come on Mike Mike, pay attention cause when those niggas come out I'm a smash all them suckers right there." Lil' G instructed from the passengers' seat while gripping the handle of his 9mm colt. "Them suckers fucked with the wrong mother fuckers this time."

"G, man I think them niggas seen us ride pass that's why they ain't come out the building yet!" Speedy replied as he watched from the back seat of the Grand Marquis they were sitting in.

"Shut your scared ass up Speedy." Black whispered as everybody bust out laughing. Speedy was always the cautious one out of the crew. Everything they did or got into, Speedy had some type of reservations about it. However, tonight was not the time to be half stepping. The Stronghold Youngin's were getting some get back at some cats from First St. for an accidental shooting of Tykisha.

Tykisha was Lil' G's girlfriend, but also the sister of Stanley and Tee. Stanley and Tee were the ones who basically raised Lil' G, taught him everything that he knew about life as well as the streets. Tee was even the one who introduced G to the hustling game not more than a year ago. Lil' G's mom, Ms. Debra was the typical single mother in the hood. She survived with Section 8, struggled to keep any kind of job, and more importantly, was addicted to that deadly thing called "Crack". She had this addiction for as long as G was old enough to understand what was going on. The one thing G didn't know was that she had been addicted to crack long before she had him and his little brother. As a matter of fact, her addiction had gotten so bad at one point that it even

1

caused Ms. Debra to lose G's little brother Kenny to the system. Today, Kenny is living with foster parents who are raising him until he turns 18, or until the courts felt like Ms. Debra was stable enough to get him back. Although, at this point it seemed like Kenny turning 18 would come first. G's dad Big Gino was down Lorton doing a 15 to 45 year bid for Armed Robbery and several weapon offenses. So he had been non-existent in G's life. All the while, G was being raised in the very same streets and neighborhood that had caused Big Gino to be doing his bid right now.

Lil' G resented his mother for losing Kenny and never ever forgave her for it. G on numerous occasions tried to get his mom to stop getting high so she could get Kenny back. Ms. Debra would do well for a minute, but before long she'd revert back to her old ways. G hated her for that, and that was one of the reasons he hung out with Tee and Stanley so much. He idolized and looked up to them like father figures, and they loved and cared for G like family. G would hang around them so much that he eventually would start to live with them in different spots. While living with them, G fell in love with their little sister Tykisha.

G was Tykisha's first real boyfriend, and she was head over heels in love with him. Puppy love I guess is what you would call it. Well whatever it was G loved Tykisha tremendously. As G progressed in the street game and started getting a little money he spoiled Tykisha buying her any and everything she wanted just as her brothers did. He was buying her so much shit that Stanley had to question G about where he was getting all this money from. G at the time revealed that not only was he hustling the coke that Tee was giving him, but also he was involved in Auto theft, boosting, robbing, and everything else under the sun. Upon hearing the information Tee and Stanley told G that he needed to slow down because he was moving too fast for a 15 year old. But after the talk, things only seemed to get worse. Until finally Tee sat G down one day and told G, "Look if you want to continue messing with our little sister you've got to slow down, and stop all that shit that you're involved in cause if something happens to Tykisha behind your mess, ain't nothing you can say to us." G understood what they were saying and calmed down for a minute, but before long he was at it again.

2

CHAPTER 2

Now G and Mike Mike had been friends since they were kids. Mike Mike lived next door and both their mothers were what we call "crack heads"! On many a night Ms. Debra and Mike Mike's mother Kathy would sit down stairs in the basement with the doors locked leaving Mike Mike and G upstairs to basically govern themselves. Over time they grew extremely close, and did everything together. If one got into trouble, the other did too. The first time they started getting into trouble together they almost got caught stealing out of the Safeway on 4th and Rhode Island Avenue. This one particular day they went inside trying to steal some meats to sell off to the hustlers in the neighborhood for a few dollars, which back then at the age of 8 and 9 years old was cool. G went inside and told Mike Mike to watch his back and let him know if at any time the security guards were headed in his direction, Mike Mike agreed. G headed to the meat section in the Safeway grabbing 4 to 5 packs of steaks and packs of chicken stuffing them inside his pants. G's little 85 pound frame now looked like he weighed 125 pounds. Needless to say G got greedy and tried to get more than his pants could hold. All the while a Good Samaritan had gotten whiff of what was going on and alerted the security guard. As the security guard approached, Mike Mike whistled to alert G, but it was too late the security guard was up on him, "Aye you! Aye you! Stop right there!" The security guard yelled rushing to grab G. G panicked and tried to place the meats back in the freezer, but it was too late. The security guard grabbed G, frisked him removing the rest of the meats from his pants. "I got you now!" the guard yelled. "Now come on here, I'm taking you in the back and call the authorities on your bad ass!"

Upon seeing what was happening, Mike Mike felt bad that G had gotten caught. Figuring if he had spotted the guard earlier G wouldn't have gotten caught so it was his entire fault, he had to figure a way to get G free. Mike Mike thought quickly grabbing an empty shopping cart and dashing to the end of the next aisle. Now at the end of the aisle Mike Mike could hear the security guard and G about to turn the corner from the aisle over. Soon as Mike Mike saw the security guard and G turn the corner he took off with the cart ramming it hard into the security guards knee full speed.

"Aaaaaaaaaaaa!!" the security guard squealed, releasing G, falling to the ground grabbing his knee.

Mike Mike looked at G, "Come on G!" He yelled as they both took off dashing out the Safeway running full speed all the way to Edgewood playground at the top of the hill.

"Thanks Mike Mike." G sighed trying to catch his breath giving Mike Mike some dap. "Man my mom would have whipped my ass if she would have found out I was stealing."

"Yeah, and I would've gotten a whipping too cause my mom know I had to be with you. Shit . . . I would have been getting a whipping for nothing." Mike Mike explained.

"Yeah, you right about that my nigga," as they hugged each other. "Let's get on home before them peoples come looking for us."

"Fo' sho'!" Mike Mike shook his head. "G you know what? We're like brothers it seems like don't it?" "We are, one for all, and all for one." G stated as they shook hands and rolled out heading back around Stronghold before their parents got suspicious.

That was the first of many things those two would get into together. Their friendship was signed and sealed.

Now how they met Speedy and Black was a story of a different color, at Langley Jr. High School Black and Speedy were jive like the shit up there. They ran with the V St. crew and terrorized all other crews that got in their way. Sometime during their 7th grade year Black developed a crush on Tykisha. On several occasions Black tried to holla at Tykisha, but was turned down on the account that she was in love with G. Black hated to be rejected and kept his pursuit up. One day G came up Langley to surprise Tykisha and walk her home from school. As she exited the building and spotted G, her face lit up with excitement and happiness. G hugged Tykisha and they all began to walk down T Street heading home, until they bumped into Black and Speedy walking up T Street. As they approached each other about to cross paths, Black stepped in front of Tykisha, "Hi, what's up Tykisha?", Black says while staring at G.

G turned to Tykisha, who had a stunned look on her face. "Black, I told you before leave me alone I have a boyfriend!" she yelled grabbing G's hand trying to hold him back.

"Now step off nigga, you heard what she said!" G emphasized while grittin' on Black.

G stepped around Tykisha trying to get to Black, "Who you talking to sucker boy? Come on out here if you want some work!" As Black and G stepped out in the street, while a crowd started to assemble around.

"So what you going do punk?" Black replied.

G laughed, and then snatched away from Tykisha charging Black knocking him back into a Ford Taurus that was parked at the curb. They went at it, while Speedy and Mike Mike mixed it up on the sidewalk. Both sides got good licks in, but neither crew would give an inch. When it was all said and done they were all taken to Juvenile Detention Hall for fighting.

At the Detention Center they were all fresh meat until their parents came to get them. Upon their arrival and being placed in the same housing unit Black was approached by some S.E. guys who tried to jump him. At that very moment Black, Speedy, G nor Mike Mike cared about what had happened between them all earlier they stuck together that night and put a whipping on some dudes from S.E.

From that time on a new respect was bought about between the 4 of them, who later became the best of friends forming their own little crew called the Young Guns. Together they ran through all the little crews growing up in that NE/NW area. Slowly but surely they started to getting into the streets deeper and deeper. Then one day Tee decided that he'd take a chance and let G hustle for him instead of having him sneak and do it for another nigga who would probably beat G anyway. G and his crew flourished in the crack game, making more money than any of them had ever seen in their lives, but with the drug game also comes war.

G and the Young Guns started to get into all kinds of little beefs throughout N.E. and N.W. DC. Things had escalated to the point where G and they had to start buying hammers to protect their turf. Anybody who's been in the streets know how it feels to get that first gun battle out your system and walk away a survivor, you feel like at that point you're untouchable, invincible and some more. So after G and them got into their first street beef with the R Street Youngins' and came away unscared, G went crazy with that pistol beefing with any and everybody. Nobody could tell him anything. G and the Young Guns reputation started to spread, and all the youngsters around the way were scared to death because G had started to play for keeps with them guns.

Until one day G and they whipped the brother of Fred from W Street, whose crew was getting a little rep in the hood too. Fred and his boys went looking for G and the Young Guns for two weeks without bumping heads. Then Saturday morning as G, Tykisha, Black, Speedy, Tamika, and Mike Mike walked to the second store on Channing Street, they were unexpectedly approached by Fred and his crew.

"Aye yo G! Let me holla at you for a minute!" Fred called out as he walked across the street with his boys in tow.

G had totally forgotten about whipping Fred's brother weeks earlier. G and they stopped, while G met Fred halfway. "Yo' what's up Fred?" G asked wondering what Fred wanted with him.

"Aye yo' G man why the fuck you jump on my little brother a few weeks back?!" Fred mentioned while seriously grittin' on G.

"First of all who you talking to like that nigga?!" G shouted while walking up into Fred's face, "and second of all who the fuck is your brother?"

"Marcus nigga!" Fred banged back. As G noticed Fred's boys starting to reach under their sweatshirts.

"Ohhh .... Shit ...., watch out G!!" Black screamed noticing what was about to happen also. It was too late; Fred, Sean, and Bam Bam cut loose blasting shots. Shouts and screams were all you heard.

"Pow ... pow ... pow ... pow ... pow ... pow ... pow ... pow ...
pow ... POW ... POW ... POW ... POW ... POW ... POW ... POW ...
POW ... POW!!!"

"Aaaaaiiiiiiiiiiiiii, Ohhhhhhh ..., get down!!!!!!" Everything seemed
to get stuck in time as bullets ripped through G, Tykisha, Mike Mike
and Black. Speedy was the only one out of the crew not to get hit. When
it was all said and done, Tykisha got hit in the side once; G was hit
twice, once in the butt, and once in the back. Mike Mike was hit in the
leg and Black got hit in the foot. Fortunately, none of their wounds was
life threatening.

However, when Tee and Stanley found out they were furious because
they had warned G about his actions and slowing down before Tykisha
got caught up in the midst of some of his shit. Now they loved G but at
that point they had to make a stance, and they forced G and Tykisha
apart from each other. Tee felt like this was the only choice they had,
before Tykisha was killed or seriously injured fucking with G. Neither
Tee nor Stanley was willing to take a chance with that relationship
anymore at that moment.

In any event after everything calmed down Tykisha felt like her
brothers couldn't tell her or G what to do, she was in love with G and that
was that. Love had blinded her and she couldn't see the danger that G
was putting her in with his dealing in the streets. All she knew was that
she loved G and nobody was going to stop them from being together.

CHAPTER 3

Several weeks after G and them got out the hospital they decided they wanted to get some get back and were lying outside some apartments parked in a Grand Marquis waiting for Bam Bam, Fred, and Sean to exit the building.

"I told y'all them nigga's saw us ride pass stupid asses, that's why they ain't coming out the building." Speedy repeated himself.

"G that nigga might be right this time, cause they been in that building a long ass time slim." Mike Mike replied peeking form under his black hoodie as he sat in the driver's seat.

"That nigga ain't right! Shit!!" Black snapped. "Them nigga's probably just in the building making some sells or something."

"Both you nigga's shut the fuck up!!!" G barked, while watching the building exits intensively. "If them suckers don't come out soon, I'm going up in there!"

Speedy looked at G like he was crazy. "G that will be suicide, them nigga's probably waiting on us."

"So what, them nigga's shot my baby. I'm killing somebody's ass tonight, believe that!!" G shouted.

No sooner G said that, Fred and Bam Bam came out the building kicking the bo bo slapping dap like they had just done something big. As they reached the bottom step and started walking down the street towards First Street they were not paying attention to G and them coming from behind them cruising up the block with the lights out.

"Aye yo' Fred!" G called out while leaning out the passengers' side window with his 9mm colt in his hand and Black hanging out the back passengers' window with a 40 caliber in his hand waiting to rip.

Fred and Bam Bam turned, "Yo' who that?!" That's when they noticed it was an ambush. "Ohhh . . . shitt!!" Bam Bam screamed ducking as they both tried to duck behind cars parked along the street.

"POW . . . POW . . . POW . . . POW . . . POW . . . POW . . . POW . . . POW . . . . !" Gun shots rang out like the fourth of July hitting Bam Bam and Fred both several times knocking them to the ground holding on for dear life.

G and they sped off heading up First Street towards the reservoir, then hitting Michigan Avenue. No sooner they turned on Michigan Avenue as luck would have it; they spotted a police cruiser coming up from behind them. "Mike Mike run it!" G screamed as Mike Mike sped down Michigan Avenue then taking a hard illegal left turn on North Capitol Street. By this time another police cruiser had joined on the chase, and soon after many more.

"Mike Mike head up by Carroll school, we can jump out and jet cross the field with these hammers!" G directed.

"Hurry up . . . . hurry up!!" Black yelled getting ready to jump out as soon as they reached Carroll football field.

"Man y'all be careful and just beep us from wherever you are." Speedy replied.

As they were approaching Carroll school they now had at least 7 police cars chasing behind them and more coming. G and Mike Mike were ready to roll as Mike Mike came to stop at the end of the football field. "Let's go Black!!" G shouted as they jumped out and started chucking through the gate and down the field with several officers many yards behind them.

Other officers surrounded the car with guns drawn while Mike Mike and Speedy were still inside. "Get out . . . get out!!" one of the officers yelled. "Step out the car and put your hands up!!"

Mike Mike and Speedy did as was told and were accosted by the by the officers and placed face down on the ground.

Shortly after the car was searched and they were questioned intensively, then taken to 6th District where they were being held until further questioning could be done. G and Black had gotten away or so they thought. They had ended up splitting up, and G found his way into a wooded area right behind Park Place Townhouse complex which set on Michigan Avenue. He knew that if he could get across Michigan Avenue he'd be home in minutes, but as he looked out from the woods he could see police cruisers all around the woods probably waiting fro him to come out. G decided to stash the gun he had used in the shooting, but kept his 380 on him just in case.

Several minutes later, G could hear the barks of what sounded like dogs and a lot of them. "Damn they got dogs." G whispered to himself. Now deciding he had to take a chance and get out the woods before the dogs found him, he made a choice to make a run for it.

G hopped the gate entering Park Place gated community right where the swimming pool was located at along North Capitol Street. Ducking and dodging between cars he found his way to the front gate facing Michigan Avenue, only minutes away from home. "Fuck!" G mumbled seeing two squad cars ride pass. "These motherfuckers are everywhere."

G surveyed Michigan Avenue and saw no police cruiser in sight. Feeling like this may be his only chance; he hopped the gate and made a run for the alley between Michigan Avenue and Girard Street. Balling across the street like a lightening rod, G made it into the alley, continuing to head towards Franklin Street, as he approached Girard Street, he spotted two police cruisers coming down the street. G paused and thought about what he should do and decided to hop inside one of the big green public trash barrels sitting in the alley. Sitting inside, G could hear the cruisers ride pass. "Sssssssss", G exhaled lifting just a tip of the top off the trash bin to see if the coast was clear.

The police had turned on North Capitol Street, witnessing this G jumped out the trash can, rushing down the alley G noticed several police cruisers sitting on Franklin Street huddled up. G stopped in his tracks, reversing and running back up towards Girard Street only to have a police cruiser turn into the alley meeting G head on. "Ohh . . . shitt . . . !" G yelled jumping the gate of the yard immediately to his left dashing towards the front yard.

"Stop . . . stop . . . freeze . . . !" Officers yelled from the cruiser that now headed to the front of the house.

[On North Capitol Street, G was running his heart out but I don't care how fast you are, you can not out run those walkie talkies.]

Five minutes later, G was apprehended on North Capitol Street and booked on suspicion of attempted murder and assault.

CHAPTER 4

Three months after being arrested Gino was sentenced to two years in a Juvenile Detention Center. Of course Gino was crushed by what he considered to be a stiff sentence, but there was nothing that he or anyone for that matter could do about it. When the Judge hit that Gravel yelling, "Two years restriction!" Gino immediately glanced over at Tykisha as tears began to trickle down her cheeks. Tykisha knew that for 2 years her heart and soul would be locked away from her. There was a blessing in all the madness though; the police never gathered enough information to bring murder charges against Gino.

Gino was off to the Juvenile D. T. C. in Maryland. Upon his arrival, he was quiet, but bitter. Gino knew he was going to be away from his family and friends, in the midst of his accession to the top, or so he thought. At that time of his arrest, Lil' G was really beginning to get the rep in the streets that he had so badly craved, and now he had to be away for 2 years.

While G was locked up doing his bid, all the little dudes that were already there had heard all about G's crazy antics in the streets, and G continued to carry it the same way locked up. G barely ever got into confrontation because a lot of the little dudes there were scared of him. This one time though G got into it with some Valley Green cats who tried to pull a move while G was in the shower. What they didn't know was that G carried his shank to the shower with him everyday. So when they tried to move on him, he came out slinging. The results were 3 stabbed up inmates, 1 critically and that wasn't G. Even the counselors at the DTC catered and pampered G. So while locked up G still enjoyed the fruits of his reputation from the streets.

During the beginning of his time, Tykisha kept a constant flow of letters coming to Gino, and Gino loved hearing from her. The letters kept Gino sane for a while, until one day Tykisha wrote and informed Gino that his brother Kenny was home and out of Foster Care. Gino's mom didn't have a phone so Gino had no way of contacting his brother. But Tykisha had informed Gino that Mike Mike and the crew had been looking out for Kenny and that he was doing fine. However, Gino knew inside that it was him that was supposed to be out there taking care of his little brother. This really had Gino mad at himself, as he started to go through a lot emotionally. Gino went into a deep funk, and found himself getting into all kinds of trouble, and stayed in the segregation unit, which is where they put you whenever you're a disciplinary problem.

This one particular time, Gino was in the disciplinary unit when he met this guy named Shadow from Virginia. Now Shadow was a huge guy that had a little rep from Virginia area, and had been at the D. T. C. now almost 9 months for distribution of cocaine, and now only had 3 more months to go before being released. Now usually Virginia guys and DC guys didn't get along, but for some reason these two took a liking to one another. They even somehow became cell mates, which was really a no-no!! However, no one was going to question Gino about why and/or how this Virginia dude ended up in his cell with him.

During their time in the cell together Shadow had mentioned to Gino how he was going to blow up when he got out, and Gino saw a lot of his dreams within Shadow. They both had a lot of ambitions about getting rich and fast. Shadow had confided in Gino the details of how he had been set up and locked up. Shadow had been set up by an undercover officer during a drug sell. Fortunately, when the sell was supposed to allegedly go down, Shadow arrived late followed by Greg his uncle. As soon as Shadow pulled into the Burger King parking lot, the undercover officers approached Shadow's car and vamped down on him. The good thing was that at the time they ran down on Shadow, he didn't have anything on him but a half ounce of crack, which was for another person. After snatching Shadow out the car and only finding a half ounce of crack, Shadow was placed under arrest, while his uncle Greg parked several cars behind him slowly pulled off and disappeared with the half of brick, which was originally for the sell to the undercover officer.

Gino had also confided in Shadow how he got locked up and what his plans were when he got out. They had gotten so close that they even talked about the possibility of hooking up once they got out and both were back on the streets. A bond was definitely formed. They exchanged phone numbers and each others home addresses just in case, cause Shadow was due to get out in less than 60 days now. While Gino had only been locked up for 9 months now, and had a ways to go, but his new found buddy was about to shine, and if he kept his word, shit would be alright especially when he got out. Gino now had a plan, he just needed Shadow to honor his word and upon his release he and Shadow would run a DC/Virginia connection pushing dope all through both states. [Let's blow up!!!!]

When they finally finished their segregation time and were placed back in general population they maintained their friendship. They hung out together, ate together, and did just about everything together. This really rubbed a lot of DC cats the wrong way. So one day some DC homies decided that they were going to rob Shadow and take all his shit. A few of them got together from Valley Green and 14th and Clifton and went into Shadow's cell one evening while he and Gino were out walking the pound. They broke into his locker stealing everything, Shadow's sweat clothes, tennis shoes, commissary, radio and everything else that was not bolted down. The DC homies figured even if Shadow was to find out who did it and mentioned it to Gino, that Gino would not take sides with the out of towner over the homies.

Later that evening when Shadow returned to his cell he noticed his lock had been kicked or broken off his locker, and upon further investigation he found out that all his shit had been taken. Shadow was mad and frustrated, but didn't know really what to do about it. He knew he wasn't the greatest fighter in the world, but would definitely defend himself if he had to. Shadow immediately thought about running and telling Gino, but later decided against it. Shadow knew that he and Gino had become close, but he wasn't sure if push came to shove if Gino would ride for him. So over the next couple of days Shadow slowly but surely started to back away from Gino, and hanging around his Virginia homies more and more. One of Shadow's homeboys later informed him that he had heard that the DC dudes were the ones who allegedly had stolen his shit. Shadow was puzzled because even though he didn't think that Gino had nothing to do with it, he figured there would be no way that Gino would go against his homeboys for him. Plus in a sense, Shadow figured that by now Gino had to have heard something about the situation, yet he had not mentioned anything about it to him yet. So Shadow continued to distance himself from the relationship with Gino, and for the life of him, Gino could not understand why Shadow had just flipped the script like that. Gino just figured maybe Shadow was going through some things or either his homeboys had gotten to him.

One day outside on the bleachers Gino was watching dudes play basketball, and working out when Jose from Clifton Terrace walked up taking a seat beside Gino. "What's up Gino?" Jose spoke while reaching out to shake Gino's hand.

"Ain't shit Jose", Gino replied shaking Jose's hand and then refocusing back on the basketball game.

"Yeah my nigga", Jose started saying pulling out a Newport cigarette lighting it up. "I'm glad you back hanging with homies again my nigga."

Gino turned to face Jose, "What the fuck you talking about nigga? I'm always with the home team."

"Nah, I'm just saying." Jose plucked the ashes from his cigarette. "You jive was playing the VA dude real close like slim. The homies thought you cut us off or something!"

"Jose!" Gino raised his eyebrows, "How in the hell am I cutting homies off when I'm with y'all niggas everyday."

"Yeah but you always bringing the VA dude with you. You know how shit is Gino." Jose was referring to the old all jail house politics of only swinging with your homies.

"Jose first of all, I'm a man." Gino stated sarcastically. "Secondly, that's my man, and I don't care anything about no fake ass codes of hanging with only homies. I do whatever the fuck I want!" Gino was agitated now rising from the bleachers, and now standing in front of

Jose. "But the dude had been acting kind of funny lately, that's the only reason why I've pulled back from the dude."

Jose snickered, which Gino didn't understand what was so funny. "Yeah that nigga probably mad about his shit."

Gino's face frowned up, confused not understanding what Jose was talking about. "What you talking about Jose?"

Jose looked at Gino with a slight smirk on his face. "Oh you don't know huh?"

"Know what Jose?!!" Gino barked feeling like something had slipped passed him.

"Man you know the homies took all Shadow shit about two weeks ago. I mean everything too, shoes, commissary, sweat shit. The whole motherfucking shebang." Jose laughed rearing back on the bleachers.

Gino was boiling inside, face turning red and everything. Gino stepped up in Jose's face which immediately stopped him from laughing as he noticed the seriousness on Gino's face. "Jose, who the fuck took slim shit??!!"

Jose stepped up off the bleachers, "Man fuck that Virginia nigga!"

Gino pushed Jose back against the bleachers making his back snap, "Jose if you don't tell me who the fuck took slim shit, I'm going to knock your bitch ass out right here!" Gino said with force.

Jose pushed Gino off of him taking his stance like he was ready to do whatever. "Gino nigga you got me fucked up! You ain't going to do a motherfucking thing to Ms. Blunt son, believe that."

"You know what," Gino stepped back, "nigga if you weren't a homie I'd dog you right now, but believe this if I find out that you had anything to do with slim shit getting stolen, I'll be back to see you. That's a promise not a threat." Gino stated as he marched off in search of Shadow.

Walking all throughout the D.T.C. Gino finally caught sight of Shadow across the gym when he peeked inside. Shadow was working out with his homies when he caught a glimpse of Gino heading in his direction. His homeboys also saw Gino heading over as they all rose to their feet waiting as Gino was crossing the gym floor. "Aye Shadow here come your man Gino," Shadow's homie Bobby commented. "I'm telling you, don't be fucking with that nigga, he probably was with that shit anyway."

16

"Look Bobby, you can't tell me who I can or can't fuck with. Like I told you before I don't think Gino had nothing to do with that shit."

"Yeah well if you feel like that, why you been hanging with us lately?" Greg, Shadow's other homie replied as Gino walked up.

"Aye Shadow . . . Shadow let me holler at you for a minute!" Gino hollered as he walked right pass the Virginia crews like they were non-existent.

Shadow walked over by the water fountain following Gino until he came to a stop. "What's up Gino?"

Gino's face was serious as he looked Shadow straight in the eyes. "Look Shadow, now ever since you've known me, I've always kept shit real with you, right?!" Shadow nodded his head. "And no matter what or who was around I always acted the same towards you, even when my homies were around, right?"

"Yeah you did that." Shadow replied.

"Then why in the hell you been acting all funny and shit lately, like you don't fuck wit' a nigga no more or something? I mean keep it real." Gino asked still looking Shadow in the eyes as his homies and everybody else in the gym looked on with anticipation of something kicking off.

"Gino mann . . . to be honest I jive been going through some shit right now, and I just been dealing with it in my own little way, feel me?"

"Well it wouldn't have anything to do with some of my homies stealing your shit, would it?" Gino asked.

"Ssss . . ." Shadow hissed, "Come on Gino!" as Gino followed Shadow over to a secluded part of the gym since all eyes were on them. "Gino you my nigga, and I can't lie to you cause you always been straight up wit' me, but yeah I had heard that some DC cats had stole my shit, but at no time did I think you had anything to do with it. I even told my homies that."

Gino shook his head in frustration, "Shadow you didn't have to say nothing, your actions towards me showed how you felt. As long as you've known me, you've never seen me steal nothing from nobody, or take advantage of anyone, that's just not my style, and to be honest I'm really fucked up that you didn't tell me about this shit from the beginning instead of acting all funny and shit. However, the bottom line is, I fucks wit' you and if a nigga steal from you, that's just like stealing from me. So come on nigga we going to get your shit back!!" Gino exclaimed as he leaned down and began tying up his timberland boots.

Shadow glanced over at his homies, then back at Gino, as they stepped off heading towards Shadow's cell. At Shadow's cell they grabbed two knives, and then proceeded over to Gino's unit. On their way down the hallway Gino asked Shadow, "Who you heard had something to do with your shit being missing?"

"Man they say Ray B. and Carlos from Third Street did it." As they entered Gino's cell grabbing his knives and ace bandages.

"Alright, that's all I need to know. We're going straight at them nigga's, asking no questions, you hear me?" Gino stated as Shadow nodded his head. "Let's go then!" Gino instructed as they strapped up heading out the door.

Inside, Shadow was nervous; DC guys had a reputation for going hard inside the D.T.C. so he knew that he would have to back Gino 100%. The one good thing was that Gino was well respected and had a lot of buddies inside as well. Now as they were about to exit Gino's unit a few of Gino's buddies spotted him and could tell something wasn't right. Birdie and Kelvin from S.W. ran and caught up with Gino as he and Shadow were about to exit the door. "Aye Gino hold up nigga!!!" Birdie shouted as they ran up. "What's going on my nigga? I see you up to something?"

"Birdie ain't nothing really slim; I just got to handle some shit. Some homies took some of my man's shit, and we gettin' that back bottom line." Gino stated.

Kelvin then jumped in, "Hold up then Gino, we riding too. Let us grab our shit." They took off running to their cells gathering their straps as well.

Once they returned, they all headed straight for the chow hall, knowing that everybody would be going to get that chicken on chicken day. The gray double doors to the cafeteria opened up and Gino entered as Shadow, Kelvin, and Birdie followed, all eyes lifted up. "Oh shit y'all something about to happen." Some niggas from 4th Street whispered.

"Watch them niggas, something is going on." Fred from Condon Terrace mentioned to his crew.

Basically everybody knew something was about to jump off. Gino and them strolled straight towards the uptown table where Ray B. and Los were eating. Sensing that trouble was coming their way, Ray B and Los immediately rose to their feet as Gino approached, but before Ray B. could make any moves Gino took off on him and all hell broke loose in the cafeteria. They all went at it for a while before the Police stormed the cafeteria with their tear gas and mace fogging up the whole entire cafeteria. Before long everyone was on the ground gagging and choking for air, which turned out to be a good thing cause that gave Gino, Shadow, Birdie, and Kelvin time to get rid of their knives and shit. But it didn't matter because the police already knew who were involved; they grabbed up everybody and escorted them straight to the Segregation Unit.

Gino and them were all cool, but Ray B. and a few of his dudes got fucked around. Nothing that serious but the point was well taken. Somehow again with Gino's influence and pull, he was able to get Shadow in the cell with him again.

After they got in the cell and were examined by the medical staff they finally got a chance to talk about everything. Gino explained to Shadow that he was offended that Shadow thought that he could have known or taken part in stealing his shit. Shadow then explained that it wasn't that, Shadow just figured that Gino wouldn't go against the home team for him. Gino then explained that if he fucks with a nigga, it was all the way to the end for him. That's when Shadow understood just how sincere Gino really was about their friendship. They got a better understanding, and decided that no matter what, they were going to be friends for life.

Deep down inside, Shadow felt like he owed Gino. Shadow knew that for real, Gino had put himself out there for him, and he would probably be gone home by the time Gino finished his segregation time and had to go back out on the line. But during those last weeks before Shadow's departure they made a lot of promises to each other, and their bond was solidified, and no one could break it now.

CHAPTER 5

After 45 days in segregation, Shadow's release date came, in the morning fat boy would be rolling out, and Gino would be losing his best friend. Gino was happy for Shadow, plus he knew that he only had a year left to finish. They stayed up talking the entire night. Shadow couldn't wait to get out, he had plans, but he wasn't going to forget about Gino in the slightest bit.

"Gino man, I leave in a few hours, but I always want you to know that you're my man slim", Shadow stated. "You showed me madd love when you went against the home team for me, and I really respect and love you for that slim. On top of that, true friendship is hard to come by; I just hope that we can continue to be the best of friends forever and not just in here." Gino just nodded his head. "My nigga when I get out, I'm going to keep in touch with you, I got all your hook ups and trust me, and you're going to be alright. Always remember when you get out, I promise you, I'll be there, like you was for me. I'm going out here and get this paper you can believe that, and ain't nobody stopping me from doing that." Shadow finished as they gave each other dap.

Gino was a little shocked at everything that Shadow had stated, and felt that fat boy was serious about it. "Shadow I believe you, and you know that I got madd love for you too. Just don't be like a lot of those dudes that get out and forget their man. I've had a lot of good men leave here promising me shit, but soon as they hit the street, it's a whole nother story. Stick to the "G" code and don't forget the struggle continues."

"Gino man, I've only got my word. That's all any man has to stand on, but I'm telling you for sure I got you slim." Shadow assured Gino.

They continued to talk the rest of the night until breakfast arrived. Shadow had been telling Gino some of what he planned on doing once he got out there, and Gino was soaking it all in knowing that his release day would be around the corner. Later that morning two officers came to the door alerting Shadow that it was that time. He and Gino hugged, shook hands and gave each other a salute, which was symbolic of their loyalty to one another. Shadow was then cuffed and escorted out while Gino had to wait his turn.

Fifteen days after Shadow left, Gino, Birdie and Kelvin finished their seg time and was headed back to the line. Gino didn't even feel the same without his partner, but he had all the information to call or write once he felt fat boy had gotten settled and back on his feet. Gino knew that being locked up for a while and then getting released took a little adjusting period, before things would be back to normal. However, when Gino got out the seg unit he concentrated on contacting Tykisha, but he had been totally unable to reach her. He constantly got messages that she was either outside or gone somewhere. Gino got frustrated and decided to write her.

Gino waited on a response that never came. After 3 months, Gino finally did receive some mail. However, the envelope didn't have a return address on it. When Gino opened it up, there it was a letter from Tykisha, and a money order receipt for $500 from Tee.

In the letter Tykisha basically explained to Gino that she still loved him and had been extremely busy with school and all. She also sent some recent photos of her, the crew, and Kenny. Kenny was not a little boy anymore Gino thought to himself as he sat there staring at the pictures. Gino continued reading the letter really just happy to know that Tykisha hadn't forgotten about him, but what Tykisha didn't mention in the letter is what Gino would later find out. For the next couple of weeks though, Gino was riding high especially happy to find out his little brother was alright and being looked after by the crew.

One day Gino was lying in the bed looking at an old Slam magazine when the homie Man-Man entered Gino's cell. "Hey what's up Man-Man?" Gino rose up to give him some dap.

"Ain't shit, just came to give you your mail. They called your name but you weren't out there so I grabbed it." Man-Man handed the envelope to Gino.

"Thanks my nigga", Gino replied.

"No problem slim, I'll see you later I've got to call baby girl you know." Man Man smiled exiting Gino's cell heading for the phone.

Gino opened the letter and began to read it.

To Gino,

My nigga I told you I wouldn't forget about you. It has taken me a minute to get back on my feet, but shit looking lovely out here. I can't wait 'til you get out. What you got 6 more months now? Whatever it is, don't worry I'll be here for you. Just write me and let me know your exact release date so I can be there.

Also, inside here are a few flicks of me and few of my many women, you know! Plus a money order for $1,000. If you need more just write me and let me know. I got to go now but write soon and let me know something.

Much respect,
Your man Shadow

Gino was happy to see his man shining and doing his thing. But more importantly he had kept his word. During Gino's incarceration he was unaware of his mom's transformation in life as well. However, he'd have to wait until he got home to see that. Tee continued to look out for Gino, while the Young Guns continued to do their thing and looking out for Kenny who now was a part of the crew.

The next few months were really rough for Gino because he had ceased getting letters from Tykisha and couldn't catch her on the phone, and things just seemed to be falling apart in his eyes. Tee still continued to send money from time to time, but hearing from Tykisha is what Gino yearned for. Shadow stayed in contact periodically and had told Gino not to forget to alert him when his released date was approaching because he planned on being there. Gino didn't know whether or not to believe Shadow but he'd have to wait and see.

Gino had been waiting for his release date so bad, he could taste it. Tykisha had basically left him for dead in Gino's eyes and he needed to know why. However, Gino had big plans, and a lot of them depended upon if his man Shadow keeping his word about what they had discussed before he was released. Shadow had written Gino and told him bits and pieces of his plans that would make them all rich when Gino was finally released. So a week before Gino's release he wrote Shadow a letter alerting him that he would be released the following week and what day and time. Gino also expressed in the letter that he really needed Shadow to be there, because he wasn't going to tell his family or nothing, he'd just surprise them when he got there.

Gino never received a response to his letter. Now he was two days away from being released and still unsure if Shadow had received his letter. He would just have to go on blind faith, and Shadow's word.

CHAPTER 6

On the morning of Gino's release he went around to all homies paying his respects leaving all his shit with the home team. As Gino headed for R&D to be processed out he had a smile on his face that was worth a million dollars. Words could not express the anxiety that was running through his veins at that moment. He had envisioned walking out into the arms of Tykisha and the rest of the crew waiting to show him a hell of a time. That dream had faded away months ago when he no longer received anymore letters from Tykisha, but dreams do come true. If Shadow was just waiting for him on the outside of those gates like he had assured Gino he would be.

Erkkk . . . , the gates opened up which would allow Gino to be a free man again. Gino stood there with two C. O. guards standing on both sides ready to usher him through. "I bet you're sure ready to get up out of here, huh Gino?" Officer Brown whispered to Gino noticing the smile on Gino's face.

"You better know it." Gino replied as the gates opened and Gino gripped the envelope with his pictures and letters inside.

The double gates finally opened up, "Okay Gino take care of yourself and stay out of trouble." Officer Brown stated as he stood there biting down on that nasty ass cigar that Gino couldn't stand. However, during Gino's time at D.T.C. Officer Brown had always been nice to Gino and helped him out as much as he could. He had always mentioned to Gino that he reminded him so much of his own son, who had died several years earlier in an accidental drive by shooting.

"I'm definitely going to try Mr. Brown. You take care of yourself as well." Gino reached out to shake Mr. Brown's hand as he stepped through the gates, back out in the world he had missed so much.

Stepping through those gates all Gino could see was cars lining the parking lot. No one appeared to be waiting for anyone as Gino continued to survey the parking lot. Suddenly a whistle came from across the parking lot maybe 100 feet from where Gino was standing. Gino turned to look over his shoulder when he spotted fat boy leaning up against a white Lexus coup LS 400, smiling and shaking his head. A giant smirk immediately came across Gino's face as he walked towards Shadow. Upon getting closer Gino saw that there were two females also in the car that Shadow was leaning up against, but at this point Gino was just happy to see his man, "What's up nigga?" Gino said as they embraced each other, and then gave each other a salute.

"Nigga didn't I tell you I'd be here for you when you got out?" Shadow asked.

Gino smiled, "You sure said that fat boy. And boy old boy am I glad you're here, because I wouldn't have had no other way home. I didn't even tell my people or nothing, I just had faith in you my nigga." Gino stated as he started peeking at the two females whispering and giggling in the car.

"Yeah right nigga! Come on Gino let's get up out of here."

"Fo' sho'!" Gino replied licking his lips still staring at the chocolate sister sitting in the back of the coup. "Fat boy who this right here?"

"Oh my bad slim; this is my wifey Tricia right here." Shadow pointed to the caramel sister in the front.

"Hi Gino!" Tricia spoke.

"Hey what's up, nice to meet you Tricia?"

"And this right here is Marquita, Tricia's sister." Shadow stated.

"Hi Gino!" Marquita replied batting her long attractive eye lashes along with her beautiful smile.

"Nice to meet you Marquita." Gino said looking somewhat mesmerized at Marquita's attractiveness.

"Shadow has told me a lot about you." Marquita stated opening the car door for Gino.

"Hopefully they were all good things," Gino looked at Shadow grinning, "well how about you finding out from me since I'm here now." Gino closed the door, now laying back in his Casanova mode.

Shadow then jumped in, "Nigga cut the bullshit out." As laughter erupted from everybody.

On their way back to DC Shadow slid the old Frankie Beverly and Maze CD in the CD player as Gino kept a constant flow of conversation going on with Marquita. Gino was really feeling himself now that he was free again. Finally arriving back in DC, Shadow took Gino up Georgetown shopping. Parking on K Street exiting the car Gino asked Shadow, "This is how you doing it big huh big boy?" Gino was speaking about the car, the money, and the way Shadow was doing it at the moment.

"Gino I told you when I got out that I was going to get this money, didn't I?" Gino stuck his lip out nodding his head.

"Yeah you sure did that Fat boy." Gino responded as he stood next to Marquita leaning up against the side of the car.

"You know what? Hold on for a minute. I almost forgot . . . I got something for you." Shadow said walking back towards the back of the car. Shadow popped the trunk open and grabbed a duffle bag out of it. Closing the trunk, Shadow returned to Gino throwing him the duffle bag. Gino caught the bag mid-air. "What's this Fat boy?" Gino asked.

"Look inside, that's you right there." Shadow replied now hugged up behind Tricia.

Gino opened the bag to the sight of what had to be at least 50 to 60 thousand dollars cash, wrapped in bundles. "This me, Huh!!?" Gino glanced up at Shadow.

"Do rabbits shit in the woods? Nigga that's just a little something to help you get on your feet. I don't believe in having a nigga underneath me. I want my man right beside me til the end."

"Shadow you know what?? I respect that . . . cause a lot of niggas talk that shit, but don't be honoring it. Feel me?!"

"My word is all I got," Shadow reiterated, "remember when you stuck by my side against your homies? I never forgot that, now it's my turn to return the favor."

"Shadow, you my nigga." Gino reached out to embrace Shadow.

After releasing each other, the girls looked at them, "Awwww . . . ain't that sweet!" The girls said in unison.

"Gino I told you about that sentimental shit nigga!" Shadow laughed. "Save that shit for Marquita." As laughter continued . . ." Come on y'all let's go shopping!"

They first headed to Players clothing store buying Gino throwback Jersey's, Sweat suits, and some Air Force One's. Leaving there, they went inside the Boss shop copping and purchasing more shit. By the time they exited Sweat Styles, everybody's hands were full. It looked as if they had been shopping all day and night with all the shit they had. Gino was just happy as he could be because he had gained his freedom and had his man, who honored his word right at his side. There's nothing more powerful than a true friendship.

Before leaving Georgetown, they went to Houston's Restaurant. Upon entering Houston's the aroma of street food again rushed Gino's nostrils while he glanced around at all the people conversing, the hostess showed them to their table, where they had placed their orders. Everybody was having wonderful conversation until this voice interrupted, "Heyyy . . . Shadow . . . Hey Tricia." A sexy attractive woman walked up to the table in her Houston's hostess uniform. She was about 5'5" short with a Halle Berry hair style that matched her smooth caramel colored skin. "I haven't seen y'all in a minute now." The woman flashed a warm smile.

"Yeah I know," Shadow said knowing that he and Tricia hadn't been back to Houston's in about three months. However, this waitress named Tracy always seemed to be the one whom waited on them whenever they did come, and Shadow would always tip her big cause she'd always do her job with a smile even when Tricia and Shadow were assholes. "Girl we just been so busy," Tricia stated.

"Well if y'all need something just let me know." Tracy smiled walking off to wait more tables.

After eating and talking some more, Shadow turned to something more serious . . . the plan! "My nigga you know we've got to talk tonight seriously right?" Shadow winked his eye at Gino.

"No doubt!" Gino stated.

"Well come on y'all, let's get up out of here, we've got a lot of shit to take care of tonight." Shadow replied placing $300.00 on the table for Tracy as they all got up heading for the door.

After exiting Houston's and walking to the car, Shadow suggested that they stop past and let Gino go see his probation officer, that way they could head straight down to Virginia and party for the night. Gino agreed as they rushed off to the probation office.

Upon arriving at the probation office, Gino got out the car, went inside and handled his business. When he reappeared, he informed Shadow that he only had to come see his Probation officer once a month, and piss occasionally. Gino really didn't care right now anyway, he had one thing on his mind, "blowing up" with his man Shadow, and that was it . . . period!!! By any means necessary.

They hit I-95 headed to Virginia cruising. While riding, Gino laid back and thought about all he had been through over the last two years, and all he planned on doing now, until he fell asleep in Marquita's lap.

Upon arriving in Newport News, VA, Shadow went straight to the Courtyard Hotel. They got connecting rooms and headed on up stairs. Gino was all smiles as he and Quita were about to enter their room, "Aye Gino, here you go." Shadow handed Gino the room card key.

"Thanks Big homie, you know I got some business to handle, right??!" Gino cut his eyes at Quita. They all chuckled.

"Yeah OK, but look we've got to talk tonight or first thing in the morning. I've got to put you down with how shit is going down. It's time to put our plan in full effect, you heard??!"

"Fo' Sho' big boy. You know I'm with you not matter what, you done already showed me you're a loyal nigga, and that's all I needed to know. I'm not even going to tell my peoples that I'm home yet, I'll wait until we get this money then I'll holla at them."

"Alright Gino," they gave each other dap and headed into their rooms.

Gino and Marquita entered the room and got settled by showering and watching a little TV. Now being as though Gino hadn't been with a female in 2 years, he was somewhat shy, but not Marquita. She laid Gino down on the bed and massaged his back, while they discussed stuff that they both had been through. Marquita opened up to Gino as well discussing her past as well as what she wanted to do in the future.

Unbeknown to Gino, Marquita was admiring his muscular build and the way he talked. Sensing that things had gotten comfortable between them Gino rolled over, as Marquita continued to talk. Suddenly Gino put his finger over her lips, and began kissing her passionately. After several minutes, their lips finally unlocked but only momentarily. Marquita then began to kissing all over Gino chest, working her way down. Once she got to Gino's dick, she tensed up a bit, paused, then began to tease him by licking it, kissing it, until finally taking it inside her salivating mouth. Gino then began to meet Quita's downward thrust with upward thrust, but she handled every bit of it. Gino was going crazy; he had never had his dick sucked like this before.

After she finished sucking his dick, she crawled up on top of Gino, mounted him and began to ride him like she was a rodeo queen. Gino was in ecstasy and Marquita knew it. She threw her head back and started to scream Gino's name. "Gino . . . Gino baby . . . Gino!" sensing that she was about to cum Gino really started pumping harder thrusts until she climaxed, "Oh baby . . . Oh baby!!!!" She cringed tightly to the bed sheets screaming.

Afterwards, Marquita got on her knees towards the end of the bed and told Gino, "Fuck me doggy-style . . . Fuck me doggy-style." As Gino stood off the end of the bed sliding his dick inside her wet pussy pounding it just as she had asked him to do, while she loved every bit of it too. In the midst of everything Marquita reached back and removed Gino's dick from her pussy, and directed it inside her ass. Marquita was a beast, and she was trying her best to turn Gino out. He had never fucked a broad in the ass, so this brought an all new excitement to the sexacade.

Marquita must have cum 2 to 3 times before they finally finished. They both were exhausted as they laid in bed now cuddled up in conversation. "Gino I want us to be really close," Marquita stated "I don't want this to be just a fuck thing."

Gino kissed her on the forehead, "Listen baby girl, I'm going to be straight up with you. Me and Shadow have some big plans we trying to accomplish, and I don't know how much time I'll have to really spend with you right now."

Marquita rose up looking Gino in the eyes, "I understand and respect your honesty. But if my sister can wait and deal with Shadow, then I can wait for you. I just want to know at least that if I wait for you, I won't be waiting for nothing."

"Marquita if you can be patient until we put this thing down, I promise it will be worth your wait. I just want to be able to get on my feet first. Shadow has looked out for me big time, but I'm use to having my own. Now once that happens we can do whatever you want to do."

"You promise Gino?" she inquired while batting her eye lashes at Gino.

"My word is my bond, if I tell you something; you can take it to the bank."

"Give me a kiss," she leaned over poking her lips out until Gino met her lips with his. "I'm so glad that Shadow introduced us."

"Yeah . . . . Me too, and I'm sure that my man feels the same way as well."

Marquita looked at Gino with a puzzled look, "Who are you talking about?"

Gino grabbed his dick as they both burst out laughing and started wrestling in the bed. Before you knew it they were back at it again. Gino was making up for lost time, 2 years locked up. Later they fell asleep in each others arms.

CHAPTER 7

It was 8:00pm when the phone rung, which startled Gino; he reached across Marquita who was still sleeping retrieving the phone, "Hello!"

"Damn! What's up nigga you sound like you drained?" Shadow teased. "What little sis' done put that thing on you like that?"

"Ain't no question!" Gino exclaimed, as he could hear Tricia in the background getting on Shadow.

"Why don't you leave them alone, you know they're getting their freak on." Tricia was commenting.

"Fuck what you talking about," Shadow replied. "They'll have plenty of time for all that. I'm trying to take my man to the club so I can show him how we really do it down in VA."

"That's your problem now, always out in them damn streets with those stank ass hoes!" Tricia shouted.

"Look I ain't trying to argue with you alright. Ain't nobody trying to be with bitches and all that, just chill out." Shadow responded.

Tricia rolled her eyes, "Yeah whatever!"

Gino cut in, "Uh . . . uh . . . uh, damn big boy looks like somebody needs to handle their business, big pimpin'." Gino teased.

"Man this broad crazy, always thinking a nigga out with some other bitches. Look though get ready I'm taking you to meet the rest of the squad." Shadow replied.

"Alright, but you got to give me a minute to get dressed." Said Gino.

"Okay, and stay away from Quita too nigga."

Gino peeked over at Quita still sleep, "Yeah I'll try." As they hung up.

Twenty minutes later Gino was knocking on the connecting doors between their rooms. Shadow opened the door, "Hold on Gino let me grab my keys and shit," as he headed back towards the bedroom.

Tricia was sitting on the couch, "Gino where's my sister?"

"Oh she still sleep Tricia," Gino answered with a jive swagger.

"I mean so what you saying, you wore her out! Cause I know she handles her business?" Tricia jokingly asked.

Gino smiled, "Nah . . . I ain't saying that, I'm just saying she sleep that's all."

"Yeah alright now, don't let Shadow get you into none of his bad habits either." Tricia replied.

Shadow was exiting the bedroom, "shut up girl!!" Shadow exclaimed. "Man don't pay that girl no mind she crazy for real. Give me a kiss, I'll see you later." Shadow kissed Tricia as he and Gino exited the room rolling out.

The club they pulled up in front of was "Chocolate City". It was the hangout spot for all the hood niggas to relax and kick back. Tonight the crowd was packed as usual, as Gino stared at all the beautiful half naked women posted up outside the club chit chatting, gossiping and scoping out their prey for the night. Finally, they parked, got out and headed inside.

As they entered the door Shadow shook hands with Ed the bouncer he knew, and strolled on inside. Music was thumpin', beautiful women were everywhere, on tables, on nigga's laps, on the stages, and I mean a man's heaven. Shadow put his arm around Gino, "Come on man, everybody over here." Shadow pointed to an isolated corner where three dudes were standing around talking. As they approached the table, Teddy Bear hollered, "What's up Shadow?!!" they shook hands. Teddy Bear was Shadow's first cousin on his mother's side of the family. They'd been close since growing up.

"Ain't shit, look this my man Gino right here y'all. This the dude I was telling y'all about," said Shadow.

"Oh yeah, what's up Gino?" Greg stated shaking Gino hand. "I'm glad you're finally home, now fat ass can stop talking about you so much."

"Yeah he told me," Gino replied. "Well at least now we can put this game down and get this money."

"No doubt!!" William shouted as they all nodded at each other. William was also Shadow's cousin; he was the son of Shadow's favorite Aunt Rita. Everybody loved Aunt Rita because she smoked weed with the crew and understood the street game. Greg was one of Shadow's best friends from back in the days. They were really tight until Shadow changed dreams to becoming the ghetto Bill Gates instead of a rapper. The streets were not for Greg until he wanted to go to college and needed the money, and the street provided that avenue for him. However, the streets took him under and he never saw the campus of Virginia State University.

Shadow jumped in, "Well listen y'all; tonight we're just having fun. Tomorrow we'll discuss the plan and shit alright."

Everybody nodded their head tipping their glasses up as Shadow was finishing up his statement, two fine ass light skinned native looking females walked up to Fat boy. One of them kissed him, while the other hugged him. "Damn Shadow! Who this be right here?" Gino said in broken English, admiring the one who looked like one of those video broads.

"Oh my bad, Gino this Peaches and Tuesday." Shadow hugged them both. "They my thugged out hood soldiers I keep close to the squad. They've been down with me from the beginning, on all levels. This my God sister Tuesday right here." Shadow mentioned as he noticed Tuesday and Gino staring at each other seductively.

Gino rubbed his hands together, "Oh yeah!" Shaking his head staring at Tuesday. "Well since we're basically family now, maybe me and Tuesday need to get to know each other a little better."

Tuesday moved over closer to Gino, "Well maybe we do need to do that then." Tuesday stood there hands on her hips.

Shadow then cut in, "Tuesday my man just got out of jail today, make sure you take good care of him. You hear me?!"

Tuesday licked her lips. "Oh yeah? I guess you really ready to hurt some bitches then huh?"

Gino hit back, "Well you know how shit is, right now I'm just trying to relax and have some fun."

Shadow saw it coming and cut in, "Look come on my nigga, you'll have plenty of time to talk and freak later on." Shadow put his arm around Gino walking him off.

They headed straight over to the bar where the female bartender Crystal awaited, "What's up Shadow?" she asked, "You want your regular?" Shadow nodded. "What does your cute ass friend here want?" She eyed Gino like a piece of meat.

Shadow looked at Gino, "What you want my nigga?"

"Hennessy and Coke," Gino responded still cooing at Crystal.

"Crystal just give him the whole bottle, that's how we doing it tonight. My man just came home today." Said Shadow.

"For real! That's good." Crystal replied while grabbing the bottle of Hennessy handing it to Shadow.

"Yeah, he from DC, so you better be careful." Shadow played with Crystal.

Finally Gino decided to speak up for himself, "So how are you doing Crystal? You don't mind me calling you Crystal do you?" Gino poured some Hennessy in his glass.

"Nah, Crystal's aiight, and I'm doing quite fine right now." Crystal said, standing there playing with her hair in a sexy way. "How are you doing though?"

"I was doing alright, but it seems like my night might have just gotten better." Gino sipped on his drink.

Unbeknown to Gino, Tuesday was walking up fast. "Uh . . . Uh . . ." Tuesday tapped Gino on the shoulder, "Gino can I speak to you for a minute?" Tuesday glared at Crystal with her nose turned up as Gino began to get up.

Shadow immediately knew where this was going and cut in grabbing Gino and walking him away from the jam. "Nigga I'm bonding you this time," Shadow started laughing, "you better calm the fuck down; you know these Virginia broads are crazy. You down here starting all kinds of shit already with these broads."

While back at the bar, Tuesday and Crystal were having a gritting competition at each other. Tuesday felt like Crystal had a habit of always trying to go after men in which Tuesday had before, or was after. So that really set her off. Tuesday was standing over to the side with a few of her buddies whispering; until Crystal made it clear she wasn't ducking anything. "Bitch you better stay behind that bar and keep serving those drinks before you get yourself hurt, for real!!!" Tuesday hollered at Crystal.

"Ain't nobody scared of you bitch!" Crystal replied while exiting from behind the bar, "you got this bitch fucked up, real talk!!"

Shadow noticed what was going down and rushed over before shit got out of hand, grabbing Tuesday and Peaches. "Come on both of y'all before y'all get into some shit and get locked up bullshitting."

Gino then stepped in, "I got her Shadow." Gino grabbed Tuesday around the waist walking her away from the commotion. Tuesday somewhat calmed down as Gino walked her through the crowd over to the table where the crew was sitting initially. Tuesday was nodding her head the whole way. Shadow stood back and watched knowing that Gino didn't really understand what he was getting himself into messing with Tuesday. She was the possessive type. On the block she's called the stalker, and for good reason. She didn't play when it came to her man. Oh well, this is what he wanted. Gino better understand that these VA broads are cut from a different cloth than those DC broads. These country bitches are crazy.

He couldn't have seen that sign when we were coming into Virginia because he would know. "Virginia is for Lovers!" Broads down this part took that phrase to heart, REAL TALK!!

Later that night the rest of the squad finally showed up. Gino and Tuesday were over in a booth secluded deep in the back. Shadow walked over interrupting their personal party. "Uh . . . Uh, excuse me," Shadow got their attention, "Gino my nigga I need to speak to you for a minute."

Tuesday just shook her head, "Shadow don't be trying to turn him into no dog like you either."

Gino stood up smiling; Shadow looked at him, shaking his head. "Damn Tuesday, where that come from?" Gino just stood back laughing to himself, only if she knew "Birds of a feather flock together." Gino said to himself.

Shadow then ushered Gino over to the table where the family was sitting and waiting. As they were approaching Shadow spotted Greg over talking to some broad and waved him over. "Okay y'all, for those of you who weren't here earlier, I want y'all to meet my man Gino. He is the latest piece to the puzzle for the plan."

Everybody said what's up and gave Gino dap as they introduced themselves. All the while Shadow was talking; Gino was still concentrating on Tuesday who was on the dance floor eyeing Gino, dancing in a provocative manner. Soon as Shadow finished with his speech, Gino couldn't wait and immediately found his way back over to Tuesday. Shadow and them just stood back and laughed because they knew how it felt to just get out of jail. A nigga be trying to make up for all the lost time. But Gino didn't know what he was in for messing with Tuesday.

Shortly thereafter, while Gino was slow dragging with Tuesday, Shadow crept on him and whispered in his ear, "I don't care what you do, but don't forget about Marquita playboy."

Gino told Tuesday to hold on for a minute as he went to speak to Shadow once again. "My nigga I had a good talk with Quita earlier today. I explained exactly what was going on with us and where I stood."

"Yeah aiight, I'm trying to . . . ," Shadow started to respond.

Gino cut him off, "Quita is going to be my little peoples, and all these other broads are going to be just that, other!"

"Gino my nigga I'm just not trying to be hearing Tricia mouth about you dogging her little sister, but at the same time do you too. Just remember when shit hit the ceiling, don't say I didn't tell you so."

"I got that Fat boy." Gino replied.

"Aiight, if you say so," Shadow laughed. "Come on let's get some more drinks." As they laughed all they way back over to the bar.

Somehow near closing time, Gino had found his way back over talking to Crystal again, trying to persuade her to go home with him for the night. Gino was unsure of Shadow's plans for the night, so he told her to hold up while he ran to check. "Hey Fat boy," Gino called out walking over to him, "What's up? What we doing tonight?"

"My nigga, I'm going over Peaches house for a little while, and I would advise you to go with Tuesday if you know what's good for you. The bitch is crazy; I'm trying to tell you. You already playing with fire, cause if she catch you talking to Crystal again the bitch liable to cut both of y'all, real talk."

Gino looked kind of shocked, "Damn big homie, I just met the broad."

"Nigga that's what I've been trying to tell you. These broads on some, if you fuck me, you stuck with me type shit."

"Oh yeah?!"

"Yeah!!!"

Gino hunched his shoulders and threw up his hands, "Well I guess I'll be going with Tuesday then huh?"

"Good choice homes, real talk. I ain't trying to be at no hospital tonight fucking with you and that lunatic." Shadow stated.

"Alright hold up let me go get Crystal's number for a later date then." Gino responded.

Shadow laughed, "Go head, but don't let that fool see you."

When Shadow and the crew left, they all headed over to the Waffle House on Mercy Boulevard across from the Hampton Coliseum. They got some carry out food and shot straight over to Peaches and Tuesday house on King Street right off Rip Rap Road, which they shared with their mom. As they all entered the house, Peaches and Tuesday mom, Kathy came from the back of the house, "Is that y'all Peaches?!" She screamed finally appearing from one of the bedrooms.

"Yeah Ma," Tuesday responded as they all took seats.

"Oh! I know y'all didn't go out to eat and not bring me nothing?" Kathy stood in the door way hands on hips.

Shadow walked over and hugged mom, "Ma you know damn well I ain't going to forget you for nothing in the world."

She kissed Shadow on the cheek, "That's why you my favorite son baby!" They all laughed. "Y'all are so rude why hasn't anybody introduced me to your friend Tuesday?"

"Oh sorry ma, my bad. Ma this my man Gino from DC. This the dude I used to tell you I couldn't wait to come home." Shadow responded.

"Okay, I remember now. Nice to meet you Gino." Kathy spoke eyeing how attractive Gino was.

"Ma don't even think about it!" Tuesday commented sarcastically.

"Ha . . . Ha . . . Ha . . . ," Kathy snickered, "What you talking about girl?"

"Yeah okay, don't play with me." Tuesday knew her mom had a habit of trying to seduce her and Peaches men whenever they had company. They always thought that their mom was trying to recapture her youth through them.

Everybody laughed knowing what she was referring to.

After they finished eating, Tuesday grabbed Gino's hand, "Come on." She stood up leading the way towards the bedroom. Entering the bedroom slow jams were coming from the stereo system. Gino immediately had a flashback to what Marquita had done to him earlier, and figured that he was in for another treat. The lights went out and the rest was history.

In the morning, Gino was the only person still asleep, while Tuesday and Peaches were in the living room gossiping about the events of last night. Shadow walked pass them shaking his head on his way to the bathroom, "Y'all don't make any damn sense." Shadow commented.

"We're not gossiping for your information," Peaches replied still snickering.

"Whatever!! Ohhh . . . Shittt!!!" Shadow slapped himself upside the head, then taking off running towards the bedroom.

"What's wrong baby?" Peaches asked as Shadow ran straight pass her into the bedroom. Peaches followed still asking what the problem was.

"Nothing . . . nothing," Shadow waved her off knowing that he had just remembered that they had left Tricia and Quita still at the hotel. Shadow looked at his watch, 10:30 a.m. "Aye Peaches do me a favor, go wake up Gino now, and tell him get dressed fast!!!!" Shadow shouted as she took off to do as he told her to.

CHAPTER 8

Minutes later they sped off down the highway where Shadow reminded Gino that they had left Tricia and Quita at the hotel. As they pulled up, Shadow knew he had a cursing out coming. They jumped out rushing to the rooms, pushing inside. Tricia and Marquita were sitting on the couch talking. Tricia's expression said it all, even before she opened her mouth. "Shadow uh . . . uh, I know damn well you ain't leave me and my sister up in the hotel while you went out chasing some bitches." Her face was steaming red, and her voice reeked anger, as she got into Shadow's face. "Now tell me you didn't . . . tell me . . . . ??!!!" She begged him to.

Shadow grabbed her hand removing it from his face, "Listen Tricia I wasn't chasing no broads, we were with the family. We partied all night and then went pass Grandma's and fell asleep by accident."

"What the fuck ever!!!!" she smooched Shadow.

All the while Gino had found his way over to Quita and had taken a seat beside her on the bed. Marquita was mad as well, but she was happier to be back in the presence of Gino, so she forgave him. After they all finished arguing and left, they stopped to eat at Tommy's Restaurant. Then dropped the ladies off, but as they dropped Quita off Shadow told her to get dressed he'd be back to get her, and to bring both of her ID's, she agreed and they pulled off.

Soon as they left Quita's, Shadow decided that he wanted to buy Gino a car, cause he knew that a fly ass whip was a must in the streets, and he wanted to make sure his man was set from the gate. Shadow took Gino over to Pamoco Car lot where Shadow was super cool with the owner, Doug. He and Shadow had been close for years, especially after the police raided Doug's lot one day for selling illegal paper tags. Doug owned the lot but he also sold coke out the back of the shop to make ends meet. On the day the police raided Doug's shop, Shadow and his uncle happened to be there buying some coke from Doug as well. When it was all said and done Shadow was a juvenile and his uncle convinced Shadow to take the beef, which he did and got nothing but a slap on the wrist for it. The police were mad because they knew what had happened, but there was no way to prove it. Doug and Shadow had been close ever since.

Gino selected a Smokey Grey Acura TL fully loaded. Doug gave Shadow a sweet deal, which he always did and the Acura was Gino's. Shadow tossed Doug a few extra thousand, and the paper work was fixed up and they were ready to roll. Shadow told Gino to get all his bags and shit out of his trunk and threw them in his trunk, they then took off.

Gino was now following Shadow and riding high. He felt like King Kong, and nothing could touch him. He had the sunroof open while he listened to Ludacris' new joint "Area Codes" play on the radio. Gino leaned his seat all the way back, and all you could see was his head cruising like he was on some gangster shit.

Shadow then went back to Quita's apartment beeping the horn for her to come out. While they waited, Gino pulled up beside Shadow and motioned for him to roll his window down. "Yo what up Gino?" Shadow asked.

"What we about to do now?"

"I want Quita to put an apartment for you in her name. She has good credit and is trustworthy, you know what I mean?"

"You sure she'll do that for me?" Gino asked noticing Quita exiting the apartment building door.

"Nigga! Quita and her sister will do anything for you and me, believe that! You think I introduced y'all for nothing?!"

Gino pointed his finger at Shadow, "You know what? You right big boy."

Now Marquita noticed that it was Gino in that brand new Acura, and shot right pass Shadow not even acknowledging him jumping inside with Gino. "Damn baby, this you?" She asked while looking around inside the coup.

"You better know it, and I'm just getting started." Gino laughed at the excitement on her face. "Nah, real talk Shadow just copped this for me."

"Oh yeah? Well I know he really fucks with you because you were all he talked about when he came home. He couldn't wait 'til you got out." Marquita stated.

"Yeah, that's what everybody keeps telling me." Said Gino.

"So what are we about to do?" Quita turned to face Gino.

"Shadow wants you to put an apartment in your name for me. Can you do that for me?" Gino threw the charm on.

"Of course," as she held her hands out, "as long as I get keys."

Gino looked at her with a serious expression, "I guess I can go for that." He smiled kissing her lightly on the cheeks.

They followed Shadow while he was on the phone calling around telling the whole squad to meet him at the stash house within the hour. It was time to stop bullshitting and put that plan into motion.

New Gate Apartments is where Shadow decided would be a good spot for Gino to live. It was a new complex, and not far from where they were going to be taking over soon. Shadow gave Quita two bundles of money and instructed her to go inside and get an apartment by any means necessary.

Half hour later, Quita came out the rental office with the keys to a two bedroom apartment which they immediately all went to look at. Shadow asked her what did she have to do, and she said nothing, just a promise of a later date. They all laughed. Gino then gave Quita the car keys, kissed her and hopped in the car with Shadow. RipRap Road was now their destination.

CHAPTER 9

Later at the stash house everybody was already in attendance when they arrived. Shadow called everyone inside so he could have the meeting that was either going to change their lives or take their lives. Inside, everybody was sitting around pondering what was about to be said, cause this plan had been kept a secret for months. Shadow and Gino entered the room, and all conversations ceased to exist, eyes got focused, bodies got to twitching, and nothing but what Shadow had to say mattered anymore. Shadow stood in the middle of the crowd, "Okay y'all," Shadow rubbed his goatee, "this is what we're going to do, we're going to take over the whole damn RipRap Road." Eyebrows rose! "Now we know these chumps think they running those streets, so we're going to have to show them that there are some new sheriffs in town. They can either get with us or get rolled over."

Gino cut in, "Let's just blast them suckers and cut the games. Those niggas might try to trick a nigga or something."

Shadow shook his head in agreeance with Gino. "Gino I thought about that myself, however, I'm trying to keep as much attention and heat off the spot. If we kill a whole block of niggas, the police will just shut the block down and it won't do us any good then. I believe if we just set a few examples then we won't have any resistance at all. These blocks are gold mines, I mean gold mines!" Shadow stared intensely into everyone's eyes. "And I don't want us to lose the opportunity to capitalize on it by doing something stupid. I'm guaranteeing everybody that if we get these blocks we'll all be filthy rich within the next few months. So are y'all with me or what??" Shadow looked at everybody as they nodded their heads and put their thumbs up.

"Now while we're moving in, we can't afford to have no slip-ups. Just so happens if you do, let us know off the break so we can try to fix the problem immediately. Listen carefully, now here are the blocks Bethel Ave., Langley Ave., Quash Street, and Wesley Ave. Bethel Avenue is the biggest, and will take more men to take down. So me and Gino will take that one, but we'll also have to put more work in to acquire and maintain it as well. Do whatever need to be done to take your blocks, rob, kill, beat down; I mean . . . you know how it goes. Nobody or nothing is to get in our way. If you have a conscience this not the place for you right now. This shit could get really ugly, so be prepared.

Now Bethel Avenue is the headquarters, so once we've taken that, the rest will fall in line. Fat Cheese, The Barlows, and Miami Dink run all other streets from Bethel. Be ever mindful that these dudes are not just going to lay down just like that, so we're going right at them off the top. After tomorrow, it will be known all throughout Newport News and Hampton that we're running shit form this point on. If you got any second thoughts, let us know now and save us the trouble cause this thing is going down with or without you." Everybody looked around at each other, but no one backed out. "Okay this will be the street assignments once we take over. Me, Gino, Uncle Tee, and Teddy Bear will hold down Bethel Avenue. Mason Street will be Donnie and Uncle Man. Quash Street will be Kelvin and AJ, and finally Wesley goes to Stevie and Greg. Now everybody meet us back here at 12:00 tomorrow and be ready!" Everybody stood up shaking hands and hugging each other, as they started leaving.

CHAPTER 10

"Let's get our shit cut," Shadow suggested to Gino. Gino rubbed his head noticing his waves were fading because his hair had been growing. "No bullshit I can go for that Fat boy."

"Yeah we've got to be fresh for tomorrow, you know?" Gino just looked out the window as they drove down the road. "Gino what you think about my plan?"

Gino rubbed his forehead like he was in deep thought, "Shadow mann . . . , I can't say. All I know is that I'm with you all the way 'til the end. We're going to ride or die together my nigga." Gino looked at Shadow to assure him he was serious.

"My nigga, I know you with me. Right now I'm doing it on a small scale, but once we get those blocks, shit's going to be lovely. Whenever you do decide to go back to DC, you'll have more money than you could ever imagine, and that's no bullshit."

"Then let's do the motherfucker!!" Gino shouted in anticipation, as they arrived at the barbershop.

Leaving the barbershop, Shadow decided to drop through few of his spots and collect some money that was owed to him. Then they went out to eat.

Marquita had headed over to Tricia's and Shadow's apartment to pick her up. Pulling up out front she honked the horn, then spotted Tricia peeking through the window acknowledging her arrival. Seconds later Tricia exited the door, rushing to the car, and jumping in. "Damn girl who shit you pushing?" Tricia closed her door, fastening her seatbelt.

Marquita smiled, "Girl, Shadow just bought this for me."

Tricia's head snapped around, "I beg your pardon! What did you say?"

"Bitch, I'm just playing, this Gino's new car."

"Damn he letting you push the whip already?? You must have fucked the shit outta that nigga!" They laughed.

"Bitch you know I always handle mines," Marquita pulled off. "Guess what else girl?"

"What Bitch?!"

"You know . . . we just got an apartment together too."

"You lying," they smacked high fives.

"Bitch, I'm locking the dick down before any of these funky ass hoes try their hand, feel me?!" exclaimed Marquita.

"I hear you girl," Tricia pulled her visor down putting lip gloss on her lips. "Get your man bitch.

"Yeah, look though I need you to ride with me so I can pick up some furniture for the apartment, alright?"

"Okay!" Tricia exclaimed smiling.

CHAPTER 11

Later Shadow and Gino were on their way home when Shadow suggested they stop pass to see Peaches and Tuesday, which Gino really didn't mind doing. Soon as they knocked on the door, Tuesday opened the door immediately jumping all over Gino, kissing his face. "Damn, will I get this every time I see you?" Gino asked smiling.

"Maybe . . . maybe not, but you'll have to come by more often to find out," Tuesday replied. "Hi Shadow." As he walked inside pass the love birds.

"Damn I didn't even know I existed," Shadow shook his head. "Where your sister at?"

"Oh she's in the bedroom." Tuesday stated as Shadow strolled on into the back rooms.

Gino pulled Tuesday down on the couch, "Listen baby girl, I need to tell you something." Gino grabbed her hands.

"Whatt . . . what just tell me . . . ," Gino put his finger over her lips.

Let me talk. Tomorrow we've got some big things jumping off, and I'll be extremely busy for the next couple of days. I don't want you to think I'm ducking you or avoiding you."

"Oh okay, I understand." She laid across Gino's chest. "Why were you looking so serious though?"

Gino bit down on his bottom lip, "Tuesday there's a possibility I could get killed tomorrow." She rose back up immediately. "But if I don't everything's good."

A slight tear fell from Tuesday's eye as she leaned over hugging Gino. Seconds later Shadow appeared from the bedroom with Peaches in tow crying her eyes out. Gino knew she had to be crying because Shadow had warned her about tomorrow. This is the life we choose, FUCK IT!

CHAPTER 12

Walking into his apartment, Gino was surprised at Quita's taste. She had dressed the apartment up super nice. She purchased leather furniture, a recliner, TV, and audio system, bedroom set, and a dining room set. Gino figured she had to have spent a considerable amount of money out the bag as good as the place looked. Quita came from out the bathroom, "Hey y'all . . . ." She walked over lightly kissing Gino and waving at Shadow. "You like what I picked out baby?"

"Fo' sho' . . ." Gino continued to walk around. "You call good money Shadow. You said she'd handle her B.I."

Shadow responded, "Nigga I told you, she knows what to do. She's perfect for you."

"I see." As Gino continued walking around.

"Gino, I just wanted to make sure all was well, I'm going to be getting up out of here. I'll see you early in the morning." Shadow pulled out his keys heading towards the door.

"No doubt, I see you early fat boy." Gino walked him to the door.

Shadow looked over Gino's shoulder at Quita, "See you sis!"

"Okay, tell my sister to call me too."

"Alright." Shadow looked at Gino, "and nigga stay away from Quita tonight." They all laughed as Fat boy exited the door.

That night Quita fixed Gino dinner and they just enjoyed each others company the rest of the night. Especially not knowing how tomorrow was going to turn out. Gino opened up in conversation to Quita revealing some of his history with Tykisha, his brother and past life to her, and she did the same. They really got a better understanding of each other that night, and by the time they went to bed Quita was sure that Gino was the man for her.

In the morning Shadow woke up early got dressed, and discussed with Tricia the danger that could possibly go down today. She began to cry, but it didn't make any difference because she knew that no matter what she said or did that Shadow was going through with his plan today. Virginia was going to be his within a matter of hours. Shadow kissed Tricia before exiting the door heading towards his destiny. Outside Shadow went to his Impala, popped the trunk retrieving a duffle bag full of artillery, then placing it in his coup and driving off. Soon as he pulled up at Gino's, he beeped the horn and Gino came straight out dressed in all black. Shadow smiled knowing Gino meant business today. Gino entered the car and they sped off to the stash house.

At the stash house, Shadow peeked at his watch noticing that they were early, so he grabbed the guns out the back and they went on inside. In the stash house Shadow set the bag on the table, disappearing and then reappearing with more guns placing them all spread out over the table. Gino's eyes got big as a mother . . . , "Gino!" Shadow called out. "Since you're the first one here, you can pick out whatever hammers you like." Shadow mentioned as he continued to place more guns on the table.

Gino surveyed the table grabbing the P-89 Ruger, and the 50 Caliber Desert Eagle. He stood there marveling at the 50 Caliber. "That's a lot of power homie; you think you can handle that?"

Gino looked up and laughed, "My nigga I was born for this kind of shit, you hear me?"

"Yeah Okay John Wayne."

While they were talking everybody started to show up slowly but surely. As they arrived everybody selected the guns they wanted and loaded up. Finally Shadow asked, "Are y'all ready or what??!!"

Everybody barked, "Yeah!!!"

"Let's do it then!" Shadow replied as they all headed for the door.

Bethel Avenue was the first destination. Initially turning on the block, Shadow spotted Cheese, Dink, and J. Barlow standing outside in front of the buildings as usual. Shadow instructed Gino to get out up the block so he could come up from behind just in case one of them suckers tried to make a run for it. Shadow and them then cruised down the block coming to a halt a few feet from the crowd, and exiting their cars. Cheese and Dink immediately turned to see who these niggas were pulling up on their block like that. J. Barlow reached into his dip for his hammer, until Cheese recognized who it was. "Nah . . . hold up y'all, that's just Fat Chris." As the crew removed their hands from the waist band.

Shadow walked up calling out, "Aye Dink let me holla at you for a second slim?" He approached with 6 of his crew behind him.

Dink waved Shadow over as he passed the blunt he was smoking to J.B. "Yo' what's up Fat Chris?"

Shadow walked up and before Dink could utter a word, Teddy Bear, Tee Tee, Kelvin, and AJ whipped out. Stunned and shocked looks came across everyone's face, as Cheese attempted to turn and make a run for it, only to run straight into Gino and that 50 Caliber. "Get your bitch ass back over there with the rest of 'em!!" Gino shook his gun motioning for Cheese to get back over with everybody else.

"Aye Yo' Chris what the fuck is going on with y'all coming up on our spot like this?" Dink mustered out as he had his hands now raised.

"Nigga y'all know what it is, I warned you suckers months ago." Shadow responded.

"Man whatever you want just take it, this shit ain't nothing to us." Cheese replied.

"Shake them down y'all and take their hammers," Shadow instructed the crew as he walked up into Dink's face. "Bitch nigga this shit ain't about any robbery, this is about Bethel Avenue period, and it's the takeover. Now I want all you bitch nigga's to listen up real good, because I'm only going to say this one time and one time only. From here on out, we're taking these blocks period. Now we're going to give you an opportunity to choose. You can join the team, or vacate and move on. Ain't no more works being sold out here unless it's ours, point blank! Now I know one or more of y'all are going to try and be slick and try your hand, which is a good thing cause we'll use you for the example."

All faces had a look of uncertainty on them, not really wanting to speak. "Aye Shadow what's all this about?" J. Barlow asked.

"Cause nigga, y'all ain't respecting the game when I tried to come through last time. Now you ain't got no choice, I'm taking." Shadow stated with emphasis.

Cheese then says, "Damn Chris we've been homies since Bad News, and this how you carrying shit now huh?"

Shadow looked around surveying the area, "Nigga you act like you ain't heard what I said!" He shouted angrily this time slapping Dink in the face with the 50 cal knocking him to the ground, losing a few of his teeth.

"Hold up . . . hold up Chris", Cheese begged as he looked down at Dink holding his mouth full of blood trying to grab his teeth. "Look man we don't want no problems, it's whatever. We ain't trying to beef with y'all."

"Good! Now tomorrow we'll be through here about the same time, y'all just be ready. If not, don't come up here no more period. If you do, I promise my man right here," Shadow pointed at Gino, "will kill you that's a promise. See you niggas in the morning." As Shadow and them just walked off hopping back in their cars and rolling out.

Next stop Wesley Avenue. Now this was going to be exciting to Shadow because he and Darryl had a long standing beef with each other, which had occurred years earlier. On Wesley Avenue there was a crap game going on, with all the major players out there. A few cuties were leaning on cars posted up, making their presence known. As Shadow and them pulled up and exited their cars, all broads started positioning themselves to be seen by this unknown crew of nigga's headed in their direction. Big Darryl noticed the crowd heading their way, and immediately his crew rose up to their feet from shooting dice. Darryl motioned for his men to be on point. As Shadow got closer and Darryl recognized who it was, anger instantly came across his face as he met Shadow halfway. "What the fuck is up nigga?!! You coming down on my block like you want some drama or something?!" Big Darryl shouted with a vicious mug on his face.

Shadow snickered at Darryl, which was like an insult, "Nah . . . hold on big boy," Shadow tried to stop from laughing. "Let me explain something to you . . ." Shadow continued to talk while unbeknown to Darryl and his crew, there were two hoopties slowly creeping up the block with tinted windows. "Darryl my nigga I've only come to warn you to get off this block. You no longer run this." Shadow commented.

"Nigga who the fuck you think you talking to???!!!!!" Darryl responded as he got all the way up into Shadow's face.

As the two hoopties pulled up with 2 gunmen leaning out the passenger side windows of each vehicle, someone from the cars yelled, "Bitch ass niggas!!!!!!!!!!!!!!!!!!!" Darryl and his crew turned to see who yelled as Shadow took off running in the opposite direction. Terror was now stuck on their faces as gunfire erupted, hitting big Darryl several times, jerking his body with each shot sending him to the ground. His body convulsed, spasm, and jerked like he was doing the Harlem Shake. Females were screaming, Darryl's men yelled out, "Run, duck, get the fuck down!!!!!!!!!!!!!!" Several of them tried to get away, but to no avail Tee Tee, AJ, and the crew wiped them out, as the two hoopties sped off down Wesley Avenue disappearing around the block.

The sight was ugly, dead bodies of males and females sprawled out all over the street and sidewalks, several injured, and some terrorized. But the message was definitely sent for sure as gunfire censed, Man Man pulled up in his SS Monte Carlo motioning for Shadow to come on. Shadow looked at Man Man, then back at Darryl's body, raising his gun once again and letting the three remaining shots from his chrome plated 9mm go into Darryl's head, then jumped in the car with Man Man, and they took off.

Mason Street here we come. While heading around there, Shadow pulled out his Uzi this time, removed the clip making sure it was full then throwing it back in. "Gino my nigga look there's this dude named Stingy that be around here, whose uncle is a police. This nigga has got to go, cause he informs his people on all the shit that goes on down the way. So let's eliminate him from the break." Shadow glanced over at Gino.

Gino nodded his head, "No problem my nigga! No more needs to be said." Gino then tightened his grip on the p-89 he was holding in his grasp.

When they slid through, Stingy was outside with several other workers serving customers as they came from all angles. Shadow peeped that nobody was conscience of what had happened at the other streets yet, cause nobody was really on point. So timing was beautiful. Shadow tapped Gino on the shoulder, "Look that's Stingy right there with the N.Y. Yankee fitted hat on serving the broad in the alley. When I give you the signal get rid of this nigga."

Gino never responded he just continued to play with the p-89 in his hand, staring at Stingy.

Shadow, Teddy Bear, Tee Tee, and Man Man then got out the car walking over to where Stingy and the other workers were. Gino waited for a minute then crept up from the back. Shadow then yelled, "Aye y'all come here for a minute!!" Workers were baffled, but came to see what was going on.

"What's up Shadow?" Marvin asked. Marvin knew Shadow since they both went to the same high school. "You know we missing customers, what you got to say?"

"Marvin," Shadow began with his facial expression changing to serious. "Since y'all are all over here now, I have an announcement. Starting tomorrow, all dope sold out here will come from us, if anybody sells some dope out here, and it ain't mines, you will be dealt with. Believe that!"

Stingy just had to open his mouth, "Shadow nigga you know damn well this Cheese and them block, and they ain't going for that." Stingy replied.

"See I knew somebody was going to be the dumb ass who challenges me. Well since you opened your mouth first, you'll be the example." Shadow winked at Gino who was now standing directly behind Stingy, P-89 right at the base of Stingy's skull. "POW-POW!!" Two shots to the head was what Stingy got as his body hit the ground gyrating. Faces were stunned and shocked, terror was everywhere, but nobody uttered a word. "Well now I hope that y'all see that this shit is not a joke, I'm serious. Again, as of tomorrow no dope will be sold out here unless it's ours understood??!!!" Shadow shouted.

Everybody just nodded their heads as Shadow and crew began to step off jumping into their cars and jetting.

Now the ride over to Quash Street was a little different cause Shadow already had one of his little men posted up waiting on Shadow's call. As soon as he spotted Shadow and crew turn the corner, V-Rock got up walking towards the curb where they would pull up to. Reaching the curb, Shadow rolled his tinted window down, as the smell of weed crept out the window. "What's up young soldier?" Shadow reached out giving V-Rock dap.

"Ain't shit Shadow," V replied leaning up against the car. "How did that other shit go?" V's eyes looked for some type of expression from Gino, but it was blank.

"Just as planned my nigga. I told you it was going down. We've taken care of everything else just have your soldiers out here and ready tomorrow morning. Nothing else will be sold out here unless it's ours." Shadow stated.

"No doubt big boy. You know I'm with you all the way. I had already taken the necessary steps around here anyway." V-Rock responded with a devilish grin on his face.

Shadow laughed, "I know you did shorty." V-Rock was a little 15-year old soldier that Shadow had watched and taken under his wing since V's mom died 2 years earlier. V-Rock was the typical young nigga in the hood with that American dream of getting rich, by any means necessary. Shadow had taught and groomed V-Rock in the drug game. So if push came to shove, shorty could handle his own. Shadow had intentionally gotten V-Rock to join Cheese's crew organization so he could learn their ins and outs, then report back to him, which is exactly how Shadow found out who ran what, and did what. He was forever grateful to V-Rock.

"Shadow don't worry man I got this block for you, alright?" V-Rock reiterated his position.

"Fo' Sho', I'll see you tomorrow." Shadow pushed the button rolling his window up, driving off all smiles.

Back at the stash house, everybody put their guns away that weren't used. While the rest was sent to be dropped in the creek. Out front as the crowd gathered, Shadow and Gino approached, "Okay y'all, I need everybody to be here first thing in the morning. We've got to package the shit up for selling. Make sure that you have all your people out there, and on point. That's it y'all. Go have some fun or something. Cause shit is about to take off for real." Shadow stated.

"Now that's what I'm talking about!" Bear yelled out as he gave AJ dap.

"Nigga I'm a show you nigga's how to stunt for real." Stevie added while imitating wiping his clothes, to imply how fly he was going to get.

Gino and Shadow hugged each other, knowing that the hard part was over with. "Let's get this money nigga." Shadow whispered in Gino's ear.

"No doubt, now drop me off cause I'm trying to try out that brand new King sized bed that I got at home." Gino commented while tilting his head.

Shadow bust out laughing, "Nigga you whipped already?"

"Call it what you want, take me home." Gino replied

"Yeah . . . yeah . . . , I need to be getting home myself. Tricia was still crying when I left this morning."

"Fat boy stop playing with that girl's head. You know she loves the shit out of you, her and Quita." Gino responded.

"Oh I know she loves me, but that's easy to do when a nigga is giving you everything. Let's wait and see if she loves me when I'm surrounded by 6-foot gun towers, or broke as a bag of rocks." Shadow stated.

"Why you looking at shit like that anyway?" Gino asked.

Shadow began to walk towards the car, "Gino my nigga, I always try to look at the reality of what shit is. At anytime the rules of the game say that you can be locked up or dead broke, just as fast as you get rich, that's if you're fortunate enough to get out before hand."

Gino understood exactly what Shadow was trying to say. "Well Shadow if we're about to get all this money you say we are, then it won't be long before we can retire huh?"

"Gino that's easier said than done. Money is so addictive, that no amount is enough."

"Well hopefully I'll be able to experience that and find out for myself." Gino replied.

"Yeah me too Gino," as Shadow grabbed Gino around the shoulders, "come on my nigga let's get home."

CHAPTER 13

"Beep . . . beep . . . beep", Shadow honked his horn as they pulled into the parking lot spotting Marquita headed in the direction of Gino's Acura. Quita turned as Gino hollered, "Aye Quita . . . Quita!!" Shadow drifted up beside her and she jumped into Gino's arms soon as he exited the car. "Oh . . . oh . . . my God," she continued to repeat kissing Gino all over his face. "Baby I'm soooo . . . glad that you're alright. I was on my way over to Tricia's now, cause she's been trippin' all day making me nervous thinking something had happened to y'all."

Gino released her from his grasp, "calm down baby girl, I'm alright."

"Boy you just don't know," she twisted her lips up. "I've been going crazy all fucking day worrying about both of y'all. And Shadow you need to get your fat ass home too cause that bitch had me worrying more than I was at first."

"Okay . . . Gino," Shadow saluted. "I'll see you tomorrow."

"No doubt." Gino gave him some dap.

"Bye Fat ass." Quita kissed Shadow on the cheek.

"Alright holla!" Shadow rolled out.

Having a hard time sleeping, Gino laid in bed with Quita lying across his chest dead sleep. For some reason Gino had Tykisha all over his mind. He laid there in bed, wondering what Tykisha was doing, and how could she have turned her back on him like that, after all they had been through. Gino wondered if she had thought of him as much as he had thought of her over the years. One thing was certain; Gino wouldn't forget the people who looked out for him, that was for sure. Shadow definitely was one person, and Tee was the other. I've got to really find a way to show them my appreciation for real, Gino thought before he dozed off to sleep finally.

Gino woke up and rolled over looking at the clock, which read 9:30am. Quita was no longer in the bed, and the aroma of breakfast food was oozing from the kitchen. "Marquita . . . Quita!!!" Gino hollered as he got up walking towards the kitchen. "Where you at girl?"

"I'm in the kitchen baby!" she yelled back.

Gino strolled into the kitchen and the sight of Marquita's nice plump ass showing through them black laced panties she was wearing gave Gino an instant hard on. Gino crept up behind her while she was cooking whispering in her ear, "Good morning baby," while his hands caressed her curvaceous body, then kissing her on the neck.

"Ohhh . . . oh . . . oh . . . wee!" She squelched her neck. "Baby you better stop before you make me burn your food. You know what I told you about your lips."

"Yeah you right, I definitely can't have you burn that up." Gino rubbed his stomach. "Cause I'm hungry as shit; you tried to work a nigga overtime last night."

She turned to face Gino placing her hands on her hips, sticking her ass out. "So are you complaining?"

"Hell nahh . . . ," Gino quickly responded as she sat his food on the table in front of him. "So what are you doing today?"

"I don't know yet baby? Why, you need me to take care of something for you?"

"Nah not really," Gino sipped his orange juice. "Just make sure that the phones get cut on today."

"Don't worry baby, I'll be here until they get here."

"Well here," Gino reached into his sweatpants pocket, pulling out a stack of one hundred dollar bills, removing 10 of them and handing them to Quita.

"What's this for baby?" she asked placing the money on the table.

Gino grabbed her hand, pulling her down on his lap, kissing her softly. Quita then straddled Gino, feeling his hard on through his sweatpants.

"That's for you sweetheart. Get your nails done or something. I'm quite sure that you'll find something to do with it, I know."

"Thank you Gino", she purred while kissing him again, but this time with more passion. Slowly she moved her hands down removing Gino's dick from his sweats to see it standing at attention. Gino moved his hands around to unfasten her bra, letting it drop to the floor. Gino then kissed her nice firm titties, then her neck, and nipples soon after as she shivered from his touch, Quita began to succumb to Gino's every whim. She thought that she was in control but boy was she mistaken.

Quita mounted Gino, whispering to him, "Put it in baby . . . put it in please . . . ." She begged and begged. Quita began to moan as soon as she felt Gino going inside her, and with every stroke and every movement she begged for more. Quita wrapped her legs around Gino and just rode the rhythm, until she suddenly spasmed and Gino knew she was cumming. After taking her to the moon, Gino grabbed her butt lifting her onto him harder and harder. He was sweating and mumbling, "I'm a . . . I'm a . . . bout to cum baby", as his body now jerked until he came all inside of her.

CHAPTER 14

The sounds of Shadow's car horn was going off outside. Gino kissed Quita bye, running out the door still half dressed, cause their episode had lasted longer than intended. "Be careful baby", she said as he was closing the door.

Gino held the door open, "I'm not fucking with you no more freak."

She smiled, "Get outta here before fat ass curse you out." Gino laughed closing the door exiting the building.

"Damn nigga", Shadow began to laugh at Gino shaking his head. "I told you to stay away from that girl. Boy she's gonna have your ass out there in a minute, watch what I tell you."

"Fuck you fat ass." Gino sat in the passengers' seat pulling his socks up.

"Why you ain't driving your car anyway?" Shadow asked.

"Cause I let Quita use it to go get her nails and shit done." Now placing his air max Nike's on his feet.

"Nigga are you crazy? She's going to make sure every bitch this side of Virginia see her in your shit, believe that. Man this shit is crazy." Shadow pulled off.

At the stash house the packaging was taken care of then divided up amongst the blocks. On there way out, Shadow's pager went off, "Hold up Gino, this little V-Rock right here. Shorty don't usually page me unless it's something serious." Shadow pulled out his cell phone dialing the number on his pager.

"Yeah who this," V-Rock answered in a panic like tone.

"This me little homie, what's up?"

"Shadow listen Dink, Cheese, and Jay are planning on pulling you a move. I don't know when or where, but it's in the works." V-Rock said in a whispering tone.

"How you know this?" Shadow asked.

"This morning they called a meeting with the old crew, and plans were discussed. So watch your back."

"Okay V-Rock, I appreciate that."

"Fo'sho, I'll be outside when you get here."

"Cool!" Shadow hung up the phone, confusion all over his face.

"What's up Fat Boy?" Gino asked as everybody came to see what the problem was.

Shadow paused as if he was thinking about something, and then looked around at everybody. "Listen y'all, I just found out that Dink, Cheese, and Jay are supposedly going to try and pull me a move."

"Oh yeahh!! . . . ," Greg exclaimed.

"Let's get them nigga's!!" Tee Tee yelled out.

"Hold up . . . hold up," Shadow raised his hand. "Don't worry about that I'm going to deal with these chumps myself personally. I need y'all to go ahead as planned and get on them blocks. If anybody have any problems, solve them with death. If shit gets too thick just give me a ring and let me know what's up. This is the first day we've got to keep our mash down on these suckers, never giving an inch initially. Alright let's roll." Everybody paired up with their partners heading towards their cars and shit. "Aye Gino and Teddy Bear let me holla at y'all for a minute." Shadow waved them over, as he discussed with them his course of action in dealing with Cheese and them.

The sun was glistening off Shadow's money green Cherokee truck when they turned onto Bethel Avenue this morning. You could see many workers posted up conversing and huddled up waiting for Shadow and them to arrive, but from the beginning Shadow didn't like the aura outside as he walked across the street towards the awaiting crowd. Probably because he spotted Cheese, Dink, and J. Barlow waiting along with the crowd of people that were out there. Gino and Bear went on as normal passing all their works out, as Shadow stood back monitoring everything, especially Cheese, Dink, and Jay. Once Gino and them passed the works out, and Cheese, Dink, nor Jay got any, Shadow caught them staring at each other with looks of uncertainty and questions. Then Cheese and them walked over, "Aye Shadow what's up? Y'all ain't giving us nothing, what part of the game is this?"

"Come on Cheese, do you think that I would treat y'all like these other niggas? Picture that!" Shadow looked at them like he was serious.

Dink then says, "Mann . . . we don't know what the fucks going on no more."

"Dink look here," as Shadow grabbed him around the shoulders walking him towards the truck. "That shit that happened yesterday is over with; we're partners now, alright?"

"Alright Shadow! I feel where you at."

"Come on y'all let's go get this shit for them," Shadow mentioned as they all now were walking towards the rides.

As they walked Cheese and them kept peeking and cutting their eyes at each other until finally Jay asked, "Where we going?"

"Nigga stop being so nervous," Shadow replied. "Didn't I just tell you we partners in this shit. Damn!!"

"Yeah you right." Dink answered attempting to quell his curiosity.

"There is one thing though," Shadow stopped at the truck now turning to face Cheese and them.

"What's that?" Jay asked

Shadow nodded towards Gino, and all heads turned towards Gino. Bear and Gino whipped out their guns. "Man hold up what's this about?!!!" Jay screamed backing up against the truck with his hands raised, while Cheese and Dink did the same. "Damn big boy I thought you just said that we were all together???"

"Yeah, you right Jay, and this is nothing personal, it's just a precautionary move. Now pat them down y'all."

"Come on with this sucker shit Shadow, this shit is crazy." Jay commented, but consented to let Gino pat him down. Gino removed a 45 pistol from Jay's waist. Dink had a 38, and Cheese had a beretta. After removing their shit, Shadow stated, "Now come on." As they jumped in the truck and Cheese rode with Bear.

Fifteen minutes later, they were at the stash house where Shadow jumped out rushing inside the house. When he came back out, he called for Gino to pop the hatch back door, where Shadow threw the backpack he had retrieved from inside the house, and then proceeded to hop back in the truck and pulled off. Cheese assumed that they were on their way back around Bethel Avenue until Shadow turned off on Mercy Boulevard and headed towards the James River Bridge. Jay and Dink looked at each other suspiciously; Dink then hunched his shoulders indicating to Jay that he was unsure of where they were headed as well. Minutes later as they were about to cross the bridge Shadow pulled over, anxiety immediately kicked in with Jay and Dink. "What's up Shadow?" Dink asked.

"Ain't nothing Dink, I just forgot something," Shadow hopped out the truck entering the rear hatch back again. Shadow pretended to go inside the bag and get something, which was really a signal for Bear to go ahead and handle his business. Shadow closed the hatch back and walked back around to the passenger's side window tapping the window where Dink sat, "Aye Dink and Jay," Shadow began to speak as Gino whipped out his 45 Smith and Wesson. Soon as Dink noticed he panicked, "Get the fuck out the truck suckers!" Gino screamed as Shadow pointed his hammer directly at Dink' dome. Slowly they exited the truck, as Shadow directed them to step around towards the back, where Bear was in route with Cheese at gun point. Cheese appeared scared as a wet leaf on a winter night, shaking so badly. "Shadow," Jay called out. "Man this shit is crazy. What the fuck is going on?"

"Bitch nigga, shut the fuck up," Shadow slapped Jay, Pow . . . ! Knocking him a few feet back as Jay grabbed the side of his face, where a red bruise immediately appeared. "Come on Shadow," Jay begged.

"You suckers thought y'all would pull one over on the old boy, huh?" Shadow commented.

"Hell nah . . . hell the fuck nah, where you hear that at?" Dink asked now on his knees at the back of the truck.

"Don't even worry about that, you'll have more important things to worry about. Like how are your families going to bury you suckers, POW . . . . POW . . . POW . . . POW . . . POW . . . , Shadow fired, then Gino and Bear followed suit. As 7 to 8 more shots rang out. POW . . . POW . . . . POW . . . . POW . . . POW . . . POW . . . !!! All three of them Cheese, Jay, and Dink laid there dead, blood and brains everywhere. "Come on y'all let's get out of here." Bear replied walking off first with Gino and Shadow right behind. Walking away Gino noticed slight movement in Jay's arm, and not knowing if he was dead or not, ran back over and squeezed off, POW. POW!! Two more shots splitting Jay's head wide open, and stepping off.

Now inside the truck as they drove off Shadow was chuckling to himself when Gino looked at him not knowing what was so funny, "What's up Shadow? I'm trying to laugh too."

"Nah it's nothing slim, I just laughed at how these suckers really tried to get at me."

"Well we ain't got to worry about that no more," Gino stated as they were crossing the bridge. "Hold up . . . hold up!!!!!" Gino hollered at Shadow motioning for him to pull over.

"What's up Gino?" Shadow turned to him.

"Give me your hammer," Gino held out his hand, as Shadow handed him his gun. Gino then jumped out the truck ran over to the bridge throwing both hammers in the water. Bear followed suit as they rolled out.

CHAPTER 15

Back on Bethel Avenue shit appeared to be going smoothly when they re-appeared form killing Cheese, Dink, and Jay. However, suspicious stares were everywhere, but no one was crazy enough to ask what happened to Cheese and them. Everybody just looked it off, charged it to the game and continued to do what they were doing, HUSTLING!

During the course of the day shit picked up tremendously, crack heads were swarming the blocks, purchasing dope and crack like it was going out of style or something. At the end of the first day, Shadow collected his money from all his runners and was ready to roll, when he noticed Gino still talking to a few niggas by the alley. "Gino!" Shadow called out.

"Yeah!" Gino turned, "what's up fat boy?"

"You ready?"

"Yeah, give me a minute." Gino was talking to one of his workers who insisted on selling to any and everybody, instead of the "Heads" that he knew. Gino instructed him to be careful, because it wouldn't do them any good if he got caught up for selling to an undercover. The worker understood and Gino left feeling better.

Back at the stash house Gino and Shadow waited for everybody to come in from the other blocks. Simultaneously, everybody started to arrive one behind the other. Gino gathered all the money bags from everybody and placed them in the truck, as Shadow called everybody up to the front porch. "Did anybody have any problems today?" he asked.

"We didn't," Tee Tee replied first.

"Nah . . . me either," Stevie then said.

"Shit went sweet as ever!" AJ answered. Everybody else just nodded their heads.

Shadow then says, "Well I must assume everybody sold out too then, huh?"

"Big Cous," Stevie spoke first. "Shit was going so fast I was getting nervous. Wesley was jumping all day long."

"Same here," AJ responded giving Stevie dap.

"I told you niggas," Shadow smiled, "these spots were like gold mines. If we can get a good run we'll be rich in no time." Shadow said as he hugged Gino, and the fam gave each other dap at the prospects of getting rich.

Shortly thereafter as everybody was departing for the day Gino spotted little V-Rock walking towards the crowd that was assembled by the curb rolling up blunts and popping them bottles, and called him over. "Aye V-Rock come here for a minute young nigga."

V-Rock told AJ to hold up for a minute as he came to see what Gino wanted. "What's up Gino?" he said as Gino gave shorty dap.

"Ain't shit shorty, I just wanted to thank you for letting us know the situation with those suckers earlier, you know."

"That shit ain't nothing Gino," V-Rock fired up the blunt that he was holding in his hand, letting out a thick wad of smoke. "I'm with y'all all the way. Shadow has always looked out for me." V-Rock then passed the blunt to Gino.

Gino shook his head, "Nah . . . Shorty, I don't fuck around." Gino never liked getting high cause he felt like, in the game he always needed to be on point at all times. Weed could cause you to get caught slipping. "Uh . . . Uh! Young nigga you remind me so much of myself when I was your age, you know that?"

V-Rock smiled, "Gino man, I'm just trying to get this money, feel me?"

"No doubt," Gino nodded his head, "get your money right first, then everything else will fall into place. Plus you won't have to depend on nobody."

"Yeah, that's exactly what I want." V-Rock exhaled another thick cloud of smoke. "Did y'all handle them suckers Cheese and them."

Gino nodded his head, laughing in the process. "You better know it."

V laughed as well, "Fuck 'hem!"

"How are you getting home V-Rock?" Gino asked.

"Oh AJ takes me home cause we live close by each other." V-Rock threw the butt of the blunt he had just finished on the ground.

"I tell you what V, go tell AJ that I'll drop you off, alright?"

V replied, "Holdup then, let me run over her to his car and let him know." V-Rock took off running.

All the while V-Rock and Gino had been conversing Shadow was standing on the porch, wondering what they had been talking about. However, Shadow knew from the body language that Gino had taking a liking to little shorty. Shadow walked over, as Gino caught glimpse of him coming out the corner of his eye. "What's up Fat boy?"

"Ain't shit, I see you done took a liking to little V, huh?" Shadow asked watching Gino's body language.

"Yeah Fat Boy, he just reminds me so much of myself. You know what I mean?"

"Yeah I know exactly what you mean," Shadow then leaned back against the wall beside Gino, "that's why I fucked with the little nigga from the beginning. Look I just talked to Tricia and she told me to tell you that Quita is on her way around here too."

"Okay," Gino responded as V-Rock came running back. "Alright Gino I told AJ, he said it's cool cause he about to go pass some freak house anyway."

"Okay, we're just waiting for my girl to come." Gino responded as he spotted his Acura turning the corner simultaneously, and pulling up in front of the house. "Spoke too soon, there she go right there. Alright Fat Boy," Gino reached out to shake Shadow's hand while Shadow was engaged in a conversation on his cell phone, "I'll see you in the morning." Shadow just nodded his head. As they walked off towards the car. No sooner Gino was about to enter the car, Shadow hollered out, "Aye Gino don't forget to get your bags out the truck!!"

"Damn!" Gino remembered that he had placed his money bags inside Fat Boy's truck. "Come on V give me a hand with these bags." They grabbed his three bags out the truck, waved at Shadow and rolled out.

CHAPTER 16

It was damn near 9:00pm when they arrived in front of V-Rock's apartment buildings. Gino shook his head at the sight of the Ford Projects where V-Rock lived. As usual it was filled with hustlers, dope fiends, crack heads, in front of what appeared to be run-down apartment buildings with busted windows, and pipes hanging from everywhere. Quita pulled up right where a crap game was taking place, never taking the car out of Drive, just holding the brake pedal just in case niggas got to acting stupid. "Okay young soldier, I'll see you tomorrow." Gino stated reaching in the back seat to shake V's hand. "Who you live with anyway V?"

"Oh I stay with my aunt. You know she a crack head, but she good peoples. I give her a few dollars here and there and she's cool. Plus she brings me a lot of sales."

"I know what you mean, believe that."

"I'm hoping that I can move out of here soon." V stared at the projects where he called home. V had been a victim to this kind of upbringing since he was 2, so he had become somewhat immune to it, but as he got older he knew he had to get out and soon. V got out the car and walked up to Gino's window.

"V-Rock I like to hear you talk like that. That lets me know you want better for yourself." Gino winked his eye at V.

"Sometimes it's just hard," V began while leaning down towards Gino's window, "but by my aunt being a 'Head' I really can't leave no money around her, you know? Every time I slip up, she burns me. I got to sleep with my shit on me now."

"If you want I can hold it for you shorty." Gino offered.

"Nah . . . I'm cool," V glanced around surveying, "but thanks Gino."

"How old are you V-Rock?" Gino had to ask, cause V seemed older but his build said he was young.

"15, but I'll be 16 in a few months."

"Yeahh . . . , damn I thought you were older than that. Okay V, we've got to go but if you want I'll pick you up in the morning."

"Yeah that'll be cool, I appreciate that."

"I'll pick you up at 10:30, be ready alright?"

"Alright," V replied then a voice suddenly called out. "V-rock . . . V-Rock, come here sweetie." Gino and V turned to see a woman who favored V-Rock, walking with a dude black as a frying pan, and both appeared to be high as a kite.

"Okay Gino, I'll holler that's my aunt. But I'll see you in the morning." V-Rock stepped off looking disappointed that Gino had seen his aunt.

Gino sat there continuing to stare at the confrontation between V and his aunt, she appeared to be asking him for something, probably a hit or a few dollars. "Gino baby," Quita broke the silence, "you must really like that boy."

"Quita you know what, I do! I understand exactly what he's going through. I was there at one time, my mom was a pipe head as well. When I was growing up I basically had to fend for myself. Fortunately, I had a few good dudes who took a liking to me, and looked out. But without them I don't know how I would have made it."

"Now I understand." Quita lightly pressed down on the gas pedal pulling away from the Ford Projects.

CHAPTER 17

At the house Gino and Marquita sat up counting money for 2 hours. Gino was extremely excited and pleased to see the first day take in. Gino instructed Quita that he needed her to go purchase a safe the next day while he was out on the block. She agreed, then Gino informed her that he didn't want any of her friends knowing where they stayed, because they would be having lots and lots of money at the spot. She then let Gino know she understood the rules to the game, and already knew what and what not to do. Gino was amazed at how sharp she was, he knew that Shadow had to have been the one who groomed her.

Later, Quita turned on the shower so that Gino could shower, and get ready for bed. Gino was standing under the hot massaging water letting it bounce off his body, when he spotted Quita's body standing outside the sliding shower door. Moments later she entered the shower, as Gino's eyes immediately locked on her marvelously shaped body. The girl had nice firm breasts and an ass like a donkey, you hear me? Marquita gently pushed Gino back against the shower wall, taking control off the break. Gino looked down at her, "Oh so you taking advantage of me?" he asked glancing into her beautiful, sensual eyes.

"Shut up," she whispered, "just enjoy yourself." as she lathered up the wash cloth, washing Gino's whole entire body. After rinsing him off, she found her way down, slowly taking Gino's hard penis into her mouth while staring him straight in the eyes. Gino raised his head in ecstasy as he placed his hand on her head urging her on. She sucked his dick with a furious passion, while playing with his balls.

Gino moaned, "Ohhh . . . baby, Ohh . . . Baby!" cause the head she was giving him was a monster. When she thought that he was about to cum she stopped, rose up, turned around and bent over. "Gino fuck me baby," she cried out grabbing both her ass cheeks spreading them so Gino could see what she was working with. Gino slid his penis inside Quita, starting off slow, with deep thrusts. Then he went deeper trying to touch her every wall. Quita stretched her arms out to brace herself from hitting her head on the shower wall. "Come on baby!! . . . come on baby!!!" she screamed as she climaxed.

Gino then grabbed her ass and pulled her to meet his every thrust as he really fucked her hard until he was about to cum. Sensing that he was about to cum from his speed of movement, Quita tightened up her pussy muscles, which made that thing feel extra good as Gino's body exploded in ecstasy.

In the bed that night Gino noticed that he was really starting to fall for Quita somewhat, he liked her swagger and style he thought. She treated him like a king and in return he treated her like his queen. Quita was 20 years old, which was only two years older than Gino, but she was far more mature than he was. She had been messing with older guys her whole life. However, she was so use to being the one in control in her relationships, but with Gino she found herself being submissive and willing to let Gino be in charge. They were a good fit.

Gino was up the next day early as he shook Marquita waking her, "Get up sleepy head. You got to make some runs this morning, did you forget?"

She rolled over pulling the covers over her head to block the radiant sunlight that came through the blinds, "Alright baby, hold up just give me five more minutes."

Gino snatched the covers, laughing, as she squirmed trying to cover her eyes. "Damn baby, I'm coming shooo . . . . t!" She rolled out the bed racing to the bathroom.

"And don't be all day in there either, sleepy head!" Gino snickered as she entered the bathroom closing the door.

Beep . . . beep . . . beep, Quita honked the horn outside V-Rock's apartment building. They sat waiting and watching to see if and when he would exit the building. Suddenly, Gino noticed this guy maybe 6

71

feet tall, stocky built, scruffy beard staring and heading in the direction of the car. Gino grabbed the handle of the Smith and Wesson that was sitting on his lap ready for whatever. Quita peeped him, "Gino Please," she reached out grabbing his forearm.

"Sssssssss . . . . ," Gino hissed, "I got this." He mentioned focusing his attention back on the guy who was now a few feet away from the car.

"Excuse me sir," the guy says approaching Gino's passenger side window.

"Yeah what the business be?" Gino stated as the crack head peeped the 45 sitting on Gino's lap and immediately he jumped back, "Nahhh . . . nooo . . . no . . . , I want no problems." He stumbled back.

"No, it's alright, come here for a minute." Gino waved the guy back over.

"I . . . . I . . . . I just had some food stamps that I was trying to sell, that's all. I didn't mean to cause no problems."

"Don't worry about that. How much food stamps do you have?" Gino asked while reaching inside his pocket pulling out some money.

"I got $100 worth, all I want is $50 for it." The guy smiled as if that would seal the deal.

"No problem, let me get them." Gino held his hand out to receive the food stamps. Gino knew crack heads were famous for running games, always get your product first, rule #103 in the hustlers manual. The guy placed the $100 booklet in Gino's hand, then Gino breezed through it to make sure it was all there. "Huh, here you go." Gino handed the guy $75.

"John John, aye . . . John John, get the hell away from that car." A voice yelled out . . . Gino snapped around to see V-Rock approaching, and yelling at the guy. "John get away from that car, you don't even know these people." V-Rock motioned for John to get back.

John stepped away still waving at Gino and yelling, "Thanks sir . . . thank you!"

"Come on young nigga," Gino told V-Rock. "Everything cool he just was selling some stamps that's all." V-Rock hopped in the car, and Quita sped off.

CHAPTER 18

"Alright baby, I'll see you later give me a kiss," Gino kissed Quita as they exited the car in front of the stash house. "Don't forget be here at 5:30 too."

"Don't worry baby, I'll be here. Y'all be careful too." Quita mentioned.

"We will," V-Rock responded.

"See you later," Gino stated as they began to head up the steps towards the front door of the stash house.

Midway up the steps V-Rock paused, looking back at Quita pulling off. "Gino man you know what, I like Quita. She seems like real good peoples."

"Yeah shorty," a smile broke across his face, "she is real good peoples, as you get to know her, you'll see."

"Aye Gino, man where you from? I . . . I mean . . . ." Gino cut him off.

"I'm from DC young soldier." Gino pushed through the front door of the stash house, V-Rock right behind him.

A puzzled look came across V's face, "If you from DC how in the hell did you start hanging all the way down here?"

"Ha. Ha . . .Ha," Gino laughed, "well shorty me and Shadow were locked up together. We got tight, and said that once we both got out that we were going to get this money together. And since he was out first, I guess this was the best move, you know?"

"Yeah I feel you, that's love right there. How is shit down in DC though?"

"It's no different from down here, everybody trying to get that money. Chasing that dollar and a dream. Maybe one day I'll take you down there. My little brother is around your age, and y'all would probably get along good."

"Oh yeah . . ." V-Rock replied.

"Yeah . . . , but I don't know how he's doing right now because I haven't talked to him or been to see him since I've been home." Gino sat down at the table with V-Rock sitting across from him. "See while I was locked up a lot of people turned their backs on me. So I'm going to wait til I'm on my feet and shining, before I go back around my way. You know what I'm saying?"

"Shitt . . . , nigga you already shining and doing your thing. You got the new Legend joint, a bad ass chick, and your own apartment, plus plenty money. What else you need?" V-Rock reached out to give Gino dap.

"Yeah all that's cool shorty, but I ain't buy none of that shit, Shadow bought all that for a nigga."

"So what, it's yours." V-Rock reiterated.

"I know what you're saying, but I just want to be able to say I got this on my own. You know what I'm saying? That's when I'm going back to DC shining for real. Maybe you can go with me."

"Yeah I definitely would like to do that."

Soon after everybody arrived at the house, and the works for the day were dished out, and then they disbursed for the day. On their way to their cars Gino hollered at V-Rock. "I'll see you later shorty."

"Alright Gino." As he hopped in the car with Stevie.

Shadow saw how Gino was really starting to get attached to V-Rock and smiled, because Shadow knew that that was the same thing that happened to him, soon as he met V-Rock. Shadow walked up, "Gino my nig', I see you done really took a liking to little shorty, huh?"

"Yeah no doubt Big Boy," Gino nodded his head, "I'm jive feeling shorty little swagger, you know. I used to be just like that. I'm going to try and help shorty out as much as I can."

Shadow smiled, "I feel you, and I felt the same way when I first met the little nigga. Why you think that I recruited him? He good peoples, and I encourage you to groom shorty as much as possible."

"I got that fat boy."

"Oh yeah, before I forget, I promised Peaches and Tuesday that we would take them out tonight too."

Gino's eyes opened wide, "Fo'sho my nigga. You know I'd love to hit that ass again."

"Alright lover boy," they laughed. "Well we'll holla at them tonight."

"Cool!"

CHAPTER 19

Bethel Avenue was jumping again today just as it was yesterday. RipRap Road as a whole was pumping from Wesley Avenue to Langley Avenue. Gino and Shadow were now clocking some major dough. On this day they were late finishing cause Shadow had brought out extra coke and dope cause he wanted to make a killing while shit was pumping so hard. Money was the bottom line, get it now and as much as you could.

At the end of the day everybody was back at the stash house when a crap game broke out. Gino had just gotten off the phone telling Marquita to come pick them up, when Shadow called him out. "Aye Gino hang up that phone nigga, and come over here so I can get some of that money up off you."

Gino laughed as he walked up, "Picture that, you ain't smooth enough to pull that off." Gino replied reaching into his pocket pulling out a bundle of money.

To everyone's surprise V-Rock was the only one throwing numbers and winning all the money at the moment. "Come on little nigga, I got your fade." Shadow stated to V-Rock as he slid the dice back to him.

"Big Boy I hate to do this to you, but you jumped out there." V-Rock responded as he threw pass after pass. I mean shorty was on fire for real and talking plenty shit too.

Finally he got off the dice, that little nigga had won about $8,000 in about 15 to 20 minutes. Gino got on the dice a few times but couldn't hit a number more than once or twice. So he just decided to start betting with V since everybody was gunning for shorty. When it was all said and done, Gino and V-Rock had shut it down.

After the crap game Shadow told everybody to put their money bags in his trunk. Gino removed his three bags and handed them to V-Rock to hold. Five minutes later Quita pulled up, and V-Rock immediately placed Gino's bags inside the car, while Gino was finishing up his conversation with Shadow. "So Fat Boy what's up, before I roll out?" Gino asked noticing that Quita had rolled her window down trying to listen.

Shadow leaned in to whisper into Gino's ear, "I'll be pass to pick you up at 9:00, and don't be in there with that lovey dovey shit with Quita either."

Gino burst out laughing, "Nigga cut it out, I'll be ready. See you later." As they gave each other dap.

Rain had just started to subside as they were riding on their way to drop V-rock off at home. Gino turned around looking over his shoulder to see V-Rock in the back seat counting all the money he had just won. "Damn V, my nigga you won a lot of money tonight, huh? Make sure you're smart with your money shorty."

V licked his fingers and continued to count his money, "No doubt Gino, I might need you to hold some of this for me tonight. I can't afford to have my aunt get hold of this here. She'll be done smoked all my shit up."

"I got you, just count it and let me know how much you want me to hold for you."

"Alright give me a minute."

In any event as Quita turned into the Ford Projects they all spotted several fire trucks, police, and other emergency responsive vehicles cluttering the street right along the building where V-Rock lived. A closer look revealed that the building V-Rock lived in, was on fire from the back side. Flames were still coming out the building, but everybody had already been evacuated. As they all got out and rushed to the scene, V-Rock immediately begun to look for his aunt. Several tenants had informed V-Rock that the last time they had seen of her, that she was being interviewed by some officers in connection with the fire. V-Rock scurried off in search of his aunt as Gino and Quita followed.

Behind all the commotion, over at the corner of the block several tenants were being interviewed by officers, when V-Rock spotted his aunt. "V-Rock hold up!" Gino yelled to stop V-Rock before he just ran over there. "Come here shorty." Gino waved him over.

V-Rock looked frustrated and confused walking over to Gino, "What's up Gino?"

"Look you don't need to be going over there, just in case your aunt is being arrested. Because if she is arrested you'll be snatched too, cause you're a juvenile in her care. You understand?"

V-Rock nodded his head, while still looking at the conversation his aunt was having with the officer. "Quita look," Gino began, "go over there and find out what's the situation with his aunt, if you can. Just be nosy act like you're interested in the situation or something. Just find out something." Gino stated.

"Alright." Quita responded as she walked off into the direction where V's aunt was being questioned.

"Damn Gino," V-Rock replied while looking at his building that was still engulfed in flames. "Man all my shit was up in there. What the fuck am I going to do now?"

"What do you think you're going to do, SURVIVE! Shit happens, and life goes on." Gino looked at V-Rock with the compassion of a father. "I got your back no matter what, you hear me?"

V-Rock just stood there shaking his head, still shook up about the whole situation overall. I guess it would be a lot for any 15-year old to digest. Shortly thereafter Quita came back and informed them that V-Rock's aunt was being taken down for questions in connection with starting the fire. V-Rock was in a daze upon hearing the information, lost in his own thoughts. "Aye Gino, can you drop me off at the 6?" V-Rock asked.

Gino was standing there hugging Quita from behind. "Shorty look, don't worry about nothing, didn't I tell you I got your back?"

"Fo'sho?" V-Rock replied truly not understanding what Gino meant.

Back at the car, Gino instructed V-Rock to get inside, as he and Quita stood outside talking. "Baby what's wrong?" Quita asked sensing something was on Gino's mind.

"Quita would you have a problem with shorty staying with us until he get on his feet?"

She peeked inside the car at V-Rock, "Baby that's your call, whatever you say is okay with me."

"You sure? I mean be honest." Gino stated as he looked her straight in the eyes to see if he could see any apprehension.

"No for real baby, it's cool with me."

"Alright come on." As they hopped back in the car.

"What's wrong Gino?" V-Rock asked as soon as they entered the car.

"Nothing . . . Nothing shorty. Listen to this, and I want you to listen good." Gino faced V-Rock so that V totally understood what he was about to say to him. "Now I ain't supposed to allow no one to know where I lay my head at, that's just one of the rules to the game. However, I'm going to break a rule this time and let you stay at our house. Please don't let me down, or make no ass out of me. I don't ever want to regret this decision, alright?"

"Gino man, I ain't gonna fuck up for real. You can count on me, I promise."

"Also this is my woman right here," Gino's eyes strolled towards Quita, which V-Rock understood. "You must respect her to the fullest at all times." Gino said with emphasis.

"I got you Gino, that's my word."

"Come on then, let's go!" Gino said to Quita as she started the car.

CHAPTER 20

It was just after 7:00 when they finished eating and Marquita was clearing the table preparing to wash dishes. "Gino, thanks my nigga, I appreciate everything that you're doing for me." Stated V-Rock.

"No problem shorty, just remember what I said." Gino reiterated, as he glanced at his watch and decided he had to hurry up and go take his shower before Shadow arrived.

"Where you going tonight Gino?" Quita asked when she heard the shower water cut on.

"Oh, me and Shadow are going to take care of some stuff, but I won't be gone long."

"Gino don't be out late, you know I can't sleep if you're not home." She said in a sexy tone.

"I won't, I promise."

Gino finished his shower and got dressed, as he waited for Shadow to show up. Shortly thereafter, Shadow's horn beeped. He kissed Quita, "I'll be right back baby." Gino whispered in her ear. He then gave V-Rock a pound and rolled out.

As he exited the building Shadow was waiting, sitting in his convertible white 64 Impala, seat laid way back. "Damn this how you doing it?" Gino mentioned.

"I mean you know, I've been known to do that from time to time." Shadow replied with a smirk on his face.

"Okay . . . okay Fat Boy. Aye but check this out I need to holla at you for a minute." Gino commented as he came around and got inside the Impala on the passengers' side.

"What's wrong my nigga?" Shadow asked as a concerned look came across his face.

"Fat Boy I jive did something tonight and I wanted to put you on point." Gino stated as Shadow nodded his head. "You know when we left the stash house we took V-Rock home, right?"

"Right!"

"Well when we arrived at his apartment building, the joint was on fire. The whole spot jive like burnt down basically, and they took shorty's aunt in for questioning."

"Okay, that's all?" Fat Boy asked.

"Nah . . . , so V-Rock didn't have anywhere to go. I decided to bring shorty back to the house, he's inside with Quita now."

"Gino I mean . . . , you made the call. Shorty's a good dude, and I probably would have done the same thing. But you've got to be extremely careful now. Not saying that he'll do something to betray you or nothing, but you understand how the rules to the game are." Shadow said as he looked at Gino with a serious stare.

"Yeah I feel you," Gino replied, "I trust the little nigga though. He's the one who put us on point that them suckers were going to try and get at you. I mean . . . I just like the little nigga anyway."

"Ha . . . ha," Shadow snickered. "Yeah I know, but under pressure you never know what he may do."

"I trust him Shadow!" Gino reiterated while rubbing his goatee.

"Well if it's cool with you, then it's cool with me. Fuck that come on let's go have some fun."

"Fo'sho," Gino responded as he exited Shadow's Impala, hopping into his coup following Shadow as they headed to Peaches and Tuesday's house.

They picked up the females and decided to head down to the Solid Gold Night Club, as they pulled up in front of the club it was packed, the line was way around the corner somewhere. Shadow informed everybody to follow him as he headed to the front of the line, then called out. "Aye Big Al, what's happening?" Shadow yelled as he held his hands up so Al could see who he was. Al was the bouncer at the door of the club. He immediately noticed Shadow. "Who dat . . . my nigga Shadow?" Al responded.

"Yeah you know who it is," Shadow answered as he handed Al something in his hand. "You know how we carry it."

"No doubt, I see you later," Al replied as he headed back towards the entrance of the club.

No sooner as Gino and Shadow walked through the double doors of the club, it seemed like all eyes and attention turned towards them. Beautiful women were posted up all over the room smiling flirtatiously, and guys were gawking at Peaches and Tuesday. Everybody from Newport News to Hampton had heard about the takeover, so the sight of them immediately sent a frenzy throughout the club. Word on the street was that, they were killing first and asking questions later. So everybody knew that they meant business.

Strolling through to their tables, many hood soldiers were hollering at Shadow and his men. Peaches and Tuesday were just enjoying all the attention that they were getting, and loved every bit of it too. Even as they all sat down the attention didn't stop.

Gino looked around before sitting down, "Damn Fat Boy it seems like everybody in here watching us, huh?"

"Well Gino," Shadow was smiling, "you know that everybody done heard about that work we put in, so it's understandable. Fuck'em we're here to have some fun and have a good time." Shadow grabbed Gino around the shoulders, "Come on let's go get some drinks my nigga."

As the night wore on all the attention was starting to bother Gino. It was okay at first, but now Gino was getting annoyed with it. "I'll be back y'all, I've got to use the bathroom." Gino rose up from the table.

Gino walked towards the area where the bathroom was located, but as he was walking he could feel some intrusive eyes watching his every move. As he glanced around, sure enough there were 3 guys who seemed to be watching him extra hard. Gino looked it off, and kept on heading to the bathroom.

After exiting the bathroom he noticed that the same 3 dudes were still watching him. Gino again shook it off, and pushed back to the table where he grabbed Shadow's shoulder to get his attention. "Aye Shadow did you bring some heat with you?"

Shadow looked around, "You know I did, I never leave home without it. Why what's up?" Shadow looked at Gino to see what the problem was.

"See them nigga's over there," Gino pointed at the 3 guys he noticed watching him from earlier. "them suckers keep looking at a nigga, like they want some problems or something."

"Are you talking about those 3 niggas sitting at the bar?" Shadow asked.

"Yeah!"

"Look that's Big Pokey, Mack, and Black, they from Walker Village. I ain't never liked them nigga's, but they've always stayed in their place, feel me?"

"Well I'm about to check and see why the fuck they keep watching my every fucking move." Gino pierced his eyes over at them, letting them know that he was talking about them.

"Fuck them suckers Gino, don't let them fuck up our night, too many bitches in here sweating us. As a matter of fact, see that broad right there with that mini skirt on standing next to the girl in the knee high boots?"

Gino spotted them immediately, "Yeah I see her, why what's up with her?"

"That's Missy and Tangie. Tangie asked me what's up with you a few minutes ago." Shadow smiled at Gino.

"What did you tell her?"

"Nothing but I guess you're about to find out, cause here they come now." Shadow mentioned to Gino. "Don't look back cause they'll know that we're talking about them."

"Uh . . . Uh . . . Uh," Missy uttered like she was clearing her throat. Gino turned to face them when Missy spoke up. "Shadow what's up with your friend? Tangie trying to holla at him! You ain't let him know?"

"Tangie can speak up for herself, can't she?" Gino asked while admiring Tangie's body.

Tangie sipped her drink, "You right, I apologize. My name is Tangie, nice to meet you Gino."

"Same here," Gino replied now moving closer to Tangie.

"I guess that was your little girlfriend that I saw come in here with you, huh?" Tangie asked as she licked the rim of her glass.

"Something like that." Gino looked up to make sure Tuesday was no where around.

"Well I take it that it's not all like that, since we're engaging in this conversation then, right?"

"I guess that depends on what you want from me?" Gino asked.

Tangie smiled, "I can be whatever you want me to be."

"I tell you what Tangie," Gino said continuing to watch out for Tuesday, "since I don't want to disrespect my female friend and cause no scene, why don't you give me your number and we all can hook up tomorrow and hang out."

"That sounds good to me," Tangie replied. "You free tomorrow Missy?"

Missy nodded her head yes, as she continued to converse with Shadow.

"She's free too, so I guess that's a bet." Tangie reaffirmed. "Plus I don't have time to be whipping nobody ass tonight." As she went off into her purse, searching for a pen, after writing her number down she handed the piece of paper to Gino. "Don't have us waiting on y'all all day either, just call and let us know something."

"Fo'sho," Gino responded, "I'll call you personally myself around 12:00 alright?"

"Okay," Tangie answered. "Come on girl," she called out to Missy, "before we have to whip some asses tonight." Missy said her goodbye's to Shadow and they stepped off.

"Damn Fat Boy, that's how bitches doing it, huh?" Gino commented as they watched them walk off.

"Nigga I tried to tell you, but you ain't listening."

"Yeah you right. Look I'm going over here cause I just peeped Tuesday with some of her friends, and I know they were talking about me."

"Alright I'll see you later," Shadow responded as he stepped off and Gino headed over towards Tuesday. Gino was approaching when he noticed Tuesday and her friends were staring at him and whispering. So naturally he assumed that they were talking about him. Tuesday broke off and met Gino halfway. "Hi baby, where have you been? I've been looking all over for you." Tuesday stated as she put her arms around Gino's neck.

"I've been looking all over for you too. I see you and your girlfriends staring and shit, what's up with that?"

"Nooo . . . , I was just letting them bitches know, stay away from mines. I don't want to have to cut no bitches tonight."

"Girl you wild as a mother . . . . ! Shadow wasn't lying about that."

"No! I'm crazy about you," she kissed Gino. "Come on," she grabbed his hand pulling him, "I want you to meet some of my girlfriends."

Later that night Gino and Tuesday were coming from the bar heading back towards the table, when Gino noticed the same 3 dudes from earlier headed in their direction. As they were all crossing paths Gino zeroed in on the niggas. "What's up Tuesday?" one of the dudes says as Tuesday ignored his greetings and kept walking with Gino right behind, but as Gino was passing the last dude, he heard one of them say, "Fuck that bitch, she ain't all that for real."

That was it, Gino snapped around. "What did you say bitch nigga?!" As everybody in the vicinity eye's turned towards Gino.

"Who you talking to slim?" the guy Gino was staring at asked.

Gino began to walk over towards him as Tuesday tried to pull him back. "I'm talking to you, if you want me to be!" Gino forcefully said now standing in the dudes face.

"Nigga I said what I said, now what?" The dude commented in an aggressive manner, while his man started acting like he was reaching for something. "Now what you trying to do?"

Big Pokey then grabbed Mack, "Come on man, that nigga don't want no drama."

Gino snatched away from Tuesday, "Yeah okay, don't get tricked. All you got to do is jump out there." As now a few dudes were getting in between them trying to stop the situation from blowing up. But by this time somebody had ran and gotten Shadow who rushed up pushing through everybody. "My nigga what's up?" Shadow asked, eyes going back and forth from Gino back to Big Pokey.

"Ain't nothing these niggas just doing a whole lot of faking, that's all."

Shadow walked over to Big Pokey and Mack, "Aye Mack so what the fuck is up, y'all nigga's know y'all don't want this for real?"

"Shadow fuck you and that nigga!!" Mack yelled out throwing up the VA sign with his right hand.

"You know what? You right. Come on y'all." Shadow replied as they all headed for the exit sign immediately. On their way out the door Shadow stopped, whispered something into Big Al the bouncer's ear, then stepped.

Outside Shadow popped the trunk and handed Gino a Tec-9, and snatched his baby 380 with an extended clip from the secret compartment he had made in his car. Slamming the trunk they walked back towards the club, "Aye Shadow, know what?" Gino paused looking around seeing that nobody was really outside. "Put the girls in your car, I got these niggas."

Everybody looked at Gino, "Are you sure???" Shadow asked.

"Yeah I just want you to wait for me somewhere at the end of Washington Avenue."

"You sure about this?"

"Yeah, I got this." Gino repeated as they all hopped inside of Shadow's car and pulled off.

Finally, the club had started letting patrons out. When the doors opened, everybody was peeking around assuming that something was about to go down. "Mack we've got to be careful, them nigga's might be out here waiting on us." Big Pokey stated as they were exiting the club.

"Pokey you see them nigga's anywhere?" Mack asked as they all surveyed the area, while everybody scurried towards their cars.

"Fuck that Mack, let's get to our cars and get them joints. I'll feel better with that heat in my hand." Pokey said with emphasis.

"No doubt, let's go y'all." Mack responded as they headed towards their car still looking for any sight of Gino, Shadow, and the rest of them.

Unbeknown to them, Gino was sitting in his car watching from a distance and waiting to make his move. "Come on bitch niggas get to your car." Gino whispered to himself while watching them and cocking his Tec 9.

Finally they approached a white Taurus wagon, as Mack reached in his pocket for the keys. "Come on nigga, we're like sitting ducks out here!!" Black screamed at Mack to hurry up and find the keys. While they all continued to look around, Mack got the keys out, opened the door, got inside then hit the automatic unlock button, unlocking their doors. Upon entering the car Mack reached under his seat and grabbed his Uzi, while Black grabbed his 9mm. "Give me that Uzi Mack since you're driving," Big Pokey stated, "you can't drive and handle that."

"Shiddd . . . , who told you that?" Mack replied, "nigga I'm a beast." Mack started up the car, but as Mack was turning the ignition to start the car, a shadow appeared out of nowhere at the driver's side window. It was too late, "Watch Out!!!!!!!!!" was all that Pokey got a chance to scream before Gino cut loose.

"POW . . . POW . . . POW . . . POW . . . POW. POW . . . POW . . . POW . . . POW . . . POW . . . POW . . . POW . . . POW!!!" Damn near emptying the clip.

"Bet you bitch niggas won't be faking no more!!" Gino yelled out as he started firing again. "POW . . . POW . . . POW . . . POW . . . POW . . . !"

Gino ripped the wagon to shreds, then disappeared into a dark alley, where he jumped inside his car and sped off down Washington Avenue. "That will teach you niggas to keep your mouths closed right there." Gino beat his chest, as he rolled out in search of Shadow and the ladies.

Now finally about 5 blocks down the Avenue, Gino spotted Shadow's Impala parked next to the gas station on the next block. Soon as Shadow caught a glimpse of Gino, he pulled out onto the Avenue and mashed with Gino right behind him.

At Peaches apartment they parked, and rushed inside. Entering the apartment they headed into the living room, and took seats. Tuesday sat down beside Gino, "You alright baby?" She asked while rubbing his cheek with her hand.

"I'm cool baby girl," Gino smiled, "don't start getting all soft on me."

"Nigga you a wild mother . . . . !" Shadow commented as Peaches sat on his lap. "Did you handle that?"

"No question! Do bears shit in the woods?" They all laughed.

"No doubt," Shadow gave Gino dap, "fuck'em I guess we'll read about them in tomorrow's paper."

"Gino baby, thank you for taking up for me like that." Tuesday said while staring into his eyes.

"No need for that baby! No nigga will disrespect you or any of us while I'm present. How did you know them niggas anyway?"

"I use to mess with one of their friends a long time ago, but I know they were just trying to show off because they seen us together."

"Well they ain't got to worry about that no more."

Shadow laughed, "Church my nigga!"

"Excuse me y'all," Tuesday grabbed Gino by the hand pulling him to follow her. "I need to speak to Gino alone for a second." As she pulled Gino out onto the patio.

Tuesday stood at the rail on the patio gazing out into the parking lot as Gino stood behind her with his arms wrapped around her neck. "What's wrong baby?" Gino asked noticing that Tuesday had something on her mind.

"Gino . . . Gino, I just don't want nothing to happen to you. Do you know I was thinking about you all day?" She said in a soft tone.

"Oh yeah, well that's a good thing."

"Nah . . . Seriously Gino I usually don't go crazy over no nigga like this, but it's something about you."

Gino giggled a little bit, "That ain't what everybody tells me about you!"

"Stop playing Gino," she playfully pushed him back. "I'm serious Gino, I'm really attracted to you, and the bad part about it is, we haven't even known each other that long."

"Well sometimes Tuesday people are just attracted to each other instantly. You believe in love at first sight don't you?"

"I don't know cause I've never had that happen to me before." Tuesday shot back as she turned to face Gino.

"Well you know what the saying is, there's a first time for everything." Gino responded as he kissed her on the forehead, then on the lips.

Shortly thereafter Shadow came out onto the patio, "come on my nigga, you got to stop all that lovey dovey shit." Shadow belted out.

"Whatever!" Gino answered waving Fat Boy off.

"Okay lover boy, come on we got to roll."

Tuesday grabbed Gino around the waist, "stay with me a little while baby, please?"

Gino slightly kissed her lips, "Baby girl you know I've got to go, but I'll call you first thing in the morning alright!"

She pointed her finger at Gino, "You promise?"

"I promise," Gino replied.

Shadow just shook his head stepping inside from the patio, "This lovey dovey shit is crazy." As he threw his hands in the air.

Outside, Shadow was leaning on his car waiting as Gino finally came out. "Damn I thought you might spend the night or something as long as you took." Shadow commented jokingly as Gino walked up. "What happen with those suckers tonight?"

"You know what happen, I crushed them suckers." Gino made it clear. "I couldn't let them get away with that shit right there."

"You right slim, now I've got to get home before Tricia kills me." Shadow says.

"Yeah me too, I'll see you in the morning." They embraced and then began to enter their cars. "Oh yeah, Shadow I might be a little late in the morning, cause I'm going to take V-Rock shopping and shit."

"Alright, I got you. Here," Shadow tossed Gino a stack of money, "use that to get some of shorty shit. I got love for the little nigga too. Don't tell him I gave you that though, alright?"

Gino hunched his shoulders, "Why?"

"You handle that, he's in your care," Shadow mentioned as he pulled off.

When Gino got home, the house was quiet as a church mouse. Gino assumed that everybody must have been sleep. On his way to his bedroom, Gino peeked in V-Rock's room to make sure he was alright. V-Rock was knocked out cold, Gino smiled, closed the door and headed into his room. Gino tried to gently open the door, so he would not wake Quita up. WRONG!, "Gino hi baby." She said sleepily.

"What's up baby? I didn't mean to wake you. Go ahead back to sleep, I was just coming in." Gino replied while removing his clothes.

"You know I can't sleep good without you here beside me," she mumbled as Gino hopped in the bed and snuggled up against her. "I'm alright now baby." She whispered as she went off to sleep.

CHAPTER 21

The alarm clock blasted on playing 50 Cents song, "In the Club".
Gino immediately rose up pushing the off button on the clock.
Wiping his eyes and trying to clear his bearings, he noticed that Quita
was not alongside him in the bed. Gino hopped up and ran to the
shower, knowing he had a lot to do today.

After exiting the shower and getting dressed, Gino went into
V-Rock's room to check on him. V-Rock wasn't in his room either. Gino
then headed towards the kitchen where he heard chatter going on. As he
entered, Marquita and V-Rock were in there talking like they were sister
and brother, which brought a smile to Gino's face. "Good morning y'all!"
Gino spoke as he entered taking a seat at the table beside V-Rock.

V-Rock responded first, "What's up Gino?"

"Hi baby, we've been waiting for you to get out the shower." Quita
kissed Gino.

Gino smiled, "Yeah I see."

"We've just been in here talking baby." Quita said as she continued
to cook the food on the stove, "This boy crazy baby, he keep trying to
get me to hook him up with one of my friends."

V-Rock jumped in, "I'm saying big homie, Quita hating on me for
real."

"Please . . . boy, you're only 15."

"So what sis, I know how to handle mines." V-Rock beat on his chest
like he was the man.

Gino decided to intervene at this point, "Damn Quita I know you ain't hating baby?" Gino jokingly inquired.

"Please . . ." She emphasized placing her hands on her hips. "Gino you shouldn't be sicing that boy up. He need to be meeting girls his own age."

Gino laughed at both of them, "V-Rock you just have to show her, you might have to pull up on one of her friends on the low by yourself. Make her a believer."

"Yup', you right Gino!" V-Rock responded.

"Gino that's bad you doing that to that boy like that." Quita said as she placed Gino's and V-Rock's plate in front of them shaking her head.

They ate, got dressed and headed down to the New Market Mall in Hampton. They got there early, so all the stores were basically empty. They hurried and shopped for V-Rock, but of course you know women, Quita just had to shop too. V-Rock picked out whatever he wanted and Gino paid for it. When they finally finished V had about 8 bags of shit in his hands, and Quita had a few herself.

Back at the car, Marquita thanked Gino and so did V-Rock. Now riding home Gino remembered something, "Oh aye V-Rock," Gino began to speak, "I forgot to tell you, when you see Shadow thank him too. He gave me some money towards buying some of your stuff too."

"Okay, no problem slim, I'll do that as soon as I see him. Thank you again too though Gino."

"Don't worry about nothing shorty, I just want you to start saving your money and stay focused."

"I will Gino, as a matter of fact all the money I came up with yesterday, I gave to Marquita."

Quita cut in, "Yeah he did that baby. I put in the small safe under the bed." Marquita informed Gino.

"Alright, she'll take care of it for you."

At 11:20, Gino and V-Rock pulled up outside the stash house. Gino noticed that everybody's cars were still parked out front, so they parked and dashed inside. As usual inside everybody was still packaging their shit for the day, and kicking it. Shadow was on the phone when Gino approached, "alright Grandma, I'll call you later." Shadow said into the phone as he hung up. "Damn my nigga you alright?" Shadow placed his hand on Gino's forehead testing to see if he had a fever. "I thought something was wrong, cause you are usually never late. You still letting that girl pussy whip you nigga?"

"Fuck you fat boy," laughter erupted. "Hell nah, I told you I had to take V-Rock shopping this morning, and you know Quita had to get some shit too."

"Oh that's right, you did tell me that last night. Did you get shorty taken care of?"

"No doubt!" Gino answered as V-Rock appeared from the other room.

"What's up y'all?" They both embraced him, "Shadow thanks too man. Gino told me you gave him some money for me."

Shadow looked at Gino, who now looked away. "No problem shorty, you're like family to me. Just do me a favor and don't disappoint Gino. He's got a lot of love for you my nig'."

"I know, I got madd love for him too." V replied as Gino smiled. "Look let me get over here and help Stevie with this shit before he curse me out. I'll see y'all later."

"Alright go ahead, we'll see you later," Shadow responded as V walked off. "Damn nigga why you tell him I gave you some money, I told you to take care of that."

"Man I ain't taking no credit for something that I didn't do. Big Boy you a good dude, and nigga's need to know who's real with them and who's not."

"Gino man that little shit was nothing."

"Yeah it was nothing to you, but for the nigga's who you be looking out for, it means a lot. Shadow you've got to understand it ain't a whole lot of good niggas out here no more. Majority of these niggas out here got some type of cruddy shit in them. You're one of the few niggas that are still keeping it 100 for real, and niggas respect that about you."

"Gino, I just try to treat niggas how I would want to be treated, you know?"

"And that's real Fat Boy, because a lot of these niggas don't care about nothing but themselves. That's why I've got a lot of respect for you my nigga."

"I feel you Gino! Come on nigga, let's go get this money. WE can talk about this shit later." Shadow placed his arm around Gino's neck and they walked off.

CHAPTER 22

Six months had gone by now, Gino and Shadow was getting major paper for real now. They were making more money than they could have ever imagined when they started out. The strips were pumping and Gino was really doing his thing and saving his money. V-Rock had even stepped his game up, saving his money instead of wasting it. The boy had bought so many clothes and shoes over the last few months that it was a shame. The only real expensive purchase he had made was a chain he had bought. A diamond crusted dog collar chain with a medallion on it that said "TRIPLE R" in all diamonds. However, what V-Rock wasn't noticing was that other niggas around Wesley Avenue were really starting to get jealous and envious of him. And we all know what jealousy breeds, envy!

It was now October and Gino still hadn't been home or even called as of yet. Sitting home watching BET's 106 and Park one day, Gino saw a commercial advertising Howard University's Homecoming the following weekend. Immediately the thought hit him, good time to finally show his face. He picked up the phone and dialed up Shadow. Shadow answered, "Hello who this?"

"It's me my nigga," Gino replied, "what you busy or something?"

"No this damn girl Tricia getting on my nerves. She answered my cell and I guess some broad must have asked for me, and she going crazy as usual."

Gino could hear Tricia ranting and raving in the background, "Don't lie Shadow, it was your bitch Peaches! Don't even worry about it though,

cause when I catch her I'm going to whip her ass, you can bet that!!"
Tricia continued to lash out.

"Damn Fat Boy, you better handle your business. Look I called
you because I wanted to know if you wanted to go down Howard's
Homecoming next weekend? You know all the bitches going to be down
there, for real?"

"Man it's whatever, I need to get away for a minute anyway."

"Alright then, it's a done deal. Plus it's time for me to let my family
know I'm home and okay. You know I'm going to stunt on that city when
we touch down, right?!" Gino excitedly stated.

"Gino I know you're still frustrated about that little shit that
happened while you were locked up, but you need to let that shit go.
Those dudes were all young when you came to jail."

"Shadow fuck all that, them niggas carried me greasy on some real
shit. Now Tykisha, she kept it real for a while, but shiiddd. Even she took
off on a nigga."

"My nigga if the only reason we're going back to DC is so that you
get back at them dudes, I'm not with that. All that's going to lead to is
beefing with some dudes you used to fuck with over some dumb shit.
Now if we're going to have some fun and party, I'm all for that, but fuck
all that childish shit!"

"Shadow I feel where you coming from, but sometimes I still think
back to how them niggas carried me. You know what I'm saying? It's just
not that easy to leave alone just like that."

"Gino look, I know exactly how you feel. Did you forget, I was down
there with you? When I came home I was mad at a lot of people myself,
but I didn't have time to be around all that negative energy, so I let that
shit go, it was time to get this money."

"Yeah alright," Gino said sarcastically, "I'm going to take V-Rock
with us too, alright?"

"Ha . . . ha . . . ha," Shadow chuckled, "that figures."

"Oh yeahh . . . , and you know I'm buying me something realll . . .
fresh to pull up into."

"Gino, I was just looking at this new Pathfinder the other day too."

"Yeahh . . . , I got my eyes on something myself. You'll see, plus
V-Rock wants to get a whip too. He told me that last month."

"Gino shorty been doing his little thing too. That nigga stay fly and fresh everyday, but what I love most about him is that, he stays on his grind."

"Fo'sho," Gino answered feeling good that Shadow had taken notice of V's progression.

"Well Gino since we're going to be gone for a few days, I've got some shit that I've got to take care of before we leave. We can cop the new joints this week some time."

"No doubt. I'll see you later."

"Alright." Shadow replied as they hung up.

CHAPTER 23

Well for the next couple of days they got their grind on, while taking care of all little errands and shit before they were to leave DC Thursday, Gino and Shadow were at the car wash when Shadow received a page. He glanced at his beeper and saw that it was Donnie, his cousin and he had put 911 behind his code. "Who's that Fat Boy?" Gino asked noticing that Shadow had immediately pulled out his cell phone returning the call.

"It's Donnie, he put in 911!"

Donnie immediately answered on the first ring, "Who this?"

"It's me Donnie, what's up?" Shadow asked.

"Shadow man the police just locked Kelvin and AJ up!"

"They did what!!! . . . What happen?!!" Shadow asked shocked at what he had just heard.

"I don't know all the particulars yet, but from what I heard so far they were on their way to the block and something happened. So I guess between the time they left the stash house, and wherever they got pulled over, they ran into some problems. All I know for certain is that they did get arrested."

"Damn! . . . Damn!!" Shadow shouted in frustration. "Look, go around Langley Avenue and find out what you can, then meet us at the stash house in 30 minutes. Nobody else got jammed, right?!"

"Nahh . . . , not that I know of."

"Alright, I'll see you in 30 minutes." Shadow replied as he hung up the phone, turning to Gino. "Donnie just told me that AJ and Kelvin got locked up this morning."

"What happened??" Gino asked.

"Don't nobody know yet." Shadow commented as he began to dial Grandma's phone number. "Hold up Gino let me tell grandma, so she can get on top of the lawyers." She answered the phone as Shadow gave her all the information he had received, then instructed her to call the lawyer to get on top of their situation immediately.

After hanging up from Grandma, Gino told Shadow that he was going around Langley Avenue and hold it down for the day. Shadow agreed that, that was a good idea, cause he was about to go grab some money and head over the stash house to meet Donnie.

When Shadow met Donnie at the house, Donnie quickly informed Shadow that Kelvin and AJ had gotten bagged on their way to the block by the Po-Po's with coke, dope, and guns still on them. Shadow was flabbergasted, "Okay Donnie," Shadow began to say, "I need you to do me a favor right now. Take these packages right here," Shadow handed Donnie a knapsack, "and I need you to hold down Langley Avenue until we find out the situation. Tell Gino to meet me back at the house later. You be careful too, especially now until we find out everything that's going on. We've got to keep shit real tight right now, hear me??"

"I got that Fat Boy." Donnie assured Shadow as he jumped in his GS 300 and pulled off.

Later that night at the stash house a meeting was called. Everybody was present when Shadow, Gino, and V-Rock walked in. "Uh . . . Uh," Shadow uttered to get everybody's attention, "okay listen y'all we've got to realign the streets for the time being until Kelvin and AJ get out. Tee Tee, I want you to move over to Quash Street with them, Teddy Bear, you and Stevie take Langley Avenue, and me and Gino will handle Bethel, understood?" Everybody shook their heads. "Now y'all be real careful out there right now. Also, on Friday, me, Gino, and V-Rock will be going out of town for the weekend taking care of some business. We won't be back until Sunday night. Greg you'll take Bethel Avenue while we're gone. Man Man will help you, alright?"

"I got you Shadow." Greg responded.

Outside walking towards their cars Shadow called Gino over, "Aye Gino, Grandma is going to court in the morning with the lawyer. She'll call and let you know immediately if they get a bond."

"Fo'sho my nigga. We've got to be extremely careful right now too. I say that cause we don't know if they were being watched. You know what I mean?"

"Yeah you right, or they could have just gotten caught up on a humble too."

"I know! Well we'll see in the morning Fat Boy. I'm out, call me later."

"No doubt." As they embraced and went off in their separate directions.

V-Rock didn't get any sleep that night in anticipation of buying his first car in the morning. V had come a long way now. He had come from struggling and living in the projects, to enjoying some of the finer things in life. V-Rock felt he had a right to feel as proud as he did about his accomplishments. It was his time to shine, he would always say.

Gino got up early himself knowing that today he would finally get a chance to shit on the niggas that shitted on him when he needed them. Fuck what Shadow was talking about Gino thought, as he brushed his teeth. "Aye V-Rock, you up in there?!!" Gino hollered.

"Yeah, I'm putting my shit on now!" V responded as he was tying up his new Timberland boots. "Do I need to bring some stacks with me now?!"

"Nah . . . , wait until we see what time Shadow wants to go to the dealership. We've first got to find out what's up with Kelvin and AJ."

"Heyy . . . baby," Marquita called out. "y'all ain't find out what happened with them yet?!"

"No, they go to court this morning. We're waiting to find out what happened now."

"Alright, I'm ready when y'all are." Quita stated as she walked pass Gino heading towards the living room.

"I'm ready too!" V-Rock responded as well. Minutes later Gino came out and they left headed for the stash house.

When they arrived at the stash house, Tricia and Quita stayed outside talking while the boys went inside for a minute. Inside the house, business was as usual. Shadow passed out the works and informed the crew that they'd probably be gone by the time they had finished today. So he just told them to hold shit down until they returned from their trip. Once finished with the talk, they all disbursed and proceeded with their own business.

As they were all standing outside, Shadow and Gino decided to go cop the new rides, while Grandma was at court checking on AJ and Kelvin. So Gino, Quita, and V-Rock shot home picked up some stacks, and soon after Shadow and Tricia showed up at their house, and then they all jetted.

At the car lot, shit was crazy, V-Rock couldn't decide what he wanted. Shadow liked the Escalade but couldn't decide on which color. Gino didn't have a problem in the world, he knew exactly what he wanted, and was getting. That brand new 735 BMW, black on black with the light tint. V-Rock finally settled on a money green 300 ZX, and Shadow got the white Escalade. Shadow knew the dealer, threw him a few extra thousand and all was being taken care of.

While they waited outside for the paperwork to get done, Quita was standing over by V-Rock talking. Shadow had Tricia already sitting up in the Escalade smiling and cheesing. While walking around the lot, Gino spotted this cute little Maxima that he thought would be nice for Quita. "Aye Quita come here for a minute." Gino waved her over.

She walked over wondering curiously what Gino wanted, "Hey baby what's wrong?" She asked approaching.

"You like this car?" Gino asked while still checking it out.

"Yeah, it's cute baby."

Gino ran his hand across the hood, "Do you want it?"

"I mean . . . Of course. You going to buy it for me baby?!!!!!" She asked voice shooting up 10 decibels.

"Alright tell Shadow to tell the dude that I want this car too."

"Alright hold on baby," she stated as she headed over to where Shadow and Tricia were sitting in the Escalade.

"What's up Quita?" Shadow asked as he saw Quita approaching.

"Shadow, Gino said to tell the guy that he wants to buy the Maxima right there too."

"Yeah . . . alright!"

Now while Quita was over talking to Shadow, V-Rock had walked over to Gino, "My nigga I heard you about to buy that joint for Quita huh?" V-Rock asked.

"Yeah little shorty, she deserves it, plus she need her own shit anyway."

"I feel you Gino, aye look though take this $10,000 and put it towards her car for me. She been like a sister and a mother to me homie." V-Rock attempted to hand Gino his back pack.

"Nahh . . . shorty, I got this. Keep your money and save it up, you hear me?"

V-Rock then shoved the bag up against Gino's chest. "Man take this my nig. Ever since I been down with y'all, everybody has always been looking out for me, now it's my turn. Do this for me, for real big homie?" V-Rock insisted.

"Yeah alright shorty, I'll do this for you." Gino accepted the bag and hugged V-Rock.

Before they left the lot Shadow was now forced to buy Tricia a new car as well. Shortly thereafter, all the paper work and shit had been completed, as the paper tags were being placed on the cars, Shadow's pager went off. Peeking at his beeper he could see that it was his grandmother. "Hold up y'all that's Grandma right here." Shadow informed everybody as he dialed up her number.

"Hello!" Grandma answered.

"Hey Grandma, what happened?"

"Oh baby their being held without bond. The lawyer was fighting hard, but all the judge kept talking about was the amount of drugs that they found, and the weapons that they were caught with also. However, the lawyer did say that they had a good chance of beating the case though." Grandma explained.

"Alright Grandma, are you alright?"

"Yes baby. You be careful out there, you hear me?!" Grandma was always concerned about her babies. She knew and understood the life they lived. She didn't like it, nor accepted it, but she was always there for them if they ever needed her for anything.

"Yeah Grandma I hear you. Also, look I'm going out of town tonight for a few days, and I'll be back on Sunday night. So when Kelvin or AJ call let them know, I'll be to see them as soon as I get back."

"Okay baby, I'll let him know. Like I said, you just be careful!!" She raised her voice to emphasize.

Shadow smiled knowing how much Grandma loved her grand babies. "Yes Grandma, see you Sunday." Shadow hung up the phone.

"What's the deal Fat Boy?" Gino asked as everybody's attention turned to Shadow.

"Grandma said that they were denied bond, but she also said that the lawyer told her they have a good chance to beat the case though."

"Well shiddd . . . , that's the most important thing. Fuck the bond!" Gino said excitedly.

"I told Grandma to tell them that we'd come see them when we get back."

"Fo'sho big boy!" as they slapped dap.

"Come on y'all, let's get up out of here." Everybody checked their shit for the tags and paperwork, and hopped in their shit. Shadow pulled up beside Gino motioning for him to roll his window down. "What's up Fat Boy?" Gino asked.

"Tell Quita that she and Tricia got to come back and pick the other cars up during the weekend some time."

"You know I already told her that, she knows."

"Alright, let's stop and pick up some stacks and get on up out of here." Shadow replied.

"No doubt!" as Gino pulled off with V-Rock right behind him, and Shadow behind him.

CHAPTER 24

Gino was laid back listening to the Sade CD he had grabbed out the house as they were cruising down I-95 towards D.C. Gino was feeling real good, as he looked in the mirror trying to make sure that his appearance was to the "T". He couldn't wait to show his ass to everybody that had turned on him. He knew that as soon as he hit Stronghold, that it was going to cause a scene, which is really what he wanted. He did really want to see Kenny and his mom, but rubbing his success in a few nigga's faces in the process wouldn't hurt either. Even though he was hyped up, he had thoughts of Tykisha weighing heavily on his mind. She was his first love, and even though she stopped communicating with him while he was locked up, Gino still loved her very much. Marquita had become an important part of Gino's life, but the love he shared with Tykisha was not even up for discussion. The love they shared was the kind that touches your soul.

Gino continued cruising on while thinking about so many things. "Damn I wonder does she think about me as much as I've thought about her over the years. I wonder did Stanley get out of jail yet? I know they'll be proud to see how I'm carrying shit now. Hopefully, I'll get a chance to see all of them. Plus I need to look out for my mom and Kenny, I got them though. Deep down inside, I really miss Speedy, Black, and Mike Mike. Knowing them niggas like I do, they still doing their thing. Fuck it, we'll see in a minute." Gino said to himself as he continued to listen to the Sade CD, but couldn't wait to get to D.C.

At about 5:45pm they finally reached Woodrow Wilson Bridge entering into D.C. Now D.C. was like a world of its own, it was nothing like Virginia at all. It was smaller in size compared to Virginia, but bigger in stature and street life. D.C. has a swagger unlike any other place in the world, it's fast and grimy in the city, and if you're slow you'll be eaten alive. Chocolate City, Dodge City, City under siege, Murder Capitol were just a few of the names D.C. was called. The entire city loved Go-Go music, fast cars, fast broads, and definitely fast money. But the one thing you could always count on, was that if anyone visited, they loved it and couldn't wait to return.

Coming across the bridge, Shadow pulled up beside Gino and signaled for him to follow him. "Damn where this nigga going?" Gino uttered as he followed Shadow, with V-Rock behind him. Shadow took Portland Street exit and went up to Martin Luther King, Jr. Avenue, then turned on Orange Street. On Orange St. Shadow pulled up in front of this apartment building that sat across from where several guys were outside hustling. They parked and got out. "Fat Boy where you going?" Gino asked with a puzzled look across his face, also watching the crowd of guys hustling that was now watching them.

"Remember I told you that I had some family down in D.C.?" Shadow reminded Gino.

"Oh yeah, you sure did."

"Come on I want you to meet my peoples." Shadow replied as they headed towards the building. Gino felt uneasy about the group of guys staring at them, as he continued to eye the crowd. Suddenly Gino noticed somebody in the crowd that he knew from D.T.C. "Hold up Shadow!" As Gino started walking over towards the crowd. Midway cross the street, a voice called out, "Aye Gino what's up nigga?!!" A guy from the crowd said as he and another guy stepped out now walking towards Gino.

"Yeah it's me, Jamaal!" the guy stated as they met up in the middle of the street embracing each other.

"Damn nigga, you done got big as shit." Jamaal responded as they released their embrace of each other.

"Cut the bullshit!" said the other guy as they all started laughing.

"What's up Earl?" Gino spoke as they shook hands and embraced each other.

"Ain't shit G, same old shit. You know?" Earl responded.

"Aye look y'all," Gino cut in, "this my man Shadow and V-Rock right here."

They all spoke to each other. "What y'all niggas out here doing?" Gino asked now leaning up against his BMW. "You know how we go," Jamaal pulled out a blunt and lit it up. "But we ain't doing it like you, I see." Jamaal admired the BMW.

"Oh yeah," Gino rubbed his goatee, "look we about to go see my man's peoples, but write your number down Jamaal so we can hook up later."

"Definitely."

Shadow then asked, "Aye Jamaal, do you know my peoples?"

Earl answered, "Who your peoples?"

"Tim, Tee Tee, Itchy and them, the Deloaches." Shadow replied. "They live in the 3542 building?"

"Yeah we know them, as a matter of fact they just left about five minutes ago. I think they went to get something to eat." Earl answered.

"Shitt . . . , well if you get a chance, let them know Shadow in town for me, and I'll try to come back pass before I roll."

"No problem, I got that for you." Earl replied.

"Huh Gino." Jamaal handed Gino a small piece of paper with his beeper number on it. "Man don't forget to get at me, for real."

"Nigga I got you," Gino then turned to V-Rock and Shadow, "I'll holla at y'all Jamaal and Earl, just be ready when I do."

"We'll be here, that's for sure." Earl responded.

"I'll be waiting," Jamaal said, "see y'all Shadow and V-Rock."

"No doubt, see y'all soon!" They responded as they all proceeded back to their cars, and rolled out with Gino leading the pack this time.

Hitting the highway, now Gino was on a new high. He couldn't explain the excitement he was feeling now, but being back in the city definitely felt good. As they came up North Capitol Street Gino started to get butterflies in his stomach, but he had been waiting for this moment damn near three years. Turning onto Channing Street, Gino immediately caught some people's attention. Niggas were gawking at the BMW, and broads were too. Then when Shadow and V-Rock followed, eyes really focused in. As Gino was about to turn in the alley Ray Ray spotted him first, "Aye Gino . . . Gino . . . !!!" Ray Ray yelled out as he caught a glimpse of Gino in the BMW. Gino peeked over, smiled, put up the peace sign while honking his horn. Ray Ray continued to call him, but Gino waved and kept it moving, pulling through the alley with Shadow and V-Rock right behind him. "Damn that felt good." Gino said to himself as he hit Evart Street, headed towards Franklin Street. Coming up the alley, Gino saw the crowd that was oh so familiar to him, when he used to be standing out there hustling and hanging with the boys. The closer Gino got, the crowd took notice and rose up, getting on point. Gino honked his horn, somewhat as a signal to let them know everything was alright. Gino came to a halt about 20 feet from the crowd, with all eyes resting on those three vehicles parking. Slowly Gino exited the car, and the homies couldn't believe their eyes.

Tee yelled out first, "Gino!! . . . Gino!!!" Tee paused to make sure his guess was right.

"Yeahhh . . . ," Gino replied as he closed his door to the BMW and started walking towards the crowd.

"Nigga!! . . . nigga!," Tee excitedly shouted. "Man come here. When you get out?" as other shout outs continued to come.

"Damn my nigga," Timmy hugged Gino, "it is you, what the fuck is up?!"

Gino had a smile on his face worth a million dollars, "What's up my niggas?!!" Gino continued to hug everybody, and giving everybody dap.

"When the fuck did you get out?" Tee repeated.

"Oh my nigga, I been out about a year now." Gino responded as he leaned up against his BMW still smiling from ear to ear. "Oh excuse me y'all, these my mens right here, Shadow and V-Rock. They some real niggas."

Everybody hollered, "What's up?!!" as they exchanged handshakes. "Just chilling, came to enjoy the weekend with my man Gino, that's it." Shadow commented.

"I see you baby boy, shining like a brand new silver dollar," Damien was scoping out the 735, "this you huh?"

"Who else would it be?" Gino responded.

"Well it's a good thing y'all came down this weekend, cause we're doing it up for real. Partying all weekend." Tee says while sipping the drink that he was holding in his hand.

"That's exactly why we came down." Gino answered as he noticed a couple of females walking up the alley. "I see some things never change, soon as they see some cars, all the freaks come out." Gino commented as laughter erupted.

Shawnee, Tamika, and Stephanie were coming up the alley to be nosy of course, typical hood rats. "What's up Gino?" Shawnee spoke while taking notice that Gino had really grew up. The last time Shawnee had seen Gino, she had known that he was still in love with Tykisha. However, it never stopped her from still trying to pursue him. Gino was no fool though, knowing that as soon as he would have slept with Shawnee she would have made sure Tykisha knew she had slept with her man.

"What's up y'all?" Gino replied while still laughing inside.

"When you get home?" Tamika asked. However, her attention clearly appeared to be on V-Rock. "Gino who your friends?"

"Ha . . . Ha . . . ," Gino chuckled. "Oh this V-Rock Mika, and that's Shadow."

Shadow was now leaning up against his truck looking like he thought he was God's gift to women. "If I may," Shadow then spoke up, "the question is who are you?" Shadow stated as he stood there twisting the tooth pick around in his mouth, checking Stephanie out.

Stephanie blushed and replied, "It all depends on whose inquiring?"

"A good man, who happens to be looking for a good woman."

"Well I'm a good woman looking for a good man." Stephanie answered as she stood back on her legs, Stephanie was extremely bowlegged.

"Let me holla at you for a minute then mami." then Fat Boy and Stephanie stepped off towards the back of his truck talking.

Over on the other side of the alley V-Rock and Tamika stepped off and started talking about who knows what. I guess V and Shadow were putting their mack down on the D.C. broads. All the while back on the front Gino was talking to Tee. "What's been up though Tee?" Gino asked.

"Man the same old shit, you know? I just moved out Fort Washington, Maryland. Me and Stanley's girl Tracy live next door to each other."

"What's up with Stanley, is he home yet?"

"Nah . . . , but he'll be home soon. Tracy still with that nigga though."

"How is Ma doing?" Gino asked.

"She's in the house, you probably need to go holla at her, she's always asking about you."

"Most definitely! Is Tykisha in the house?" Gino asked waiting to hear the response.

"Nahh . . . she's not in the house, but she's home for the weekend. You know she's a freshman at Virginia State University and doing pretty good too."

Gino was shocked to hear that, because she had never informed him that she was going to college or even had aspirations of attending college. "Damn that's good Tee." Gino said.

"Lil' G . . . excuse me," Tee chuckled, "I mean Gino, you know that girl is going to go crazy when she sees you."

"I don't know Tee," Gino said while rubbing his goatee thinking about what would happen when he did finally see Tykisha, "man it's been a long time."

"Nigga that girl still got your pictures hanging up in her room, ain't nothing changed," Tee insisted, "as a matter of fact her and Monique just left about 5 minutes ago. Ain't no telling where they went to."

"Well let me go in here and holla at Ma." Gino stated as he began climbing the steps peeking over his shoulder at V and Shadow, still so called macking.

Gino entered the house closing the door behind himself, as he glanced around in the house that used to be his second home. Things basically still looked the same, but there was a picture of Tykisha at her graduation that Gino got caught up staring at. He could see from the photo how much she had grown up. She was amazingly beautiful, and had developed a well defined body to go along with her looks. As Gino proceeded on he called out, "Hey Ma . . . Ma! . . ."

A faint voice replied, "I'm in here!" Ma yelled from the living room, where she was watching Oz on cable. When Gino entered the living room, Ma was excitedly happy to see him. A big smile immediately came across her face, "Gino is that you? Boy you better get over here and give me a hug." Ma reached her arms out hugging Gino with the motherly love she always showed him. "Ohhh . . . Lord boy you done really grown up haven't you?"

"Ha . . . Ha . . . ," Gino snickered like he used to do when he was a kid, "nah Ma, I'm still a young man." Gino took a seat beside her on the couch.

"You really look nice Gino. So I guess that was you who pulled up out back and parked, huh?"

"Yeah . . . me and a couple of my buddies just came down from Virginia for the Homecoming and stuff."

"When did you get released? I always used to ask Tykisha and Tee when you were supposed to be getting out, but no one knew exactly when."

"Oh Ma, I've been home," Gino was saying as he spotted a picture of Tykisha on top of the T.V. with the whole crew, but there was something that Gino noticed about the picture that wasn't sitting too well with him. Black had his arms around Tykisha and it looked a little too cozy for Gino's liking.

Ma snapped Gino out of his daze, "So you've been home all this time and you're just coming to see me?!! I should spank your butt boy." Ma teased.

"Nah . . . , it wasn't like that Ma." Gino caught his composure after studying the picture. "I just wanted to get myself in order before I came back around, that's all Ma.

"Well Gino," Ma rubbed her left hand across Gino's cheek, "I'm glad that you're home. You know I've always considered you like a son to me. You know you just missed Tykisha too, her and Monique just went to the hair dresser about 15 minutes ago. She should be back in an hour or so."

"Yeah Ma, I really need to see her." Gino glanced back at the picture of the gang that was sitting on top of the T.V. again. The sight of Black hugging Tykisha in that manner just wasn't settling right in Gino's stomach.

"Well Gino I don't want to hold you up too long baby, but make sure you come back and see me before you leave town again, you hear me?" Ma replied as she hugged Gino once again.

Gino whispered in her ear, "I will Ma."

"Promise?!"

"I promise Ma," as Gino released her, "talk to you later."

"Okay." Ma waved as Gino exited the living room, on his way back outside.

Walking down the steps Gino saw Tee sitting inside the BMW scoping the joint out. Soon as Tee saw Gino he waved him over, "How much you pay for this joint Gino? I jive like this mother . . . !"

"Man I gave them peoples $52,000!" Gino stated like it was nothing, which it really wasn't to him. Gino was sitting on major paper now and doing his thing.

Tee raised his head, sticking his bottom lip out, while rubbing his chin. "That's right young nigga, stunt! You know that's me right there." Tee pointed to the brand new Range Rover parked several cars up.

"Whew!!!!!!!!! . . . ," Gino exclaimed. "See that's that big boy shit right there. You got to be still doing your thing, huh?!"

"Somewhat, you know how it is?" Tee says as his pager went off. Tee peeked at the number, then placed his pager back in his pocket. "She don't want nothing."

"Yeah Tee, we down VA doing our thing. Shit is pumping like crazy, you hear me? Shit so sweet, it scares me," Gino explained, "I just been saving up my money, cause I know how this game goes, feel me?"

"Fo'sho young nigga." Tee responded.

"Tee let me ask you something," Gino looked around so as to make sure no one else was in ear shot distance. "What's up with my little brother?"

"Gino to be honest," Tee looked Gino square in the eyes, "I can't really tell you. All I know is that he be hanging down 4th Street with Black, Speedy, and Mike Mike."

"Oh yeahh . . ." Gino exhaled, while rubbing his chin.

"But the last I heard, he was doing alright. You know Terrell be down there with them too."

"Alright then," Gino nodded his head, "well Tee let me get up out of here, I need to stop pass my moms and see how she is doing. You know she hasn't seen me yet either."

Tee nodded his head, "Yeah slim you ain't going to believe it when you see her," Tee had a peculiar look on his face, "I'm just going to let you see for yourself."

Gino immediately thought the worst. He remembered her state when he left, and if she was anywhere near that, he knew it could be ugly. "Yeah . . . it's like that, huh?" Gino asked.

Tee just shook his head, "Go see for yourself."

By this time Shadow and V-Rock had gotten Tamika and Stephanie's numbers and shit, as they hopped in their cars about to follow Gino up to his mom's. Gino pulled up beside Tee, stopped and rolled down his window, "Aye Tee what y'all doing tonight?"

Tee was filling his cup up again with some more Remy, then turned around to answer Gino. "Man we're going to see Essence tonight at the Metro Club. Why what's up?"

"What time y'all leaving?" Gino asked.

"About 12:30 a.m. I guess."

"Alright, we're going too then! Don't leave without us."

"Fo'sho!" Tee answered as Gino rolled his window back up and pulled off.

CHAPTER 25

Knock . . . knock . . . knock, Gino knocked on his mother's front door. Gino looked around at the exterior of the house, which looked pretty good compared to how he remembered it when he last left. But he knew that this could all be a fake out, shortly thereafter a faint voice called out, "Who is it?" from the other side of the door.

Gino paused for a second, looking back at Shadow and V-Rock. "It's me Ma."

"Gino is that you baby?" The door quickly opened. "Oh baby . . . baby!!!" Ms. Debra screamed as she rushed over hugging Gino, "Baby where have you been?"

Gino was shocked at what he was seeing, his mom looked really good. "Hold on Ma, let me in first." Gino stated as they all stepped inside with V-Rock being the last one and closing the door. "Hey Ma, these are my two friends Shadow and V-Rock."

"Hi gentlemen, how are you? God Bless!"

"We're doing fine." They both replied.

"Have a seat!" Ms. Debra took a seat, and Gino sat beside her. Gino was staring and looking around in amazement and shocked at how his mom had gotten her shit together.

"So Gino when did you get out? Because I called the Detention Center months and months ago, and they informed me that you had been released." She commented as she looked intensely into Gino's eyes.

Gino turned to face his mom, "Ma when I got out, I went to live down Virginia with my man right here." Gino looked at Shadow, as Ms. Debra caught eye contact with Shadow as well. "I just wanted to get myself together before I came back around."

"Gino you still should have called somebody and said something. Your brother has been worrying me sick about you."

"I know Ma, but things turned out for the best this way. Plus things were moving so fast when I got out, it was just crazy."

"Well . . . I mean where are you staying baby?" Ms. Debra asked.

"Ma, I lived down Virginia. I got my own apartment."

A slight smirk came across her face, "You got your own apartment?" She commented remembering that Gino was not the same little boy he was when he left, he was 18 and on his own now.

"I do live with a female though Ma." Gino stated as he watched her face for a reaction.

Ms. Debra paused for a minute, "My . . . my . . . my, you don't have any kids yet, do you?"

"Nah Ma . . ." Gino answered smiling. "I'm glad to see that you've gotten yourself together though."

"Yes Lord . . . baby by the grace of God I was able to get my life back in order. Right now I'm working at National Airport and I've been clean now over a year. I went into rehab for about 6 months and everything worked out for the best."

Gino stood up and walked over to a picture of Kenny, he spotted picking it up. Staring at the picture Gino wondered how he was doing, and marveled at how much Kenny had grew up from the looks of the picture. "What's up with Kenny Ma?" Gino asked while his eyes were still intensively locked on the photograph of Kenny.

Ms. Debra walked up and placed her hand on Gino's shoulder. "Well Gino he's just like you use to be. He's hard headed, but fortunately he hasn't gotten in any trouble as of yet. But if he doesn't start getting his act together and get back in school, I don't know what's going to happen to that boy."

Gino sat the picture down, "Where's he at now Ma?"

"He's probably down 4th Street with his little buddies. Well your buddies."

"Ma . . . I've got to see him. I really need to talk to him."

"Baby . . ." Ms. Debra looked at Gino, "please do, before he gets into some trouble."

"I got that Ma." Gino walked over picking up his keys from the couch. "Ma I'll be back, I'm about to ride down 4th Street and see if he's there right now." Gino hugged his mom and began to walk towards the front door with Shadow and V-Rock right behind him.

At the door, Gino reached for the door knob when the door pushed opened almost hitting Gino in the head. Quickly Gino reacted raising his hand to stop the door from striking his face. "Aye . . . aye!" Gino echoed as the door swung open and Kenny walked in. "Kenny . . . Kenny" Gino replied as time seemed to freeze momentarily while Kenny and Gino stood there just staring at each other.

"Gino what's up dog?!!" Kenny broke the silence first grabbing Gino as they embraced each other. "Man when you get out?" Kenny asked.

"Nigga . . . nigga, just hug your brother right now." Gino replied as they continued to hug each other, until Gino finally released Kenny.

"Gino man, you know a nigga been waiting for you to get out. Where the hell you been?"

"Yeah I know, I was supposed to be here for you when you got out slim. That's my bad, but you know how shit happens. I've been out for a minute now, I live down Virginia with my mans and them right here." Gino turned to Shadow and V-Rock. "Look this Shadow and this V-Rock."

Kenny shook their hands, "What's up y'all?"

"Ain't too much." V-rock stated.

"Kenny listen we really need to talk, you know." Gino cut in. "Aye Ma, I'm going to take Kenny with me for a while, you don't mind, do you?"

"No baby." Ms. Debra answered. "I know that y'all have a lot of catching up to do. Go ahead, but don't forget what I asked you to do Gino."

"I got that Ma." Gino replied grabbing Kenny by the shoulder. "Come on Bro' let's roll."

"Fo' sho', my nigga!"

"Damn my nigga." Kenny uttered as they were about to enter the BMW. "You doing it like this huh?"

"You know it." Gino answered as he hit the unlock button unlocking both of their doors, and they hopped in. Gino started up the car and pulled out with the crew in tow.

They decided to all go shopping, and Potomac Mills Mall was their first stop. While at the Mall they all went shopping crazy. Leaving the Mall they all had both hands full of shit. Kenny was smiling and was just as happy as he could be. All his wishes had finally come true, his brother was home, and they were back together. Shit was on and popping now!!

Next stop was the Embassy Suites out College Park, where they all got suites with Jacuzzi's and waterbeds included. Entering the elevator, the door closed and Shadow asked, "So what's on the agenda for the night Gino?"

"Oh my nig, we're taking you to the Go-Go. Believe this, you gonna love it, real talk."

"Yeah I heard all about them Go-Go's, I just never had a chance to attend one."

Kenny then jumped in, "V-Rock you really going to love it, man the bitches go crazy in there. No bullshit!"

"I can't wait." V-Rock commented as the elevator door opened and they stepped off heading towards their rooms.

"Look y'all," Gino spoke as he cracked the door open to his room placing his bags inside. "go ahead and take y'all showers and shit, be ready by 12:00 so we can meet up with Tee and them."

"Alright!" everybody said in unison as they were entering into their rooms then doors closing.

CHAPTER 26

Later that night as they were all riding to meet Tee and them, Kenny was riding with V-Rock, which definitely smelled like trouble from the beginning. About 12:15, they arrived around Stronghold immediately noticing that everybody was outside drinking and conversing as usual. Gino and them parked, got out and walked over when Gino spotted Tee, "Tee what's up my nigga?"

"Ain't too much, what's up with y'all?" Tee responded while giving everybody dap. "We've been waiting on y'all niggas."

"No doubt." Gino picked up the Remy and poured himself a cup then handed the bottle to Shadow who did the same. "We ready whenever y'all are."

"Aiight, but before we go, you know Tykisha's in the house and she wants to see you." Tee alerted Gino.

Gino took a gasp as if he had just had the wind knocked out of him. "Oh yeah . . ." Gino paused to catch his thoughts for a moment. "Well let me go holla at her for a minute before we jet." Gino suggested still nervous as could be.

"Hold on, I'll call her out here." Tee stated as he walked up to the front porch calling his sis. "Tykisha . . . aye Tykisha!"

Shortly thereafter the screen door opened, and Tykisha walked outside. "What Tee, you ain't got to be calling me like that either." Tykisha responded as she momentarily spotted Gino, and instantly took off running down the steps, and jumping instantly into his waiting arms. "Gino . . . Gino," she repeatedly said several times as they continued to hug each other. "When did you get home baby?" she whispered in his ear, while they still were in each others' grasp.

Finally releasing each other, Gino just stared at her for a few seconds, as she eyed him down. Gino then mumbled, "I've been home. I live down Virginia now, but I see you're still looking good as ever."

"Thank you," she blushed, "you're still cute as ever yourself. Why am I just hearing from you Gino, if you've been out all this time? This how you treat me now?"

"Nah shorty, it's not like that. I've just been trying to get myself together, that's all."

"This your car?" Tykisha asked probably because Gino was leaned up against it. "Oh you too big for me now, huh?"

"Come on Tykisha, you know me better than that," Gino explained while taking the back of his left hand and rubbing Tykisha's cheek. "no amount of money could change who I am, you should know that better than anyone."

"Gino I was just messing with you." Tykisha teased as she continued to blush while playing in her hair like a little girl in love all over again.

"Aye Gino, come on man!!!" Tee screamed out from his car, as everyone was now waiting on Gino. "Nigga you got all weekend to talk that lovey dovey shit, right now let's go!!"

"Mind your business Tee!!" Tykisha screamed while staring at Tee with a look that would kill. "Oh so they're waiting on you, huh?"

Gino smiled, "Yeah something like that, but we need to talk Tykisha."

"I know, maybe we can hook up tomorrow. What you going to be doing?"

"Uh . . . uh" Gino bit down on his bottom lip. "How about I pick you up about 12:00 noon tomorrow?"

"Alright, I'll be waiting!" She remarked as she leaned in and kissed Gino lightly on his lips. Gino melted inside like it was his first kiss all over again. Finally they broke away, "I'll see you tomorrow Gino." Tykisha stated as she slowly walked away, headed back towards the house.

Gino was speechless, all he could do was watch her sashay up the steps as she entered the house. After catching his composure Gino opened his car door, got inside, and pulled off following the crew as they headed to the Metro Club.

All during the drive to the club, Gino couldn't get Tykisha off his mind. However, Tykisha was at the house still savoring the sight of the man she first loved and the man she gave her virginity to. Tykisha also had another issue that was bothering her, which she knew she had to inform Gino about. She knew it would hurt him, but she had to be honest. Tykisha had been in a relationship with Gino's old friend, Black for the last 6 months or so. It wasn't meant to happen, it just did, and no matter what, she knew Gino was going to be furious.

Outside the Metro Club you would have thought the party was outside, instead of inside. There were BMW's, Lexus', Mercedes', and all kinds of cars lining the street and in the parking lot with scores of females looking, "Oh!" so good. Guys were dropping their best rap game on freaks trying to set that late night freak session up for the hotel after the Go-Go. "Damn Gino, shidd . . . we ain't even got to go in, I like what I see right out here." Shadow continued to survey the females all over Bladensburg Road on their way to the front door of the club.

"Fatboy calm down, I promise you, you haven't seen nothing yet." Gino replied as they met Tee and them at the front door of the club.

"Come on y'all." Tee said as they all paid the $15 entrance fee and entered inside the 'Metro Club'. Women were shaking their asses all over the place. Rare Essence Go-Go band had the club jumping as usual, and it had just gotten started. Immediately Shadow, Gino, and Tee headed towards the bar to get some drinks. Kenny and V-Rock stopped and got caught up talking to some First Street cuties that they had bumped into. The rest of the crew all went out onto the dance floor partying with all the females in attendance.

"Damn Gino you weren't lying champ, these broads like that, you hear me?" Shadow mentioned while eyeing a group of females over by the pinball machines.

"Down boy," Gino patted Shadow on the back, "you better be careful fucking with that crew right there. They call their selves the Lolly-pop honies. I don't think I got to tell you why they call themselves that either, huh?" Gino and Tee both busted out laughing. Gino knew the females that Shadow were eyeing, Mechelle, Kim, Felecia, and the rest of their

119

crew were well known gold digging broads, who had a reputation for turning niggas out and partying.

"Gino you ain't hip your man?" Tee asked as he and Gino were still snickering at Shadow.

"Tell me what?" Shadow had a dumbfounded look on his face wondering what he had missed out on.

"Mann . . . ," Gino was still laughing at this point too, "it's nothing Fat Boy, Tee was just messing with you."

"Oh . . . Oh . . . okay, I thought I missed something." Shadow tried to read their expressions to see if they were playing some kind of joke on him.

"Nah . . . nah for real Shadow." Tee commented as this slim, caramel, wavy haired broad walks up behind Tee and covers his eyes from behind.

"Guess who?" A soft voice said.

Tee reached behind and grabbed the girls' ass and immediately knew who it was, "Come on Freeda!" Tee shouted.

"How you know it was me?" She asked innocently, which she definitely wasn't.

"Ain't nobody got an ass as soft as that!" Tee exclaimed, as Shadow stood back admiring the figure on this girl. She was stacked like a stallion, beautiful, and had titties like Pamela A., but what niggas didn't know, was that she was notorious for working niggas out their money, and/or setting them up for other niggas to get at them. However, she had been cool with Tee for years and never ever had tried anything cruddy with him or any of his buddies.

"What's up with y'all tonight?" Freeda asked as she caught Shadow eyeing her up and down.

"Same shit." Tee replied. "Look this my man Gino and his man Shadow right here."

"What's up Freeda?" Gino replied.

"How you doing Freeda?" Shadow inquired with a smooth tone.

"Nice to meet y'all." Freeda responded without ever losing eye contact with Shadow, who was locked on her for sure. "Well I'll see y'all later, let me get back over here with my girlfriends. See y'all." She hurriedly scurried off to a crowd of her friends sitting at the other end of the bar. Shadow watched as she met back up with her friends and they all started exchanging conversation, at which point all eyes turned towards Tee, Gino, and Shadow. That moment Shadow had his mind made up, she was his target for the night.

Later that night, Rare Essence started hitting one of their old grooves, 'Work The Walls!' Almost instantly the girls went crazy. Gino was interlocked with this female named Tammy, who was shaking her ass so hard against Gino that they were basically dry fucking, you know what I mean? When Gino had a chance to look around, he spotted Shadow dancing with freak ass Freeda, and she was putting it on him too, and Fat Boy was enjoying every bit of it. However, Gino knew what kind of broad Freeda was, but he didn't want to spoil Fat Boy's night. So Gino kept quiet and decided to let Shadow find out on his own, unless Freeda got out of control.

"Work the walls . . . work the walls, yeah!" Tammy screamed as she continued to grind harder on Gino, and Rare Essence was pouring on thick too. Gino knew that he had to take Tammy to the Mo'Mo' after all this, she had him aroused and ready to go now for real . . . for real!

Now sipping his drink standing by the pinball machines, Gino spotted Sean, an old friend of his from Montana Avenue. "Aye Sean!" Gino called out as Sean was walking pass with a group of his buddies from the Avenue. Sean quickly turned to see who had called his name.

"Who that?" Sean asked as he was trying to figure out who Gino was through the dimly lit club. "Gino? . . . Gino?" Sean said as he began walking up towards Gino. "Is that Gino from Stronghold?"

"And you know this mann . . . !" Gino stated as they embraced each other. "Long time no see nigga."

"No bullshit." Sean replied checking Gino out. The last time Sean had seen Gino, he was still up and coming in the street game. Sean had been messing with Tykisha's older sister Monique during the time Gino first started messing with Tykisha. "Nigga where you been?"

"Slim you know I had gotten locked up. I just came home about a year and some change ago." Gino explained. "And now I'm living down Virginia. Niggas it's super sweet down there."

"Oh yeahh . . ." Sean's antennas immediately went up. "Sweet like that, huh? Shidd . . . I might have to come down there and snatch a few of them suckers then, huh man?!"

"I tell you what, if I find something sweet or need you to get a nigga, I'll give you a call."

"That's a bet!" Sean winked his eye at Gino. "Huh, write my number down and hit a nigga sometime." Sean wrote his number down on a napkin that was on the bar and handed it to Gino.

"I got that slim, I ain't going to forget you." They hugged, gave each other dap and Sean stepped off.

Gino was now in line waiting on his chicken dinners, when the female Tammy found her way over to him. "Gino order me a pork chop dinner please? Cause I do not feel like getting in this long ass line." Tammy whispered as she placed her arm intertwined with Gino's. Gino was still lusting off her body and damn sure wasn't going to deny her anything right now.

"What you doing tonight Tammy?" Gino asked.

"I'm trying to see you, unless you're scared you can't handle this." Tammy said with a devilish look on her face.

"Scared . . . scared?!" Gino chuckled. "Yeah whatever then, we'll see who's scared of whom tonight then."

"Stop talkin' about it, and be about it then." Tammy replied as she squeezed Gino on the ass.

"Yeah aiight." Gino smiled. "Soon as these dinners get ready, I'ma let my partner know I'm out."

"Good, can't wait." Tammy licked her lips and stood in front of Gino as he hugged her from the back, dick bone hard all on that ass.

"Gino, let me holla at you my nigga!" Shadow's voice echoed from somewhere, as Gino and Tammy both turned around. Fat Boy was approaching with Freeda not far behind. Gino just laughed, "Stop laughing" Tammy said smacking Gino on the arm. Gino knew Freeda had worked her magic on his man, who thought he was the slickest thing since Formula one oil. "What's up Fat Boy?" Gino asked.

"Mann . . . Mann," Shadow sighed, rolling his eyes towards Freeda. "Yeah I'm about to roll back to the hotel, feel me?"

Gino looked at Freeda, and chuckled. "Yeah okay, I feel you big boy. But I'ma bout to roll myself, so hold on for a minute and we can jet together."

"Fo'sho . . . . !"

CHAPTER 27

Back at the hotel Gino was sitting on the bed shirtless watching Tammy come up out those Guess Jeans that were so tight, you'd think that she painted them on her ass. The girls' ass was simply put, "AMAZING", and she had dimples that would melt you. After removing all her clothes she approached Gino, walking up the mattress like a cat. "You sure you're ready for this?" she purred while lightly kissing Gino on the stomach and then his chest.

Gino mumbled, "I guess we'll soon find out." They interlocked fingers and Gino laid back like he was the King.

Tammy mounted Gino slowly easing Gino inside of her warm, wet pussy. She moaned with each deeper stroke. After finally getting in sync together they humped each other like two wild animals. Gino watched Tammy's every facial expression, and body movement, which only intensified his desires. Moments later Tammy sped up her thrusts down onto Gino, which let him know that she was about to climax. "Aye baby!! Aye babyyyy!!! This your pussyyy!!! This your pussyyyyy!!!!!" is all you could hear Tammy screaming as she climaxed. Tammy's pussy was feeling so good to Gino at this point, that he could no longer hold back. "Come on baby . . . come on baby . . ." Gino repeatedly sighed as he was punishing Tammy's pussy until he busted off. This was just the beginning of a long night of ecstasy.

Ring . . . ring . . . ring . . . ring. The phone rang startling Shadow, waking his fat ass up from his sleep. He reached across Freeda who was still dead asleep retrieving the receiver, "Hello!"

"Get your fat ass up nigga!" Gino laughed.

"Damn my nigga what time is it?" Shadow's faint voice uttered.

"Nigga it's after 11 o'clock a.m. What you let the broad work you like that?" Gino teased.

"Picture that!"

"Look," Gino started to say, "I'm about to make a run into the city for a minute. If you need me just call me, aiight?"

"Yeah I'll do that." Shadow yawned still tired from Freeda working that nigga's ass. "I got to run pass the Mall myself."

Gino was laughing like shit inside, he knew Freeda would never have been with that nigga if it wasn't something in it for her, believe that. "Yeah I bet you do. Don't let that bitch hit your pockets too hard."

"You got me fucked up." Shadow answered jokingly.

"Yeah I bet I do, see you later." Gino responded hanging up the phone and exiting the hotel to take Tammy home.

CHAPTER 28

"Where the hell were you last night?" Gino was on his cell phone talking to Kenny as he was pulling up in front of Tykisha's house beeping the horn. Moments later she appeared and hopped in the car as Gino was ending his conversation with Kenny. "Aiight then Kenny, I'll see you later. I'ma call you when I get back.... Love you too champ!" Gino hung up the phone.

"Hey baby girl!" Gino spoke, while turning and leaning over to kiss Tykisha.

"Good morning to you too." She smiled as Gino pulled off. "Did y'all have fun last night?"

"Yeah and no," Gino turned the A/C up, "it would have been better if I had spent last night with you."

"Well . . . if you felt like that, then why did you leave me?" Tykisha was trying to make Gino feel guilty in a teasing way. "Nah, I'm just playing baby, where are we going?"

"Have you eaten yet?"

"No . . . I haven't." she replied.

"You want to go out and get something to eat?"

"Gino, I don't care what we do as long as I'm with you." She responded while placing her left hand on Gino's thigh.

Later at Denny's Restaurant they were seated and served by a sexy sister looking to be about 21-22 years old, that Gino made sure not to even peek at. Tykisha would probably slap the shit out of him and the broad. While eating Gino broke the silence between them, "Tykisha honestly speaking," Gino wiped the food from his mouth, "you know I still love you right?" Tykisha's eyes slowly rose to meet Gino's. "I mean ain't no sense in me faking. It is what it is, I was just fucked up at the way you carried me while I was locked up. I jive felt as if you left a nigga hanging, real talk."

Tykisha paused as if she was gathering her thoughts before she spoke. "Gino . . ." she wiped the food from her mouth with her napkin. "How could I forget you, after all we've been through. You were my first love, and the person I gave my virginity to. You always have and still do have my heart and soul. However, as time went on our letters were less frequent to each other, the phone calls became non-existent, and I felt like things slowly started to change between us. Nevertheless, that never changed my love for you." Tykisha explained emotionally. "And then Gino what really shocked me, was the fact that I knew you had gotten out, yet you failed to contact and/or come see me. So I figured that you had moved on with your life."

Gino sipped on some of his soda wetting his dry mouth. "Tykisha let me explain to you what happened." Gino was saying as Tykisha reached across the table grabbing Gino's hands. "When I was locked up I met this dude named Shadow. He was the fat guy with me yesterday. When I got released, he came and picked me up and showed me madd love. So I decided to go stay down Virginia with him, until I could get back on my feet."

Tykisha wiped a tear from her face, "Gino you still should have called me or something. I would've never done you like that. Do you know I still have your pictures hanging up in my room til this day?"

"Tykisha I love you too, and I always will . . . ." Gino was saying when Tykisha cut him off.

"Gino . . . Gino," she began as Gino wiped a stream of tears from her face.

"What's wrong? Why you crying like that?" Gino asked.

Tykisha put her head inside her hands momentarily. Gino put his hand under her chin raising her head back up, looking her straight in the eyes. "Gino I've got to tell you something." Tears were streaming down her face at this point. "I know you're not going to like it, but I've got to be honest with you."

Gino could see whatever it was, was painful by the look on her face. "What is it baby girl?"

Tykisha took her thumbs placing her braids behind her ear as she began. "Gino, like 6 months ago, me and Black started talking . . ."

Gino immediately jumped in, "What you mean talking, talking like friends or boyfriend/girlfriend?" Gino asked as his voice began to rise with every word.

"Gino baby . . . I . . . I thought that you had moved on." Tykisha mumbled.

"So Tykisha you're telling me that you and Black are messing with each other right, huh?" Gino asked with a puzzled look on his face. Tykisha put her head back inside her hands again, and began crying hysterically. "Tykisha I asked you a question? Are you and Black fucking with each other like that or what?!" Gino repeated once again.

Raising her head, she answered. "Yes Gino!"

Gino stuck his bottom lip out nodding his head, rocking back and forth in his chair. "Tykisha that's crazy," Gino began, "but hey I can't be mad at you. I've known for years that he's liked you. I still feel like you could've found somebody else to be with. But fuck it . . . , if he makes you happy, then I'm happy for y'all."

Tykisha got up and walked around the table taking a seat beside Gino. "I know what you're saying baby. It was not the smartest decision, but it was not intentional. He just be with Terrell and them, and they be over the house all the time and it just somewhat happened."

Gino removed his hands from Tykisha's grasp, placing both of his hands back behind his head and now begun staring at her intensely. "Tykisha you ain't got to explain nothing to me. I'm just glad that you gave me a heads up." Gino sighed. "Honestly speaking, I have someone in my life as well. Her name is Marquita, and we live together down Virginia. And no, I'm not just saying this because of what you just told me about you and Black. I just figured since we're being honest with each other, I might as well lay everything on the table."

Tykisha's whole body language changed. "Do you love her?"

"I'm not sure, love is a sensitive word. I know that I do care about her, but I don't know if I'm in love with her though." Gino explained. "Do you love Black?"

"Gino honestly speaking I like Black a lot, but I don't think I could love another man as long as you're still alive. We started from nothing and built everything together. Love is just so confusing sometimes."

Gino was nodding his head understanding exactly what she meant. "I know what you mean Tykisha."

"So Gino, what are we going to do about you and I?"

Gino paused, stood up and reached for Tykisha's hand. She happily grabbed his hand. "Come on." Gino replied as he left some money on the table for the meal and they exited the restaurant.

Gino headed straight back to the hotel, where fortunately the house keepers had cleaned up the room from the night before with Tammy. Immediately upon them entering the room, Gino pushed Tykisha against the wall kissing her passionately while rubbing all over her body. Finally releasing her lips from his grasp she whispered, "Sssss . . . do that again."

"Say please . . . , pretty please." Gino teased.

"Please . . . pretty please." She obliged as Gino tongued her down. His hands were all over her like an octopus. After making it over to the bed, Gino laid Tykisha down as he stood up and removed his clothes, while she lay on the bed doing the same.

Gino climbed back on top of her as she moaned, "Stop playing with me, I want you." Gino then raised her legs up damn near behind her head and slid his dick inside. Within seconds Gino was deep inside her, as she winced and quivered with Gino's every motion. Gino was hitting all her G spots as she exhaled, and sighed, "Oh baby . . . oh baby, I miss you sooo . . . much. Please don't stop . . . don't stop!" She repeated. Seconds later she began to shiver violently, and screaming . . . "Baby!! Baby!! Baby!!!" She grabbed the sheets and balled them up in her hands to avoid scratching Gino's back up. "I'm . . . I'm . . . I . . . ." was all she could utter before her body orgasmed.

Still going, Gino was now about to reach the mountain top. He began biting down on his bottom lip, locking his arms underneath her back, onto her shoulders. "Baby . . . baby," Gino mumbled. "I'm cummm . . . ." Was all he could get out before he hit pay dirt. The orgasm felt so good that Gino caught a Charlie horse, and had to pull up shortly thereafter.

Tykisha chuckled at that, as she cuddled up next to Gino until he could get himself together.

Shortly after that as they laid in each others arms, Tykisha began to cry. Gino didn't want to ask why, figuring that she was just feeling guilty about what they had just done. Gino caressed her in his arms, not uttering a word, as they fell asleep in each others arms.

Gino was first to wake up in the morning, he shook Tykisha to wake her. "Get up sleepy head." Gino teased.

"What . . . what . . . baby." she replied rolling over trying to shield her eyes from the sun rays coming through the window. "I'm up . . . I'm up!"

Gino rolled her back over towards him, then kissing her. "Let's talk." He suggested as he now had gotten her attention. "What are we going to do now?"

"Gino I don't know, but I love you sooo . . . . much." She stated while rising up from under the covers to meet Gino face to face. "Why does life have to be so complicated?"

"Baby girl I can't answer that question, it just is." As she lay back against Gino's chest, in his arms until they heard a knock at the door. Gino rose up, grabbed his sweatpants, and went to answer the door. "Who is it?" Gino called out as he walked towards the door.

"It's me Gino." Shadow's voice echoed from the other side of the door.

Gino opened the door, "What's up my nigga?!!" Shadow yelled as he pushed through the door.

"Ain't shit, just chillin' with Tykisha." Gino replied closing the door behind Fat Boy.

"Nigga you was talking about me the other day, what you still doing in bed. I know you ain't whipped this morning are you?" Shadow joked, as they both bust out laughing. So . . . what's up for the day?"

"The Homecoming game is today, then later tonight the after party."

"Yeah, that sounds like a winner to me. What time we leaving out?" Shadow asked.

"Well give me about 30 minutes to get dressed. Then I've got to drop Tykisha off . . . !" Gino smiled. "You ain't let Freeda hit those pockets too hard did you?" as laughter erupted again.

"Never that . . ." Shadow responded as they continued to laugh. "But you can bet, I got my money's worth, that's for sure."

"Yeah . . . yeah . . . yeah," Gino waved him off, "Fat Boy stop faking."

"Fuck you Gino," as they hugged, "look I'll be in my room, just call me when you're ready."

"Aiight." Gino replied as he walked Shadow to the door. Shadow exited and Gino headed back into the bedroom.

As he entered the bedroom, Tykisha was headed to the shower, "Where you going sweetheart?" Gino asked, grabbing her from behind.

"If you don't mind, I'd like to take a shower," she said in a sexy tone, "unless you have something else in mind."

Gino chuckled to himself, "Nah . . . baby girl go ahead and handle your business." Gino kissed her on the forehead. "That was Shadow at the door, and he's waiting on me to get dressed anyway."

"So what are y'all doing today baby?" Tykisha asked as she entered the bathroom.

"We're going to the football game, then probably the after party at the Republic Gardens."

"So when are we going to finish our conversation Gino?"

Gino paused for a second not sure of what to say.

"Did you hear me Gino? When are we going to finish our conversation?" Tykisha repeated herself.

"Yeah . . . yeah, I heard you baby." Gino answered. "I guess we'll have to figure something out."

"You sure?"

"Yeah I'm sure." Gino responded while reaching to grab his cell phone, which was vibrating on the table. It was Kenny so he answered. "Hello! . . . ."

CHAPTER 29

Later that evening they attended the football game, which Howard won 14-7 over N.C. A&T. That night the after party was a smash hit also. Any and everybody that was somebody was up in there. Women galore, more than a nigga could fathom, and they were dressed to impress. However, all night long no matter what Gino did, his thoughts always somehow shot back to Tykisha. Gino still couldn't figure out, how or what he as going to do about his dilemma with her, but he was trying his best to get the thoughts of her off his mind. He still felt somewhat betrayed, but the love he had for her would never go away. Gino decided that he was just going to have some fun tonight, and worry about that when the time came. So he hooked up with this female named Kyia, while Shadow met some female named Misha, and they left later that night and headed back to the hotel.

Sunday morning came around too fast, Gino thought to himself as they were in the midst of riding back to drop the females off. That's when a thought hit Gino, "Damn! I haven't seen Kenny or V-Rock in over 24-hours now. Them little mother . . . . niggas out acting a fool I bet. I've got to ride pass 4th Street and see if they're down there."

Turning off Rhode Island Avenue onto 4th Street with Shadow right behind Gino, they pulled up in front of the arcade, and Gino immediately spotted V-Rock's 300ZX sitting out front. Gino and Shadow parked, got out, and strolled into the arcade looking for those two. Glancing around the arcade Shadow commented, "Them little mother . . . . been gone the whole weekend."

"Believe me, I know." Gino responded as they walked around still surveying the arcade for those two. All you could hear was Backyard Band blasting out the speakers inside, with females and guys posted up talking and conversing, while some people were serving customers. "Damn Gino I don't remember arcades down my way ever being like this." Shadow remarked.

"Yeah, a lot has changed. Do you see any signs of those two anywhere?" Gino asked as they continued looking around. Suddenly Gino pointed towards a crowd standing by the door. "There they go. Aye Kenny!! . . . Kenny!!!" Gino called out as they walked over.

Kenny and V-Rock looked up simultaneously, "What's up Gino?" Kenny replied stepping out to give his brother some dap.

"What's up with y'all?" V-Rock then stated.

"Mann . . . where the hell y'all niggas been at? We haven't seen y'all two in damn near 24-hours." Gino said.

"You know how it is bro." Kenny rolled his eyes towards the two females standing behind them watching Kenny and V-Rock's every move. "I jive been showing V-Rock around the city. Then we hooked up with some cuties from the Quarters, and you know . . ." As V and Kenny gave each other dap.

"Yeah aiight nigga come on outside, let me holla at you for a minute." Gino hugged Kenny as they all walked outside the arcade.

Outside they walked over by Gino's BMW, when Gino spoke up. "Damn Kenny, I thought that we were going to spend some time together." Gino says as he noticed the same two females from the inside of the arcade, now outside still eyeing them all.

"Yeah Gino, but I thought you wanted me to show V-Rock around the city." Kenny said as he leaned up against the BMW beside Gino. "So what's up now then?"

"Well, we're really short on time right now. We've got to get back down Virginia to tend to some serious business, feel me?"

V-Rock then cut in, "Gino man, come on let's stay a few more days?"

"V you know I would love to, but you know what's going on back home. We've got to get back as soon as possible." Gino reminded V of the seriousness of their operation down Virginia.

"Well let me go down Virginia with y'all." Kenny suggested as he looked around to see everyone's expression.

Gino looked at Shadow to get somewhat of a feel of his reaction, which was blank. "Kenny look . . . I'll come back and get you." Gino stood there rubbing his forehead. "That's my word, soon as this business down VA has calmed down, aiight?"

Kenny shook his head understanding whatever was going on had to be important. "Look V, you and Kenny meet me back at Ma's house in an hour, okay? And Kenny don't have V late!" Gino sternly stated.

"Aiight . . . I got that Gino." Kenny replied as he pointed at something behind Gino and them. They all turned, "Look who just pulled up?"

Gino turned to see Black, Speedy, and Mike Mike exiting their cars. All kinds of emotions started to hit Gino at once, frustration, angriness, happiness, excitement . . . I mean a rush just came over him. Gino continued to watch them closely as they approached. "Looky . . . looky here, my nigga Gino!!!" Mike Mike screamed out as they walked up and immediately embraced each other.

"Damn nigga when did you get out? What the fuck is up for real?" Speedy replied as they also embraced each other.

After breaking their embrace, Gino says, "Ain't shit y'all, what's been up?"

"Nigga fuck all that, what's been going on with you? I see you done stepped that thing up real swell now, huh?!" Speedy was checking Gino out.

"Nahhh . . . , just a little something, you know? I've been missing you niggas. When I got out I went to live in Virginia for a minute to get myself together." Gino was talking to Speedy, but caught himself staring at Black, who at this point hadn't said a word to Gino yet. "But you know I still got madd love for y'all niggas, no matter what!"

"Damn . . . Kenny told us that you had copped that new joint too!" Black finally broke the ice first, referring to the 735 BMW Gino was driving.

"Man that ain't shit! For real . . . for real, your hands are better than mines." Gino locked his eyes with Black, who was now looking confused. "Especially now that you're fucking with my old girl, huh?" Gino's voice got really cold.

"Hold up, let me explain slim." Black was trying to say before Gino cut him off.

"Black listen, there's no need for explanations. She already told me everything, it's cool. I just want you to know one thing though Black." Gino at this moment was smiling. "Were you wondering where she was all day yesterday?" Gino paused to wait and see Black's response, which never came. Black just hunched his shoulders. "Well just in case you were, I wanted to let you know that she was with me. So now you don't have to wonder anymore. And just to let the record reflect, if I wanted her back, you couldn't stop me."

"Fuck you nigga!" Black screamed out as he tried to approach Gino, but was cut off by Mike Mike. "Nigga you ain't like that!"

"Well ask Tykisha if I'm like that then." Gino smiled sarcastically. "Fuck you too nigga! . . . come on y'all let's roll." Gino, Shadow, V-Rock, and Kenny all stepped off hopping in their cars.

CHAPTER 30

Inside mom's house, Gino had taken Kenny upstairs to talk with him. Gino sat him down and explained what had happened pertaining to his whole situation, and why he wasn't there for Kenny when he got home. Kenny understood and explained to Gino what he had been doing, and what his future plans were. Gino then stopped Kenny, "Look take this," Gino handed Kenny $20,000 in a knapsack, "start doing your own thing. I want you to stop fucking with those dudes you been copping from. Save your money, and take care of mom cause I'll be back to get you soon as Virginia calm down, alright?"

Kenny set the money on his bed, and hugged his brother. "I got that Gino."

After finishing their conversation, Gino said his good-byes to his mother, promising her that he'd stay out of trouble and that he'd be back to visit soon before walking out.

Deciding that he couldn't leave D.C. without saying good-bye to Tykisha, Gino headed over to her house. As usual, when he pulled up everybody was outside trying to be apart of that American Dream, "Getting Rich". Exiting the car, somehow Tykisha must have sensed his presence, cause soon as Gino said what's up to Tee, Tykisha came out the screen door to the house. Gino saw her smile and he lit up like a star in the sky. "What's up baby girl?" Gino said as they embraced.

"Hi Gino, how are you?" Tykisha blushed.

"I'm fine . . . Aye Tee hold up for a minute I need to speak to Tykisha."

"Go ahead slim, handle your business." Tee excused himself, and they walked over beside Gino's car.

Gino leaned up against the BMW, while turning to face her. "Baby girl listen," Gino grabbed her hand, "don't say nothing just listen. I'm about to head back down Virginia to take care of some stuff, but I'll be back soon." Tykisha's eyes watered! "Now when I come back, I want you to know that you'll be mines again, and that's that, you hear me?" Tears continued to stream down her face, Gino grabbed her pulling her close. "Stop crying, here take this . . ." Gino handed her a stack of money.

"What's this for . . . I'm alright." She said barely audible.

"Didn't I say, don't talk." Gino leaned over kissing her passionately and meaningfully. When he finally released her, he didn't utter a word. He opened his car door, stepped inside, glanced at her one last time, and pulled off with Shadow and V-Rock following.

As he pulled off he watched out of his rear view mirror and saw her wiping the tears from her face and he knew then, that he had to come back and get his baby . . . and soon.

CHAPTER 31

Upon arriving back in Virginia, Gino pulled up beside Shadow and motioned for Fat Boy to roll his window down. "Yeah, what's up Gino?" Shadow asked as they sat at the light.

"I'll see you in the morning, we heading back to the house, aiight?"

"Fo'sho, see you in the morning." Shadow replied as the light changed and they all pulled off.

At the apartment, Gino and V-Rock both parked their cars, and grabbed their bags, and headed on up the steps into the apartment. Soon as Gino opened the door he hollered, "Aye Quita!! . . . Quita!!!" as V-Rock closed the door.

"It does feel good to be home." V-Rock says setting his bags down and plopping down on the couch.

"Hi baby . . . Hi baby!!" Quita came rushing out from the back room, jumping straight into Gino's arms.

"Damn if it's like this, then maybe I should go out of town more often!" Gino smiled.

Marquita immediately looked down at all the bags, "Oh I know my baby got me something." She started peeking in the bags at Gino's feet.

"So what if I didn't?" Gino teased.

"Then you'll be sleeping on that couch tonight." V-Rock busted out laughing. Gino reached and grabbed one of the bags and handed it to Quita. "Thank you baby." She purred with excitement. Pulling the contents out, Gino had gotten her a Louis Vuitton handbag, with the shoes to match. "Thank you baby!! Thank you!!" she hugged and kissed Gino repeatedly.

Gino grabbed the rest of his bags and started to head for the bedroom, when Quita says, "Gino I'm glad y'all are back baby . . ." Something in her voice didn't sound right, Gino could tell. As he dropped his bags and turned to face her. "Why . . . what happened baby?"

"Ever since y'all left town, it's been non-stop shooting around RipRap. The whole weekend has been crazy."

Gino's face went blank, "Did anybody get shot, that you know of?"

"Baby I didn't go around there to find out, my friend Danyell told me that about 3 or 4 people had gotten shot though. However, she didn't know exactly who."

"Oh yeah . . . , thanks baby. Hopefully nobody from the fam got hurt, if so Fat Boy will call me. Come on, let's go to bed." As they strolled towards the bedroom.

Shadow was on his way home when he decided to stop pass his grandmother's house before heading home. Opening the door to his grandmothers' house, Shadow's belly felt funny, and he could sense that something just wasn't right. "Aye Grandma! . . . Grandma!!" Shadow called out as he walked through the house.

"In the den baby." Grandma answered.

"Hi Grandma." Shadow leaned over and hugged his grandmother, and kissed her on the cheek.

She sat back in her chair, placing her sewing material by her side. "Baby I'm soo . . . glad you're home." She coughed momentarily. "Ever since you've been gone things have been haywire around here."

Shadow sat down, "What happened?"

"Your cousin Stevie got robbed and shot yesterday, but he's alright." Shadow's eyebrows rose up. "I went to see him, and he knows who done it, but he's not telling anyone anything until he talks to you."

Shadow sat there rubbing his chin listening to the information, "as long as he's okay, that's all that matters Ma. I'll go see him first thing in the morning."

"That's not it baby," Grandma proclaimed, "Trustin and Torey also got shot. I don't know all the specifics, but you need to get some order back around here, before somebody really gets hurt, okay?"

"Got you Grandma." Fat Boy got up and kissed grandma on her forehead and began to head for the door.

"I mean what I said Shadow!"

"Got you Grandma . . ." as he jetted.

Jumping inside his car, and pulling off, he immediately dialed up Gino. V-Rock answered. "Hello."

"V let me speak to Gino right quick!" Shadow insisted.

Shortly thereafter, Gino picked up the phone, "What's up Fat Boy?"

"Man I jive like got to really holler at you on some important stuff. A lot of little shit went down while we were out of town."

"Yeah I heard, Quita was telling me. You need to meet up right now?"

"Nah . . . , I'll see you first thing in the morning. Just come early, I hate talking on these phones." Shadow commented.

"Fo'sho, see you in the morning." They hung up.

All night long Gino nor Shadow got any sleep. Gino was now standing out front of the stash house sipping on some coffee he had just bought from the 7-11, when he spotted Shadow's truck pulling up. "Piss . . . , this shit is nasty." Gino hissed, throwing the coffee cup on the ground as Shadow walked up. "What's up nigga?" Gino spoke as they gave each other dap.

"Ain't too much, come on let's go in the house so we can talk." Shadow led the way.

Inside the house, Fat Boy explained the whole scenario that Grandma had informed him about. Gino stood there listening, arms crossed with a serious look on his face taking it all in. "Fat Boy, I suggest we go see Stevie and find out exactly what happened from the horses mouth."

"No doubt, but let's see what everybody else has to say when they get here." Shadow suggested as Tee Tee entered the house, closing the door behind him.

Tee Tee was shaking his head the whole time he walked up. "Mann . . . . , I'm glad y'all back. Things really have gotten out of control 'round here, real talk!"

"Yeah we heard, what happened?" Shadow asked.

140

Tee Tee explained, "I really don't know everything, but somebodies squad has been trying to get at us. All of us have been ambushed or shot at by these suckers during the course of this weekend."

Shadow barked, "Who's the niggas?!!!"

"I believe it was those Queen Street niggas, Bam, Deon, Baby D, Mike B, and the rest of the squad. They act like they were trying to take control of the blocks or something."

"Oh yeahh . . . ," Shadow replied nodding his head, "don't even worry about that, we're going to take care of them TODAY!!" Shadow looked at Gino, as Gino threw his hands in the air.

Noticing that everybody was starting to arrive, Shadow called everybody into the back room. "Listen up!" all noise ceased! "Everybody go ahead back to your blocks as usual, don't change a thing. If anybody comes through, blaz'em, no hesitation! Me, Gino, and V-Rock are going to handle them nigga's today, aiight?"

Teddy Bear then spoke up, "Shadow all the money for y'all is back at my crib."

"Don't worry about that right now, we'll get that later. Right now let's get hold of these streets again. Shit getting ready to get real ugly round here." Shadow mentioned as they all disbursed.

Shadow went down the basement and came back up with a double barrel sawed-off shot gun, a street sweeper, and 2 mac-11's. He handed V-Rock the bag, "Let's go!" as they all marched outside.

CHAPTER 32

They drove over to Queen Street but noticed that none of the guys that they were looking for were out there. Frustrated, Gino suggested, "Look Shadow . . . since them niggas ain't out here, I'ma send a message through the ones who are out here . . . . that we're back!"

Shadow asked, "what you got in mind?"

"Just sit right here for a minute," Gino said. "V-Rock come with me."

Shadow sat and watched as they exited the car and walked down the street towards a crowd of dudes that were hustling in front of the building, next to the alley. While they were walking Gino whispered to V-Rock, "Follow my lead." As Gino adjusted the sawed-off shotgun inside his sweat pants.

"I got you." V mumbled back as he watched Gino's every move walking in front of him.

Approaching the crowd, Gino yelled out, "Aye yo . . . y'all got some smoke over there?!!!"

It was like 8 workers out there, just so happen one of them responded, "Yeah we got that, come on over." He waved for Gino and V to cross over to their side of the street. Walking across the street, Gino noticed that they were watching him kind of funny, and wondered if they had spotted the sawed off on his side. "Follow me." The guy said as he led them into an alley where they served all their customers. The guy then reaches down into his underwear pulling out a sandwich bag full of $30 packages of weed.

"Let me see one of those champ." Gino says taking the package, opening it up and smelling the sticky icky. "Yeah . . . boy, this shit smells good."

"Best on the block." The guy replies feeling like he had just wheeled in another sell.

"No doubt." Gino answered fake like, reaching into his pocket for the money. "Sike a Boo Boo!!" Gino shouted out the blue scaring everybody as he whipped out the sawed off.

"Ohhhhh . . . shittt!!!!!!!!!!!!!!!!!!!!!!!!" the guy yells trying to make a run for it, but it was too late, V-Rock was letting loose, "POW . . . POW . . . POW . . . POW . . . POW . . . POW . . . POW . . .", then Gino joined in the fireworks, "Boommmm . . . Boom . . . . booommmmm . . . !" All you could see was niggas dropping like flies in screams of desperation. Feeling like the message was sent, they took off running towards the car, where Shadow was waiting. They jumped in, and Fat Boy quickly pulled off.

CHAPTER 33

Two days later, Shadow and Gino were riding pass Burger King on the Boulevard, when Shadow spotted what looked like Bam's truck, or so he thought. "Aye Gino," Shadow pointed to the truck as they were riding pass slowly. "I swear that looks like Bam's truck right there." Shadow then pulled inside the car wash across the street down the block a bit from the Burger King.

"Are you sure Fat Boy?" Gino asked.

"I can't say to be 100%, but if it is, this could be our lucky day!" They sat in the car wash watching patently to see if their prayers were answered. Fortunately they didn't have to wait long, minutes later Bam, Deon and two female associates exited the Burger King. "Damn Gino they got two freaks with them right now."

"And?? . . . What that mean?" Gino glanced up at Shadow. "Them niggas getting it, and anybody with them getting it too." Gino pulled out his 9mm colt.

Bam and them hopped in his truck and pulled off, with Gino and Shadow following not far behind. As they followed them it appeared that Bam was headed around Queen Street. Not much longer after that, they would learn that their hunch was right, as Bam turned onto Queen Street cruising down the block. Gino gripped the handle of his Colt that was lying on his lap. Gino then checked to make sure that one was in the chamber, and then he clicked it back. Halfway down the block Bam pulled over and began to park. Unbeknown to him, his life and his buddies' lives were about to change forever, and in a matter of seconds now. Soon as Bam turned the ignition off, Gino pushed the electronic window button letting his window come all the way down. Shadow then pulled up alongside of Bam's truck, as Gino's arm quickly extended out the window. "Aye Bam!!" Gino yelled catching everybody's attention in the truck. Bam turned, and fright was all over his face. "Ayeeeee!!!!! . . ." he screamed out trying to duck inside the truck. "POW . . . POW . . . POW . . . POW . . . POW . . . POW . . . POW . . . POW . . . POW . . . POW . . . POW . . . POW . . . POW!!!!!" Gino emptied the clip inside the truck, as Shadow screeched off leaving a blood bath on Queen Street.

CHAPTER 34

Weeks later Gino and Shadow were finally getting things back under control like they were from the beginning. Little did they know, but down in D.C. Kenny had started to really step his game up to a whole nother level. He took the money that Gino had given him and did well for real. In any event, when Gino left D.C., Kenny somewhat fell out with Black, Mike Mike, and Speedy. Black was mad at the fact that he knew Tykisha had been with Gino sexually while he was in D.C., and being as though Gino wasn't around he took his frustrations and anger out on Kenny.

Soon after Gino left town, Black confronted Tykisha about the insinuations that Gino gave him. She told Black that she was with Gino, but not in that manner, which she knew was a lie. Tykisha informed Black that she was only with Gino to explain the whole situation, before somebody else did. Black didn't believe Tykisha at all, and they fell out before she went back to school. Black was steaming mad at the fact that he couldn't confront Gino on the situation, so over time he would constantly try to pick little arguments and fights with Kenny. But by this time Kenny was blowing up, and his name was ringing all over N.E. Now you know how money makes a nigga head get real big, so Kenny told Black the last time, "Back up before he had to do something to Black for real." Black definitely didn't take that too kindly.

One day while Kenny was coming through 4th Street to pick up some money and drop off some packages, Black and Mike Mike spotted him and waved for him to come holla. "What's up Kenny?" Mike Mike spoke as he and Black observed Kenny passing out some packages to his people.

"Ain't too much Mike Mike," as they exchanged dap, "just coming through to take care of a little business, you know?"

Black stood back watching, twirling a straw that was in his mouth. "Oh so you too big for us peons now, huh?" Black said in a slick tone.

"Black look." Kenny sighed . . . "you know me better than that. Why we got to keep going through this? You know I don't like to fuck with my niggas on a business tip, too many headaches."

"I told you Mike Mike." Black began, throwing his hands towards Kenny. "This nigga done got brand new all of a sudden, cause he getting a little money slim."

"Fuck you Black!!" Kenny shouted with force. "Nigga I'm doing me. Don't be mad at me cause Gino came back to town and took your girl. For real . . . for real, you ain't have no business messing with her from the beginning anyway."

Mike Mike grabbed Black from approaching Kenny, "Bitch nigga, he ain't done nothing for real! You see who she still with punk."

"Yeah whatever, don't fool yourself." Kenny chuckled.

"Yeah aiight, keep running your mouth, and I'ma see if I can't fix it for you." Black responded trying to get out of Mike Mike's grasp. "Let me go Mike Mike."

Mike Mike then shouted, "Both you niggas shut up!! Just leave that shit alone, I'm serious Black."

Kenny leaned back against the wall, "Mike Mike mann . . . , you know that you and Speedy always been cool with me. I'm not going to waste no more of my time arguing with this fool, cause I know for real, it ain't about me. That stuff with Gino and Tykisha, is their business. I never even told Gino that Black was messing with her from the beginning, cause I didn't want Black to feel like I switched up on him. But now I see that no matter what, I can't satisfy his feelings, and I ain't going to try no more." Kenny walked up and shook Mike Mike's hand. "See you later folks." Kenny stepped off heading towards his car.

"Mike Mike I'm telling you, I'ma end up fucking that nigga up. He's doing a lot of faking." Black said as they watched Kenny walk towards his car.

"Black what you need to do is calm down. Come on let's get up out of here." Mike Mike stepped off with Black following.

Kenny had a few sections of the city on locks now, Edgewood . . . 4th Street, and a few more here and there. He was really getting that cash flow now, and wasn't letting nothing get in his way.

Tykisha had gone back to school, but had Gino on her mind everyday, and he definitely had her heart. She had felt bad about the way things had gone with Black, and felt as if she had to make a decision and soon. Did she want Black or Gino, were her thoughts. Gino had a woman, but she knew if she decided to be with him, Gino would be with her. "Oooooo . . . ." she hissed while holding her head inside her hands. "I don't know why does love have to be so complicated. I love Gino, but we've been separated so long I don't know if he's the same person. Black's been here for me, and I know I'll feel bad if I leave him just like that. However, it's not fair to be with him, and still be in love with Gino. Why can't life just be simple, hopefully things will work out.

CHAPTER 35

Back in Virginia shit had settled down, and RipRap was back pumping again. Money was pouring in and things were really looking good. Grandma had called Shadow and informed him that Kelvin and AJ needed to see him, so he and Gino had to take an unpleasant trip back to the BIG House today.

Barbed wired fences, Correctional Officers, and getting patted down, brought back all the memories that Gino had wanted to forever forget about prison. Especially as they were being searched and patted down entering Tidewater's Detention Center. Single mothers, baby mothers, children, mothers, fathers, family and friends were jammed pack in the visiting hall waiting to see their loved ones. Gino and Shadow took a seat at a table way over in the corner, trying to be as far away from the crowded table areas as possible.

Shortly after taking their seats, Kelvin and AJ appeared from behind the electronic sliding doors entering the visiting hall. They both appeared to be mini celebrities in the joint, cause damn near everybody in the visiting hall spoke or hollered at them while they were in the process of reaching the table where Gino and Shadow awaited on them. Finally as they reached the table, they all embraced each other. "What's up y'all?" Shadow says. "Oh . . . yeah, y'all niggas look like y'all been putting in major work on that pull up bar, what's up with that?"

"I mean you know how it is." AJ remarked, "what's up with y'all niggas?"

"Same old shit, we just came back from D.C." Shadow replied.

"Yeah we heard about them niggas fakin' out there too." Kelvin mentioned.

"Yeah . . . but them peoples taken care of, you hear me? . . . Done!" They all looked at each other with sneaky eyes, which let everybody know they were dead.

"Well look Shadow," Kelvin scooted his chair up between Gino and Shadow. "Mann . . . you know them feds came to see us yesterday, asking me and slim a lot of questions about different murders, beefs, and other stuff that's been happening around the way."

Gino and Shadow's expressions both changed instantly, "Oh yeah!! . . ." Shadow glanced at Gino. "What else were they saying?"

"That's basically it, they act like they really trying to gather some information on you and Gino." Kelvin then says.

"Fuck!! . . ." Shadow reared back in his chair. "This shit is getting crazy."

"Calm down Fat Boy." Gino grabbed Shadow around the shoulder. "Man them peoples searching, if they had something for real, they wouldn't be asking all these questions. They would have came and got our black asses by now, real talk.

"Yeah I guess you right, slim." Shadow then commented to AJ and Kelvin. "If anything else occurs, just call Grandma like before, and give me a heads up, aiight?"

"Fat Boy look," Gino pointed to a sexy female that was sitting with her boyfriend or male friend. "don't you know her?"

"Yeah nigga, you don't remember her?" Shadow chuckled. "That's the broad I met when we was down Langley Avenue that day."

"Okay . . . now I remember." Gino smacked himself in the head.

"AJ what the lawyer talking about?" Shadow asked.

"He said that shit look alright, but we just might have to sit until trial, which is a few weeks away you know?"

"No doubt." Shadow shook his head. "Did y'all get that money I gave to Grandma?"

"Yeah . . . , we cool with what's on our books though, but don't forget to send the broads to see us next week some time." Kelvin reminded Shadow.

"You got that." As they all stood up and hugged. "Let us get out of here, but call if y'all need anything." Shadow said as they shook hands and exited the jail.

CHAPTER 36

The next morning at the stash house Gino and Shadow issued a warning to everybody that they'd have to be extra careful. Shadow explained the situation that Kelvin and AJ had informed him about the day before. After the conversation, everybody understood and went on out about their regular business. Gino caught Shadow walking to his car and pulled up on him, "Aye Fat Boy . . . mann . . . I'm telling you, I'm not going back to jail, that's out the question, feel me? Them people will have one hell of a time trying to lock me back up. I'm serious about that slim, on everything!"

Shadow opened his truck and threw his works inside on the seat. "Gino my nigga believe this, I know exactly how you feel. That's why I ain't going to panic or nothing, hopefully shit will work itself out."

"It don't matter to me Shadow, they can question me all they want." Gino shook his head in disagreement. "I ain't going out like that! Shidd . . . maybe it's time for us to close up shop. We got plenty money, I mean what else is there to chase."

Shadow stood up placing his hands in his pocket as if he was thinking about something. "Gino mann . . . , I wish it was just that easy."

"It is," Gino sternly looked at Fat Boy. "we can shut down shop out here, and move business down D.C. What's hard about that?"

Shadow listened intensely, "That sounds like a good idea." Shadow stood there rubbing his chin.

"Yeah I bet it does sound like a good idea, especially when you're trying to get some more loving from that freak ass broad Freeda nigga."

Laughter erupted from the both of them. "Yeah I'm hip to you Fat Boy." They continued to laugh.

"So what's wrong with that Gino? They say it's only tricking when you don't got it."

"You know what?" Gino pointed at Fat Boy, "you right." As they laughed some more.

CHAPTER 37

O ver the next couple of weeks everybody was cautious in their dealings and actions. During this time V-Rock had started to really do his little thing. He had all the young niggas around the hood extremely jealous of him. He stayed fresh to death, and was getting major play with all the little hoodrats now. Gino was really proud of the little homie, cause V was doing things the right way, and how he wanted to do it. What Gino really liked the most about V-Rock, was the discipline he showed at such a young age when it came to saving his money, and not wasting it. The only real vice shorty had, was shopping. The boy shopped damn near everyday it seemed like, however that was a vice that couldn't be handled.

Several days later over at Gino's house everybody was there, Gino, Shadow, Tricia, Marquita, V-Rock, and his new bun Lisa. They all came up with the idea to take a vacation down Miami Beach for a few days. Tricia and Marquita made all the arrangements and accommodations, while Gino, Shadow, and V went to take care of business. They would be leaving that evening.

Later that evening at the stash house Shadow was on the phone with Tricia when she informed him to be home by 7:00 pm cause their flight was scheduled to leave at 8:00 pm that night. Shadow hung up the phone, waved Gino over, and explained to him what Tricia said. "Alright I'm ready now for real." Gino responded.

"I told her to call V-Rock, and she had informed me that she had already done that. So let me holla at Bear, then we can roll." Shadow walked off down the steps to meet Teddy Bear who was out front.

"Aye Bear!!" Shadow yelled out as he walked up on Bear conversing with Tee Tee. "Look we're about to go out of town for a few days and I need you to hold shit down. Can you do that for me?"

"I mean . . . , you know I got that, but you remember what happened the last time y'all left town." Bear reminded Shadow.

"Yeah . . . yeah, so what! I'm leaving you in charge this time, and if shit get sticky, deal with it. Then contact me and let me know the situation." Shadow instructed Bear.

"Aiight," Bear and Fat Boy shook hands, "I got that Fat Boy."

At 7:20 p.m. that night V-Rock still hadn't showed up at the apartment. Everybody was sitting around figuring V-Rock was just being the same irresponsible kid he was at times. They called his cell phone, no answer. This was crazy!

Gino was pacing back and forth from the balcony to the living room, watching to see if and when V pulled up. Whenever he did decide to arrive, Gino definitely was surely going to lash out on his ass. "Aye Shadow something's got to be wrong." Gino stood at the balcony window looking out over the parking lot. "That little nigga would have called me by now, real talk Fat Boy."

"That nigga probably out shopping somewhere and done forgot the time." Shadow said as he sipped on a glass of water.

"Anytime I've ever called V, or left a message on his voice mail, shorty has always called me straight back." Gino was saying as he entered the bathroom.

Unbeknown to them when V-Rock was leaving Wesley Avenue the po-po's had rolled up on him. They blocked his car in, drew their weapons and snatched his little ass out of his car. After placing him face first on the concrete. "Hello . . . , how are you doing Mr. Daniels?" the sergeant at the scene leaned over saying to V-Rock.

"Man what the fuck y'all messing with me for, I ain't done nothing." V-Rock barely could speak cause his face was buried in the ground.

The sergeant then instructed the officer holding V-Rock to lift him up to his knees. "Well . . . well . . . well, Mr. Daniels." The sergeant began by saying, "we were just in the neighborhood and decided to come pay you a little visit, and ask a few questions. You don't mind do you?

"Sir I don't know anything." V stated as he noticed several officers peeking inside his car, and several more surrounding him.

"You don't even know what I'm going to ask you Mr. Daniels." The sergeant looked to see if he could sense any fear in V. "You don't mind if we search your vehicle, do you?"

"Go ahead," V-Rock nodded his head. "Ain't nothing in there."

"Well let us be the judge of that," the sergeant replied as he nodded his head for the officers to go ahead and search V-Rock's car.

As the police were searching his car, V-Rock was thinking about being late to meet Gino and Shadow. V knew they'd think that he was out fucking around. Then suddenly one of the officers exits V's car hollering, "Bingo . . . Bingo . . . !" The officer had a 38 pistol dangling from his index finger. "Look what I have here?" The officer was showing the pistol to all the other officers there as well as the sergeant.

V immediately yelled, "That ain't mines!"

"Well who the hell else does it belong to then?" The sergeant barked at V-Rock. "My officer sure as hell just got that out of your vehicle."

"Mann . . . . that ain't mine. Y'all put that there." V snapped.

The officer holding the gun then bent over top V's face and whispered, "Maybe we did, maybe we didn't. But who do you think the jury would believe? You, or 4 officers here who've been on the force probably longer than you've been living? You won't stand a chance boy, you hear me?"

V just sighed, "SSSSSs . . . . , this shit is crazy!"

The sergeant then spoke. "Well Mr. Daniels," V-Rock then spotted the sergeant winking his eye at the other officers standing around. "I'm feeling really good today, so I'm going to do you a big favor Mr. Daniels, and in return you're going to do me a favor, understood?"

The sergeant nodded his head and glanced up at the other officers, whom were all standing around with smirks on their faces. "Now I already know you hang out with these two guys Gino and Shadow, correct?" V just sat silently. "I'll take your silence as a yes. I know y'all are close, I just need you to tell me what the hell is going on with this beef between RipRap and Queen St."

"Sir, I don't know what you're talking about." V straight lied.

156

"Mr. Daniels don't play me for no damn fool. I don't believe you really want to get on my bad side, do you?"

"I swear . . . I swear, I don't know nothing. If I did I'd have no problem letting you know for real." V tried to make the sergeant believe his story.

The officer then stood V up as they all surrounded him. "Son listen to this, I'm going to make this gun disappear that my officer just found in your car." The sergeant was saying, "and I'm going to believe you're not lying to me, when you say you don't know nothing. But the next time we meet, you better have something for me, or I'm going to make your life a living hell around here, and put you away for a long time, you hear me?"

V-Rock exhaled, "Ssss . . . , yeah deal!"

"Take the cuffs off," the sergeant instructed the officer holding V-Rock. "Now if you try and play me Mr. Daniels, I'll make sure that your life is a living hell from here on out, believe me when I say that!"

"I won't believe me, I won't!" V-Rock responded as the other officers were getting back into their cruisers. "Damn these motherfuckers are trying to play a nigga dirty for real, they must want Shadow and Gino bad. Fuck!!!!!" V said to himself as he watched the police pull off and leave.

V-Rock then jumped inside his 300 and was pulling off as well. However, as he was turning off of Wesley Avenue, he noticed that there was a car tailing him. "Shitt . . . . , them fucking cock suckers trying to follow a nigga." V mumbled to himself as he decided that there was no way he could head to Gino and Shadow. So he just decided to ride around until he could either shake them, or they'd get tired and just give up.

V-Rock rode around for damn near two hours before he was able to shake the feds completely. Now back at the house they had figured out by now that something had to really have happened as late as V was now. He was well over 2 hours late. As they were still patiently waiting to hear something, the phone finally rang breaking the silence. Tricia was closest to the phone at the time so she grabbed it immediately, "Hello!"

"Tricia this V, where's Shadow and Gino?" V whispered into the phone.

"Noooo . . . . , the question is where are you?!!!!" Tricia yelled as Shadow snatched the phone from her grasp.

"V-Rock! What the fuck is going on shorty?!!"

"Shadow . . . Shadow listen, meet me at the stash house right now."

"Alright, where you at?" Shadow asked.

"I'm about 10 minutes away from the stash house, just meet me there." V-Rock hung up.

Shadow removed the phone from his ear, throwing it on the couch. "Come on Gino!" Shadow grabbed his keys with Gino following, "Tricia we'll be right back." as they left out.

Fifteen minutes later when Shadow and Gino pulled up, V-Rock was standing out front leaning up against his car. Noticing their arrival he looked around and stepped towards them as they got out of Shadow's car. "What's up soldier?" Gino immediately asked.

"Come on walk with me," V led the way over to the playground across the street. Stopping by the swings, V turned and faced them. "Listen y'all . . . when I went around Wesley to make a few pick ups before our flight, I was stopped by the police."

Shadow sighed, "Sssss . . . ."

V-Rock continued, "Man they trying to find out something about y'all, but they were also asking questions about some murders that had happened around RipRap and Queens Street. When I told them that I didn't know anything, they told me that they knew I knew something because I hung out with y'all."

"What did you say?" Shadow asked.

"I ain't crazy, I told them yeah I knew y'all, but I said that you guys never discuss anything with me. They got mad and tried to plant a gun in my car. Real talk."

"They did what?!" Shadow was shocked at what he had just heard.

"Yeahh . . . , they put a gun in my car, then tried to black mail me for some information. I just stuck to my story and the officer said, he was letting me go this time, but the next time they saw me I'd better have some information for them or else."

"This shit is crazy! . . ." Gino replied as they all stood there in silence for a minute.

"Oh and guess what else," Gino and Shadow both immediately looked at V. "When I left the Avenue, them son of a bitches were trying to follow me. That's why I was sooo . . . late. I drove around for two hours until I got rid of them."

"Good thinking young nigga." Shadow responded now snapping out of his daze. "Is that all they said?"

"Yeah . . . but somebody is talking big time homie, they asking too many questions." V suggested.

Everybody stood in silence watching the cars drive past thinking and contemplating. After several minutes, Shadow spoke first, "Gino we really need to lay low for a minute. Tomorrow morning I'll get Tricia and Quita to make some new reservations, and we're out of here for a while." Shadow then stated, "Gino maybe it's time for us to get up out of Virginia period."

"You might be right Fat Boy," Gino nodded his head in agreement.

CHAPTER 38

The next morning all six of them flew to Miami, Florida. However, while they were in Miami the police were back in Virginia stepping their pursuit up too. The feds went throuhout RipRap, Bethel, and everywhere else questioning any and everybody. In the process of them shaking up a few people, they were also making the strips 'HOT', which meant that not much money was being made out there. Everybody and their Mama knew that it would make Gino and Shadow upset, but there was nothing anybody could do.

Down in DC, Kenny continued his rise in the drug game. Kenny now had a brand new 535 BMW, and an apartment in Park Place, which was gated residence located on Michigan Avenue. Everybody in the city knew that if you were living in there, you were sure nuff getting some paper. Kenny had one thorn in his side though, 'BLACK'. He and Black had been going back and forth at each other, and the tension between them had become monstrous. Kenny could've been gotten Black knocked off, but he knew that Black had grown up with Gino. On top of that, Black was one of the guys who looked out for him when he came home. So he just took it, for the time being.

One day, Kenny was passing through Stonghold and happen to see Tykisha standing out front of her house. Kenny pulled over, parked and got out. Tykisha sat down on the bottom step and waited for Kenny. "What's up lil' sis?" Kenny said as they hugged each other.

"I'm doing fine, but you're the one everybody talking 'bout." Tykisha teased.

"Nah . . . , don't believe that." Kenny took a seat on the step next to Tykisha. "So how have you been?"

"I'm alright, . . ." as silence creep momentarily. "Have you heard from Gino, Kenny?"

"Nope," Kenny replied, "I haven't seen or heard from him in about a week now. But when I talked to him last week, he said that he'd be back up here soon."

Tykisha sat there staring at the cars riding pass North Capital St., "Kenny I need to see him. Black is getting on my last nerve about Gino. All he keeps throwing in my face is that Gino told him that we were together."

Kenny snickered a bit, "Y'all were right?!"

Tykisha pushed Kenny over. "You know we were stupid, why you even ask me that? Kenny I just don't want to cut Black off just like that. He's been there for me when I needed a friend too."

"Well Tykisha you know how you and Gino feel about each other, right?" She nodded her head. "It's not fair to be with Black while loving and thinking about Gino, feel me?"

Tykisha placed both her hands over her face. Kenny pulled her hands down as he noticed now that her eyes were becoming watery. "Kenny I know it's not fair, but what can I do? Gino has a girlfriend too."

"So what . . . ," Kenny reared back. "What that got to do with you telling him how you feel and what you want? That is what you want, right?"

"My heart is telling me yes Kenny," she wiped the tears from her eyes. "but I don't want Gino and Black beefing about this stuff."

Kenny stood up off the steps, "Tykisha you know Gino can handle his own. Do what you suppose to do."

"Kenny you know I love your brother, right?"

Kenny looked Tykisha straight in the eyes. "He really loves you too."

Tykisha finally broke a smile. "Did he tell you that Kenny? Keep it real!"

"Tykisha I said he really loves you too," as they both smiled at each other. Seconds later a car pulls up in front of them and comes to a screeching halt. Tykisha and Kenny's attention immediately turned to see who was exiting the car, and wouldn't you know it . . . it was Black. He slowly exited the car and was strolling in their direction. "Tykisha what's up girl? I see you standing there by yourself." Black was saying as he walked up, and then stood beside Tykisha, while staring Kenny up and down.

"Black stop acting like that," Tykisha mentioned as soon as she saw what Black was doing.

"Nah . . . baby, it's not like that, Kenny know what the fuck I'm talking about, don't you champ?" Black was trying to clown Kenny.

Kenny bit down on his bottom lip, as he tried to calm himself down. "Look Black I don't know what's your problem, but I ain't fittin' to sit here and try to figure it out either. Whatever it is, just deal with it nigga!"

"Yeah whatever then, but deep down I know you know what I'm talking about. Ever since your brother left you a little something, you been acting funny as shit. Nigga that shit ain't nothing. You left your own boys hanging."

Kenny stood there shaking his head. "Black listen to this for the last time. I told you that I didn't want none of my men hustling for me. However, I also told you, that if any of y'all needed anything to just let me know, and I'd handle that for y'all . . . didn't I?"

"Nigga I ain't been asking you for nothing, and I ain't 'bout to start now!!" Black shouted.

"You know what Black, you right." Kenny then walked up to Tykisha. "Listen lil' sis I'm outta here, when are you going back to school?"

"I'm leaving tomorrow, why?" Tykisha asked.

"Nothing, you just be careful and remember what I said." Kenny mentioned knowing it would bother Black.

"Alright Kenny, you be careful yourself, you hear me?"

"Tykisha . . . ," Black grabbed her around the shoulders, "come on baby before I say something I might regret. Black took Tykisha's hand leading her on up the steps.

Kenny got in his car, started it and rolled his window down. "Aye Black! . . ." Kenny called out as Black turned to see what Kenny wanted. "If you wasn't Gino's man, believe me I would've been gotten that ass, believe that." Kenny then rolled his window back up and slowly began to pull off.

"Whatever sucker, let that be the reason!" Black yelled back as Kenny was driving off. Black then turned to face Tykisha, "Kisha why you keep talking to that nigga for anyway?! You must be using him to send messages back and forth to Gino, huh?! Don't play with me girl! I'll kill both of y'all! Now try me!"

Tykisha stopped in her tracks turning to face Black. "Look Black me and Kenny were not discussing Gino for your information. He just happen to stop pass cause he saw me out front. In any event, who are you to be questioning me like you my father anyway? I told you before, I'm grown and I can talk to whomever I want. What you need to do is stop worrying about Gino so much, and focus on handling your business!!" She snapped with much attitude.

"You right . . ." Black said sarcastically. "That's why the next time I see either one of them suckers I'm going to do just that, handle my business." Black replied before storming down the steps and hopping in his car. As he screeched off, Tykisha stood there just shaking her head.

When Kenny left Tykisha's he rode pass his mom's house to see how she was doing. Of course she gave him the third degree about being out in them streets. As always, Kenny denied being in the streets, then excused himself to use the restroom. Upstairs instead of going to the restroom Kenny snuck into his mothers' bedroom and placed $5,000 in her night stand. Kenny knew that she wouldn't take it no other kind of way. Kenny loved his mom despite what had happened in the past, she had changed her life around and was doing really well now. All she wanted was her baby's to get out that street life, which they both kept denying. She knew them streets were dangerous and vicious. Kenny came back downstairs, kissed his mom on the cheek, let her know that he'd be back soon, and left to go take care of some business he had.

CHAPTER 39

Down in Miami, Gino and them were having the time of their lives spending plenty cash and enjoying the comforts of the warm weather and lovely sights. They partied at all the hot spots during the week and on Saturday they went to the Spider Club, which set right directly on the beach, and kept celebrity crowds inside. This night, Magic Johnson, Alonzo Mourning, Vivica Fox, Brad Pitt, and many other stars happened to stop through. Shit was happening down Miami, believe that. Later in the week they all went to Disney World and enjoyed themselves even more. These were just some of the perks they were afforded with getting money.

One day while lounging on the beach watching the girls swim, Gino said to Shadow, "Man we need to get one more good push slim and get the hell out of Virginia before it's too late."

"Gino my nigga," Shadow spoke from behind his Gucci shades and sipping on some Gin and juice. "I was thinking along those same lines myself. What do you want to do about the girls?"

Gino sipped his Strawberry Daiquiri, "Man we can keep them down in Virginia, but we can't stay here. See cause what's going to happen is, the police are going to squeeze the right mother . . . , and they're going to tell everything. You know how the game goes."

"I'm feeling you on that my nig'," Shadow commented still watching Tricia and Quita. "So when we get back, we're going to make one last run, and then we out, right?"

Gino tilted his head, so he could see Shadow over the top of his shades. "You better know it. There's one thing though, when we roll I'm taking V-Rock with me?"

Shadow nodded his head, "That figures, I know you love little shorty."

"You better know it." They gave each other dap.

Knowing that Kelvin and AJ's trial was starting Monday, they jumped on a plane Friday and headed back to Virginia. During the flight, Gino had noticed that he hadn't seen V-Rock or Lisa since the flight had taken off. "Aye Baby," Gino called Quita who was listening to her IPod, "have you seen V-Rock or Lisa?"

"Nah . . . Sweetheart, I been dozing off back and forth."

"What about you Shadow, you seen shorty?"

"Mann . . . the last time I seen that nigga, they were headed for the restroom, I think. That was about 30 minutes ago." Shadow stated.

"I hated leaving Miami Baby," Tricia mentioned.

"Girl what you talking 'bout?" Marquita replied.

"I'm glad you had such a nice time baby," Gino kissed her.

"Gino." Shadow tapped him form the seat behind him, "There's that little nigga right there." V-Rock and Lisa were now coming down the aisle way.

"Aye V, let me holla at you for a minute soldier." Gino said as Lisa stopped and took her seat, and V proceeded back to see what Gino wanted.

"Yeah, what's up Big Homie?"

"Nigga where you been?" Gino asked as V began smiling, while peeking over his shoulder at Lisa who was blushing at V.

"Well you know," V began to snicker, ". . . you know I had to find out about that Mile High Club Jay-Z always talking 'bout, you hear me?!"

Laughter erupted, as V-Rock gave Gino and Shadow high fives before heading back to his seat. Young and Wild!!!

CHAPTER 40

The next morning Gino woke up at 11:30 a.m. As he rolled over he noticed that Quita was still sleep. So he got up and showered, then went to wake V-Rock, so he could get up and dressed. Twenty minutes later they were speeding down the Avenue towards Bethel. Gino had already informed V-Rock of their plans of getting out of Virginia, and V said that he was down. V-Rock knew that in DC he and Kenny could hook back up, which of course we know meant trouble!

Shortly thereafter as Gino pulled up on Bethel with V behind him, Gino spotted Greg standing on the porch. He rolled his window down, "Hey Greg!" Gino hollered.

"Yeah, what's up Gino?!" Greg replied.

"You seen Shadow this morning?"

"Yeah that fat nigga just left about 15 minutes ago. I think he said he was heading over to the stash house."

"Okay, thanks Greg. How did shit go while we were out of town?" Gino asked.

"It's been crazy, but I'll let Fatboy tell you when you see him."

"Aiight, I'll see you tonight."

"Fo' sho!" Greg replied backing up from the car waving at V-Rock as he rode past.

CHAPTER 41

"They did what?!" Gino was asking Shadow to repeat what he had just told him.

"Gino mann . . . , while we were gone the feds were shaking the blocks up, questioning and pressing people for information about us. The shit was sooo . . . bad, that they slowed the money flow up."

"Damn . . . !" Gino shouted. "Fatboy that probably was their plan from the beginning. That way they could try to draw us out. What we got to do is lay real low and chill out for a minute."

"You might be right." Shadow leaned up against the side of the house, catching Teddy Bear attention who was walking up. "Aye Bear check this out," Shadow was pondering his thoughts, "from now on you'll be our go between for everybody and us. We're still going to come pass the stash house maybe periodically, but we're no longer coming through the blocks unless necessary. So y'all will have to collect the money and deliver the packages."

Bear nodded his head, "Okay . . . I got that Fat Boy."

"Also, I need you to let everybody know under no circumstances to talk to the feds about nothing. And if anybody's caught doing so, it's on."

"I got that." Bear answered.

"Bear, where's the money stashed at?" Shadow asked.

"At my house, you need it now?"

"Yeah . . . , V-Rock do me a favor . . ."

V cut him off, "I got that Fat boy. I'll meet y'all back at the house."

"Cool, Gino come on let's ride pass the lawyer's office now." Shadow mentioned as they rolled out.

The intercom buzzed on the secretary's desk. "Beep . . . , Yes Mr. Davis?" The secretary responded hanging up the phone. "You can go in now Mr. Thompson."

"Thank you ma'am." Shadow answered as he and Gino got up and headed towards the office door. Pushing the solid oak doors open to the office, Mr. Davis was sitting behind his desk rambling through some paperwork.

"Come on in gentlemen, take a seat." Mr. Davis found the documents he was looking for. "Well gentlemen, I have some good news for you!" A broad smile came across Gino and Shadow's face. "I had a meeting with the prosecutor two days ago pertaining to Kelvin and AJ's case. During out discussions we came to an agreement on a lot of things. The main thing being that AJ and Kelvin were pulled over without probable cause. We can prove that because there was never a traffic violation or citation ever written pertaining to them being pulled over."

Shadow then cut in, "Well how come they searched their car?"

"Let me finish Mr. Thompson. Therefore the stop was faulty, any and everything found after the search of the car was obtained illegally and unconstitutionally. So on Monday they'll be released."

"Yeah that's right." Shadow blurted out as he and Gino gave each other dap.

"Hell yeah!" Gino was rubbing his hands together.

"Hold up . . . Hold up a minute." Mr. Davis interrupted their celebration. "There is something that you guys need to know though. The reason that AJ and Kelvin were pulled over was because they wanted to question them about y'all two." All smiles immediately faded away. "So I suggest tomorrow, that you guys not attend their court appearance. Stay out of the lime light, because right now y'all are some pretty important people downtown."

"I mean . . . I mean, what they questioning people about us for?" Gino asked.

"That there is a question that I can't answer, but whatever it is for, it must be pretty serious." Mr. Davis implied.

They both stood up, "Okay thanks Mr. Davis, we appreciate all your help", Shadow was saying, "also, I would like for you to represent me and Gino if something was to ever happen to us. I'll pay you in advance if need be."

Mr. Davis smiled and stuck his hand out for Shadow to shake. "There's no need for all that Mr. Thompson, we've been dealing with each other a long time. If any problems so happen to arrive, just have someone contact me."

"I'll definitely do that, thanks again." Shadow commented as they walked out.

CHAPTER 42

"Shadow is that you?" Tricia called out from the bedroom where she was ironing.

"Yeah baby, who else would it be? Somebody else has the keys to my house?" Shadow responded as he and Gino sat down.

"You always got something slick to say fat ass." She joked as she walked over and took a seat on Shadow's lap.

"Yeahh . . . , but you love something else fat too," Shadow teased as they shared a kiss, "listen baby, I need you to do me a favor."

"What's that baby?" she purred.

"Well you know that AJ and Kelvin getting out Monday, right?"

"Noo . . . baby, you didn't tell me that."

"I'm telling you now girl." Tricia slid off his lap taking a seat beside him. "So look we're throwing a party for them. I need you and Quita to go down to the 1851 Club and let Mack know I want to throw a party on Monday, alright?"

"Uhhhh . . . baby, you know I hate that nigga ever since I told you he tried to talk to me before he knew I was your girl, uhhhh . . . ." Tricia squelched her face.

"Come on Tricia, that nigga ain't gonna do or say nothing crazy to you no more, alright! He knows now!"

"Yeah okay, what else?"

"Tell Mack that I'll pay him whatever, just get me 5 of his best dancers."

"You just got to have some strippers, nasty ass self." Tricia rolled her eyes.

"Girl shut up, you know it ain't no party without the strippers. Also let Mack know we want Fred to DJ the party. He already knows whom I'm talking about. Let him know that I'll be getting Flames to perform as well."

Gino then asked, "Who's Flames big boy?"

"Oh . . . , Flames is a young nigga from the hood who's been trying to make it in the rap game. The nigga's the truth, but he just can't catch a break. I got him though, we've been close since way back in the day when we tried to form a rap group together. We used to battle all the time, until I got tired of waiting for that break and got into the drug game. But I've always encouraged him to continue on, and never give up. That's why every time I see that nigga I throw him a few stacks."

"Damn big boy, I didn't know you could rap!" Gino replied.

"Gino that shit was years ago . . . I mean years!"

"You probably could have been the next Heavy D." Gino and Tricia both bust out laughing.

"What you laughing at Tricia?" Shadow asked as he was still laughing himself. "you were still sweating a nigga back then too."

Finally catching a break from laughing, Tricia says, "I love you no matter what baby." As she tried to hold her laugh in.

"Look go ahead baby and y'all take care of that. Me and Gino got some other stuff we've got to attend to alright?!"

Tricia got up grabbing her purse, "I'll call you when I get back."

"Okay, ohh . . . make sure you and Quita let all your little hoodrat buddies know about the party too."

"For your information, my buddies aren't hoodrats. You got my friends mixed up with Peaches." Tricia slammed the door walking out.

"Damn Cuz!" Gino laughed, as they got up and left soon after.

CHAPTER 43

"Beep . . . beep . . . beep," Shadow honked his horn to get Dexter's attention. Dexter and Paris looked over. "Whaaatttt? . . . , is that Shadow? Nigga you better get up out that car and come holla at your peoples!!!!" Dexter yelled out.

Shadow parked and they got out, strolling towards the building where Dexter and Paris were posted up in front of, "Damn my nigga! What the fuck is up?!!" Paris greeted Shadow and they all gave each other dap.

"Ain't shit y'all. Aye this my man Gino right here." Gino shook their hands.

"Yeah boyy . . . , we heard about how you done took over BadNews. What you too big for a nigga now?" Paris commented.

"That's crazy, y'all know I always got love for y'all niggas." Shadow replied.

"I can't tell, you ain't been around to holla at yo folks." Dexter says while taking a seat on the bottom step of the building staircase.

"Slim y'all know a nigga jive been super busy, feel me?"

"Yeah we heard about all the drama and stuff."

"Where's that nigga Flames at?" Shadow asked knowing that those two were never too far behind him.

Paris was now rolling a blunt, "Mann . . . , that nigga on his ways round here now. I just hung the phone up with him 5 minutes ago."

"Yeah cause I need to holla at that nigga, for real." Shadow wiped his forehead with his little rag. "You know I'm throwing a party Monday at the 1851 and I want him to perform."

"Fo'sho', you know he'll do anything for you. As a matter of fact there he go right there." Dexter said as Flames was pulling up in his black Tahoe. Flames parked and got out, immediately spotting Shadow . . . his man. "Man . . . man . . . man, look what the wind done blew my way." Flames joked as they hugged each other.

"Man I feel blessed to be in the presence of a rap star, for real." Shadow commented as he stood back admiring all the ice and jewelry Flames had on.

"Yeah I wish, shiddd . . . you the one the streets talking about." Flames glanced at Gino, probably figuring or assuming this was the dude Gino he had heard about. "Everybody still talking about the take over in RipRap. Maybe I'm in the wrong business, huh man?!"

"Don't fool yourself, keep doing what you doing, and I know you'll catch that break you need, then maybe I can get a job with you." They all laughed.

"So what brings you round the way?" Flames asked now lighting up the blunt that Paris had just handed him.

"My nigga I need a favor . . ." Shadow suggested.

"Just name it, you got." Flames quickly responded.

"I'm throwing a party Monday at the 1851, and I need you to perform for me."

"Now come on my nigga, you know you got that, no questions asked. What time is the party?"

"It's at 9:00, you can perform anytime after 11:00. Plus I need you to bring some of those groupie broads that you got . . . along too. Spread the word that the party will be jumping and live for me aiight?"

Flames blew a thick cloud of smoke out from the blunt, "I got you big Homie."

"How much will this cost me?" Shadow knew Flames wasn't going to accept none of his money, but he had to ask anyway.

"Nigga you my man, all the shit you done for me . . . I can't charge you nothing even if I wanted to." Flames knew that he could always count on Shadow if he ever needed something. No questions asked, just huh!

"Aiight homie!" Shadow and Flames hugged each other. "I'll see you Monday. I've got to make me a few runs, but thanks again my nigga." Shadow stated as he and Gino turned and walked towards the car.

After entering and starting his car, Shadow pulled up beside where Flames and them were standing, "Aye Flames!" Shadow called out to catch Flames attention.

"Yo' what's up homie?" Flames turned towards Shadow, as soon as Flames glanced at Shadow, he noticed Shadow throwing something out the window towards him. Immediately, Flames knew it was some money, but before he could catch it and return it, Shadow pulled out in a blazed speed.

"Damn it! This nigga do this shit every time. Come on y'all I got a surprise for that nigga on Monday, watch what I tell you." Flames waved his hand for Dexter and Paris to come on as they jumped into his truck and rolled out.

CHAPTER 44

All weekend long things went pretty normal, besides the fact that Shadow and Gino didn't show their faces not once.

Monday rolled around before you knew it, and Gino, Shadow, Tricia, and Quita got up early to do all their little running around and errands in preparation for the party. All the while, in court, just like the lawyer had said Kelvin and AJ were released, after leaving the court building Kelvin and AJ headed straight over to Grandma's house, and immediately paged Shadow. Upon Shadow seeing Grandma's number he quickly called back. "Hello!" Shadow's Grandmother answered.

"Good morning Grandma, did everything go aiight?" Shadow asked.

"Hold on baby." Grandma then handed Kelvin the phone.

"What's up big Cuz?" Kelvin shouted into the phone.

"Okay . . . okay, glad to hear that you're home." Shadow replied.

"Thanks Big Boy!"

"No problem, you're family. I'll always be here for you. Look Tricia will be through to pick y'all up in a few, just sit still."

"Got you! AJ said what's up too."

"Tell him I said what's up, and I'll see y'all in a minute."

"Aiight!"

Shadow hung up and dialed Tricia, "Hello!" she answered.

"Tricia where you at?" Shadow asked.

"I'm around the Avenue talking to Stevie baby."

"What the fuck?!!" Shadow's voice was raising with every word. "What are you doing up on that Avenue. What did I tell you about being up there?"

"I was looking for you," she sighed, "I paged you 4 or 5 times and you still hadn't called me back. So I came up here."

"Get the fuck from up there, NOW!! You hear me??!" Shadow shouted so loud that Stevie was in the background and heard Shadow's every word.

"Yes . . . but,"

Shadow cut her off, "I need you to go past Grandma's house and pick up Kelvin and AJ. Then meet me at the stash house in 30 minutes, you hear me?!"

"Yeah I hear you," Tricia sucked her teeth, "but you ain't got to talk to me like that either."

"You better be glad I don't slap the shit out of you, for real . . . for real."

"Whatever! I'm on my way." She stated hanging up the phone.

"Gino my nigga this going to be one hell of a party tonight." Shadow said to Gino as they stood outside the stash house watching the neighborhood.

"Yeah my nigga, this will be a night that we won't forget. I gave Quita some money to go shopping and shit early this morning."

"Huh . . . that ain't nothing. Tricia got her outfit yesterday."

"Shadow," Gino rubbed his head looking crazy like something was on his mind, "what about Peaches and Tuesday??"

"What about them, ain't nothing we can do? They going to be there, best believe that. We just got to play it smooth, that's all I can say." Shadow was talking when he caught glimpse of Tricia turning the corner with Kelvin and AJ, "There go AJ and Kelvin right there."

They both focused on the car as Tricia parked, and they got out. "What's up big Homie?" AJ stated as they both walked up hugging Gino and Shadow.

"Gino what's happening?" Kelvin asked as they all stood there conversing for a few moments, until Shadow told them to hold on.

"Aye Tricia come here," Shadow watched as she walked over with plenty of attitude. "What's wrong with your face? Don't make me mad, you hear me?"

Tricia sighed, "Whatever Shadow."

"Go head home and get ready for tonight. I'll be there in about 2 hours."

"Yeah aiight," she sucked her teeth again, "cause we need to talk seriously."

"Aiight we'll deal with that when I get to the house." Shadow rushed her off, as he watched her get in he car and roll out.

Shadow then turned to the crew, who were watching everything anyway, "Come on y'all, let's go shopping."

CHAPTER 45

At 9pm, Gino was ready and Marquita was still getting extra cute to show off. Gino hollered form the living room, "Quita have you heard from V-Rock yet?!!!"

"Yeah baby, he called while you were in the shower. He said that he was on his way."

"Beep . . . beep . . . beep", a car horn was sounding off outside. Gino peeked out of the balcony to see if Shadow had changed plans and had come past his house. "Is that him baby?" Quita asked.

"Nah baby, I don't think so. I don't see his car out there."

"I'm on my way out anyway baby." Quita replied.

"Yeah right, you told me that 20 minutes ago."

Surprisingly though while Gino was talking Quita turned the corner dressed in a tight ass Bebe mini skirt show casing her sexy legs, with a Bebe body shirt to match showing off her nice firm breasts.

"Damn baby girl! Whew!! . . ." Gino wiped his forehead teasing Quita. "What you trying to get a nigga caught up tonight?"

"Shut up boy, you so stupid," as the car horn went off outside again. "Damn I wish whoever they waiting for would hurry up, so they could stop beeping that damn horn." Quita said.

"Come on baby." Gino handed Quita her purse as they headed for the door.

"Thanks baby." She grabbed it as they exited the apartment.

In the parking lot Gino and Quita were headed to Gino's car when Gino noticed a car in the parking lot that he assumed had been beeping the horn making all that unnecessary noise. Suddenly a voice called out from the vehicle. "Aye Gino! . . . Gino! . . . Gino!" All the while the car was moving in Gino and Quita's direction. Quickly Gino shoved Quita behind him as he began to reach for his 9mm tucked in his waist.

"Hold up . . . hold up," a familiar voice cried out as a cream colored Porsche was slowly coming to a halt a few feet away from Gino and Quita.

Gino took a second look and saw that it was V-Rock sitting behind the wheel of the Porsche, as it finally came to a halt a few feet in front of Gino. "What's up Big Homie?" V-Rock was saying as he stepped out the Porsche shining like a new silver dollar.

"Oooh . . . . wee . . . ! Young nigga this a bad mother fucker right here!" Gino stated as he started to check out the Porsche, as it was glowing from the glare of the street lights.

"Boy don't you ever scare me like that ever again, you hear me?!?!" Quita shouted as she stepped out from behind Gino.

"I'm sorry sis, my bad. Y'all like my new joint?" V-Rock asked as he turned to face the Porsche. V-Rock really wanted Gino's approval because it always made him feel better when he knew Gino approved of something he did or said.

"Boyyy! . . . you done stepped your game up with this one here for real." Gino said as he marveled at V's taste. Then they embraced each other.

"You better know it!" V was happy as a kid in a candy store.

"I see you done got a new chain and everything, huh?! Do your thing young nigga." Gino was excited for V-Rock. "Who that riding with you?"

"Oh this my new wifey Stacy," V-Rock walked them over to the passengers side window, "Stacy this Gino and my sister Quita."

"Hello, nice to meet you." Stacy replied, while Gino saw that V-Rock's social status had stepped up just like his paper game.

Marquita quickly replied, "Nice to meet you too."

"Come on y'all Shadow is waiting on us." Gino stated as they got in their cars and sped off.

At Shadow's house, Shadow was just as excited about V-Rock's new ride. He was also very proud to see the growth in shorty's game. He congratulated V-Rock and told him to keep doing what he was doing. V-rock thanked Shadow, and then they all jumped back in their rides and headed to the party.

Tonight was the night. All type of cars lined the club and the club's parking lot: Acura NSX's, BMW 850's, Corvette's, Hummers, etc. Seeing this, Gino suggested that they let the girls out in front of the club to enter while they went to park. As Tricia, Marquita, and Stacy stepped out the cars they were loving all the attention they were receiving. Tricia and Quita understood the attention came from who their men were in the streets, but they ate it up anyway. "Damn, do you see all these motherfuckers trying to get in the party Tricia?" Quita said as they walked up towards the front door passing a line full of people with hello's and well wishes.

"Do I see them? How can you miss them bitch?" Tricia replied as Bam Bam the bouncer spotted Tricia.

"Come on up here girl, what you back there waiting for?!" Bam yelled out removing the chain restraints to let them through.

"No, Shadow was parking the car, I was going to wait for him, but . . ." Tricia answered.

"Come on in here girl. I'll tell Shadow I let you in already. This crowd out here is crazy." Bam Bam stated, ushering them inside.

The weather was warm for the girls to show what their mama's gave'em, and that's exactly what they were doing.

"Ooh wee . . . ," Gino excitedly squealed, grabbing Shadow's arm and squeezing it, "look at those six bitches over there." He pointed to a group of girls who called themselves 'The Sixty Second or Less Bitches'. All six of the girls were wearing fishnet body suits, different colored thong panties, and bra's underneath with six inch peep toe stilettos. Their motto was the head, the pussy and the ass was so good, you'd cum in sixty seconds or less.

"They setting it out tonight!!" Gino shouted, as he noticed all the extremely attractive females walking to the front of the club about to receive VIP treatment and be allowed in without standing in the long ass line. Music blared out of the club when the bouncer opened the heavy wooden door. "Hurry up my nigga let's park these motherfuckers, I've got to get inside." Gino said as Shadow hurriedly parked the Black on

Black Deuce and a quarter he was driving. Gino had the Money green 72 Impala out tonight, and V-Rock was in his Porsche. They paid one of the valet's an extra hundred dollars to have their cars parked right in front, as they rushed inside.

The Deejay was pumping Biggie Smalls, 'One More Chance' and had the dance floor packed with women gyrating their hips and shaking their asses, vying for the attention of the money getters. Bottles of Moet, Don Perignon, and Crystal were on every table.

"Shadow ain't that the nigga Styles from Richmond?" V-Rock asked as they fought to get through the crowd to their table in the packed club.

"Yeah that's him." He pointed to a booth against the wall packed with niggas getting lap dances from some strippers.

"That's them 41st niggas right there. I heard they had Tidewater locked down with coke and weed." Gino mentioned to Shadow passing the 41st crew.

It looked like a player's ball get together with everybody who was somebody in attendance. Before reaching their table with the girls, Shadow was congratulated by several people he knew every step of the way, giving him props for throwing such a hyped party.

Tricia wiped sweat from her brow, "Damn Baby, is everybody in here or what?"

"Yeah baby it looks like the whole crew's in here tonight for real." Shadow replied. "Have y'all spotted Kelvin and AJ yet?"

Marquita pointed, "Over there Shadow." She pointed over by the wall where a gang of nigga's from Newport News were posted up.

"Come on Gino let's go holla at these niggas." Shadow led the way.

Kelvin and AJ were sitting at a table surrounded by at least 5 females, laughing and talking. "Here comes Fat Boy and Gino." Kelvin said while nudging AJ. They got up to meet them halfway.

"What's up my niggas?!" Shadow yelled out, spreading his arms to embrace Kelvin.

"What's up Cous?" Kelvin replied while they hugged. Then AJ and Shadow embraced.

"Nigga I see y'all enjoying yourselves." Gino stated, rolling his eyes towards the cuties still sitting in the booth.

"Oh Fo'Sho' . . . this party is the shit, and we're going to enjoy every bit of this, believe that!" AJ commented.

"Aiight! Y'all do that, we just wanted to come holla. Do y'all thing, this party is for y'all. We'll see you niggas later on." They all gave each other dap and Shadow and Gino disappeared into the crowd.

While mingling through the crowd Gino grabbed Shadow's arm, "Look Fat Boy." Gino called out spotting Peaches and Tuesday looking good as ever and headed in their direction.

"Oh shit . . . See if you see Quita and Tricia anywhere?" Surveying the crowd they didn't see them no where in the immediate area.

"Hey baby." Peaches said as she gave Shadow a hug and light kiss.

Shadow grabbed Peaches' ass, "What's up sweetheart? I see you looking good for daddy tonight."

"Oh yeah . . . , it's still like that." She said turning around poking her ass out.

"Gino you know I've been missing you baby," Tuesday said while hugging Gino and giving him a quick kiss, then wiping her lip stick off his lips, "I'm sorry."

"It ain't nothing, don't worry about that. Damn girl you gonna hurt something tonight ain't you?" Gino stated looking Tuesday up and down.

She blushed, "Cut it out Gino, I'm already spoken for."

"And who might that be?"

"Oh you don't know? Maybe I should find him then?" she said sucking her lips.

Gino grabbed Tuesday and pulled her close, whispering in her ear, "Girl don't make me kill nobody up in here," licking her ear when he finished.

"Ohhh . . . don't do that, you know how I get, and if you ain't ready to give it to me now, don't start something that you can't finish."

"You right." Gino replied while backing up from her a bit.

Suddenly a crowd of people started to assemble by the door, and before you knew it, you could hear women screaming. All eyes were on the crowd as it started to move towards the middle of the floor. "Shadow what you thinks going on?" Gino asked.

"I don't know, but let's find out. I ain't letting nobody fuck up our night like that."

Pushing through the crowd and getting closer to the action, Shadow finally noticed what the commotion was all about. "Flames!"

"Gino that's that nigga Flames, that boy keeps a crowd around him. I should have known. Come on Gino . . . that nigga got his whole Buck Roe Crew coming through the door with him." Shadow and Gino continued to weave their way through the crowd.

Shadow got up close behind Flames and grabbed his shoulder. Flames stopped, turned around, and noticed it was Shadow. "Give me some love my nigga!!!" Flames screamed out as he and Shadow embraced each other.

"Thanks for coming my nig'. Damn I see you still got all the bitches sweating you still, huh? I guess some things never change." Shadow teased.

"I mean you know how it go. I love the bitches and they love me back." They all bust out laughing.

"I feel you on that," Gino responded, "look I'll see y'all two later on I'm going to find that broad Crystal. She was looking good as hell tonight." Gino said as he gave them both dap and stepped off, leaving Flames and Shadow to talk.

Gino knew exactly where Crystal was standing because he had spotted her looking oh sooo . . . . good while they were talking to Peaches and Tuesday earlier. "Bingo" Gino said to himself as he spotted Crystal still standing in the same spot with a group of her friends in the second booth from the stage. As he got closer and closer, Gino was trying to figure out a way to approach her, knowing she probably was still upset that he had gotten her number and never called. Gino grabbed a glass of Don Perignon from one of the waiters and just headed on over.

Noticing Gino heading in her direction Crystal started whispering to her girlfriends.

"Damn I know she talking about me," Gino thought as he walked up, sipping his drink, and locking eyes with Crystal. "Hello ladies, how are y'all doing tonight?" Gino spoke while still locking eyes with Crystal.

Everyone replied, "Hello Gino!" But they noticed that Gino and Crystal were still staring at each other.

Finally after several seconds Tasha says, "Damn is anybody going to say anything?"

Everybody looked at Gino, "Excuse me ladies, Crystal can I speak to you for a minute? If you don't mind?" Crystal gave a light smile as she scooted around exiting the booth. Gino grabbed her hand and led her away.

Gino passed the bar on the way grabbing both of them glasses of Moet, then walking her to a secluded table way in the back away from the crowd. "It's crowded in here tonight, huh?" Crystal stated as she took a seat across the table from Gino.

"Yeah, too crowded for me." Gino commented while reaching his hand under the table touching her thigh.

A slight smirk came across her face, "you better stop before your little girlfriend sees you."

Shocked at the comment Gino revved back, "Hold up . . . where did that come from?"

"Oh I'm hip to you and Marquita. It's not a secret around town, she let everybody know what was up that day she came pass the hair shop driving your BMW. I mean I ain't mad at you."

Gino paused considering what direction he wanted to go in at this point, "Yeah that's my little peoples right there, I ain't going to lie about that, but that ain't got nothing to do with me trying to see you."

"Gino you full of shit!" She replied, "you say that shit all the time, but hey . . . if she got you pussy whipped, ain't nothing wrong with that."

Gino laughed, "Picture that!"

"Well you sure didn't call my number, so what's the problem then?" Now reaching her hand under the table feeling his bulge through his Linen shorts.

"I tell you what . . . ," he paused cause she had his dick in her hand stroking it. "Oh so you playing like that?"

She licked her lips, "It's only playing if it's a game, I'm serious."

"I tell you what . . . what are you doing tomorrow?"

"I go to work, why? What you about to make another promise you can't keep?"

"I swear, tomorrow I'm picking you up from work. That's on everything."

"Yeah whatever!!" She smacked her lips as she removed her hands from his shorts, leaving his dick standing at attention.

"I'm serious this time Crystal. What time do you get off?" Gino looked at her as if he meant it this time.

"Gino look, I get off at 12:00, and if you're not there by 12:01 I'm outta there. You will not have me looking like no fool waiting around for you."

"I swear, I'll be there for real!"

"You better! Well let me go now, before your little girlfriend see us together. I ain't got time to be fighting over a nigga whom I haven't even fucked yet."

"Oh . . . Yeah . . . . !"

"Yeah!" Crystal replied as she leaned over to whisper something into Gino's ear. "OH . . . and so you'll know . . . , I've got white liver."

"Damn skippie!" Gino said to himself as he watched her walk off across the floor shaking her ass in them tight ass black Versace jeans. "Goodness gracious, the lord truly blessed that girl for real. I'm going to fuck the shit out of her tomorrow." Gino said to himself.

CHAPTER 46

Later that evening, Shadow headed up onto the stage about to introduce Flames for his performance, when he spotted Flames and Marquita engaged in a conversation that didn't look kosher. Low and behold not only had Shadow spotted them talking, but Gino had saw them 15 minutes prior to that, when the conversation first started. Gino was smoking madd, but held his composure and decided if that's how she wanted to play it tonight, then that was cool with him.

In any event, Shadow approached them though, "Aye Flames my nigga you ready?"

Flames nodded his head, "Let's do it my nigga."

"Excuse me for one second Flames, Marquita let me holla at you for a minute." Shadow said stepping a few steps to the side, as Marquita followed.

"What's up Shadow?" Quita asked.

"Now I want you to listen to me and listen to me good Marquita," Shadow began to speak staring into her eyes, "you like family to me Quita, but you know that you're out of pocket right now, and you know that damn Gino is a fool. Don't be no dummy playing with that dude feelings like that."

Her face immediately frowned up, "Shadow what are you talking about, we were just talking, what . . ." she spoke in a soft tone.

"Yeah okay, I'm telling you, if you betray Gino I'm not getting into the middle of that bullshit."

"Shadow please . . . please, don't make something out of nothing," she begged.

"Yeah aiight," Shadow replied as he stepped off heading towards the stage leaving Quita standing there.

Walking towards the stage Shadow was mumbling to himself, "Damn it . . . I should've known that dumb bitch was going to do that. I should've told Gino that they use to talk back in the days. Fuck . . . . !"

"Good evening everybody," Shadow shouted into the mic as cheers erupted. "First let me thank all of you on behalf of my family and friends for coming out to this party tonight. Hopefully all of y'all are enjoying yourselves. Well I don't want to hold y'all up too long, so with out further or do, let me introduce to y'all the hottest rapper out of Virginia, my man, my homie, Flames!!" as the crowd went crazy.

Flames strolled out on the stage, with the beat dropping to his hit song, 'This Is For My Homies'. The crowd was rocking and singing along to his song.

Gino and V-Rock made their way over by the stage area standing right beside Shadow, "Damn Big homie, your man Flames is nice. He spitting that shit." Gino slapped dap with Shadow.

"Yeah I told you he was nice. What's up V-Rock? I ain't seen you all night young nigga." Shadow said.

"Shadow that nigga been getting his swerve on all night." Gino said hugging V-Rock around the neck.

"My nigga's, I got about 5 bitches thinking they going home with the kid." Said V-Rock while giving both of them some dap.

On stage, Flames was burning it up, keeping the crowd in a frenzy. He ran through most of his local hits, and some of his new shit as well. Gino stood there beside Shadow talking to himself, "Slim is all that, just like Shadow said." Gino looked over and saw V-Rock rocking to the music and enjoying himself as well. "This is what living is all about. Shitt . . . plenty money and women at our dispense, what else could a nigga ask for." Gino thought as Flames ended his song, 'Ho's and Bitches'.

"How are y'all doing up in here?!" Flames asked the crowd, as chatter erupted with nigga's throwing up gang signs and everything. "Listen y'all back before I blew up some what, when I was struggling to get on,

I had a partner, and this nigga can rap his ass off. So what I'm going to do since this is a special occasion, I want to bring him up here and take it back to when none of this shit was possible. Aye Shadow!! . . . Shadow!! Come on up here!" Flames shouted as the whole crowd looked towards where Shadow, Gino, and V-Rock were standing.

Shadow was stuck, "Come on Flames don't do that, I ain't rapped in years."

Flames waved Shadow up, "Come on my nigga!" Flames continued to urge as the crowd started yelling, "Shadow!! . . . Shadow!! . . . Shadow!! . . . Shadow!! . . . Shadow!!"

Gino laughed, "My nigga go ahead up there and give the people what they want."

Slowly Shadow started to climb the steps onto the sage, as the crowd was going crazy in a frenzy. Soon as he got to the top step, the beat kicked in to a song they had made together called, 'It's a Cold World Outside". The crowd continued to cheer as Flames and Shadow embraced each other center stage. Gino was standing beside the stage waiting to see if Shadow could really rap. Flames blazed the first verse with some hot lyrics, then the hook came in and it was Shadow's turn.

"Aye yo, it's Big Chris the Hitler, watch how I spit ya, tell your whole crew fuck you and I'll get back wit ya.

Got gats for combat, sling cracks on RipRap. Toting Tec's, getting vexed, never fucking the same sex.

So stay out my way fake cats, cause I hate snakes and rats. Bodies I dispose, revolvers I reload, I hate nigga's that talk shit then wanna fold. I run with nothing but murderers and soldiers, I thought I told ya, it's a cold world outside." As the hook came back in.

"Damn this nigga can really go," Gino thought to himself, "this nigga suppose to be in the studio, and he out here bullshittin' with these streets."

It was time for Shadow's second verse and Gino wanted to see if Shadow could deliver like that again.

"Nigga's in the street acting like they real, about to get theirselves killed. I got 16 shots and they headed straight for this grill.

Got this crew calling saying aye yo big Chris chill, but already they got me on some ill shit, ready to kill shit. So I tell his man it's something that's got to be dealt wit.

I don't know why he want to try his gangsta out on me, because I let my guns do the talking, my bullets do the walking, homicide do the chalking. Keep running his mouth he'll end up in a coffin, I don't see happen very often, so back up off me, cause I ain't no softie."

The hook came in once again. Gino was in awe, he couldn't believe what he had just heard. Everybody was buzzing over the scene, two Virginia nigga's making it from two different worlds. Plus a lot of people couldn't believe that Shadow could rap like that.

As Shadow and Flames exited the stage they were both still amped up. Nigga's from all over were giving them props, and big ups. Gino made his way over through the madness, "Aye Shadow, you think I can get a minute in with you big rap super star."

Shadow smiled and hugged Gino, "Stop playing my nigga, anytime for you."

"I mean . . . I didn't know you were also a big rap star. Damn I swear I didn't know you could go like that."

Shadow hunched his shoulders, "Gino . . . man all that was old shit."

Flames then walked up, "That nigga lying Gino. This Fat nigga is a beast on the mic."

"Come on with that bullshit Flames," Shadow fired back.

"Believe me I know now Flames," Gino responded, "Nigga we've got to talk tomorrow."

"Yeah . . . yeah . . . yeah, whatever . . ." Shadow said grabbing Gino and Flames around the neck. "Right now all I want to do is enjoy the rest of the night." As they all smiled and disappeared into the crowd.

It was damn near 2:00 in the morning and Shadow was getting tired as shit, plus he was somewhat drunk. He decided that he was ready to go, and went in search of Gino. He found Gino coming out of the bathroom talking to Bear, "Aye Gino!" Shadow called out catching Gino's attention.

Gino looked, saw that it was Shadow and came over to see what was up, "What's wrong Big Boy?"

"Nothing . . . nothing like that Gino. I was just wondering had you seen Tricia?"

Shadow stood there for a second, "you know what?" Shadow placed both his hands behind his neck, "Fuck that bitch slim. Something going on with her and Stevie and I know it. That's my cousin, and I know that nigga like a book."

Gino now had a puzzled look on his face, "you sure Fat boy?"

Suddenly a voice echoed out across the room, "Gino! . . . Gino! . . . . Gino! . . ."

Gino turned to see Marquita coming in his direction. Gino glanced at Shadow, Shadow looked back at him, all the while she sashayed her way over, reaching her arms out for a hug, "Hey . . . baby!"

Gino halted her hands, looking at her like she was crazy. "Listen Quita, don't come over here with that baby shit now. Take your ass back on over there with your little friend Flames."

A mystified look came across her face, "Gino what are you talking about?"

"Bitch I saw you all cheet . . . . cheeing up in that nigga Flames face, but I ain't mad at you, I know how the game goes. Do what you do."

"Gino don't act like that . . ." she begged as Gino just walked off. Marquita then approached Shadow, "You fat bitch what did you tell him? I know you said something!!" she screamed causing a scene.

"I ain't said shit to him, I guess you did all the talking yourself dumb ass!"

"Shadow . . . Shadow!" tears began to form in her eyes, "I swear I didn't do anything."

"I mean . . . I don't know what to tell you. I ain't the one you should be explaining yourself to."

"Whatever Shadow . . . you full of shit."

"Have you seen Tricia?" Shadow asked.

"I don't know," she sucked her teeth, "maybe if you tend to your own business and leave mine alone you'd know where she was."

Shadow walked up, grabbing her by the neck and shoving Quita against the wall. "Now I think you better watch your mouth," Shadow stated in an aggressive tone, "you like family, but I will slap the shit out of you. Now show off if you want."

Releasing her, Marquita began to cry while walking away, "Fuck you Shadow!" She turned and stated before disappearing into he crowd.

Kelvin was sitting back watching the whole situation from a distance. Sensing that Shadow was a little too drunk, Kelvin came over to holla. "What's up Fatboy?" they shook hands, "I see you still got it with that rap shit my nigga."

"Kelvin mann . . . , that shit was all in fun. I just wanted everybody to enjoy themselves."

While they were conversing, Peaches walked up, grabbing Shadow around the waist from behind. "Guess who?" she said in a sexy tone.

"Ummm . . . ummm . . . ummm . . ." Shadow pretended to be thinking.

"Don't make me slap the shit out of you negro!" Peaches replied.

Shadow snickered, "Ohh . . . Ohh I know, it's Peaches."

"Keep playing," she said now standing in between he and Kelvin, "excuse him for a minute Kelvin I want to dance with Shadow."

He kissed her forehead, "Anything for my baby." As they scooted out to the dance floor.

The club was still packed; Tricia was over in the corner with a pack of her girlfriends gossiping about the events of the night. "Girl did y'all see Tyrone from BadNews?" Tamika asked, "That nigga got it going on now, huh?"

Francine sipped her drink, "Mika that nigga is old news, I had him 2 months ago, and the dick is not all that."

Laughter erupted, "Bitch how much money did you work him out of?" Tricia asked.

"I'm a good girl," Francine said, "I don't kiss and tell."

"Fuck you then bitch," Crissy shouted as more laughter persisted, "Aye Tricia girl, is that Shadow with that bitch Peaches from Bad News?"

"Where?" as all heads turned to see, "Oh no . . . I know he didn't bring that slut bitch in here like that, and disrespect me." She commented as she scooted around trying to get up from the table.

"Damn," said Tamika, "he playing you like that girl?!"

Out from under the table now, tying her hair in a bun, Tricia says, "I don't know, but somebody about to get their ass whipped." She then stomped off with her crew right behind her.

Shadow was in the middle of the floor slow dragging whispering sweet game into Peaches ear, until he noticed split in the crowd. "Hold up . . . hold on Peaches." They separated their grasp. "Something's going down."

Watching the crowd moving closer and closer to where they were standing, Shadow spotted Tricia leading a pack of females, heading in his direction. "Look at this simple ass broad." Shadow thought to himself knowing that she was about to come over and make a scene.

"Uh uh . . . you fat bitch, I know you ain't disrespecting me like that with this little slut right here!" Tricia screamed walking up with her crew.

"Bitch! Who you calling a slut?!!" Peaches barked back trying to get around Shadow.

Shadow held her back, "Hold on Peaches let me handle this please." Shadow then turned to face Tricia, "Now look Tricia don't make me do it to you, don't come over here with that bullshit, I'm warning you. Go ahead back and find Stevie somewhere, y'all always together anyway."

Tricia frowned her face, "Nigga what the fuck are you talking about?"

"You figure it out; I ain't got it being too hard at all. What part of that you don't understand?" Shadow stated while reaching for Peaches hand. Soon as they turned to walk off Tricia ran up from behind grabbing Peaches by the hair and punching her in the face with several jabs, and punches. By the time Shadow was able to break them apart, Tricia had gotten the best of Peaches. Even after separating them and the music had stopped you could still hear Tricia and her girls, "Whip that bitch ass!!! . . . Whip that bitch ass!!!"

Finally catching her composure, Peaches lunged at Tricia, but Shadow grabbed her. "Look let that shit go baby please." Shadow begged Peaches.

"Uh . . . uh, I'm going to whip that bitch ass. Where's Tuesday at?!!" Peaches shouted, while glancing through the crowd for her sister.

Tricia was standing with her friends like she wanted some more wreck, "Fuck you and your sister bitch, and if I catch you around Shadow again I'm going to whip that ass some more, hear me??!!!"

Shadow then walked over to Tricia, "Won't you go ahead now, before you make me mad. I'm warning you shorty."

"Fuck you Shadow!!!!" she screamed.

Before she knew what had happened, Shadow reared back and slapped the shit out of Tricia, knocking her back into the crowd. As she staggered to catch her balance, she stood there holding her face looking stupid and says, "Oh I know you didn't just slap me because of that bitch!" as she patted her lips to see if they were bleeding.

Shadow replied, "Nah . . . I ain't smack you because of her, I smacked you cause you don't know what to say out your mouth."

By this time somebody had alerted Gino to what had occurred, and he rushed up grabbing Fat boy by the shoulder trying to calm him down. "Aye Fat boy come on, this shit ain't bout nothing, just let her be."

Shadow looked at Gino's expression, "You know what, you right Gino." Shadow then looked around, "Where's Peaches at?"

"I just sent her and her sister to the car. I told Bear and Man Man to handle that for me." Gino responded, "Come on Fat boy let's get up out of here anyway."

Shadow shouted out to the whole crew, "We out y'all!" As everybody started exiting the club. On there way out the door, another scuffle was in the process of breaking out between Richmond crew and Suffolk Virginia crew. They started fighting probably over some dumb shit as usual. Gino and Shadow ignored the commotion, and pushed on out the door.

As they approached the entrance of the Omni Hotel in Newport News, Gino felt a little guilty about leaving Quita stranded at the party like that, but felt like he had been disrespected, so his actions were justified. So he just washed his conscience off as everybody got their rooms, and headed in for the night.

Back at the club, Tricia and Quita couldn't believe that they had been carried like that, but hey . . . Now they had to find a way home. Tricia knew inside that she had fucked up, and fucked up bad. "Quita I think I went too far out there this time," Tricia was explaining to Quita, "Girl Shadow was mad as hell tonight."

Quita shook her head, "Bitch fuck that we need to be finding us a way home."

"Hold on . . . I'll see if Stevie will take us home."

"You ain't learned your lesson yet . . . . That's how we got into this situation now."

Minutes later, Tricia spotted Stevie outside heading to his car, "Hey Stevie . . . . Stevie!" Tricia called out catching his attention sticking his key in his car door Stevie looked up, "Yeah what's up Tricia?"

Tricia held her hand up, "Hold up for a minute please!"

"What's up shorty? I thought you had rolled out." Stevie asked. "What you still doing here?"

"It's a long story Stevie . . . Shadow left me."

Stevie's eye brows rose, "Why he do that?"

"Because I was talking to you, can you believe that?"

"Me . . . me?" Stevie pointed to himself. "What?? . . . I ain't done nothing wrong . . . What the hell he trippin' off of?"

"Yeah well I feel the same way, but hey he won't listen to me. Maybe you need to holla at him. Listen though, right now Stevie me and Quita need a ride home."

"I got you shorty, where's Quita?"

"Hold up, let me go get her." Tricia dashed back inside the club to find Quita.

Arriving at Quita's apartment first, Quita noticed that Gino's car was not parked outside. "Thank you Stevie," said Marquita, "and I'll see you tomorrow girl."

"Okay I'll call you when I get into the house." Tricia replied.

"Tricia don't do nothing I wouldn't do." Quita teased as she closed the car door exiting the car.

"Fuck you Quita!" Tricia yelled out the window as she waved goodbye just before Stevie pulled off.

Driving Tricia home, Stevie and Tricia talked, but no funny business went on. They pulled up at the house, she thanked him, and he agreed to holla at Shadow about the situation the next day.

Entering into the house, Tricia waved Stevie off letting him know that she was inside, and he drove off.

Back at Marquita's, she was now going crazy paging Gino, blowing up his pager. However, she would never receive a response. She knew that Gino was furious and felt disrespected. Quita figured that Shadow had mentioned to Gino that her and Flames were old lovers. "Damn it!! I was only talking to him though. I can't lose Gino, that's my baby. I've got to find a way to get through to him, hopefully before he does something stupid."

CHAPTER 47

In the morning, Tuesday was awakening to find Gino sitting on the edge of the bed staring at her. "Good morning sleepy head! How you feelin'?" Gino leaned over to kiss her.

"I'm doing fine Gino, especially anytime that I'm with you." She sat up in the bed and then noticed the cart of food sitting at the foot of the bed. "Ohh . . . that's so sweet Gino, breakfast in bed, a bitch could get spoiled with all this."

"Well we worked up a hell of an appetite last night. So I figured you could use a big breakfast, know what I mean?" Gino grabbed a tray of food off the cart placing it on Tuesday's lap.

"Thank you baby," she was smiling from ear to ear, "you think I can get use to this?"

"You think so?" Gino rubbed her cheek, "well what if we moved in together and you could wake me up like this on a regular basis?"

She finished sipping her orange juice, "Gino what are you insinuating? Please don't play games with me. You know how I feel about you."

Gino picked up the spoon and fed her some eggs, "I'm not playing, I need a good woman by my side. I just ain't got time for no bullshit, you know?"

"Gino I told you from the beginning I wanted to be with you. I've been patient, giving you your space and played my position, so I'm waiting on you."

Gino paused, rubbing his hand across his goatee, "Listen let me check on a few things, and then I'll let you know something for sure this week."

"Gino please . . . don't get my hopes up for nothing." She purred.

"I won't" kissing her on the forehead when suddenly someone knocked on the door. Gino got up and headed for he door, "Who is it?!" he yelled.

"It's me Gino," Shadow's voice echoed from the other side as he opened the door. "What's up my nigga?" Shadow shouted as he and Peaches entered the room.

"Damn." Gino closed the door, "I see y'all up bright and early this morning."

"Yeah we just eating a little breakfast in bed, you know." Gino replied leading the way back into the bedroom.

"Heyyy . . . y'all." Tuesday spoke as they all walked into the room.

"Okay girlfriend, breakfast in bed. Now that's what I'm talking about." Peaches teased, taking a seat on the bed beside Tuesday.

"Shadow have y'all eaten?" Gino asked taking a seat.

"Noo . . . not yet!"

"Well you might as well order room service, and we all can eat up in here. Call V-Rock too and tell him to bring his ass up here, he's in room 132."

While waiting for V-Rock and the food to arrive Gino pulled Shadow into the other room. They both took seat as Gino stared at Shadow, "Look here my nigga, I'm going to be straight up with you, I really haven't been able to sleep all night. I had two things on my mind. One was the shit that Marquita pulled, and the second is that I didn't know that you could rap like that."

Shadow thought for a second, "Gino my nigga, I hadn't rapped in years before last night. It was just a spur of the moment type thing."

"I understand all that big boy, but you're nice. If you could focus on your music totally I know you could make it. Shadow right now we've got more money than we could have ever imagined having. My nigga we can get up out this shit and put our concentration into this music thing. We can pump CD's and tapes, like we pumped this drug shit."

197

Shadow sat up in his chair, "Gino man, I've been in this business before, and it's a shrewd industry. Lots of up's and down's, and broken promises."

"I can believe that," Gino sat up now looking Shadow straight in the eyes, "but there's a major difference now . . . money!!! Back then you didn't have the money or resources you have now! No let me correct that, we have now. The last time you were mainly depending on some label to do this and that. This time we have all the resources at our expense. We can take some money buy a big ass house, and build a studio inside."

"Gino, I'm telling you slim, this shit is not as easy as it looks."

"Shadow let's just give it a try. Nothing beats a failure, but a try. Plus you know the feds are looking and watching our every move. At least this move is a positive one. We can still continue the run until the end of the month, which is 2 weeks away. But let's try to walk away while shit still good. I ain't trying to go back to jail big boy, that's on some real shit."

Shadow smiled, "I definitely feel you on that slim, but let me be the first to say, if shit don't work out, don't say I didn't warn you!"

Gino extended his hand to Shadow, "Nigga don't worry about that we'll find some other artist as well. We might even start our own label."

"Now that sounds like a good idea," Shadow replied, "well look Gino let's talk about that shit later on, right now, I'm hungry as shit, let's go get something to eat." Standing up they gave each other dap and strolled off in search of something to eat.

CHAPTER 48

That afternoon after dropping the girls off Gino and Shadow both knew it was time to head home and face the piper. "Big boy what're we going to do with the girls?" Gino asked.

"Slim . . . I don't know about you, but I'm fitting to back all the way up off Tricia for a while and just do me."

"I was just saying the same thing to myself. I even asked Tuesday would she like to move in with me."

"Gino why don't you go get Tykisha? You know that she still loves you and wants to be with you."

Gino thought for a second. "My nigga I thought about that, but right now I don't have time for the drama with that dumb ass boyfriend of hers. I should've killed that nigga for even having the audacity to mess with her from the beginning anyway. But he and I go back too far, and even though they left me for dead, my heart won't allow me to do nothing cruddy to this nigga."

"I feel you slim," Shadow emphasized, "that's exactly how I feel about Stevie with Tricia situation. I can't do nothing to him about Tricia cause he family. So I'm just severing my ties before I trip out."

"No doubt, maybe I should just go up her school and see her, huh?"

"Shitt . . . , you might as well. She's right up the street at Virginia State, right?"

"Yeah but . . . !"

"Yeah but nothing. If you talking about starting with a clean slate, then that's where you need to start slim. Real talk . . ."

"I don't know big boy. She might not want to leave that nigga Black."

"Well one things for sure, there's only one way to find out . . . ask!!"

"You got a point there champ," Gino hugged Shadow, "tomorrow let's go talk to the lawyer about starting our record label. See what we have to do?"

"That's a bet Gino."

"Also we need to look into getting two new houses. Get the realtor to see if he could get us two houses side by side, that way we can build the studio in one, and use the other one as the business office until we get this thing poppin'."

"Fo'Sho'! I'll get Grandma on that first thing in the morning."

"I guess while you're doing that, I'll take a trip up to see Tykisha. Plus I'll see if she can help us out in any kind of way being as though she's in college majoring in Communication. Who knows I might just get her to come home with me huh? What you think about that?"

Shadow chuckled, "Now that's what happening champ!"

Now all the while Gino and Shadow were planning their departure away from the game, V-Rock was establishing himself a little crew of niggas that were going to take over Wesley Avenue when Gino and Shadow retired from the game. V-Rock was getting a lot of jealous looks from niggas in the hood that hated how he was shining. However, V-Rock was so happy and feeling untouchable that he was not able to decipher between the genuine niggas and the fake niggas. While being down with Gino and Shadow, V-Rock maintained his block with an iron fist. V-Rock always had his money straight, and he was extremely loyal to the fam. If push came to shove, V-Rock would die for the fam. All V-Rock did was brag to his friends, male and female, about his big brothers. V-Rock was now a major figure in the streets, and was sitting on major paper. Nobody could tell him anything, he was Ghetto Fabulous.

All the years that he struggled living with his aunt and going through all those changes were in the past. He was on top of his game for sure and flaunted it for everybody to see. Gino understood a lot of V-Rock's actions because he came from a similar background. Gino was raised in a house where his mom also was on crack and he had to fend for himself. So Gino surely knew what V-Rock was going through. The only difference was that Gino never had that kind of money at the age V-Rock is now. Unfortunately, V-Rock wasn't ready to leave the game just yet. Hopefully they could convince him to get out too.

When Gino finally got home, Marquita was sitting in the living room waiting on him. Upon entering the apartment, Gino saw Quita sitting on the couch. Throwing his bags on the floor, he glanced at Quita and began to stroll towards the bedroom.

Rising up off the couch Quita says to Gino, "Oh . . . so it's like that?" Gino ignored her and kept walking, "I know you heard me Gino!!" she yelled.

Gino stopped . . . turned around and just stared at her for a second. "Listen Quita I ain't got nothing to say . . . . !"

She cut him off, "Gino I don't know what the fuck is your problem, I haven't done anything wrong. Why you acting like that?"

"If you don't know, then I guess I don't either." Gino smiled then shook his head. "Quita look . . . I ain't mad at you! And you don't owe me no apologies for nothing."

"Gino you're lying, I know you." She walked up close to Gino attempting to hug him.

Gino knocked her arms down, "What did I say?"

"Yeah . . . I heard what you said, but your actions say something different." Now she moved in front of the door to stop Gino from entering. "Gino I just want to clear everything up."

Gino again tried to pass her, "Look shorty there's nothing to clear up, everything's cool."

"Well where were you last night Gino?"

Gino headed towards the bathroom, stopping at the door and looking back. "I'm about to get in the shower, let's leave that shit alone. I don't feel like talking about it now, and that's . . . that aiight?" Gino entered the bathroom and closed the door behind him.

While taking his shower, Gino had thoughts of Tykisha running through his head. He wondered if she thought of him as much as he thought of her, and at that moment he decided that he would give her a call at school and see what would happen. "Shit . . . maybe I could talk her into coming home and living with me. I could buy her a car, or give her the Acura, but I've got to convince her to be mine again first and foremost. Damn! . . . let me call Tee and get her number. Plus I need to contact Kenny as well."

Out the shower feeling rejuvenated Gino called his mother, got Kenny's pager number and beeped him. While waiting for him to call back, Gino turned on BET to watch some videos, and soon after Gino's cell phone vibrated. Buzzz . . . . !

"Hello!" Gino answered.

"Gino, what's up my nigga?"

"Ain't shit Kenny, how you know it was me?"

I didn't, but soon as I heard your voice I knew who it was."

"Oh okay! What's going on with you? I hear you done stepped your game up down there." Gino mentioned.

"I mean . . . you know . . . a little something something."

"That's right young nigga, get that money. What's been going on with Ma?"

"Gino she doing real . . . real good, but she stay on my back about getting out the streets and going to church. Come on my nigga, picture that."

Gino laughed, "Well young nigga, she ain't telling you anything wrong. I'm about to be through with this street shit myself."

"What you talking 'bout Gino?!"

"Yeah Kenny, we're about to get into this music shit and leave these streets for the birds. This shit getting too hot up here. We supposed to be going to see a lawyer tomorrow about starting our own Label."

"Oh yeah . . . you for real huh?"

"Real as a heart attack Kenny."

"You know I be writing raps and shit too right?"

"Come on Kenny man, we're not fucking with no popcorn shit. We messing with that heat."

"Nigga I got heat, no bullshit. I've got a box full of raps already written in Ma's basement."

"You serious?"

"No bullshit, I can go slim."

"Yeah alright, then get your shit together and soon as everything fall into place, I'll send for you. Don't come up here embarrassing me either nigga."

"Gino . . . I write rhymes like fine wine, believe that."

"Yeah alright, we'll see."

"Aye . . . aye . . . you know Tykisha been asking about you?"

"Oh yeaahhh . . ." Gino commented with a curious tone in his voice.

"Yeah she been coming home from school almost every weekend, and every time I see her, she's asking about you. As a matter of fact about 2 weeks ago she even admitted to me that she's still in love with you."

"Yeah . . . Kenny I'm still in love with her too."

"But boyyy! That nigga Black," Kenny's voice now got aggressive, "is on some other shit. He still be throwing that shit in her face about what happen the last time you came down here."

"Kenny that's some real sucker shit!"

"Yeah you and I both know it, but the dude is out of control. If I didn't know y'all were best friends at one time, I'd been have gotten that nigga's head knocked off, hear me??!"

"Kenny what's up . . . , and don't lie to me either?" Gino asked.

"Gino I just think that the nigga jealous of me, you know when you hit me off right? I just took off and started doing my own thing."

"Okay . . . , and??"

"Gino I told Black, Mike Mike, and them that I didn't want none of my friends hustling for me. I wanted to separate my business from my friendships. Anyway, when I started getting money, the nigga just always have something slick to say about everything. Slim the nigga really be pushing my buttons, especially as of lately. See I know his real anger isn't with me, cause he's doing his thing too. It's really about you and Tykisha, because even when I started getting a little money I told all them niggas if they needed anything, to just holla at me. I just didn't want to deal with them on a business level."

"Kenny listen . . . Fuck that nigga! You're my brother and you don't owe nobody an explanation for anything you do. The next time that nigga jump out there; do what you got to do. If he's disrespecting you, handle your business."

"Gino, the bad part about this whole shit is, I still got mad love for the nigga. I just know how niggas get when it comes to that love and them females. So I jive try to be sympathetic to that, you know what I'm saying?"

"Yeah you got a valid point Kenny. As a matter of fact I'm about to call her up. You know she's only 20 minutes away from me. I'm going to get my shorty back slim."

"That's right . . . that's right my nigga get what's yours." Kenny shouted into the phone. "What are you going to do about the girl you're living with down there?"

Gino chuckled again, "I'm about to drop her like a bad habit, you hear me?"

"Fo'Sho' my nigga!" Kenny replied, "I know that you and Tykisha definitely love each other, so do what your heart tell you to. What's up with V-Rock?"

"Oh man that nigga done bought a Porsche, and doing his thing. He talks about you all the time. Are you ready to come up here yet?"

"Gino to be honest, I'm ready to get away from here soon as possible. I'm tired of this shit down here. I've got a little money saved up so I'm cool."

"I tell you what; you can come up here next weekend and stay awhile. I believe that we'll be headed back to DC before too long. These police are on our ass up here, so I'll send V-Rock to get you Friday. Just be at Ma house at 6:00pm, and don't be late."

"I'll be there Gino."

"Aiight, I'll see you then, I got to call Tykisha, but don't forget 6:00pm Friday."

"Fo'Sho' see you then." As they hung up the phone.

Ring . . . Ring . . . Ring . . . "Hello!"

"Hello, may I speak to Tykisha please?" Gino asked.

"Who's calling?" a female voice responded.

"Gino!"

"Ohh . . . you must be the Gino she's always talking about."

"Oh yeah . . . well I guess I am then, whom am I speaking with?" Gino asked.

"Oh . . . I'm sorry my name is Teresa."

"Okay Teresa, would Tykisha happen to be around?"

"I'm sorry Gino; she's not here right now."

"Okay thanks a lot Teresa," Gino was about to end the conversation, "as a matter of fact Teresa can you do me a favor? I'll pay you if need be."

"I don't know, what is it?"

"I would like to come see Tykisha, but I don't want her to know I'm coming."

"Alright . . . listen Gino; we're having a get together of sorts tonight for our fraternity over here. You can catch her definitely then. I'll just keep her here until you get here."

"Thank you Teresa, I appreciate that." Gino replied, "Oh before I go let me ask you a question? Are you involved with anyone at this moment? I've got a nice buddy of mines . . ."

She cut him off, "No thank you Gino. I have a boyfriend, but thanks for asking."

"Okay . . . I just had to ask. Teresa what's the address?"

"2241 Road Way Drive Petersburg, VA"

"I got that, thank you again Teresa. I'll see you tonight."

"You're welcome."

"Bye . . ."

Later that evening, Gino was on his way over to see Tykisha, not knowing how or what to expect. All he knew was that, he wanted her back and that was that. Along the way, he stopped past and picked her up some flowers, which would be a sweet gesture he figured.

Pulling up in front of 2241 Road Way Drive, Gino got nervous a little bit. He grabbed the bouquet of flowers and headed on up the door, and rang the door bell. Seconds later the solid wood doors to the house opened up, and a nice looking petite size sister was standing there, "Hello, you must be Gino." The sister says.

"Yes I am," Gino answered, "and you must be Teresa."

"Of course I am," she smiled, "look Tykisha's in the living room with some of our sisters. She doesn't have a clue that you're coming."

"Thank you Teresa . . . oh yeah" Gino reached into his pocket pulling out a bundle of money handing it to Teresa, "here you go, thanks for helping me out."

She pushed Gino's hands away, "No thank you, I don't want any money. That's my girl."

"Teresa take this, you're in college and anything may come up."

"Nooo . . . Gino," she said shaking her index finger, "I'm fine."

"Please take this," Gino continued to urge her to take the money.

"Gino just get in there and get your girl." She stated while pointing her finger towards the living room, and watching as Gino walked off.

Gino got to the opening in the living room door and just stood there watching as the girls were having a discussion on the effects the war was having on the economy. Gino's eyes were glossy as he stared at Tykisha's gorgeous face, and banging body. Boy!!! She had really become an attractive young woman. Finally one of the sisters caught sight of Gino out of her peripheral view standing at the door way, "Umm . . . umm . . . excuse me sisters." As everyone at that moment caught her insinuation and glanced up.

"How may we help you?" One of the sisters asked, just as Tykisha spotted Gino. Shocked and stunned were written all over her face. She looked like she had just seen a ghost.

"Excuse me sisters," Tykisha then cut in, "this is a friend of mine." Tykisha then stood up, still staring at Gino's face.

"Tykisha . . . who is that girl?" One of the sisters asked, while the other sisters whispered amongst each other.

Tykisha didn't hear anything they were saying as she scurried over to Gino, hugging him immediately. "What are you doing here Gino?" Tykisha asked in a whisper tone.

Gino was standing there blushing, "I'm here to see you, what else?"

"How did you know where I lived?" she was asking just as Teresa was turning the corner with a suspicious grin on her face.

Gino looked at Teresa, "Thank you Teresa!" Gino stated as she stood there smiling. "Oh . . . here baby these are for you." Gino handed Tykisha the flowers he had bought.

"Thank you sweetheart." She replied while smelling the yellow orchards.

"Excuse me sisters, this is Gino. Gino these are my sorority sisters."

They all spoke, "Hi Gino!"

"Hello, how are y'all doing ladies?" Gino responded.

"We're doing fine." Sister Mika stated.

"Well if y'all don't mind can I borrow Tykisha from y'all for a few minutes?"

Mika responded, "Sure go ahead."

"Thanks a lot," Gino then grabbed Tykisha's hand, "come on baby girl let's take a walk."

Out front on the porch, Gino leaned up against the wall, as Tykisha stood on the top step staring out across the campus. Gino broke the silence first, "So how have you been doing Tykisha?"

"I've been good, just studying a lot and thinking about you."

"Well . . . I'm sure you know that I've been thinking about you also, cause I'm here, huh?" At this point, Gino walked up into Tykisha's face grabbing both her hands. "Tykisha listen I don't want to play no games or waste not time with this rambling on and stuff. I'm just going to be straight up with you." Gino voice was serious, "Tykisha you know I've always loved you and I've never stopped. I know that even though we've been separated for some time now, none of our feelings or emotions changed. I still love you today as I did back before I went to jail. I'm tired of playing this cat and mouse game. I want you to be my girl again, and I don't care nothing about that nigga Black or what he did or none of that shit. I want you back."

Tykisha was crying as Gino took his hand and wiped the tears from her face. "Gino . . ." she sniffled, "I've been wanting to say all the things you just said to me, to you. However baby I was scared of your response. Gino I love you more than you know and I've never stopped loving you. I want to be with you so much my soul burns. Nothing would make me happier than to be your woman again, now and forever!"

Gino grabbed Tykisha pulling her close, moving her braids out of her face placing them behind her ear, then kissing her lips softly as he opened her mouth gently probing with his tongue. The magic was still there.

Shortly thereafter Tykisha pulled away and whispered, "Hold up for a second Gino." She dashed inside the house and up to her room. When she returned minutes later she held up a chain Gino had given her before he had went to jail. They both immediately laughed.

"Girl you still got that chain?"

"Gino I never let it go."

"You are crazy," Gino continued to laugh, "Give me a kiss."

Times had changed, but some things stayed the same. "Gino let me ask you a question," said Tykisha, "what about the female that you're living with?"

Gino chuckled, "Tykisha I'm through with her, we had a major fall out about 2 days ago and that's over with. On top of that I'm leaving the hustling shit alone too baby!"

"Gino that's good! Real good."

"Yeah . . . me and my man Shadow about to start up a Record Label."

"That's really good; maybe I can help you out. You know I'm majoring in Business Management."

"That's just what we need too, but I thought you were majoring in Communications."

"I switched majors." She replied.

"Alright big shot. Look . . . let me ask you something else?"

"What's that Gino?"

"Would you like to come live with me?"

Tykisha placed her hand on the side of Gino's face, using her thumb to rub his cheeks, "Of course Gino, I would love to come live with you."

"Well I'm going to get a house somewhere out here in Virginia soon, but I want you with me now."

"Gino, how am I going to get back and forth to school?"

"Don't worry about that, I've got a car for you . . . and if you don't like it, shittt . . . I'll just buy you another one."

Grabbing Gino around the neck Tykisha whispered, "Yes baby . . . yes baby I'd love to move in with you. Nothing would make me happier."

Gino later told Tykisha to contact a realtor about purchasing two houses close in proximity, price was no objective. She agreed to get on top of it first thing in the morning, and Gino told her he'd bring the Acura Legend pass the next day.

CHAPTER 49

Back in Bad News now, Gino flew over to Shadow's house. However, when Gino arrived he noticed that no one was there, so he decided to just head home. Upon pulling up in front of his house, immediately he spotted Shadow and V-Rock's cars parked out front.

Opening the front door to the apartment, Gino saw Shadow and V-Rock playing Madden 2000. "What's up my nigga's?!" Gino hollered as he was closing the door.

"Nigga you know what it is. Come on over here and get some of this ass kickin' I'm giving out." Shadow barked.

"Come on now Fat boy, you know damn well you can't beat me in no Madden." Gino took a seat between Shadow and V-Rock.

"Yeah okay . . . you talk a good game. Put your money where your mouth is. You see what I'm doing to your boy don't you?" Shadow teased.

"You ain't doing nothing Fat boy, you ain't up nothing but a touch down." V-Rock then says, "as a matter of fact, where you been Gino? I ain't seen you all day."

Gino then scooted up between the both of them, "Yeah my niggas I went to get my bun back." Gino was whispering.

"Hold up for a minute V-Rock." Shadow says while placing his controller down. "Who we talking about Tykisha?"

"You motherfucking right, and it's all good." Gino was smiling from ear to ear. "Where's Marquita?"

210

"Nigga stop all that whispering shit," Shadow began laughing at Gino, "she ain't here, her and Tricia probably out doing something, who knows."

"Oh yeah before I forget, Tykisha's going to get on top of the houses for us first thing in the morning too. You ain't even got to worry Grandma now."

Shadow nodded his head, "Now that's the kind of woman we need on our team right there."

"Also, I mentioned to her about the Label and she says that she can help us out. You know she's majoring in Business Management. Plus she was so excited when I mentioned that I was getting out of the game. That's my baby right there Fat boy."

Shadow continued to nod his head, "Yeah slim that's good to hear, because we're going to need all the help we can get."

"Fat boy, I'm out of here the first chance I get too. Quita can keep this spot; I'm just not going to be here with her."

V-Rock then asked, "Have you told her that yet?"

"Are you crazy shorty?" They all started laughing, "We all know she's going to go bananas on my ass. I ain't no fool."

The next day they all went to see the lawyer about starting their label. The lawyer agreed to set everything up for them, but not without a hefty fee of course. They had taken Tykisha with them, and she was all over the lawyer asking many . . . many questions. They agreed to put her down as the CEO of the Label. The name of the Label would be RipRap Entertainment. The lawyer said to give him a week and he'd have all the necessary paperwork done. They all thanked him and left.

As they were all leaving the lawyer's office, Tykisha informed them that she had spoken to a realtor, whom had informed her that he'd get back to her later in the week about her inquiry.

"Gino look, I'll see y'all a little later, I've got to go holla at a few niggas I know about beats." Shadow was saying as he was jumping inside his truck. "We're going to need all the help we can get."

"That's a bet, cause me and Tykisha are headed up to her school to speak to some people about working the boards and production. This dude she knows is supposed to be pretty nice, but we'll see."

Shadow started up his truck, "That's good, see if he's trying to ride or what."

"Fo'sho', holla later." Gino waved as Fat boy pulled off.

Shit was starting to fall into place. Over the last couple of days everybody that they talked to was interested in being a part of the Record Label, especially a newly formed Label. Plus everyone was assured that the money would be there to push their records and all. Tykisha introduced Gino and Shadow to this young eccentric jazz singer named Blue, whom went to school with Tykisha. Blue had a beautiful voice, and they had their second official signing to RipRap Entertainment. They had acquired a few production people and a few beat makers. Now all they had to do was wait until the realtor came through with the houses.

Things had been moving so fast that Gino had forgotten all about Kenny coming up the weekend. So Gino decided to call Kenny and postpone his visit until after the houses were purchased. Kenny understood and Gino assured him that it wouldn't be long and that he'd call as soon as the houses were acquired.

The following Monday the Realtor finally called Tykisha and told her that he had two houses beside each other separated by yards. One was $170,000.00 and the other one was $150,000.00. They purchased both spots and it turned out to be perfect for what they wanted to accomplish.

Over the next couple of weeks Gino and Shadow got both houses fixed up, and purchased all the furniture and stuff. In the basement of Shadow's house they decided to build the studio, and they put the business office inside Gino's house, that way Tykisha would have access to the office at anytime, and Shadow would have access to the studio at anytime. Things worked out just right.

CHAPTER 50

One month later, the studio and the office were finished being built, all that was needed now was office furniture, computers, file cabinets, etc. In the studio they just needed to purchase all the studio equipment.

Now all the while this was going on, word on the street spread quickly throughout RipRap that Gino and Shadow were really through with the streets and were launching their own Rap Label. Marquita was still staying at the apartment, but she and Gino's relationship had all but gone to the dogs. Gino really didn't care what she did; he just wanted her to leave him alone. Gino moved all 3 safes out the apartment and put them at the new house. Gino knew that sometimes broads got to acting crazy, especially when they're scorned and/or hurt. Shadow had met him a new cutie anyway named Carmella and he was spending all of his free time with her, everything was looking up at this point.

Early one morning, Gino woke up thinking about Kenny and decided that he wanted to see him. So he called V-Rock up and told him that he wanted him to got pick Kenny up for the weekend, and V was more than happy to oblige.

On Friday morning, the lawyer called Tykisha and informed her that they were all needed at his office ASAP. Immediately they all hustled over to the lawyer's office to find out what was wrong. Upon arriving at the office, they were surprised to be handed the official papers to launch RipRap Entertainment legitimately. They were all extremely happy and surprised. As they left, they thanked the lawyer and couldn't wait to get home to tell everybody it was on and popping.

On Friday evening, Tykisha called a meeting with everyone associated with the Label. They decided that on Saturday morning they would all take a trip to New York to order all the equipment needed for the studio, and everyone's presence was requested. Shadow felt that everyone needed to get what they wanted so they could get the best beats, best sound, and have the best voices coming out of the speakers.

Friday night V-Rock arrived at the house with Kenny. As Kenny entered the door, he was in awe of how his big brother was living it up. "Yeah Kenny I told you we about to blow this music shit up. So I hope that you're ready to spit that fire, cause tomorrow we're going to purchase all the equipment and stuff for the studio. The people just finished putting the finishing touches on it yesterday." Gino stated.

Kenny was smiling from ear to ear, "Gino man I'm ready believe that."

"Kenny your bedroom is upstairs," Gino pointed, "aye V-Rock show him where his room is."

Grabbing one of Kenny's suitcases V-Rock says, "Gino don't wait up for us tonight either, we're going to hang out aiight?"

Gino looked at V-Rock sternly, "V-Rock I'm telling you don't have Kenny miss us in the morning."

"I won't," V-Rock stated, "come on Kenny let's put your shit up, and get up out of here."

Soon as they left Gino knew they were going to get into something, he just didn't know what.

V-Rock took Kenny around Wesley Avenue and RipRap. While driving through, he mentioned to Kenny, "Yeah homie you know Shadow and Gino got out the game and left all these streets to the kid. If you want, me and you can get down together."

Kenny looked out the window pondering his thoughts, "V . . . man I don't know, I told Gino that I'd give this shit up too."

"Kenny man, all you got to do is come through, pass out your work, and pick your money up at the end of the day. It don't get no sweeter than that."

"I don't know V, let me think about it. I know this Porsche bad as a motherf . . ."

"Kenny man, I'm telling you, I'm doing it like that." V-Rock winked his eye at Kenny.

Little did V-Rock know, but niggas around RipRap had been planning on snatching him the first chance they got. All BJ and Raymond had been waiting for was the right opportunity. V-Rock had gotten so big headed that he was not taking niggas serious, and many . . . many people felt like smashing V-Rock would be the perfect way to get back at Shadow and Gino.

On this particular night BJ and Raymond had all the intention on grabbing him. Fortunately, Kenny was with V-Rock this night and it threw everything off. So they prolonged it another day knowing V-Rock wasn't going anywhere. Everybody was not as intimidated as they were before because Gino and Shadow had long stopped showing their faces on the block. On top of that, the word had spread that they had left the streets and were concentrating solely on their music thing. However, V-Rock wanted those blocks, and it would be hard to get him to change his mind.

The next morning everybody met up at the house, but guess who was still asleep . . . Kenny! Gino went up to his room and woke him up, and rushed him to get dressed. Soon after, they all headed down to the spot in New York that supposedly had top notch studio equipment. Going through the store, everybody thought they knew what they wanted, but saw other things that were new and up to date like the MPC 4000 sampler, the Connoisseur Mixer, the new Korg Kontrol 49 Keyboard, and other digital equipment. Gino and Shadow spent so much money that it was a shame. Gino said to himself, "Shit! All this money we're spending this shit has to work out."

They paid for everything as well as for the delivery and installation. The manager had informed them that he couldn't have the equipment delivered until the next day. So they all headed home with much anticipation and excitement. Instead of going straight back to the house, they all decided to go out to eat, relax and have a little fun. Later after eating they all went back to the house, and everybody decided to spend the night so they could be there in the morning when the equipment arrived.

All night long, Gino couldn't sleep, because he was excited about getting this music shit off the ground. When the morning did finally arrive, Gino went downstairs; he found out that he was not the only one who couldn't sleep. Everybody was wide awake and antsy. They all decided to head over to Shadow's and wait for the delivery truck. Shadow and Carmella were up spending some quality time together. Gino really liked Carmella and felt like she was good for Shadow. Finally the people arrived at 9:00a.m.

Around 3:25p.m., almost 6 ½ hours later, all the equipment was finally installed and hooked up. Gino decided that he was tired and was going to lie down for a while.

When he woke up it was 10:00p.m. and he was feeling rejuvenated. Gino got up and headed back over to the studio. Soon as he hit the door he could hear sounds coming from the basement. As he was touching the bottom step he could see exactly where all the noise was coming from, Shadow, Kenny, and V-Rock were into a freestyle battle. The shocking thing about it was that Gino saw that Kenny really could carry his own, and Gino thought, "Damn this shit might just work for real . . . for real!"

All during this time Gino and Tykisha had become super tight again. They were closer now than ever before. She was living at the house, and still attending school. Gino stood at his bedroom door one morning just staring at her sleeping, "Damn I love this girl," ran all through his mind. "I don't know why I've been thinking about this, but Tykisha still hasn't told Black yet, that we are together. Shit I can't say nothing; I still haven't told Marquita the truth yet either. Fuck it; I just want a clean break away. Quita can't complain anyway I still let her live rent free, and she has a brand new car. I would never take that away from her, I just wanted the relationship to be over. I hope she got the picture with the way I left things. Hopefully one day I can be straight up and tell her to just move on."

Tykisha had stopped going home on the weekends and was dedicating her free time to the Label and getting their relationship back like it was, all the while Gino loved every bit of it.

With the passing of the days, they all stayed in the studio 24/7 just trying to bang out some hot joints. Day in and day out, everybody was dedicating their time to making this shit jump off. Kenny even had made a couple of hot tracks, but make no mistake about this . . . Shadow was the DMX of this Label. The Label would make or break off of Shadow. We had an R&B singer named Blue, whose voice sounded like Erykah Badu. However, her song writing was not that good. So Gino enlisted the help of some ghost writers to help her out.

They decided early on that their main focus would be Shadow first and foremost. They wanted to see what kind of buzz they could get from him, and go from there. One day Kenny and Shadow made a song together that they knew was hot. The name of it was, 'Real Niggas . . . Do Real Things!' It was some of the hardest shit Gino ever heard, and everybody else felt the same way. The song was reminiscent of what Jay and Eminem did on the Renegade track. Now if they could get a few more joints like that to go along with that track, the album would be a smash hit. Then surely it would only be a matter of time before major Labels would come knocking.

A few weeks had passed and the routine hadn't changed, studio . . . studio . . . studio . . . all day everyday. One day Tykisha calls a meeting and tells Gino to alert everyone to be present. Gino walked over to the studio and of course everyone was hard at work. Gino spotted Shadow in the corner with a pad and pencil penning some more lyrics, "Aye Fat boy what's happening?" Gino extended his hand for a hand shake. "I just came to let you know Tykisha has called a meeting this evening. She said to make sure you're there." Shadow kept nodding his head like he had some lyrics in his head he was repeating, "Damn Fat boy did you hear anything I said?" Gino asked.

"Yeah . . . yeah I heard you Gino my nigga. I just had this thought in my head and I didn't want to forget it."

"Man you need to take a break Shadow; you've been working extremely hard on this album."

Setting his pencil and pad down, Shadow sat back in his chair. "Gino man, I done got that feeling back again, and I just want this album to be a hot joint. A lot is riding on my shoulders."

Gino looked at the seriousness in Shadow's face, "I feel you big boy, but we've got to get all our paperwork and shit together as well. We've got to make sure that we don't have any slip up's. You know how these feds are on nigga's asses about starting these Rap Labels with drug money."

"No doubt . . . no doubt," Shadow nodded his head, "I'll be there."

"No. Everybody has to be there, the whole crew." Gino noted.

"Fo'sho Gino I'll let everybody know, but let me get back to this track right now aiight?"

"Aiight Baby Heavy D." Gino laughed.

"Yeah okay . . . I got you Gino, Fuck you!" Shadow shouted as Gino ran out giggling.

At the office that night, Tykisha pulled out the contracts for everyone. Every artist, Technician, Producer, Beat Maker, etc. even her contract to be CEO, and Gino's for Co-CEO. Tykisha informed everyone to look over their contracts before they signed them, but if they were unsure about anything that they could get a lawyer to overlook it before they signed. However, everyone agreed that everything seemed in order, and signed the contract.

Gino was last to sign his contract. He smiled and looked up at Shadow, "Hey Fat boy it's all official now, you know that right?" Gino said handing Tykisha her pen back. "It's on and poppin' for sure, you digg?"

"Yeah Gino my nigga I can't wait."

"It won't be long now. As a matter of fact, everybody listen up . . . tomorrow Tykisha and I will be going to purchase all the materials needed to press our own CD's. So once we finish, we can press them and get them distributed throughout the region. Don't worry about any of that, let us . . . Management handle that part. Shadow will be the first artist out on RipRap Entertainment and everyone else will follow. Everybody's project will get the same amount of attention and work, as we want everybody to be successful. Okay y'all let's get to work."

As everyone was departing, Gino called Shadow, "Aye Shadow hold up a minute."

Shadow stood at the doorway waiting as Gino gathered some papers and came over, "What's up Gino, something wrong?"

"Nooo . . . NO . . . ," Gino hugged him as they walked out the door, "Man can you believe this, we're really about to do this shit?"

"No question Gino! You done got me inspired and serious about this shit, once again."

"Shadow I want you to be successful, because you are extremely talented and I know you can do it. Look though, some time within the next couple of days we need to buy a couple of caravans too. Then get our Label name painted on this side, with a hell of a system inside. That'll be great for promotion and advertising, plus help pushing the album and the Label."

"What does Tykisha think?" Shadow asked.

"She says that we need to target Virginia, Maryland, and DC first. If we can get some type of buzz from your single, then we can push more CD's and tapes. Of course we'll have to get a few radio spins, which will get the streets to talking. If that happens, then you know we on."

"Gino I'm feeling that 100%! Plus I'm with you all the way. So go ahead and purchase the van tomorrow."

"Also, when are you going to take care of the guys we left in the streets, you know they looking forward to that."

"Don't worry about that let me handle them. You and Tykisha take care of the van and stuff, I'll handle everything else."

"Alright, Fo'sho'! . . . Later!!"

CHAPTER 51

Two weeks later the album was coming along nicely, and being away from the streets started to feel good to Gino, but as with all things, every time you try to get away from shit, something always pull you back.

One day while picking up his money, V-Rock was confronted by BJ and Raymond. "Damn lil' V, that Porsche tight as shit shorty." BJ commented.

"Yeah just a little something . . . something." V-Rock replied as he was exiting the car closing the door.

"Aye look though V, we got this dude in the building who's trying to get a half a key of raw." Raymond expressed.

V asked, "Does he have the money now?"

"Yeah he always straight, he comes through on a regular."

"Aiight . . . hold up then." V-Rock began walking around to the trunk of his Porsche popping it open, but as he leaned inside to get the raw, BJ pulled out his 9mm Smith and Wesson and struck V-Rock in the back of the head. V staggered back holding his head, then hitting the ground hard. Looking up, V-Rock noticed BJ standing over top of him, "BJ what the fuck is going on nigga?" V-Rock barked while still hold the back of his head.

"Shut the fuck up lil' nigga!" BJ and Raymond had rage in their eyes. "Get your bitch ass up and get in that truck." At that point a white MPV slowly pulled up with the side door opened up. BJ and Raymond forced V-Rock inside, as the driver pulled off.

There were two other men inside the van, whom looked extremely familiar to V, but he couldn't place their faces. While they were riding along Raymond tied V-Rock's hands and feet up, then placed him on the floor of the van. They drove around Queen Street then took V-Rock inside an abandoned building and slammed him to the ground.

Once inside the building, V-Rock was whipped viciously. He was beaten so bad that his arm was broken, his shoulder dislocated, and had his ankle crushed with a sledge hammer. He was now on the ground crying and yelling mercifully.

When they finally finished torturing him, they laid him on his back and taunted him. "Yeah nigga," BJ spat, "you been gettin' real big headed around here lately. I remember a time when you were quiet as a church mouse. Now you done got under Shadow and them, and you done got too big for your britches boy. I know y'all didn't think that I was going to let y'all get away with killing my folks and there was not going to be no get back, uh uh . . . . ain't happenin'!"

They all stood around V-Rock just in case he tried something. BJ then stated, "Now listen V-Rock I like you little shorty, and this shit wasn't intended for you. Unfortunately, you got caught up in the mix. Now I'm going to give you a chance to live, but you only get this one chance . . . one time and one time only!"

Looking down at V-Rock at this point was almost unbearable. Blood was everywhere and he was whimpering in pain. Raymond then kicked V-Rock, "AYYYY!!!!!!!!!!!!!" V-Rock screamed out in pain, his whole body had been abused.

"What you kick shorty for dumb ass?!!!" BJ screamed out at Raymond. Raymond at this point was pulling a gun out pointing it straight at V-Rock, "Hold the fuck up nigga!!!!" BJ yelled at Raymond. "What the fuck you think you doing nigga?!!!!!!!"

"Man let me kill this nigga and get his over with!"

"Raymond chill the fuck out and let me handle this aiight!!!" BJ screamed, then turned his attention back to V-Rock. "V-Rock we really don't want you shorty, we want Shadow and the dude Gino. So if you tell me where them niggas living at, I'll let you live, but if you don't work with us, then I'll have no choice but to kill you too. Don't be no dummy . . . do the smart thing and give me the info."

V-Rock knew that there was no chance in hell that he was going to be left alive, even if he did give them the information cause the rules to the game don't go like that, death was definitely coming and V-Rock could sense it. Plus V knew when Shadow and them found out what happened they'd go crazy killing all of them, "Aye look," V-Rock began as he was whimpering and holding his ankle in pain, "BJ man I told you I don't know where them nigga's living at for real. They never discussed that with us workers, only each other." Raymond picked up the sledge hammer again and smashed V-Rock's other ankle. "Ahhhh!!!!!!!!!!!! AHHH!!!!!!!!" V-Rock cried out, as he was squirming all around on the ground in all sorts of pain.

There was no way that V-Rock could take too much more of this punishment, it was only a matter of time. BJ then bent down over top of V-Rock, "Listen little shorty this is your last time I'm giving you to save your life. Where do those niggas live?!!!" BJ barked in a vicious tone. V-Rock was still in so much pain he couldn't even answer. "Where do they live boy?!!"

V-Rock knew that he was going to die anyway at this point, and he knew hat if gave Gino and Shadow up that they would probably be killed as well. So he realized that he was in a no-win situation, and made a decision at that moment. Slowly V rolled over on his back and looked up at BJ, who was waiting to dish out some more punishment. "You know what BJ . . . Fuck you pussy boy! I told you I don't know where they live, and if you don't believe me, then tough shit! Do what you gotta do, but you know they coming. I will be avenged, believe that, cause the thing we know is that the streets do talk, it's only a matter of time."

BJ laughed at V-Rock, "Wrong answer baby boy!" BJ lifted his 9mm from under his shirt.

"BJ you know that I would never betray them dudes under no circumstances. Them the only niggas who ever kept it real with me, so do whatever. I'm a die man. Death before Dishonor!"

Raymond then cocked the handle back on his 38, and he and BJ both pointed their guns straight at V-Rock's dome. "Here's for your loyalty fool!" BJ said as they let loose, POW . . . POW . . . POW . . . POW . . . POW . . . POW . . . !!!!!!!!!!!!!

When it was all said and done, V-Rock's head was opened up like a watermelon and splattered all over the floor. Shortly thereafter as they all began to exit the building, Raymond stopped over top V-Rock's dead body and hog spat on V's quivering body. V-Rock was dead, but he was true to his men, and died proving his loyalty.

CHAPTER 52

Back at the studio, things were all good, Kenny was over in the corner working on a few tracks. While Shadow was in the booth laying down some adlibs for a few songs. His album was damn near complete, he only needed like 2 or 3 more songs. Around 10:30 that night, Shadow's pager went off 5 times back to back. Looking at the number it was Teddy Bear, Shadow picked up his cell phone and called back immediately. Bear answered on the first ring, "Yo Shadow!" Bear answered.

"Yeah what's up Bear?!"

"My nigga . . . something's wrong!!" Bear yelled.

"What? . . . What's up?"

"Listen I just got a call from somebody who told me V-Rock's car is outside on Wesley Avenue sitting with the doors open left unattended, and V-Rock is no where to be found. They say his car has been sitting like that for at least 4 to 5 hours now."

"Are you sure?'"

"Yeah Shadow that's the message I got."

"Bear do me a favor," Shadow replied, "Get the fam together and meet me on Wesley ASAP!!"

"Aiight!" Bear responded hanging up the phone.

Shadow immediately yelled out, "Gino come on!!!!!" rushing up the steps.

Trailing behind him Gino asked, "What's up . . . what's wrong Fat boy"

"It's V-Rock!!!!!"

"What happened?!"

"I don't know yet, just grab a hammer." Shadow grabbed his Desert Eagle, Gino his 45, then they jetted towards the door.

"Gino! Gino! Gino!" Tykisha screamed noticing something wasn't right.

Gino turned at the door way, "What's up baby?"

"Where are you going? What's wrong?"

"I don't know yet, something's wrong with V-Rock."

"Come on Gino, hurry up!!!!!" Shadow hollered from the car.

"I got to go Tykisha!" Gino said moving out the door.

"Gino! Gino I'm going too then." Tykisha urged.

"Baby . . . no stay here, you can't."

"Gino you're not leaving me ever again, I'm going." She insisted.

"Aiight come on. I don't have time to arguing with you."

Closing the door, Gino forgot Kenny. "Aye Kenny!!!! Aye Kenny!!!" Gino hollered upstairs, "Come on hurry up, and grab that 9mm out my drawer!!!!!"

They all rushed down to Wesley Avenue. Turning onto Wesley the fam had already assembled there. Shadow pulled up and hopped out immediately noticing that V-Rock's car was sitting at the curb, with his trunk still up. When they took a closer look, they also saw that the keys were still in the ignition. Gino knew V-Rock would never leave his car unattended unless something was desperately wrong. When they checked his trunk, he had mad dope still sitting inside. So they figured who ever or whatever had happened, it couldn't have been a robbery. Gino was now panicking, "Shadow we've got to find out what happened to shorty!" Gino stated sensing the worse. His eyes were starting to get watery already Tykisha noticed, grabbed and hugged Gino.

"Baby everything's going to be alright. You hear me?" Tykisha whispered.

"Tykisha I can't let nothing happen to shorty, I'm supposed to protect him."

"Gino he's okay stop thinking like that."

Tears were now coming down Gino's face, "Tykisha that's why I wanted shorty to walk away from this shit, but shorty was hard headed."

"Baby stop crying," Tykisha said wiping the tears from his face, "V-Rock probably had to jump out and run or something. We don't know yet baby."

Gino stood there nodding his head, "Uh uh baby, them suckers waited until a nigga got out the game, and pulled some shit like this. I know it, I can feel it."

Shadow jumped in, "Don't worry about nothing Gino, if one of them nigga's touched shorty in any kind of way, they will pay dearly for sure, you hear me?" Shadow said sternly.

Figuring it wasn't no sense in standing there all night, Shadow suggested that they all go back to the house and wait and see what happened. Riding home Shadow felt his cell phone vibrate in his pocket. Reaching to grab it, Shadow answered, "Hello, who this?!"

"Hey what's up big homie?" Greg said in an excited tone.

"Look I'm around Queen Street over Tanisha house."

"Aiight . . . so what's the problem?" Shadow said in a nasty sort of way.

"As I was leaving, I noticed the police outside in front of one of the abandoned buildings. When I went to see what the problem was, the police were just keeping everybody away from the building, but there was this one officer was asking everybody questions about a killing that had occurred. He had this chain in his hand that he held up asking anybody if they knew someone who had a chain like the one he was holding. The chain had a charm on it just like the one V-Rock had. I don't know of nobody else who had a chain like that, and so I'm figuring that it might be V big boy."

"Greg listen, see what you can find out. We're on our way," Shadow said as he hung up the phone.

Around Queen Street Police were everywhere, and I mean everywhere. So as Shadow and them pulled up, they knew that they could not go down to the scene because they probably would be arrested. Instead they sent Kenny and Man Man down to find Greg and investigate the situation.

Several minutes later when Gino saw them headed back towards the car he spotted Greg crying from a distance, and immediately he knew the news couldn't be good. Gino leaned on the car and began to cry, as

Tykisha consoled him. Greg, Kenny, and Man Man all walked up with tears in their eyes. "What's the word?" Shadow asked.

"Shadow man . . . Shadow . . . I hate to say it," Greg started to cry harder, "but I believe it was shorty. Not only that, whoever done it, knocked shorty head damn near off literally!"

Man Man cut in, "When they bought the body out, I told them that I possibly might know the person to let me see if I could identify him, but one of the officers said that I wouldn't be able to tell that way because the face was totally disfigured and destroyed."

"Damn! Damn!! Damn!!!" Gino banged on the hood of the car as everybody just stood there and cried knowing that the worst had occurred.

This was extremely hard and painful on Gino, he was going crazy. No one could control him, and for a second Shadow saw that killer look in Gino's eyes again.

Standing at the corner away from the crowd, Shadow called Kenny over, "Kenny listen to me, Gino's going to lose it. Believe what I tell you, I've seen this look in his eyes before."

Kenny looked over at Gino, "Shadow . . . man, whoever did this, Gino's going to take special interest in getting even himself. What we need to be doing is find out who's responsible, so we can deal with it as fast as possible."

"Don't even worry about that, I got that. Come on let's get everybody and get out of here." Shadow responded as they walked over and told everybody, "Let's roll."

That night at the house it was quiet and somber. No one wanted to talk, they just wanted revenge. Shadow left and went home, but this would be a long night for all of them. Hopefully tomorrow would be a better day.

Tykisha hadn't slept all night, worried about Gino's feelings and emotions. So as soon as the city morgue opened up she called down and claimed the body. She informed them that she would come down and make all the arrangements, noting that due to the severity of the disfigurement of his face, that she wanted the body cremated. The mortician agreed, and she informed him she'd call back when all the other arrangements were made.

Around RipRap things were extremely quiet for the next couple of days. Any and everyone were on eggshells knowing retribution was definitely coming, but nobody knew when or who.

Shadow and Kenny lost focus on their music for a minute, but all the other artists kept things moving. Tykisha was really on her job as CEO, plus she was Gino's comforter as well, as he really needed it during this time. Over the passing days all Gino did was think about V-Rock, and how he was suppose to protect shorty. Gino just couldn't get V-Rock off his mind, because he felt like it was his fault for allowing shorty to stay in the streets when they got out. However, he also knew that V-Rock didn't want to leave the streets alone, no matter what Gino told him. In any event, Gino was going to make sure V-Rock's memory lived forever, and there would be hell to pay for his murder.

Today was V-Rock's funeral, and Gino didn't know how he was going to make it through the day. However, Gino sat in the front row looking at V-Rock's closed casket as everybody tried to cheer him up, and gave their condolences. Gino sat there saying to himself, "Damn them niggas really dogged my man out. I got them though shorty believes that. Somebody will pay for this."

All the RipRap crew had gotten T-Shirts made with 'We'll Always Miss You!' printed on it along with V-Rock's picture. The funeral was packed; I mean shorty must have touched a lot of people during his short life. Old, young, male, and female they all came out and showed love.

Shadow was taking it hard as well. Shadow basically raised V-Rock coming up, and Fat boy felt somewhat responsible for his death. Shadow walked over to say something to Gino, "Gino my nigga you aiight?" Shadow whispered in Gino's ear.

Gino rose up hugging Shadow, "Big homie that was some fucked up shit them suckers did, you know that right?"

"Fo'sho," they released their embrace, "but we'll get them. Alll . . . . Shit . . . ." Shadow mumbled as Gino turned to see what he was referring to.

Gino grabbed his head, "Ohhh . . . Lord, not today, of all days" Gino whined spotting Marquita and Tricia coming in the door of the funeral home.

"Oh well Gino," Shadow mentioned, "ain't no sense in hiding, they know what the fuck is going on, but Tricia better not try to start nothing with Carmella I'm telling you."

Gino stood there staring at Marquita who hadn't spotted Gino as of yet, "Fat boy I know Marquita's going to try and make a scene. You know it, and I know it, as a matter of fact I'm going out front with Tykisha now." Gino walked over to Tykisha taking her hand, and heading outside. Fortunately Gino was able to get outside without incident.

"Gino, what's wrong? Why you rushing outside like this?" Tykisha asked with a complex look on her face.

"Look baby, I'm going to be straight up with you." Gino looked her in the eyes. "The girl that I use to live with and mess with just arrived at the funeral."

Tykisha sucked her bottom lip, "Gino I knew something wasn't right. I was watching you and Shadow the whole time. I noticed the body language and the facial expression on both y'all faces when they came through the door."

"Tykisha I just wanted to give you a heads up, just in case she tries to make a scene."

Tykisha kissed Gino softly, "Look baby I know how to conduct myself as a woman. There's a time and place for everything. You don't have anything to worry about, okay?!"

"I know, but you don't know her like I do."

"Gino it really don't matter to me how she acts, I know how to act accordingly. If she crosses the line, I'll deal with her later."

Gino smiled, "See that's why I love you so much." Gino hugged her.

"Uh . . . uh . . . uh . . . ," a voice choked behind them. Gino turned around and there was Marquita, "Hello Gino!" she said in a sarcastic tone.

"What's up Marquita, how are you doing?" Gino stated, Tykisha grabbing Gino's left hand.

"Oh, I'm doing fine. I'm sorry about what happened to V-Rock, you know he was like a little brother to me too."

Inside, Gino knew she was telling the truth. She and V-Rock had become close during the time he had lived with them, "Yeah . . . I know Quita, he loved you too."

Silence hung in the air for a few seconds, "Gino let me ask you a question." Quita asked, "Why haven't you been returning my pages. I know you been receiving them."

"Quita, a lot of shit has been going on, and I've been extremely busy."

"Gino you don't have to lie to me," as her eyes glanced over at Tykisha, "I know that's your little girlfriend."

Gino held his frustration in, "Quita listen, you know things were not working out. That ain't no secret. I still pay your rent, and I allowed you to keep a brand new car."

"Gino, I don't care nothing about that stuff," she hollered, "the way you carried me was not cute!"

"Aiight . . . aiight you may have a point there, but what's done is done."

"Yeah Gino, but that don't make it right. You could have been straight up with me."

Shadow had come out to the front of the church, and stood back watching the whole scene; making sure things didn't get out of hand. He could hear them arguing, but didn't know what was being said.

"Gino excuse me," Tykisha then cut in, "look baby come on, the service should be about to start."

"Excuse you!" Quita hissed, "Don't you see us talking?!"

Tykisha chuckled, "Yes I do, but you ain't talking about nothing. So Gino let's go." She pulled Gino's hand and they started walking towards the church.

As they were climbing the steps Gino wanted to look back, but kept moving until Quita yelled out, "Gino so you walking off like that huh?"

Gino turned slightly, "I'll talk to you later Quita."

"No you'll talk to me now or never!!" She screamed back as Gino finally reached the top step approaching Shadow.

"Oh well then . . ." Gino waved to her while turning to walk in the church.

"That's why I got some information on what happened to V-Rock!"

Gino, Shadow, Tykisha, and Carmella all stopped dead in their tracks and turned around. Gino's whole facial expression changed.

He pulled away from Tykisha and headed back over towards Quita, "What did you just say Quita? I know I ain't hear what I think I heard you say!" Gino was still swiftly approaching Quita at this moment.

"Nahh . . . don't come see what I want now." She sarcastically stated, "keep walking with your little girlfriend. I thought you might change your mind, huh . . ." Quita mumbled under her breath, not knowing she had just woke up a stone cold killer for real . . . for real . . . .

Gino walked up to Quita, "Did you say that you knew something about what happened to V-Rock?" Gino's face was now blank and cold.

Marquita placed her hands on her hips, "So what if I did?"

"Quita please listen to me and listen good." Gino's aura was extremely serious at this point as he grabbed Quita around the neck and began to choke her. "Now bitch stop playing these games with me, if you know what's good for you, I'm telling you!" All the while Gino was talking his grip had tightened up around her neck more and more. She was beginning to blank out as he was choking the life out of her. She was gasping for air and foaming out the mouth until Shadow ran over and jumped in, grabbing Gino and trying to get him to release her neck. Tykisha joined in as well, Gino's hand was so tightly gripped around her neck, and she fought to stay conscience.

"Gino! Gino!, let her go man!!" Shadow yelled while trying to loosen Gino's grip on her neck.

"Please baby, let her go." Tykisha begged until finally Gino let her go. At this point Gino was steaming mad and out of control. "I'm telling you . . . I'm telling you, Fat boy I'll kill her." Gino was saying as Shadow pulled him away from Quita.

"Look calm down Gino, you're out of control right now slim," Shadow was saying to Gino. Gino momentarily calmed down and then Shadow turned to Quita. "Look Quita right now is not a good time to be playing games aiight. If you know something about V-rock, let us know right now."

Quita was just getting back to her feet, trying to compose herself. "Fuck that! And Fuck y'all Shadow!!" she screamed still trying to catch her breath.

Gino walked over, "Shadow, Tykisha, and Carmella, listen go ahead inside the church. Let me speak to Quita by myself for a minute."

Shadow looked at Gino, "Are you crazy? Do you think I'm that stupid?"

"Nooo . . . for real Shadow, her and I need to air some things out anyway."

Marquita was just standing off to the side waiting to see what was going to happen next.

"Aiight Gino, come on y'all let's go inside." Shadow said to Tykisha and Carmella.

"Baby . . . Be careful please." Tykisha said as she kissed Gino on the cheek, then turned to walk towards the church.

After they all entered the church, Gino turned to face Quita, and she knew the game was over. "Marquita look, I know that you're still upset about the situation, and you're right I could have handled it differently, but I didn't. I never complained not once about your shady dealings with the dude Flames, nor the rumors that I had been hearing. I chose to still pay your rent and let you keep the car. Not at no time have I threatened to take that away from you, but now you're telling me that you have information about who killed V-Rock and you're holding back. Especially after he gave up $10,000 of his own money towards that car you're driving right now. How does that weigh out? Explain that to me."

"Gino I know all that, but I've been calling you all week long and you refused to answer my pages. So what am I suppose to do, you already carried me about something you assumed that I did, which I didn't."

"Quita this is neither the time nor place do deal with that, I need to know what you know about V-Rock's murder."

"I've got this girlfriend name Freda who lives around Queen Street. She fucks with this dude that be hustling around there from time to time named, 'Big O'. He mentioned to her that him and some of his buddies got some get back on some RipRap niggas for killing some of there people. I'm assuming that V-Rock was who he was referring to."

"Where does this broad stay Quita?"

"She lives at 3345 Queen Street two buildings away from where they found V-Rock's body. The nigga, 'Big O' drives a blue Acura Legend too."

Gino stared at Quita for a second in silence, "Quita thank you for your help, and I'm sorry about everything else, aiight?"

Her eyes began to get watery, "Gino I'm cool. I just miss you."

"Marquita you're a good woman, but I know in my heart something was going on or is still going on between you and the dude Flames, and you know I can't accept that, under any circumstances."

"Gino I swear . . ." Gino placed his hand over her mouth.

"Marquita stop . . . I don't want to argue with you. I tell you what . . . I'll be pass the house this week and we can talk aiight? Is that cool?"

"Yeah Gino." She batted her eyes as Gino hugged her and placed something in her jacket pocket to her suit.

Breaking their embrace, Gino then headed inside the church while Marquita reached in her pocket to see what Gino had placed in her pocket. She realized at that moment, Gino placed a bundle of money in her pocket. She looked at it, wiped the tears from her face, put it back in her pocket and headed back inside the church as well.

Upon leaving the church, Gino was informing Shadow about what Quita had told him. Shadow wasn't surprised but knew he'd get to this nigga Big O, whoever he was.

CHAPTER 53

Shadow pulled up on Queen Street parking his truck behind somebody's Mercedes that was sitting in front of the building where Freda supposedly lived. Shadow and Gino laid low waiting for hours so it seemed. Shortly after 2:00a.m. their prayers were answered when Gino spotted the Blue Acura Quita had said Big O drove, pulled up and parked two cars in front of them. Gino surveyed the area, which was clear, no one was outside. Watching Big O's car, Gino noticed that the nigga hadn't got out his car yet. "Shadow what the fuck you think that nigga doing?" Gino asked.

"I'm not sure Gino, but it looks like this sucker on the phone. He probably calling his little bitch to let her know that he out front."

Gino then raised up trying to get a better look when he noticed that Big O was doing exactly just that, talking on the phone. "Talk now nigga cause you'll never make another call after that." Gino whispered to himself as he cracked his side door and crept out on his way towards Big O.

Big O finally hung up his cell phone and began to exit his coup when out of nowhere Gino appeared snatching O's car door open with his gun pointed straight at O's head. "Ohhh . . . Shit!!" O screamed jumping back.

"Get your bitch ass out that car!" Gino instructed 'O'. Scared to death, 'O' followed Gino's instructions, but soon as he exited the car Gino smacked him in the head, knocking him straight to the ground with his 45 Smith and Wesson.

"Ouch!!" Big O belted out from the ground. When he finally rolled over, Gino was standing right over top of him, gun ready to release. "Hold up main man . . . ," Big O began to beg immediately, "Please don't kill me . . . please." Big boy now has his hands up in front of his face, as if that was going to do something.

"Look O, don't make me kill you, you're not who I want." Gino spoke with his 45 pointed straight at Big O's head.

Shadow slowly pulled up alongside, "Get in that truck!" Gino instructed Big O, and he followed directions.

As they were driving along, Gino then says to Big O, "Look here big boy, I know you're not behind the killing of my little man V-Rock, but I know you played a part in it. All I want to know is who made the call, that's it, that's all."

O was shaking and trembling, "Listen man I swear to God that wasn't my call." O replied.

"Who's was it then?!" Gino screamed moving the 45 closer to O's head.

"It was BJ and Raymond's call," he belted out, "they wanted to get some get back for what y'all did to Big Darryl. Plus they wanted to take their blocks back. V-Rock was just a pond in their game to get at y'all."

"So you're telling me that BJ and Raymond killed V-Rock right?"

"Yeah I was standing right there, I saw the whole thing. Raymond even spit on your shorty before we left."

"He did huh?" Gino smirked, "Well I appreciate your help, and since you helped me out, I'm going to help you out."

Big O looked up, "Man thanks, I swear if you ever need me again just let me know."

Shadow turned off on a side street several blocks away from Queen Street. "Pull over right here." Gino requested to Shadow.

The truck came to a stop at the corner of 5th and Hampton Streets, "Aiight O, you can get out right here." Gino said.

"Thanks man . . . really thanks." As he turned to get out of the back passenger side door.

POW . . . POW . . . POW . . . !! Three shots exploded into the back of O's head, as Shadow sped off racing home.

A few days went pass and the hunt for BJ and Raymond had turned up nothing so far. Gino was getting frustrated, until finally the break they had been looking for finally came. One night Bear was at Chocolate City, the strip club, when he thought he spotted BJ and Raymond posted up. Not really getting a clear look, he moved close to make sure. "Bingo" Bear mumbled to Greg, "There go those niggas Raymond and BJ right there." He pointed over by the bar.

"Oh shit . . ." Greg hissed. "You're right, call Shadow."

Bear pulled out his cell phone and called Fat boy immediately. At the house Shadow and Gino were watching the old Tupac DVD, 'Above the Rim', when Shadow's phone vibrated on the table. Shadow grabbed it and answered, "Yeah . . . who this?"

"Aye Cous . . . ," Bear announced, "guess who I'm looking at right now. Them two stupid ass niggas BJ and Raymond. These two dummies got to be the either crazy or stupid, they're here at Chocolate City."

Shadow rose up out his chair, "Are you sure?"

"Sure as a heart attack."

"Who you with?" Shadow asked.

"Me and Greg together, why?"

"Look, watch those niggas for another 5 to 10 minutes and get out of there. We'll handle it from there aiight?"

"Fo'sho' . . ." click the phone went dead.

Inside the club was packed tonight. Lap dances, private sessions in back rooms, crap games, everything was everything. Greg and Bear sat in one of the booths way in the back, but just out of sight of BJ and Raymond. "Bear it's going to get ugly in here in a few minutes, you know that don't you?" Greg said while finishing off the last of his drink.

"Shittt . . . , you think I don't know that. I'm just glad we'll be getting the fuck out of here in a few minutes, before the fireworks start."

"No doubt . . ."

Over at Raymond and BJ's table they were laid back just chillin' as usual. "BJ who that cutie right there?" Raymond pointed to a sexy chocolate thing dancing extremely seductive just a few feet away from their table.

"Nigga that's freak ass Natalie, everybody's had a piece of that." BJ said as everybody started laughing.

"I second that notion," Tyrone mentioned, "she suck a dick so good, she make a nigga toes curl up." Laughter erupted once again.

"Oooh wee . . . ," BJ shouted, "I must have gotten cheated then cause she fucked me good, but I never got a chance to get the head, you hear me?" High fives went to everybody.

"Tyrone come on," Freddie said, "let's go holla at those broads from Hampton."

"No doubt . . . , we'll holla at y'all later." Freddie said to BJ and Raymond giving them dap and then walking off.

Gino and Shadow finally arrived and were headed inside dressed in black hoodies, and tight fitted wave caps. Shadow knew the bouncer whom he called in advance and alerted that he needed to be let in the back door. The bouncer of course obliged for a few stacks. The back door was left cracked open, and work was about to be put in, for real.

"What time is it?" BJ asked Raymond.

"It's only 12:30," Raymond stated while looking at his watch. "Why? What's up?"

"Man I'm tired as shit for some reason, I'm 'bout to roll."

"Nigga we just got here," Raymond responded, "here take this, it will help you feel better." Raymond reached across the table handing BJ a freshly rolled blunt he had just rolled up.

BJ took it under his nose smelling it. "Now that's what I'm talkin' bout, right here." BJ said as he reached in his pocket for his lighter. He lit the blunt, inhaled hard, and let out a thick cloud of smoke in the air. "Now this some bomb shit here homie, real talk." BJ laid back.

"Yeah, that's my shit right there, ain't no nigga on this side of VA got chiba like that." Raymond beat on his chest as they passed the blunt back and forth getting high as a kite.

Suddenly Raymond looked up, and it was like he was staring at a ghost standing in front of him. Raymond was frozen stiff staring at these two faces that were in front of him.

Raymond then nudged BJ under the table, "What nigga?" BJ said as he finally noticed the look on Raymond's face. By the time he looked up it was too late, Shadow and Gino both whipped out from underneath their hoodies, and shots got to blazing. POW . . . POW . . . POW . . .

POW . . . POW . . . POW . . . POW . . . POW . . . POW . . . POW . . . POW . . . POW . . . !!!

People were screaming and running for cover as shots continued to bust off, POW . . . POW . . . POW . . . POW . . . POW . . . !! There was a mad rush of people trying to exit the club; it was damn near a stampede. You could hear people yelling, "Get down!!!" "Duck!!!!", "Stay down!!!" All you could hear was what sounded like several different guns going off simultaneously, and continuously.

The gun shots finally stopped, and Shadow tapped Gino, "let's go". They dashed for the back door, and disappeared through the alley. Inside the club, bodies were everywhere. BJ and Raymond were both slumped over dead in their booth, and several other bodies were spread out all over the floor. It was a blood bath.

The next morning Gino and Tykisha watched the early morning news when a report from the shooting came on.

Last night at Club Chocolate City there was a terrible shoot out, leaving 13 people dead, and several more wounded. The owner of the club says he's never had anything like this happen before at the club. He says he normally promotes nice clean entertainment, and couldn't understand why anyone would bring that kind of violence to his club. The identities of those being killed are being withheld, because some families have not been notified. There are no suspects and no witnesses. This is Kelly Strong reporting for Channel 6 Morning News . . . .

Gino twirled the tooth pick in his mouth, sitting on the sofa thinking. "Tykisha baby I'm through with this shit," Gino commented, "I'm out of this shit all the way this time. I don't want nothing else to happen to anyone that I love, me and Shadow are just going to concentrate on this music thing and see where it takes us."

She lay in his arms, "Gino I'm so happy to hear that baby, but I understood what you had to do out of respect for V-Rock. I'm just glad it's over and handled."

"Me too baby."

CHAPTER 54

The sun was shining through the blinds waking Gino up at the crack of dawn. Sleepless anyway, he decided to get up and head downstairs to the office to get caught up on some Label business he had been missing out on. Downstairs going through paperwork that was stacked up on Tykisha's desk, it seemed like everything was in order. Then Tykisha appeared, "Good morning baby," Tykisha spoke entering the office. "Why you didn't wake me up when you got up?"

"It was no need baby, I couldn't sleep anyway. So I just decided to come down here and look over whatever I've missed the last couple of weeks."

"Well let me fill you in." She took the chair opposite of Gino. "They started mixing some of the songs for Shadow's album. His tracks sound very good too baby. I believe Shadow can really carry the Label sweetie.

"Yeah baby, I've been telling him that for a while now."

"The album is almost basically finished; he just needs a radio song, and maybe one for the women. Kenny's been working really hard as well."

"I'm glad to hear that," Gino replied, "how's Blue been coming along?"

"She's doing okay; her song writing is getting better. She did record a song with Kenny that's crazy. It sounds something similar to that old Ja'Rule and Lil' Mo song. You've got to hear it. Other than that everybody been working extremely hard."

"Alright baby girl, I see you on top of your game." Gino smiled then leaned in kissing Tykisha, "Come on let's go back upstairs."

"Yeah I bet you do," Tykisha rose out of her chair and sat on Gino's lap. "Whatever you had in mind for upstairs can be handled right here. What you think?" She purred at Gino.

"I don't know, maybe . . . maybe not, but I got no problem finding out." Gino stated as she kissed him passionately, letting her take over his world.

The next couple of weeks they all were working extremely hard on this music shit. Tykisha was trying vigorously to make some connection with different labels and radio stations. All the while the rest of the crew kept banging out tracks and mixing. Finally, they got all the songs recorded for Shadow album, and only needed to mix them, and tweak it.

One night while they all were in the studio sitting around they listened to all 15 tracks recorded for Shadow's album. They had to decide which one would be best for the first single, because it had to be a hit. After listening to several tracks they all decided on this track called 'Ride Wit Me'. It was a hustler anthem and definitely for the streets. So the next couple of days the producers and technicians tightened that song up. They couldn't expect nothing less than a hit.

CHAPTER 55

"Come on Carmella you taking forever!" Shadow yelled out from downstairs. "I've been waiting on you for 20 minutes now. You're pretty with whatever you have on anyway."

"Baby you can't rush beauty," she was stating while coming down the steps, "don't you want your woman to look nice when we go out?"

Shadow just stared at her beauty as she came down the steps; at that moment he knew he had a sure head turner. "Baby you gonna get a nigga caught up over you."

Carmella was blushing, "Shadow shut up boy and come on, Gino's been waiting on us."

"Alright come one sweetie." Shadow opened the door for Carmella.

"Thank you love." Carmella replied in a sweet tone as they walked out heading towards the car.

Shadow opened her side door first, allowing her to enter. Then ran around to his side of the car and was about to enter when all you heard was, "Errrrrr . . . . Errrrrrr . . . Errrrrrr . . ." car tires screeching to a halt. Immediately police officers dressed in several different uniforms and from different agencies jumped out screaming, "Put your hands up!!! . . . Put your hands up now!!!!!"

Shadow looked out to see a flock of police officers everywhere, ATF, Virginia State, Park Police, and all other Po-Po's you could think of. Shadow raised his hands as instructed and then was placed under arrest, and carted off with escorts following. Carmella in shock, jumped out the car, ran inside and immediately called Gino.

"Gino your phone is ringing baby." Tykisha informed Gino while he was using the bathroom.

"Answer it for me sweetheart, I'm in the bathroom." He replied.

"Hello." Tykisha answered the phone.

"Tykisha!! Tykisha!!! . . . They just locked up Shadow!!" Carmella was screaming into the phone.

"What????!!! Who . . . DID WHAT??!!!" Tykisha babbled. "Carmella calm down I can't understand nothing you're saying. Now what happened?"

"We were going to get in the car to come meet y'all when the police rushed the house and car locking Shadow up."

"What did they say?"

"That's just it!" Carmella echoed, "They didn't say anything, they just cuffed him and took him away I was sitting in the car."

"Where are you at now?" Tykisha asked.

"I'm at my house."

"Aiight, look meet us at Shadow's grandmother's in 15 minutes."

"I'll be there, see you."

"Hey baby, who was that?" Gino asked returning from the bathroom. "What's wrong with your face sweetheart?"

"Gino . . . baby," she sniffed, "they just locked Shadow up."

"Who did? For what?"

"I don't know, I just told Carmella to meet us at Grandma's in 15 minutes. Come on I'll fill you in as we're riding."

"Let's go then." As they dashed out the house rushing to Grandma's house.

While at Grandma's, Carmella informed everyone of what happened, but it still didn't answer their question of, what for. Gino contacted the lawyer that Shadow retained in case of emergency, who said he would find out what Shadow had been arrested for and would call them back within 30 minutes.

Twenty-two minutes later the lawyer called back with the news that Shadow had been arrested for murder. He agreed to represent Shadow, and told Gino he'd meet them at the arraignment in the morning.

That night, Gino couldn't sleep. He got up about 3:00 a.m. and stood by the window staring out at the streets just thinking to himself, "Mann . . . oh man I can't believe this, we got out of the game to avoid shit like this. We can't win for losing the police still on a nigga back, damn! Shadow just completed his album, and now he's in the box for God knows how long. This shit is crazy." Finally Gino was able to get to sleep, but the sooner he closed his eyes it was time to get up for court.

Gino was not going into the court building for fear that the police could possibly be looking for him as well. Tykisha, Carmella, Grandma, and other family members were going inside. In the court room, the bailiff called "Christopher Thompson vs. United States." Shadow stepped around by his lawyer as the clerk announced that Shadow was being charged with First Degree Murder in the homicide of Darryl Hopkins. The judge asked the prosecutor what was their position on the bond. Their response was to deny the bond because Shadow was a flight risk as well as a threat to the community. The judge went along with that and Shadow was held without bond. Timing is a motherf . . . !

After the court appearance, Tykisha spoke to the lawyer in private, where he informed her that he really didn't have any information yet, but would contact them as soon as he finds out anything. Tykisha then called Gino on the cell phone, "Hello . . . Yeah what happened?" Gino said immediately into the phone.

"Gino they held him without bond baby." Tykisha relayed first, "and the lawyer said that he really didn't have anything as of yet, but he'd call you as soon as he did though."

"Man . . . man . . . . MAN!!!" Gino shouted. "Where you at Tykisha?"

"I'm on my way outside now. Why?" she asked.

"Nothing . . . nothing . . . just come on baby."

"Okay I'm on my way."

Two days later Gino was watching "Real World" on MTV when the phone rang, "Answer that baby I'm washing my hair!" Tykisha yelled from the bathroom.

"Aiight I got it," Gino got up grabbing the kitchen phone, "Hello."

"You have a collect call from Tide Water Detention Center, if you would like to accept the call press 5 now," the recording stated. Gino immediately pressed 5 knowing it had to be Shadow. "Beeppp . . ."

"Hello Shadow?!" Gino asked excitedly.

"What's up my nigga?" Shadow replied. "Nigga this shit is crazy."

"That's exactly what I've been saying all day my nigga," Gino responded, "I miss you big boy."

"Yeah I miss you too slim, I can't seem to win for losing."

"I know what you mean. Man what those people talking about?"

Shadow paused for a second, "Look Gino you know I've never liked these phones. I need you to come see me."

"I got that, when can I come?"

"My visiting days are Friday, Saturday, and Sunday. Bring Carmella with you too."

"I got that, she been doing alright though. She over at the house now." Gino mentioned.

"Yeah I talked to her a few minutes ago. Aye Gino guess what?"

"What? . . ."

"I called Tricia this morning right, and she had the nerve to tell me she pregnant."

"She what?"

"Yeah . . . ," Shadow repeated. "That's the same thing I said, but I did hit her a few times after we had broken up."

"Oh well champ that might be you then. You know she ain't shit, why was you still fucking her anyway?"

"Gino you know how it is, I still jive got some love for her."

"Well all I can say is you better get a blood test soon as possible." Gino suggested. "Look though, I'll be over there Friday morning aiight?"

"Fo'sho' . . ."

"Keep your head up and let me know if there's anything that you need. I'll have Tykisha send you some stacks today . . . Holla."

"Holla . . ."

All during the week long, Gino and the crew concentrated on finishing up Shadow's CD. Gino was in the studio night and day. Kenny was halfway through with his album and it sounded pretty good as well. Gino was happy that Kenny had gotten out of the game along with him and Shadow. Gino and Tykisha had become super tight again, and she hadn't been back home since they got back together, neither did Gino. Soon they would both go back through the city.

Friday came around and they were now sitting in the visiting hall waiting for Shadow to come out. Tykisha, Gino, and Carmella sat for about 10 minutes before Shadow came out in an orange jumpsuit, smiling as he and Carmella embraced and kissed. "Uh . . . Uh . . ." Gino cleared his throat, "we are back here too you know."

Shadow and Carmella both let each other go laughing, "Come here my nigga," Shadow stated as they embraced. "I ain't forgot you and Tykisha, come here too."

Gino sat down, "Big boy you know I'm fucked up about this whole shit, we got out the streets to avoid this kind of shit from happening."

"Gino don't sweat it, you know how this shit goes. Everything happens for a reason, I'll beat this shit."

"What the lawyer talking about?" Gino asked.

"He said that he'd be through here this week some time and we'll discuss everything then. So as soon as he let me know something, I'll let you know what's up."

"Shadow you know your album is completed right?" Tykisha mentions. "We'll begin pressing your CD's and tapes next week. Hopefully your single will be released soon. I just wish that you were out of here."

"I do too Tykisha, but shit will work out."

"Tykisha has already spoken to a few radio stations that are willing to break your single," Gino says, "so we'll see what happens."

After being at the Tidewater Detention Center for several weeks, Shadow had bumped into a lot of niggas who despised him and some who loved him. Shadow was pretty popular and being as big as a house you couldn't miss him. He drew attention no matter what he was doing. This particular day Shadow got called for a legal visit. He jumped up and got ready. On the way out of the unit, the officer patted him down and he proceeded to his legal visit.

Shadow entered the room, as his lawyer stood. "Hello, how are you doing Mr. Thompson? Have a seat."

"I'm alright Mr. Jordan. How are you doing?" Shadow asked taking a seat.

"I'm doing quite well, thanks for asking." Mr. Jordan opened a folder that was on the table. "Well Mr. Thompson I received the government discovery package. There are some good things and some bad things you need to hear. Which one do you want first?"

"The good news." Shadow quickly chose.

"There are 3 potential witnesses in this crime, unfortunately 2 of them are now deceased. So they will not be able to use their testimony against you, nor any previous statements they may have made. You can't cross examine a dead person." He inhaled/exhaled looking at some document. "Now the bad news is, there is still one potential witness in this case that's alive and willing to testify. Do you know a guy named Michael Downs aka 'Freaky'?"

Shadow nodded, "No sir!!"

"Well he's the last potential witness against you, that's what their basing their whole case on. They don't have any weapons, no physical evidence, only this individual linking you to the crime. Hopefully I'll be able to have my investigator track him down, and find out something that we can use against him on the stand. Well Mr. Thompson, do you have any questions?"

"No sir, Mr. Jordan. I'll try to see if anyone I know is associated with or knows this individual, and I'll let you know something."

"Okay I'll be in contact Mr. Thompson."

"Thank you," Shadow said as they shook hands and Shadow headed back to the block.

While heading back to the block, Shadow couldn't believe that Freaky would go foul like that. Even though I killed his partner I figured he keep that thing in the streets, best man wins. I guess I was wrong, that niggas whole family has been raised in the streets. Oh well, it is what it is. I just got to let Gino know what's up. Either Freaky dies, or I go to jail, simple and plain. Freaky had to die . . .

Entering the unit Shadow noticed the block was in somewhat of an uproar, huddles of dudes were conversing about something, as Shadow walked in he found out just what the uproar was about. "Hey y'all look whose back?" Fred called out as everyone turned to look at Shadow entering the unit. "Shadow my nigga they just played your song on 105.1 in Bad News nigga."

Shadow waved him off, "Fred stop playing like that nigga."

Bob from Bad News then cut in, "No bullshit Shadow, he ain't lying. They were the first to break your single, 'Ride Wit Me'."

"No shit?!" Shadow asked.

"No shit my nigga."

Everybody was coming up giving Fat Boy prop's for his joint. Shadow still couldn't believe it. "Damn that nigga Gino ain't even tell me my shit was going to be on the radio that fast. He told me the album was complete and all, but damn! I got to call this nigga."

Shadow headed straight to the phones calling Gino's house, but didn't get an answer. So he dialed Gino's cell phone, Gino answered. "You have a collect call, if you want to accept the . . ."

"Beeep . . ." Gino pressed 0 before the recording even finished. "What's up my nigga, big rap star nowadays?!!" Gino yelled out.

"Gino what's going on my nigga? I heard they played my song on the radio today. What's up with that?"

"You know what's up, RipRap Entertainment. That's what's up!" Gino said with excitement. "Yeah Fat boy I think we chose the right single."

"I'm saying, how did all this shit go down that fast? I . . . I mean." Shadow was stuttering.

"Shadow just because you're in there we ain't stopping no show. We kept that thing moving along. You are about to become a star boy, believe that. We pressed plenty of CD's and Cassettes of your joint, then Tykisha got at a few radio stations to see if they would give your single a try. After listening, a few gave us the thumbs up, and you see what happened. You're going to be the shit my nigga."

"Man some of my nigga's heard the joint, I missed it cause I was on a legal visit."

"Yeah it's hot big boy. The phones have not stopped ringing since the song broke this evening. Tykisha says she has taken many phone calls concerning your song, album, and your whereabouts. We've got the street teams out pushing . . . pushing your CD's and tapes. Plus we've got a deal with all the local mom and pop record stores to carry your joint as well. Fat boy I just need you to do one thing."

"What's that? Just name it." Shadow immediately asked.

"Tomorrow I want you to call the radio stations who broke your record. Here's the numbers write it down. They're already looking forward to your call. When you call in, just be straight up about being locked up. However, let the people and the fans know you'll be home soon. By you being locked up it will give your album much street credibility, and help you to sell more albums. Let them know that your album can be purchased on our website, www.RipRapEnt.com. Make sure you thank the people of Virginia for supporting you, especially the radio stations for giving you this opportunity."

"No doubt Gino, I got that. Listen I need you to come see me tomorrow."

"No more needs to be said, Tykisha will be there first thing in the morning."

"OK thanks my nigga, she'll have a message for you. Thanks again for handling that business for me slim."

"Fat boy you my man, if you succeed, we all succeed. Nigga we fam, just wait til you get out, then we really going to blow this shit up, you hear me?"

"Fo'sho'"

"Chill out, and Tykisha will see you first thing tomorrow. Aiight?"

"No doubt, talk to you later."

Later that night Shadow was getting out the shower when Babbalou called him, "Fat boy let me holla at you for a minute."

"What's up Bab?" Shadow walked up to Bab's cell.

"Close the door, and listen to this my nigga." Shadow closed the door and tuned into the radio. People all over Bad News were calling in requesting to hear Shadow's song again. Fans were asking when the album was dropping, and where could they purchase a CD.

"Bab I still can't believe this shit," Shadow mentioned, "I haven't heard it myself yet."

"Well you better get up to your cell and get your radio, cause they are going to play it in a minute."

"Aiight, I'll holla back." Shadow grabbed his shit and ran up to his cell so he could catch the song.

Lock down came and they still hadn't played the song yet. So Shadow just put his hand behind his head listening to his Walkman and laid back. Around 10:15 Shadow finally heard the intro to his song come on. Niggas in the unit started knocking on his wall, and yelling for Shadow, but Shadow couldn't hear any of them, cause his headphones were on full blast. The hook came in, and he knew this shit was for real. Sitting there listening, Shadow realized his dream was coming true, and it was for real this time.

CHAPTER 56

The next morning just as Gino said, Tykisha was at the jail at 8:30a.m. During the visit Shadow had explained everything that the lawyer had told him about the nigga Freaky testifying against him. Shadow informed Tykisha where Freaky lived, who he hang around, and even his hanging spots.

Shadow then thanked Tykisha for all the help with the album, and the label. She told him not to worry, she just wanted him out of jail. Shadow thanked her again and just stressed the importance of Gino getting that message. She hugged Shadow and let him know that she would definitely inform Gino about what was going on, and she departed.

Over the next couple of weeks the street team, Gino and Tykisha were pushing Shadow's music, image and the Label extremely hard. The song had picked up a little following all over Virginia. It was that street anthem, and every car from Newport to Hampton was pumping the song in their rides.

After two weeks of independently selling the album, it had sold damn near 8,500 copies just locally. Gino and Tykisha were still out putting flyers and posters up everywhere. They even went out to different clubs and got them to play Shadow's shit.

Then they decided that it was time to try and broaden their scope and see if they could get a buzz in other areas. So she sent the Street Team to New York to push CD's and tapes while they were headed to DC. They hadn't been back home since they got back together, and prior to them going home Tykisha had already made a few contacts in DC to play Shadow's song, and some others to at least listen to it. So off they went headed to the Chocolate City.

Back in DC the city was in the middle of a heat wave. It was 102° the day they arrived. They immediately went to get some hotel rooms at the Ramada Inn downtown. Kenny was happy to be back in the city as well. Tykisha and Gino got their room, while Kenny and Blue got their rooms. Upstairs Gino asked Blue and Kenny to come to their room before they got settled.

"Take a seat," Gino told Blue and Kenny, "Listen now y'all, even though this is homecoming of sorts for me, Tykisha, and Kenny, we're not here for socializing. We've got work to do, we've got to hit every club, radio stations, strip and more, to see if we can get Shadow a buzz in the city. I'm going to pay some kids to put up some flyers and posters around the city. Pushing Shadow is our primary objective. Remember if Shadow blows up, Kenny you and Blue will have an easier time with your albums. Again this is not a social visit." They both nodded their heads as if they understood.

"Anything else Gino?" Kenny asked.

"No y'all can go, I'll see y'all tomorrow."

"Aiight see you."

The next day Gino slept until 12:00pm, then got up and got dressed. He called Kenny and Blue who had already left out. So he and Tykisha decided to head around Stronghold first. Tykisha needed to see her family, she hadn't in months. Pulling up around Stronghold Tykisha saw her brother Stanley who had been locked up for the last five years.

As soon as the car stopped, she jumped out running, "Stanley! Stanley! Stanley!" while jumping into his arms.

"Hey sis! What's up baby girl?" He said in a muffled voice. One thing Gino always liked about their family was that they were all close.

While Tykisha was talking to Stanley, Gino slid over to holla at Tee, Binky, Terrell, and Damien. Gino told them all about Shadow and what they were doing, and everybody copped a couple of CD's just on G. P. "Aye Gino let me holla at you for a minute!" Stanley yelled out.

"Aiight," Gino responded, "Hold up y'all, I'll be right back."

Gino walked up as he and Stanley hugged, "Damn boy you ain't little G no more, huh?" Stanley said.

"I mean you know I couldn't stay small all my life. When did you get out?"

"I've been out for a minute now. I just been laying low, but I hear you done went down Virginia and blew the fuck up my nigga."

"Stanley man," as Gino grabbed Tykisha around the waist, "I'm not even in the streets no more, I'm a legitimate business man now. I started a record label with Tykisha and Shadow as my partners." Tykisha nodded her head as to say he was telling the truth.

"That's good Gino cause this shit is getting grimier by the day. You know they just locked the whole Kennedy Street crew up on conspiracy cases."

"Oh shit! Yeeaaaah? The city hot like that, huh?"

"You better know it, they locking up any and everybody. Tykisha tells me that y'all are back together again too, huh?"

Gino glanced at Tykisha as she blushed. "Yeah you know she's always been my baby, plus we living together down Virginia as well."

"That's good slim," Stanley replied as they shook hands, "Aye sis, let me speak to Gino alone for a second aiight? Go holla at Ma, she's been worrying about you lately anyway, cause you haven't been calling."

"Okay." She answered kissing Gino on the cheek before running off inside the house.

"Yeah . . . what's up Stanley? What's on your mind slim?" Gino asked really interested in finding out what Stanley had to say.

"Yeah Gino, you know when I was locked up down Occaquan, I saw your father, right?" Gino's expression went blank and motionless.

"Oh yeah . . . Well what's up with him?" Gino's voice sounded timid.

"Well he's aiight slim, but he really wants to get in contact with y'all."

"I mean . . . ," Gino was lost for words and got to babbling, "I'm saying, how can I contact him Stanley?"

"If you want I got his information in the house. I gave him my word that I would say something to y'all when I ran across either of you.

And I've got to keep my word. Hold up a minute." Stanley then took off running into the house.

Tykisha had already entered the house to talk to her mom, and now Gino was left outside by himself with thoughts of his father now on his mind. Gino was glad to know that his old man still cared, and thought about them, so Gino figured he'd give it a try and see how the relationship would work out. He knew it would be kind of odd at first, but fuck it . . . Gino understood that he only had one mother and one father, and he wasn't about to let them get away, not like that. Finally, Stanley came back out, handing Gino a piece of paper. "Thanks Stanley I really needed this." Gino replied looking at the piece of paper.

"Yeah Gino he really wants to talk to you, and he cares about you and Kenny."

"Yeah I feel you slim," Gino answered, "I just need to explain a lot of things to him, and I know he has a lot of questions for me as well."

"Hopefully y'all will connect." Stanley gave Gino dap.

"Fo'sho'!"

When Tykisha came back out the house they rolled out cause they had a lot of work to do. First they went to all the record stores all over DC trying to get Shadow's CD in the public eye. Then they went past a few radio stations in the city to see if they could get some play.

Later that night they shot past the Metro Club, and Gino bumped into a few buddies he hadn't seen in a long time. One of his old buddies he bumped into Gino thought could come right in handy, Sean B., Gino knew he would need somebody to knock off Shadow's witness in his case, and Sean was the perfect man. Sean had a rep in the city for killing niggas for recreation or for hire and that's what Gino needed at the time. Sean and Gino stepped to the back of the Metro Club and talked for a minute, then they agreed to go past Eddie Linens on Bladensburg Road to grab a bite to eat.

At Eddie Linens, Gino and Sean got out and took a walk, leaving Tykisha to order the food. "Yeah Sean what you been up to slim?" Gino asked.

Sean stopped at the corner of 17th and Bladensburg Road and leaned up against the stop sign. "Same old shit slim," Sean replied now looking

Gino in the eyes, "you know they just locked up everybody around Montana on a conspiracy case, right?"

"Yeah . . .", Gino paused shaking his head, "well look remember I had mentioned to you a while back about some sweet nigga I knew down Virginia?"

"Yeah . . . yeah, you sure did. Why what's up you ready for me?"

"Fo'Sho' . . . I've got this nigga for you, but the only thing is I'm not sure what kind of dough this punk sitting on. However, I've got $20,000 to make sure that this punk disappear, feel me?" Gino winked at Sean.

A grin instantly came across Sean's face, "Gino you know I'll handle that for you my nigga. I need to get out of town for a minute anyway, hot as it is up here right now. When you talking about handling this?"

"Well I'm heading back down VA probably Sunday. Is that aiight with your schedule?"

"No doubt, that's good timing for real," Sean began rubbing his hands together, "here write my number down so you can call me whenever."

"Come on," Gino started walking, "I've got a pen in my car."

They walked back to Gino's car, exchanged numbers and Sean rolled out. Tykisha stared at Gino as he entered the car, she could sense something was devilish. "Please don't . . . I'm begging you baby. I cannot afford to lose you again."

Gino kissed her on her forehead. "I won't baby, come on let's go."

At the hotel that night, Kenny and Blue informed Gino and Tykisha on all the areas they had covered, that way they wouldn't be covering the same areas twice. Kenny and Blue had basically covered all the N.W. area, while Gino had covered N.E. area. Gino explained to them that they'd be going over S.E., while he wanted them to cover S.W. They agreed, and were on their way out the room when Gino spoke, "Aye Blue come here for a minute." She came over to where Gino and Tykisha were sitting as Kenny began to follow her, "I said Blue, Kenny."

"What's up Gino?" She asked noticing Gino and Tykisha smiling.

"Where did you sleep last night?" Gino asked.

"I . . . I . . . . I, why you asking me that anyway Gino?" She asked defensively.

"Gino man cut that bullshit out," Kenny cut in, "What you trying to put a nigga out there or something?"

"No . . . No . . . no . . ." Gino and Tykisha were cracking up laughing. "Man do y'all thing, like Tupac said, I ain't mad at ya!"

"Shut up Gino." Blue replied as her and Kenny left, knowing their secret was out the bag now.

CHAPTER 57

"Ring.... Ring... Ring...."
"Yeah who this?' Bear answered his phone.

"It's me Bear," Gino spoke.

"Oh what's up Gino? Where you at?"

"Taking care of a little business for Shadow. Listen though I need you to do me a favor?"

"Name it!"

"You know the dude Freaky right?" Gino asked.

"Yeah why?"

"Well you know he's the one ratting on Shadow's case right?"

"Hell no! I ain't know all that!" Bear stressed.

"Anyway, don't tell anyone yet, I don't want the nigga to get spooked and disappear. What I need you to do is find out where he's hanging at, and where he's living. Shadow had given me some information, but when I checked it, things had changed."

"Fo'sho, I'll get right on top of that."

"Remember, don't tell anybody yet. I should be back Sunday night."

"Aiight, I got you. See you then."

"Okay." As they hung up.

After the phone call Gino felt a lot better, because now he felt like his man Shadow would be coming home. Gino went to the bedroom with Tykisha and they crashed for the night.

In the morning, they all went to White Corner for breakfast and then headed out on their promo work. Tykisha and Gino went past a few spots in S.E. where Gino knew a few niggas that would support the album, M.L.K., Barry Farms, Condon Terrace, and that whole area over there. Gino got as many soldiers as he could to cop the album, and from the feedback he was getting the joint was tight. This was all they needed to get a buzz going. Gino and Tykisha felt good about that cause they knew that even though DC listened to rap, DC is and always will be Go-Go music's home.

They headed through Howard University and got some support, then went past the Howard Radio Station, where Tykisha knew the D-Jay. Gino hit him off with a few stacks and he agreed to play Shadow's single. Once leaving there, Gino felt like they had gotten a lot accomplished for the day, and decided that he wanted to stop past his mom's house. He hadn't seen her since the last time he was down in DC.

"Knock . . . knock . . . knock . . . !" Gino knocked on his mom's front door, "Who is it?" Gino's mom yelled from inside the house.

"It's me Ma!" Gino replied, as she opened the door.

"Hi baby," she hugged Gino as he stepped pass her entering the house. "Hello Tykisha, I haven't seen you in a while." Now hugging Tykisha.

"Hi Ms. Debra, how have you been doing?" Tykisha asked taking a seat right beside Gino on the couch.

"I'm doing pretty good baby. I've been blessed." Ms. Debra replied.

"Uh . . . Uh . . . Uh . . ." Gino interrupted, "I mean is anybody going to talk to me?"

Tykisha slapped Gino's shoulder, "Shut up boy."

Ms. Debra smiled at them, "So are you two back together?"

Gino looked at Tykisha, "You wanna tell her, or do you want me to?" Gino asked Tykisha. Tykisha pointed at Gino, "Yeah Ma, we're back together."

"That's good, really . . . really good baby. I'm happy for you two."

"Aye Ma," Gino cut her off, "you know Stanley just came home from Lorton, and he gave me my father's information. He said that Dad wants to talk to me."

"That's good baby. Where's Kenny at?"

"Oh he's riding around with his girlfriend passing out and selling CD's."

"Why is he doing that?" Ms. Debra asked with a confused look on her face.

"Well you will be proud to know that your sons are no longer in the streets. We stopped months ago, and we now have our own Record Label. Our first artist just released his album, and we're down here promoting him."

"Baby, I'm sooo . . . happy to hear that. I'm proud of the both of y'all."

"No Ma, we're proud of you." Gino responded. "You have come a long way. You overcame a drug addiction, and turned your whole life around. You're the best." Gino stated getting up and giving his mom a hug and kiss. Ms. Debra couldn't contain herself and started crying. "Ma stop crying!"

"I'm just so proud of my babies," she sniffled, "Y'all have made something of yourselves without an ounce of my help."

"Ma, I forgot to tell you, Kenny's album will be out by the winter time too."

"Gino please," she smiled, "that boy can't sing a lick."

"No Ms. Debra," Tykisha jumped in, "he raps, and pretty good too."

"Ohhh Lorddd . . . , please help my babies."

"No Ma," Gino reiterated, "that boy can really go."

"Well I'm just glad my babies out them streets, anything but that!!"

"Ma where's your car? I didn't see it outside."

"Baby I had to get rid of that thing, if it wasn't one thing it was another."

"So how are you getting around?"

"I just make do baby, the Lord makes a way."

"Ma . . . Listen, before I leave town again I'll get you something to drive around in. Don't even worry about that."

"Okay baby." She responded.

Gino grabbed Tykisha's hand pulling her up, "Aye Ma we've got to get out of here before it gets too late, but I'll stop by to see you tomorrow before I go."

"I'll be here," she rose to her feet. "I get home between 4:00pm and 4:30pm baby.'

"Alright we'll see you sometime after that." Gino stated as they were all headed towards the door.

"Tell Kenny to come see me too before y'all leave." She mentioned.

"I'll definitely do that Ma." Gino kissed his mom.

"See you later Ms. Debra." Tykisha hugged Gino's mom and they exited.

Leaving Gino's mom's house, they cut through the alley deciding to shoot past Tykisha's house as well. As they pulled up, Gino noticed a big crap game going on. Tee, Stanley, Damien, Kenny, Blue, Cecil and a few others were stooped down shooting craps.

"Tykisha look," Gino pointed to the crap game, "look at Kenny, he got that girl over here shooting dice and everything."

"I see him baby, she probably in love with that boy."

"I guess they having fun so fuck it, come on." Gino said as they got out and walked over towards the crap game.

Gino went straight over to where the crowd was while Tykisha headed inside the house. The game was going back and forth for a minute, then Tee started to win all the money. More and more people started to arrive and before you knew it, damn near 20 soldiers were going at it. All of a sudden guess who pulls up, Mike Mike and Black! Nobody noticed them because Kenny was on the dice and talking cash shit to everyone. "Four one for the poor one!" Kenny shouted shooting at the dice trying to hit his point.

"Come on young nigga!!" Gino screamed. "I'm trying to win some of this money back!"

"Bet $200!!" A familiar voice screamed out.

Gino looked up and saw it was Black. Gino paused for a second, "Damn nigga where you come from?"

"Me and Mike Mike just pulled up." Black replied, "You bettin' or what?"

259

"Hold them dice Kenny I got me one." Gino stated calling Black's bet for the $200. "Do what you do now young nigga." Gino told Kenny as he threw the dice.

Kenny threw the dice, until finally he crapped out.

"I knew I had something sweet!" Black yelled out as he picked up Gino's $200 off the ground.

"Oh yeah?" Gino commented, "you got that. What's up Mike Mike?"

"Man ain't shit, just doing the same old shit as always."

"I hear that," Gino replied giving them some dap.

"Kenny told us y'all done got out the streets and fucking with that music shit now huh?"

"Yeah no doubt, I got tired of dealing with all the bullshit. Plus I ain't trying to go back to jail."

"Fo'sho!" Black responded.

"Where's Speedy at?" Gino asked noticing Speedy was nowhere around.

"Oh mann . . . you ain't heard? Speedy got killed 2 months ago riding his motorcycle."

"Damn!" Gino grabbed his head with two hands. "That's crazy. Well I'm glad to see y'all alright though."

As they were talking, Tykisha came back out the house and headed over towards the crowd, not knowing that Black had pulled up. Black immediately spotted her, "Aye Tykisha!" Black was calling her as he started walking in her direction. "Damn baby where you been? You know a nigga been calling all over town looking for you. What's up like that?"

Tykisha walked up and calmly began, "Look Black first of all who are you talking to like that? I've told you before I'm not your child."

"Yeah okay . . . whatever! You know I miss you baby girl." Black was now taking a cop. "I'm just saying, you been ducking a nigga or something? Cause every time I call your room they say you're not there."

"Well that's because I don't live there anymore."

Black's face frowned up at this point. "What you mean? Where you living at then? And more importantly, why I don't have the new number?"

Tykisha looked at Gino, who was now standing beside her. Gino then looked at Black, "What the fuck is going on, both of y'all looking crazy at each other!!" Black yelled out in an aggressive tone, sensing something wasn't right.

Gino then looked at Black straight in the eyes deciding it was time to get the whole story out in the open. "Black listen Tykisha lives with me now, and we're back together."

"What the fuck you mean she living with you, and y'all back together? Is that true Tykisha?!!" Black asked.

Tykisha slid up and grabbed Gino's hand, "Yes Black that's what it is. I'm back with Gino."

Black's face turned black/blue he was so mad. "I knew you wasn't shit anyway!! You just like all the rest of these freak ass DC bitches!!!" Black shouted.

Instantly at that moment Gino took off on Black, punching him in the jaw knocking him to the ground. Gino was on him like white on rice. Mike Mike and others were trying to break it up, but when Kenny spotted Mike Mike he thought that Mike Mike was trying to aid Black. So he took off on Mike Mike, hitting him in the back of the head.

Total chaos erupted in the alley. "Aye . . . Aye!!! Aye y'all!! Break this shit up!!!" Tee screamed as several people tried to help Tee intervene. Gino had Black on the ground trying to stomp his teeth out of his mouth, until finally Tee was able to pull him off Black. "Come on Gino!! Come on Gino!!!" Tee shouted as he pulled Gino away from the crowd.

"Tee!! Come on let me go!!" Gino barked as he continued to try and get loose. "That nigga need his ass beat, keep doing all this fakin' around here!"

Damien and Binky were able to separate Mike Mike and Kenny. Kenny then ran over tried to steal on Black, which set it off again, shit was going crazy. Finally after several more minutes Tee and them were able to separate everybody and get control on the situation. Gino then called out, "Tykisha! Blue! Come on let's get out of here." They all rushed over to the cars, entered and jetted.

The whole ride back to the hotel was silent, Tykisha felt bad because she felt like it was all her fault that the fight had occurred. Gino was upset about a couple of things, but as always he bottled it up inside. Arriving at the hotel Gino entered the room and headed straight for the shower.

Exiting the shower Gino seemed to have calmed down a bit. He entered the bedroom, and laid down beside Tykisha, "Hey baby," Gino put his arm around Tykisha's neck, "I'm sorry about that whole situation back at the house. I should've handled that a little better than that, but I feel like he went a little too far. I'm not letting anyone disrespect you, it just ain't happening."

"Gino, I understand. I just feel bad because I caused all this mess."

"Look don't feel like that. You know and I know, that . . . that was destined to happen anyway. I'm just mad because I'm trying so hard to get away from this type of shit, but I just keep getting caught up."

Tykisha sat up, now facing Gino. "Gino I don't want you to get in no more trouble, especially behind me . . ."

Gino cut her off, "Tykisha you're my girl and I'll defend you until the end. That's just who I am. I just can't allow that, you hear me?!" Gino grabbed her face with both hands as he passionately kissed her. "Come on baby let's get some rest, we have a long day ahead of us tomorrow."

Back around the way Black and Mike Mike had finally made it home and had decided that the next time they saw Gino or Kenny it was on, and the outcome would definitely be different.

CHAPTER 58

The next morning Gino got up early because he knew that they would be heading back to Virginia, and he had to purchase his mother a car before the left town. So he told Tykisha to stay at the hotel and pack everything, so as soon as he got back they could leave. Gino left heading down to Kenny's room, knocking on the door. "Bang . . . bang . . . bang . . ." Kenny opened the door, "What's up Gino?" Kenny asked as he closed the door behind Gino.

"Come on Kenny get dressed we've got to go get Ma a car today. I forgot to tell you last night, that her car broke down."

"Aiight, hold on champ." Kenny said as he began walking back towards the bathroom. "Aye Gino, I've been trying to buy Ma a car for the longest, but she wouldn't accept it, talking about devil's money . . . you know!"

"Mann . . . , you know how mom is, you got to use diplomacy."

"Yeah, I guess you right, we'll see."

All of a sudden the bathroom door swings open, and wouldn't you know it, Blue comes out walking. "Aye Kenny baby can you come dry my back please?" Blue was sounding all sweet until she looked up and spotted Gino standing in the hallway with Kenny.

Gino glanced at Blue's half naked body, and that's when she took off. "Oh . . . . Shit!!!!" She yelled as she tried to cover up and get back inside the bathroom.

Gino laughed a tad bit to himself, "Come on back out here girl. I don't care nothing about y'all messing around. You think I just knew about y'all?? Picture that!"

Seconds later the bathroom door reopened and Blue came out somewhat looking embarrassed and shy this time. "Shut up Gino, I wasn't running cause you know we mess around. I was running cause some fool forgot to tell me we had company."

Kenny quickly spoke up, "Baby I didn't know you were coming out the shower, I'm sorry. Look though, me and Gino about to go take care of some things. But while I'm gone pack our stuff cause soon as we get back, we're leaving alright?"

"Okay Kenny, give me a kiss." She replied as Kenny kissed her before they left.

They went and purchased their mom a Taurus Wagon, and dropped it off to her. Mom was happy and glad to see her babies. They all talked and discussed Gino and Kenny moving back to the city in a few months. While at mom's Gino paged Sean, who called straight back. "Hello." Gino answered the phone.

"What's up Gino? I've been waiting for you to call."

"Yeah I had to take care of a few things, but that's done now." Gino replied. "Look meet me in front of McKinley Tech in 20 minutes."

"I'll be there." Sean responded hanging up the phone.

They talked to mom a little while longer, then they had to leave. Pulling up in front of McKinley, Gino spotted Sean sitting in an Acura NSX all white. Gino pulled up beside Sean, waving his hand for Sean to follow as they headed back to the hotel picking up Tykisha and Blue to head back to Bad News.

Riding back to Bad News, Gino realized he hadn't spoken to Shadow all weekend long, but he had hoped that everything was alright, cause Gino was on his way back with the savior for Shadow's case. The exterminator who gets rid of rats, Sean! Somebody Gino knew would get the job done, and the best part was that he wouldn't have to get his hands dirty.

In Bad News they all headed straight to Gino and Tykisha's house. Upon arriving they noticed the Street Team Vans parked out front of Shadow's house, so that meant they were all back as well. Entering the house they all dropped their bags, "Kenny show Sean where the guest room is," Gino instructed Kenny, "so he can get unpacked."

"Aiight!" Grabbing their bags heading up the steps.

Later after unpacking and getting settled Sean came back downstairs entering the living room where Gino was watching reruns of the Jamie Foxx Show. "Damn Gino, nigga you living it up down here huh?" Sean asked taking a seat in the recliner next to Gino.

"You want something to drink?" Gino asked.

"Noo . . . I'm cool." Sean replied.

"Yeah Sean, I told you it's sweet down here. We tore these niggas off down here for a good minute, stacked up our cake, then just decided it was time to get out. Shit started to get too hot down here. You feel me?"

Sean nodded his head, "No doubt."

"As a matter of fact Sean, the nigga that I want you to get at, he's telling on my partner that's locked up now."

"Oh yeah?" Sean said sarcastically.

"Yeah we smashed one of his men and I guess to get some get back, he doing it like the rest of these bitch niggas do, turn to the law!!"

"Oh yeah, I'll take special care with him." Sean replied taking in all that Gino was saying.

"Sean to be honest, I don't care what you do with that hot ass nigga, Just as long as he doesn't come to court on my man."

"Gino my nigga, you ain't got to worry about that. He's dead as we speak!" As they continued to converse late into the night.

In the morning, Gino and Tykisha took the bags of money they had accumulated in DC downstairs and put it in the safe. Tykisha checked all the messages they had, and there were many. Mostly in support or questions about Shadows album and whereabouts. When she checked the web emails, there were over 300 purchase orders for the album that had come across within the last 48-hours. That's when they knew that we had something special.

Later that morning Sean finally woke up and came downstairs, and Gino showed Sean how they had transformed the basement into the business office for RipRap Entertainment. Gino then informed Sean to hold on while he paged Teddy Bear to see if he had the information that Gino needed on the nigga Freaky.

About 10 minutes later Bear called back, "What's up Gino? When did you get back?" Bear asked.

"We got back last night, but I was too tired to call you. I just waited until the morning to check and see what you had for me. Did you find out any information that I asked you about?"

"Yeah I found out where the nigga Freaky living at, and where he's hanging out at now. I can tell he ain't got a clue yet, cause I saw him at the Virginia Tech game Saturday."

"That's good, that means he should be easier to get at, give me the address."

"1424 Fuller Drive, Petersburg, VA."

"I got that," Gino replied, "Have you talked to Shadow?"

"Yeah, he waiting for you to come back so he can holla at you about something."

"Aiight Bear, I'll holla at you later."

Now off the phone, Gino relayed to Sean the information. Gino then asked Sean to hold off a minute and not to move yet. Sean didn't seem to understand why, but agreed. They then slid over to the studio to see what was poppin', and to see what happened while the street team was up New York.

Entering the studio, Gino found Kenny working on some songs of course with Blue right by his side. Gino spotted Melvin, who was the head P. R. man. Melvin saw Gino and waved him over. "Come on Sean," Gino said as they walked over into Melvin's office. "What's up Melvin?" Gino asked closing the door behind them. "How did shit go up New York?"

"Gino, shit was bananas up there. The buzz we got was unbelievable. We even got the broad Wendy Wiles, who is the top D-Jay on the evening show to break the single for us. The phone lines lit up soon as the song ended, people wanting to know who this dude was, and where they could purchase the album. We sold over 4,000 copies in the streets of New York alone. If we would have had more copies, we could have sold more, but the reception was crazy."

"Yeah!!" Gino shouted in excitement. "That's what I'm talking about Mel. We sold about 2,500 copies in DC and the buzz was great down there too. Where's the money from the sales?"

"Right here." Melvin pulled a tote bag from under his desk handing it to Gino.

"Melvin let me ask you another question. Who's album do you think would be best to get out next? Who's really ready?"

"Gino from what I've heard Blue's album is not really where I would like for it to be just yet, but Kenny lacks a complete album. However, Kenny does have the most completed songs and he has that hot single I believe with Blue."

"Okay Melvin, tell everybody I want them to put all their concentration and efforts into Kenny's album and making it the best that they can."

"I got that," Melvin noted, "anything else?"

"No, not right now. I've got something that I've got to take care of that's important. I'll see you later."

"Fo'sho." Gino and Sean departed, dashing up the steps.

At the office later that night Gino and Tykisha had calculated how many units of Shadow's album had sold so far. They found out that they had moved damn near 20,000 copies in less than 2 ½ months without any real help from distribution. So they decided that they would continue to push the album until things slowed down. Hopefully by that time, Kenny's album would be ready and could ride off the success of Shadow's album. Things were working out better than they had planned.

CHAPTER 59

The following weeks, things were the same, and Shadow's trial date had been set. It was only 3 weeks away. Gino had deliberately not let Sean kill Freaky off the break, cause he wanted Freaky to feel comfortable and think that nobody knew he was telling. That way he would be easier to get at. Gino had already informed Shadow not to worry, everything was being taken care of, and all he had to do was just lay back and be patient.

One day Gino and Sean were riding around chilling when Gino received a call from Tykisha, "Hello what's up baby?" Gino answered.

"Gino! Gino!" she paused, ". . . please come home right now!"

"What's wrong baby?!" Gino's voice rose.

"Just get here fast!" Tykisha commanded.

"Okay I'm on my way." Hanging up the phone Gino whipped the car around heading back towards the house.

Arriving at the house Gino noticed there weren't any police cars so he figured, fuck it . . . it couldn't be but so bad. They jumped out the car and rushed into the house. "Tykisha! Tykisha! Where you at?!" Gino yelled as he entered the house.

"I'm in the basement baby!" she replied.

Gino and Sean rushed down the steps, when they noticed two white men in business suits standing outside their business office in the basement. Tykisha walked up, "Excuse me Mr. Jackson and Mr. Smith, I need to speak with my boss for a second." Tykisha stated to the two men standing in the doorway. Tykisha then grabbed Gino's hand and led him into their office.

Entering the office Tykisha closed the door, "Tykisha what's up? Who the hell are those people out there?"

"Calm down baby, those two guys are from D-Jam Records and they are here to offer us a deal to join their label. They've heard all about Shadow's album, and they are willing to re-release his album with a big promotional push behind him this time. Plus they're offering us a three album deal worth about 2 million dollars up front and loads of incentives on the back end."

Gino was rubbing his head, "What . . . did you . . . . just say?" Gino was stuttering.

"2 million dollars baby." She repeated.

"Are you serious???!!"

"Yes baby, these people are for real!"

"Listen call them in here, let them know that we're extremely interested. However, we would like to have our lawyers look over the contracts and then we'll contact them as soon as the lawyers tell us everything is straight."

Tykisha went and did what Gino had told her to, and they agreed to the terms. When Tykisha returned to the office with the contracts, they couldn't believe it. They were really going to make big time and it was for real. Gino decided that he didn't want to tell anyone until after the deal was signed and official, so he made Tykisha agree to keep things quiet.

A few days later, Gino felt like it was time to get the nigga Freaky handled, so he called Sean down in the basement and explained everything to him. Then he reached behind his desk and pulled out a knap sack handing it to Sean. Inside was the $20,000 he had promised Sean to handle Freaky, and making sure Freaky never showed his face at that court house. Sean took the money, they shook hands and Gino mentioned to Sean that they would hook back up at a later date cause Gino was moving back to the city shortly anyway. They hugged, shook hands, then Sean took off.

The next couple of days Gino and Tykisha worked so hard to make sure that the contracts from D-Jam Records were proper. They didn't want to lose their creative control, but needed that major label push behind their artist, if they really wanted to make it. Gino never heard anything from Sean since the night he left, and when he asked Bear about what happened, Bear stated that after he showed Sean where Freaky lived, Sean instructed Bear to leave and that he'd handle the rest on his own. So Gino really didn't know what had happened, or if anything had occurred. Gino didn't want to call Sean as if he doubted his work, so he just let it be until Shadow's court date to see what would happen.

Shadow's court date was now two days away, Gino was praying for his man to come home. They had stopped communicating as much because of fear that the phones were being monitored. Plus Shadow knew Gino had his back until the end. Shadow's album continued to sell pretty good, RipRap Entertainment had moved over 25,000 units and were receiving calls asking for Shadow to be on remixes and everything. Gino and the crew had a lot invested in him coming home in 2 days. Gino remembered Shadow had done it big for him when he had got released, and now Gino wanted to return the favor. Gino and Tykisha later arranged a meeting with D-Jam Records' Executives and signed the deal, two million dollars up front, creative control, and 3 albums. The money was to be forwarded into an account within 24-hours. When they left the D-Jam offices, they had smiles all over their faces because their dreams finally were coming true. All the hard work had finally paid off.

CHAPTER 60

On the way home, Gino was thinking about the surprise he had waiting for Tykisha when she entered the house. As they entered the house, Gino stopped at the door grabbing Tykisha's arm, "What? What baby?" Tykisha asked noticing a funny look on Gino's face.

"Look I want you to go upstairs to the bedroom." Gino replied now smiling.

"Why, is something wrong baby?"

"No . . . No . . . No . . . Just do this for me."

"Okay." She responded placing her brief case on the floor at the bottom of the stair case, and heading up the steps. She peeked back at Gino when she reached the top step.

"Go ahead girl, stop being a scaredy cat." Gino laughed.

She walked to the bedroom door and opened it, and a huge smile just came across her face as she saw rose pedals all over the floor leading a trail to the bed. As she followed the trail inhaling the sweet smell of the roses, she noticed on the bed there was a small box on the bed surrounded by a gang of white roses. She walked over to the bed and just before picking up the box, she looked back at the doorway, noticing Gino standing there nodding his head smiling. Tykisha picked up the box, and her eyes immediately began to get watery. She slowly cracked the box open, now shaking a tad bit from being nervous. Opening the box she noticed it was an engagement ring, she stared at it for a minute, shaking continuously. When she turned to look back at Gino, he was right behind her on one knee. He reached out for her hand, which she gladly placed into his palms, Gino began by saying, "Tykisha you know I love you more than anything in the world. You've always been the love of my life, now I want you to be my wife. Will you marry me?"

Tykisha looked Gino straight in the eyes crying, "Yes baby . . . Yes baby." She replied as Gino removed the ring from the box and slid the ring onto her finger. Rising to his feet Gino took both his hands, placing them on Tykisha's face using his thumbs to remove the tears from her eyes. "I love you girl . . ."

"I love you too." She responded as Gino leaned in kissing her softly and passionately. After finally breaking their embrace Tykisha held her hand up looking at the rock she now had on her finger, "Baby this ring is so beautiful." She continued to marvel at it.

"It ain't nothing, when it pertains to my baby." Gino replied knowing he had paid a whole lot of money for that 3ct. rock she was now wearing. They kissed again and spent the rest of the night in each other's arms.

The next day, Gino told Tykisha to make some arrangements to have an album release party for Kenny's album, and the re-release of Shadow's album 'True Soldier'. She suggested the Dream Club in DC and Gino agreed. Gino also informed Tykisha to make sure that the D-Jam Executives were there, and as many radio personality hosts and music industry people as she could get. They scheduled the date to be two weeks away. That would give them time enough to tweak Kenny's album, and have it completed. Plus Shadow can add a few new tracks to his album before the re-release under D-Jam Records. Tykisha understood everything and went to work immediately.

Gino stayed in the studio with Kenny to make sure that he continued working hard on his album. Gino reiterated how important it was for Kenny's album to be finished and tightened up within the next week and a half. Gino didn't want to tell any of them about the deal yet or the party. Kenny had reassured Gino that he would be finished in the next couple of days. Gino also didn't inform anyone that while he was down DC visiting his mom, that he had given her some money to obtain two new houses for him and Shadow. He didn't want anyone to know, so it would be a surprise to everyone. When Gino had called his mom the day before, she informed him that she had the keys to the new houses already, and the deal was final.

That evening when Tykisha arrived back at home, Gino was waiting. She let him know that she was not able to get the Dream Club because of a prior engagement, but she did get Club Thatz's. So at least that part was taken care of, and now they had a big day ahead of them, Shadow's trial was scheduled to start the next day. So they went to bed early knowing they would be up at sunrise.

CHAPTER 61

"Urg . . . Urg . . . Urg . . . Urg . . ." The alarm clock went off at 6:00a.m. Gino rolled over stopping the clock from making that annoying sound. "Damn I hate this clock," Gino said rising up out the bed, noticing that Tykisha was nowhere in sight. "Tykisha . . . Tykisha." Gino called out.

"Yes baby," she replied. "I'm in the bathroom washing my face." She hated lying to Gino cause she was in the bathroom holding her stomach from some kind of stomach pain she was having. She had been throwing up for two days, and decided she had to go get checked out.

She finally got herself together and came out the bathroom, "Are you alright baby?" Gino asked looking at her concerned.

"Yes baby" She answered. "You better come on you know we got to get out of here."

"Alright." Gino responded rushing pass heading to the bathroom to take his shower.

Down at the court building, Gino was somewhat nervous but he was hiding it real good. You know it was a macho thing. Walking down the corridor to the court room Gino spotted Tricia and Marquita standing against the wall, about 10 feet from Teddy Bear, Grandma and the rest of the family. "Tykisha you see that?" Gino mentioned.

"Huh . . . It don't surprise me." Tykisha replied grabbing Gino's left hand, exposing her rock that Gino had just given her.

"Just ignore her baby, we're here for Shadow today."

"You right." As they proceeded on over to the family.

Inside the court room, Shadow's case was called and he was brought out. "Big boy look good", Gino thought to himself. "It looked like he had trimmed down a bit, probably working them weights and burpies all day."

Taking his seat Shadow glanced back at Gino before sitting. Gino winked his eye, and Shadow winked back taking his seat beside his lawyer. The judge then entered and sat on the bench, "Are you ready to proceed?" The judge asked the prosecutor.

The prosecutor stood, "Judge Brown I'm having problems locating my star witness. We have been attempting to serve a subpoena for weeks now, but obviously he avoiding us."

The Judge lowered his glasses looking sternly at the prosecutor, "Is your client reluctant to testify?"

"I'm not sure Your Honor. He has expressed reservation previously about testifying against Mr. Thompson for fear of retaliation."

"I tell you what I'm going to do," the Judge placed his glasses back on, "I'm going to post pone this trial date until the 14th by that time you should've been able to find your witness. However, since your client has expressed reluctance to testify in this matter, and based on the seriousness and danger involved, I'm going to issue a bench warrant also."

"Thank you Your Honor." The prosecutor replied closing his folder.

Then Shadow's lawyer began to argue vigorously for a mistrial, but was denied. Gino and everybody was disappointed, and Shadow had to head back over to the Detention Center. Gino was crushed, he just knew his man was getting out, but at least he knew Sean handled his business. No witness, No case!!

Over the next week or so, Gino concentrated on putting together his surprise for Shadow. Gino and Tykisha took a trip down to DC, where Tykisha could finish taking care of the party arrangements. All the while, Gino and his mom went to take a look at the houses she had purchased for him. They went to look at Shadow's house first, which sat on 16th Street, N.W. right down the street from the Carter Barron. Four bedrooms, 2 bathrooms, a swimming pool, Jacuzzi, a two car garage, a backyard that looked like it was half a football field. Gino figured since he had a garage he had to put something in it. So he rode out to the Mercedes Dealer and purchased a brand new Black on Black, 600 Mercedes Benz. Gino felt like he owed Shadow this, after all the shit Fat boy done for him when he came home. It was Gino's turn to return the favor. Gino took the Benz and parked it in Shadow's garage. That way it would be a double surprise.

After taking care of that, mom showed Gino where his new house was, which was only about 4 blocks from Shadow's on 16th Street, N.W., 3 bedrooms, 2 bathrooms, a den, 2 walk-in closets, a basketball court, and a garage. Gino really liked it and thanked his mom for all her help. Closing up Gino decided that they needed to head back cause Tykisha should be finished her running around. While heading back to the house, Gino called Tykisha on her cell phone. "Zzzzzz . . . . Zzzzzzz" Tykisha's phone vibrated as she answered. "Hello."

"Hey baby, where you at?" Gino asked.

"I'm on the way back to the house. Are you there?"

"No! But I'll be there in a minute. Why you sound like that, are you okay?"

"Yes," she replied, "I'm just tired baby, but I wanted to get everything taken care of for the party. It's going to be huge baby. I also got some posters and stuff to advertise the party. Tee said he will have somebody put them up for me soon as I drop them off."

"Okay sweetie, but you need some rest. So meet me at mom's house now. We're going home so you can get you some rest, before you get burned out."

"I'm fine baby." Tyksiha repeated.

"No you're not, meet me at the house. I'll be there in 10 minutes."

"Okay." She responded hanging up the phone.

Fifteen minutes later, Tykisha arrived at the house, and Gino saw that Tykisha looked just as he thought, burnt out. So he put her in the car and headed back to Virginia, after thanking mom for everything again.

The next day at the studio, Gino walked in and everybody was sitting around listening to tracks off of Kenny's album. Gino took a seat next to Kenny, snapping his fingers to the song that was playing. When the track ended clapping erupted, "Yeah! Yeah!" People screamed.

"Aye Boss," Melvin called out, as the clapping continued.

"What's up Mel?" Gino replied smiling at everybody's excitement.

"That's it, Kenny's album is finished."

Gino nodded his head smiling, "Completed huh?" now looking at Kenny.

"Finished . . . finished! Yeah you heard that!" Kenny snapped as they gave each other dap.

"Hold up y'all," Gino motioned for Travis to turn the music down, "Listen, first off I want to thank you all for all your hard work, but I have a major announcement that I will be announcing next week on the 15th. So next week everybody clear your calendars for a couple of days, cause we'll be taking a trip to DC. Keep working hard, and hopefully Kenny your hard work will pay off for us and you."

"Thank you Bro'! I hope so too." Kenny stated, as Gino walked out. Puzzled looks were on everyone's faces, wondering what the announcement was all about.

While Gino was in the studio, Tykisha snuck to the doctor's office to get checked out without Gino knowing. Upon arriving she was nervous because she had been sick for the last couple of weeks, throwing up, and nauseated. Soon as she got in the office the doctors ran a few tests and took some blood work to see if they could find out what the problem was. The doctor then informed Tykisha that when the results come back, he would call immediately. Tykisha left feeling a lot better knowing that she had gotten checked out.

CHAPTER 62

It was two days now before Shadow's trial, Gino and Tykisha were at home watching TV conversing. "Baby I can't understand why these people go on these talk shows and embarrass themselves like this." Gino stated.

"Gino, you took the words right out of my mouth." She responded. "Why would I go on Maury Povich and take a lie detector's test knowing that I'm lying and cheating on my husband."

"Yeah . . . cause if you ever cheat on me, I'm killing you off the break, I'm telling you." As they both started laughing. "Tykisha when do you want to get married baby?"

Tykisha got up under Gino's arm, "Gino I'm ready to get married as soon as possible. You're my heart and my world."

"I tell you what then," Gino lifted her chin up with his finger gazing into her eyes. "I can't get married without my man Shadow being my best man, but soon as he gets out, we'll get married. Alright?"

"You promise?"

"I promise baby." As Tykisha's cell phone went off.

"Bleep . . . . Bleep" Tykisha rose up grabbing it off the couch walking into the kitchen to get away from the noise. "Hello." She answered.

"Good morning, may I speak to Ms. Tykisha McCray?" A voice replied.

"This is she."

"Oh I'm sorry, this is Dr. Brown," he began, "I'm sorry if I interrupted you."

"No no Doctor, I was just messing around with my boyfriend."

Gino then yelled out, "Tykisha! Tykisha!"

"Excuse me one second Dr. Brown," Tykisha replied, "Yes baby." Answering Gino.

"I'm going to make a run right fast I'll be right back."

"Okay, I'll be here. Be careful."

"I will." As she heard the door close behind Gino.

"Excuse me Dr. Brown." She apologized.

"No problem. Well I have some good news for you Ms. McCray," the doctor stated pausing a bit, "we've found out why you're having morning sickness, nausea, and throwing up."

"Thank you Lord." Tykisha mumbled.

"Well Ms. McCray it gives me the great pleasure to let you know that you're pregnant." Total silence entered the phone for a few seconds. "Ms. McCray you still there?"

"Yes . . . yes . . ." Tykisha responded in shock, "Dr. Brown, are you sure?"

"Sure as I'll ever be, your results say that you're about 6 weeks now. Have you had a period this month?"

"No sir, but my periods are irregular so that didn't stand out."

"Well Ms. McCray congratulations, and you need to make an appointment with my office as soon as possible so I can check you out. Okay?"

"Yes, I'll get on top of that, and thank you again Dr. Brown."

"No problem, see you soon." Click . . .

Tykisha was stunned, and immediately started thinking all types of crazy stuff. She sat on the couch rubbing her stomach, "Damn I wonder how Gino feels about having kids. I don't even know if he wants kids. What am I going to do about school? Will he still want to get married? Maybe this will be my special present to Gino. I love him so much, and I know I'll love our baby."

All the while, Gino was headed over to Shadow's lawyer's office. Stepping into the office the Secretary ushered Gino straight in, cause Mr. Jordan had been waiting for him. "Thank you Sarah," Mr. Jordan replied as she closed the door behind herself. "Hello Mr. Ward, have a seat." Gino sat down in the big leather swivel chair across from Mr. Jordan.

"Thanks Mr. Jordan."

"Well Mr. Ward I have some wonderful news for you." He paused rubbishing through some papers. "I had a meeting with the D.A. yesterday and he informed me that the charges against Mr. Thompson will be dropped."

Gino fake looked surprised, "What? . . . Are you sure?"

"Sure as I can be, they have been unable to find their witness, and without the witness, there's no case. Seems pretty simple doesn't it." Mr. Jordan commented sarcastically as if he knew what had happened to the witness.

"Mr. Jordan, I'm just glad that my man is getting out. That's all that matters to me. I'll have something extra for you after court too. We appreciate all your help and assistance Mr. Jordan."

"You're more than welcome Mr. Ward. I'll see you in court then." Mr. Jordan said standing up reaching his hand out to shake Gino's hand.

"I'll be there." Gino responded as he exited Mr. Jordan's office.

Leaving Mr. Jordan's office, Gino was so excited. Things were really starting to come together. At that moment Gino decided that he was going to tell the family about the party for Shadow and Label in DC. So Gino shot over to Grandma's house and called everybody over. After they all arrived, Gino informed them about the party and the signing to D-Jam Records, and wanted them all to be there. Gino told all of them to be ready the next day cause he would make arrangements to have all of them transported to DC without Shadow knowing. They were all shocked and happy for them, and agreed to be ready to leave the next day.

Next Gino had to do something he didn't want to, but what he felt was the right thing to do. He went to see Tricia, and even thought this wasn't one of Gino's favorite people, he understood she could possibly be having Shadow's child. As he pulled up at her apartment, he was still hoping he was doing the right thing. "Fuck it!" He hissed as he hopped out his truck, walking towards her apartment building.

"Knock . . . knock . . . knock" Gino tapped the door and nothing happened for few seconds. Then suddenly she responded, "Who is it?"

The door slowly crept open, and immediately Tricia's stomach caught Gino's attention. It was sticking out showing every bit of her being 7 months pregnant. "Damn . . ." Tricia said, "What did I do to deserve this visit from you?" Tricia said in a sarcastic tone.

"Tricia look, I'm not here to go through no drama shit with you. Just listen to me for a minute. You know that Shadow's supposed to get out tomorrow right?"

"No I didn't know that, all I heard was that he was supposed to start trial tomorrow."

"Well look, he's getting released tomorrow, and I'm throwing him a party in DC to celebrate our signing to D-Jam Records. So I came by to invite you, and see if you would like to come."

Tricia stood there for a second, I guess figuring how she wanted to respond. "Gino I know that you don't like me, which is cool with me, and I know you think that I fucked Stevie, but I didn't. I love Shadow and this is his baby. Believe me when the baby is born, I won't have a problem giving him a blood test just to prove my point. But to answer your question, yes I would love to come to the party."

Gino half way jive believed her, "Okay look, be over at Grandma's house tomorrow at 10:00a.m., I'll pick y'all up over there."

"Alright, I'll be there, thank you Gino." She pleasantly replied.

"No don't thank me, thank Shadow, and just to let you know so we won't have to ever have this conversation again, I know you fucked Stevie, because Marquita told me the day after V-Rock's funeral."

Tricia's whole facial expression changed, as Gino walked away. Gino laughed to himself heading to the car, knowing he had just lied to see her expression. He just wanted to see how she responded and from her body language, he felt like she told on herself.

CHAPTER 63

"Gino everybody downstairs waiting on you baby." Tykisha mentioned to Gino as he was finishing up a conversation on his cell phone.

Gino spoke into the phone, "Yeah okay, I'll be pass there this evening. Thank you." As he hung up the phone. "Tykisha what's up baby?" Gino walked up hugging her.

"Nothing sweetie! I was just telling you that everybody's waiting on you downstairs. Who was that on the phone?"

"Nobody important," he replied, "Come on let's get down there to this meeting."

Downstairs in the office, Gino called a meeting with all the members involved with RipRap Entertainment. Finally entering the office with Tykisha leading the way, Gino was smiling from ear to ear. "What's up y'all?" Gino commented as he headed to his seat.

"What's up Gino?" Kenny and Marcus spoke.

"Heyy Gino." Blue and Mesisha spoke

Melvin just nodded his head, and everybody else just waved. Gino took his seat at the head of the table with Tykisha by his side. "Good afternoon everybody," Gino began, "I'm glad that everybody was able to make it, I have an announcement that's about to blow RipRap Entertainment straight to the top." Everybody started to look around at each other. "A few days ago Tykisha secured RipRap Entertainment a deal with D-Jam Records. The deal is worth a lot of money, as a matter of fact this morning I received a call from the bank alerting to me that 2 million dollars had been forwarded to our account, from D-Jam Records."

"Gino did you say 2 million dollars?!!!" Kenny shouted.

"Yes I did, 2 million dollars." As everybody started giving each other high fives. "Look we've got a 3 album deal. They want to re-release Shadow's album with big promotional push. Then Kenny's album will be next with Blue's album soon after. To show our appreciation Tykisha has some bonus checks for all of you."

"Yes siree buddy!!" Melvin yelled out, while rubbing his hands together.

"Lord have Mercyyy!" Blue commented.

"Hold up for a minute y'all," Gino commented, "there's more, today we all will be heading to DC for an album release party for Shadow's re-release. However, Kenny we will have you perform your first single at the party also. Everybody and anybody in the music industry will be there, so it's our time to shine. So everybody be ready to leave in 2-hours, we'll leave from here. See y'all in 2-hours." Gino got up and he and Tykisha rolled out.

When Gino left the studio he was so happy, because he knew this was his meal ticket to leave the streets forever. He couldn't wait to tell Shadow about everything. Gino jetted over to Grandma's house to pick her and family up. When they got there it looked like a family reunion with all the cars lining the street in front of Grandma's house. They all followed Gino back to his house where they waited until the rest of the people going arrived. Not much longer after that, everybody was back and they headed to DC.

They all ended up in DC by 4:30 that evening. Gino first took them to get hotel rooms and get settled. After getting everybody settled Gino alerted Tykisha that he needed her to take a ride with him, as they both jumped in Gino's Escalade and he pulled off.

Fifteen minutes later, Tykisha was wondering where they were going, Gino had not mentioned anything as of yet. Soon Gino pulled up in front of this residence on 16th Street and parked. Gino got out, and waved his hand for Tykisha to follow. She exited the truck and closed her door, "Gino where are we going?" she asked as Gino grabbed her hand.

"Shhhh . . ." Gino pleaded, walking up towards the front door. Gino then pulled the keys out of his pocket and stuck it in the door.

"Baby who . . .", she replied before Gino cut her off.

"Tyksiha baby . . ." he began to speak as they entered the house. "This is our new house baby."

Tykisha turned to look at Gino, placing both her hands over her mouth. "Are you for real Gino?" Gino just smiled and nodded his head. "Oh my Godd . . . baby." She responded hugging Gino.

"Come on baby, let me give you a tour." Grabbing her hand leading the way, he showed her all throughout the house. Finally Tykisha felt like it was time to surprise Gino. Entering one of the bedrooms that Gino had tabbed as a guest room, Tykisha jumped in, "Yeah baby, I really like this room right here." Tykisha replied. "It's big enough to fit all that baby stuff."

Gino's face squelched up, as he turned to face her. "What baby stuff? Where did that come from?"

"Baby I think that this will be a cute baby's room. What you think?"

I mean . . . , you never mentioned anything about you wanting a baby."

"Gino so what are you saying, that you don't want kids?"

"No . . . no . . . no . . ." Gino explained, "I love kids, you just never mentioned it to me, that's all."

"So are you saying that you do want kids?"

"What I'm saying is, I want whatever you want. That's what I'm saying."

"Well Gino you need to get ready," she started rubbing her stomach. "Cause we're about to have a baby. I'm pregnant!"

Gino was shocked, "You're what??!!!"

"Yes baby . . . Yes I'm pregnant. I found out last week when I went to get checked out."

"Are you serious Tykisha?"

"Yes baby." She grabbed Gino's hand placing it on her stomach. "We're having a baby."

"Yes! Yes! Yes!" Gino shouted. "Tykisha I love you so much baby. We really about to be a family huh?" Gino hugged Tykisha, whispering into her ear, "you know my mom is going to be really excited about this."

"Mine too," Tykisha looked at him, "but I think I'm more excited than both of them put together."

"Give me a kiss." Gino and Tykisha locked hands and gently kissed each other. "Here baby." Gino handed Tykisha her keys to the house. "Come on I need to show you something else." As they locked up the house and left.

Five minutes later Gino came to a halt in front of another residence, "What you think about that house right there?" Gino asked pointing to the house slightly to the left.

"It's beautiful baby," glancing back at Gino. "No . . . that's not ours, I bought that for Shadow."

"Ohhh . . . weee . . . baby," she covered her mouth, "he's going to love it."

"Yeah it has everything too, I just wanted to do something big for him. When I came home he looked out for me big time."

"He'll love it baby."

"That's not it, though." Gino pulled out the remote control to the garage. "Watch this," as Gino pushed the button and the garage door rose up exposing the brand new 600 Benz parked.

"Ohhh . . . baby you got that for him? Shadow will love that."

"Yeah I owe him that Tykisha," Gino stated as he laid back in his seat. "Tykisha I love that dude. He's a real nigga, and I'd do anything for him."

"I know baby," she rubbed his face. "He feels the same way about you."

"I know! Look though come on I've got to get back down Virginia so I can pick him up from court tomorrow morning. But I need you to stay here and keep an eye out on his family for me. I'll be back first thing in the morning, soon as they release Shadow."

"Gino, I want to go with you." She hissed, putting on her puppy face.

"Come on baby, please don't look at me like that. Somebody has to stay here with his family, they don't know their way around DC baby."

"Kenny can stay with them baby."

"Baby you know as well as I do, that we can't keep that boy away from Blue longer than 2 minutes. So how is he going to watch somebody."

"Alright Gino, but baby please hurry up back." She begged.

"I promise," he kissed her, "come on let me drop you off cause I don't want to be on this road late tonight."

"I love you Gino."

"I love you too." As they pulled off.

CHAPTER 64

All the way back down Bad News, Gino thought about how surprised
Shadow would be when he found out about everything. "I know
that fat nigga will be hyped up." Gino thought to himself. "Especially
when I tell him I'm getting married. Then Tykisha's pregnant too, and I
know when he sees that crib he will go bananas, plus the 600, he won't
know what to do with himself. I ain't even going to tell him about the
deal until the party. Shit going to be crazy. Ooooh . . . weee!!!!"

When Gino arrived back in VA it was almost 9:00p.m. so he headed
straight to the house so he could call Tykisha before she got worried to
death. After calling Tykisha, Gino got something to eat and jumped
straight in the bed, until his phone rang. "Ring . . . Ring . . .", Gino
answered, "Hello."

"You have a collect call from Tide Water . . ."

Gino pressed the 0 cutting off the recording, "What's up Fat boy?!!"
Gino shouted into the phone.

"Ain't shit my nigga," Shadow replied. "Just waiting to see what
happens tomorrow, you feel me?"

"Man look, I told you don't worry about that." Gino reiterated.

"Have you spoke to the lawyer Gino?"

"No he's been ducking me, but I'm not concerned. You know how
things have a way of working there way out, feel me?"

"No doubt . . . no doubt", as they both snickered. "Aye Gino, you
know I hate these phones, but I just wanted to check and make sure shit
was aiight."

"You know I got that my nigga."

"Aye have you spoken to Grandma? I've been calling her all night and she hasn't been answering the phone."

"Nope . . . As a matter of fact I haven't spoken to her in some days now. She's cool though."

"Aiight then slim, I'll see her at court tomorrow."

"Fo'sho," Gino said knowing she wouldn't be there. "I'll see you in the morning champ."

"No doubt . . . see you!"

They both hung up as Gino hopped in the bed knowing that after tomorrow there would be no turning back. Smooth sailing from there on out.

All night, Gino couldn't sleep, he tossed and turned until finally he looked over at the clock. "Damn it's only 4:30 . . . shit! I can't even sleep." Gino mumbled to himself. "Fuck it I might as well get up and go down to the office and look over some paper work and stuff." Gino rose out the bed deciding to do just that.

Opening the door to the office, Gino noticed just how long it had been since he had been in the office. Tykisha had spiced things up with some decoration changes and everything. Gino took a seat behind his desk, when he noticed a copy of Kenny's album sitting on his desk. Gino smiled, while nodding his head. He picked up the CD and placed it in the stereo system and pushed play.

After a few tracks had played Gino realized that Kenny's CD was really good. Then track #5 came on, and unbeknown to Gino it was a song dedicated to V-Rock called, 'I MISS YOU!' Gino listened to the song as tears began to rush down his face. Gino really missed V-Rock, and the song reiterated that fact. When he finally got finished listening to the whole CD it was 7:00a.m. At this point, Gino decided it was time to get ready for court, so he turned everything off and went to take a shower.

Now out the shower and dressed, Gino made a few phone calls, then grabbed his truck keys and left heading down to the court house. Walking into the court house, Gino was strolling with that swagger, that aura about himself that lit up a room. He couldn't wait to show Shadow all the stuff that he done for him, and the Label. Walking down the hallway towards the courtroom, noticing Gino, Mr. Jordan approached him, "Good morning Mr. Ward!" Mr. Jordan spoke while shaking Gino's hand. "I guess you're feeling pretty good this morning, I might imagine, right?"

"Mr. Jordan you can't even imagine how happy I am right now."

"I know what you mean. Have you mentioned anything to Mr. Thompson yet, cause I haven't ?"

"Nope I didn't say anything . . . nothing at all. I wanted it to be a surprise."

"Good . . . . , well let's get in here and get him out of there." They shook hands and headed into the courtroom.

Inside the courtroom cases were being called left and right, finally they called Christopher Thompson vs. United States. Shadow was then ushered in from the holding cells in the back. Upon entering the courtroom, Shadow immediately surveyed the room to see who was all here in support of him. He spotted Gino instantly as he continued to glance around for everybody else. Unfortunately, no one else was there, which hurt him, and his expressions told it all.

Gino could tell Shadow was upset, but he never wavered, Gino just winked at Shadow, as Shadow took a seat beside his lawyer. The prosecutor then rose, stating that there would not be a trial in this case, due to the fact that they were unable to locate their star witness. Without the witness they knew that didn't have any chance of getting a conviction. So the judge dismissed the case and informed Shadow that he was free to go. Gino immediately stood up with a smirk on his face that let Shadow know that Gino knew all the time. Shadow then shook hands with is lawyer, Mr. Jordan, and then headed over in Gino's direction.

When they finally reached one another, they immediately embraced. "Thanks for everything my nigga." Shadow whispered into Gino's ear.

"Shit ain't nothing big homie. I've been waiting for this day to come, you know what I'm saying champ, as a matter of fact let's get up out of here, I hate these court rooms."

"Yeah you got a point there, I hate them too." They hugged one another again as they exited the court room and boarded the escalator on their way to the parking garage.

"Damn this garage packed with BMW's you see that Fat boy?" Gino was saying as they noticed quite a few BMW's on their way to Gino's truck.

Then as they were walking, out the clear blue Shadow just stopped, and stared at Gino intensively. Gino looked up at Fat boy, "What?! What's up?" Gino was trying to figure out what was going on with Shadow at this point.

"Man where the fuck is everybody at? That's crazy, you telling me you the only one who came to support your boy, that's what you're saying?"

"Nigga fuck that I'm here, that's all that matters."

"You know what," Shadow pointed at Gino, "you're right . . . . Oh hell nahhh!!!!" Shadow yelled out, "I know you ain't doing it like this, are you my nigga?" Shadow was referring to the new money green Range Rover Gino had just purchased.

"Nigga you know how we do, if we ain't going to do it big, then we ain't going to do it at all." Gino replied as he opened his door and then unlocked Shadow's side. "Ain't no sense in faking you know?" Reaching over to give Shadow dap.

"Oohhhh weee . . . nigga, you killing them with this joint right here." Shadow stated as he marveled at the TV's and extra shit Gino had installed.

"Nigga this ain't nothing, just watch and see." Gino proclaimed as he pulled off.

"Oh yeah Gino, I need you to do me a favor right fast too."

"What's that?"

"You got some money on you?"

"Why? What's up?" Gino asked while sliding the new Jill Scott CD into the CD player.

"I need to run some money pass my man people's house. I promised that nigga I'd handle that first thing soon as I got out."

"Look, you got the dude information? Cause I'll just have Tykisha to send him a money order first thing in the morning."

"Nah Gino, I gave him my word I'd do it on my way home. The nigga fucked up in there slim, and he need that ASAP."

Gino reached in his pocket and pulled out a knot of money, handing it to Shadow. "I think that's about $1,500."

"Shitt . . . that's good enough. Go around Langley Avenue right quick that's where his girl live at."

"Yeah aiight!"

"Turn right here", Shadow instructed Gino, "now pull right by that first building right there."

All the way around Langley Avenue Gino wanted to tell Shadow about the surprise, but he held his composure even thought it was killing him. Gino just wanted to get as far away from Virginia and fast as he could. "Hurry up nigga," Gino commented, "Don't get in there running your mouth. You know how you love to talk."

"Fuck you Gino." Shadow replied opening his door heading up towards the house.

Shadow knocked on the door and waited until a pretty chocolate sister appeared. Gino watched as they conversed for a second then disappeared inside.

Gino sat restlessly outside in the truck wishing Fat Ass would hurry up. Suddenly Gino saw these two guys standing beside the next building. Their faces seemed extremely familiar, but Gino and Shadow had been away from the streets for a minute now so Gino looked it off as just being nothing.

But the longer Gino sat there, the more suspicious he got of the two dudes standing out there, especially knowing that he wasn't strapped. Finally the door to the house opened as Shadow came out, waved goodbye and was headed back towards the truck. Gino immediately started the truck, and as Shadow got half way down the walk, Gino hollered. "Come on Fat Boy! Let's go!" Shadow just laughed, putting his middle finger up to Gino.

Suddenly Gino noticed that the two dudes that were standing by the building were now moving swiftly also, and in Shadow's direction. As Shadow reached the bottom step a voice called out, "Aye Shadow!"

Shadow pivoted to see who was calling him, "Yeah who that?"

"What's up?" Two dudes were speed walking towards him. He quickly turned and made a run for the truck when he saw their right hand reach underneath their sweatshirts.

Time seemed too slow to a crawl, it created the impression that the awaiting truck was a football field away. In his mind he was moving as slow as William 'The Refrigerator' Perry in the 40-yard dash.

"Shadow!!!!!!!!" Gino screamed.

Even his best friend's voice seemed to come to him in a slow prolonged scream. Two yards away Shadow thought, "I MADE IT". A smile spread across his face when he snatched the truck's door open.

"PLOW-PLOW-PLOW-PLOW-PLOW-PLOW-PLOW!" Gun shots rang out as hot, burning pain peppered Shadow's lower and upper back just before he jumped into the truck.

Gino screeched off, crashing into the parked cars blocking their escape, pushing them out of his way. He cleared enough space to maneuver and then speed off down the street. Out of his peripheral vision he saw Shadow faced down leaning forward on the dashboard. "Shadow!" His best friend didn't move nor respond. "Shadow!" G reached over and pulled Shadow back into the seat, "Shadow wake up man . . . wake up Shadow." He cried fearing the worst, "you're going to be alright. Stick with me big boy. We're going to the hospital." Tears began to roll down Gino face. "Just hold on."

Shadow's eyes fluttered open. "G," he called out barely louder than a whisper, "you my nigga. I got mad love for you slim."

"I got mad love for you too. Shadow man, I wanted to tell you. Everybody is in DC waiting on you. I didn't tell you because I wanted it to be a surprise. We just signed a record deal worth over two million dollars," he chuckled, nodding his head as tears continued to stream down his face. "Shadow we did it! We made it big boy!"

"Why—why?" bubbles formed in the blood coming from Shadow's mouth when he spoke, "Why ain't you tell me?"

"We wanted to surprise you. Come on Shadow stay up. Don't blank out on me. This can't end like this. No way, no how."

Shadow's eyes were blinking. He was fighting to keep them open. "Please Shadow!!" G shouted. "Hold on! Tricia is in DC too and she's carrying your baby. You got to hold on for her and your baby."

"I'm . . . . not going . . . . to make it." Shadow stated while blinking out.

"Don't talk like that! Come on man. We came too far." G stated.

During the midst of everything Gino hadn't noticed that he'd been shot as well. He was so concerned about Shadow and that was all that mattered. As Gino continued to drive, he noticed Shadow had blanked out again, so he reached over to pull Shadow back in his seat when he lost control of the truck. "Ohh . . . Shit!!!" Gino screamed noticing he had lost control. He tried vigorously to regain control, but none the less the truck smashed into a tree. A loud screeching sound, sounded off from the truck smacking the tree knocking Gino semi unconscious. As Gino lay there in the truck going in and out of consciousness, he flashed back to all the fun he and Shadow had together. All the partying they had done, he thought about the first time he met Shadow in jail as a light smile came across his face. Gino thought about how they never really got a chance to blow that music thing up. 'Damn it can't end like this', Gino thought to himself with blood trickling down from everywhere as he finally blanked all the way out.

Two weeks later Gino finally came out the coma he had been submerged in for the last two weeks. Tykisha was right there holding his hand looking into handsome face as he slowly tried to recapture all his senses. Gino's mom was standing on the other side of the bed, squeezing Kenny's hand in excitement, as she mumbled, "Thank you Lord . . . ."

Finally regaining enough of his senses tears started to form in Gino's eyes, as he squeezed Tykisha's hand.

"Hi baby", she whispered smiling from ear to ear.

"Tykisha . . .", he mumbled "where's Shadow baby?"

Tykisha glanced back at mom and Kenny, who's expressions were puzzled at how she should respond. Gino's eye's pierced at Tykisha as well as mom and Kenny. "Tykisha where's Shadow?" Gino repeated, voice sounding a little stronger now.

Tykisha rubbed his arm, "Gino just relax baby you just come out of a coma."

Gino must have mustered up all the strength he had left as he snatched away from Tykisha, catching her off guard, "Tykisha just answer the question please, where's Shadow?"

Tykisha rubbed Gino's forehead, "Baby . . . Baby", she stuttered, "I'm so sorry . . . Shadow didn't make it."

Silence surrounded the room as if the whole world had stopped for just them few minutes. Gino's eyes began to swell as a constant flow of tears came down his face. No one said a word they all just sat there consoling Gino. Sometimes life takes some hard turns, we just have to be able to withstand them and continue to fight. The game is no joke.

CHAPTER 65

Four months later.

"This is it baby. Everybody is waiting for us outside", Gino said to Tykisha as he took hold of her left hand and stared into her brown loving eyes. "your hands are sweating boo . . ." he teased.

Tykisha smiled and then kissed his lips. "I know," joy was in her voice. "I'm nervous . . . and excited," she rubbed the palm of his hand with her finger tips; it was wet, "your hands sweating too."

"Yeah cause I'm nervous and excited!" They both chuckled.

Chants from male voices in unison of "Gino" and chants from female voices in unison of "Tykisha" one after the other with the intensity of a high school pep rally poured through the closed church doors.

"You ready?" Gino asked smiling.

Tykisha looked back over her shoulder, focusing on the spot where she had stood before Reverend Macklin and God and said "I do" to the man she loved-her soul mate. A joyful tear sprung from her right eye. She wiped it away with the back of her hand that held her bouquet of flowers. "Yeah baby, I'm ready."

Together they pushed through the oak doors onto the top landing of the church steps, into the sunlight, into an eruption of applauses and smiles.

"That's right Gino!"

"You go girl!"

"You the man!"

"Tykisha, you look beautiful!"

The bridesmaids and female guests, and the best man and male guests were all gathered together, females on the left side, males on the right side of the lawn.

Passing cars blew their horns congratulations as Gino and Tykisha quickly descended the stairs making their way to the 600 Benz with "JUST MARRIED" placards taped to the doors, hood and trunk.

"Cover your eyes", Gino cheerfully yelled to Tykisha over the competing noise; loud cheers and blowing horns. "Rice is coming from everywhere." They were being pelted by rice from both sides.

The rain of rice stopped once they reached the sidewalk and stood next to their car. They turned to face their relatives and friends.

"We want to thank all of you," Gino said to the smiling crowd, "for coming to our wedding and for making today special."

"And we love y'all!" Tykisha happily added.

"We love y'all too!" a female guest hollered back. The crowd giggled and clapped.

"Fellas, I hope y'all ready for this." Gino turned to Tykisha, "Give me your leg boo."

Tykisha stuck her right leg out and hitched up her wedding dress a few inches. Whistling sounds came from lips as Gino reached under his wife's dress, up her leg, pulling the white laced garter-belt down and off.

Laughing, Gino advised, "Get your own wife!" The crowd broke in laughter.

"Men y'all know what this means for whoever catches this garter-belt." Gino couldn't help but to be hit with the fragrance of Chanel perfume as he held the garter-belt so the men could see it. That was his favorite perfume and Tykisha knew it. They made eye contact, he smiled and she winked knowingly.

A male guest yelled, "Don't throw that belt, you keep it!"

Gino ignored him and tossed it. The high arching white garter-belt glided through the air like a gracefully white dove. To the amusement of the women, all the young men scattered, bumping into each other, tripping over and pushing one another to get as far away from the descending garter-belt as possible.

"I got it!" Tykisha's uncle Henry, fifty-five years old, tight too small tuxedo on, and a jheri curl screamed, rushing to catch the unwanted surprise. The crowd of women laughed and laughed as Henry jumped up and down, holding the garter-belt. "Whoever catches that bouquet I wanna marry today." He broke out doing the robot dance, arms mechanically and stiffly moving up and down.

Tykisha screamed, "Ladies!!" She tossed the lovely bouquet of sweet smelling flowers in to the air. Unlike the men, the females rushed and shoved to get into position to catch the prize. Shoes were kicked off, hats were tossed and sunshades were thrown aside.

"Ouch!!"

"Watch out!"

"It's mine!!!"

When the dust cleared Shadow's fat aunt Missy had the bouquet. All six feet, two hundred ten pounds of country chocolate that she was, held the bouquet of flowers proudly. "We fittin' to get married today right?!!" she hollered over to Henry.

The crowd burst out with laughter. Men and women fell on their backs, holding their stomachs laughing.

"Beep . . . beep . . . beep!" A dodge caravan going south on North Capitol Street beeped it's horn as it passed the wedding congregation in front of A.M.E. Church.

"Beeeeeeeeep!" a Honda Accord traveling in the opposite direction blew it's horn.

Gino opened the passenger's side door of the 600 Benz. Tykisha blew kisses and waved bye as she climbed inside.

"Have fun!" Kenny yelled to Gino.

"Take care of each other!" Ma Grady and Ms. Debra hollered as Gino ran around the front of the car to the drivers' side.

"Don't expect to hear from us for at least two weeks." Gino said to the crowd of smiling faces.

"At least two weeks!" Tykisha repeated to the crowd.

As Gino was waving goodbye, he began to notice the smiling faces fade and grow into looks of horror and fright. It was like being in a Stephen King movie. One second you're looking at a happy, smiling, congratulating and accepting crowd. Then next they're scattering away from you because you transformed into a monster without knowing it.

People in the crowd were pointing at him, eyes were wide, hands clasped over mouths, and some fell to the ground.

A loud piercing scream of "Noooooo!!!!!!!!!!!" came from Kenny's mouth as he raced to reach Gino.

In that instant, Gino realized that the crowd wasn't pointing at him, but behind him. They didn't fall to the ground, they dove to the ground. Gino quickly spun around. A late model Mazda 626 had stopped in the middle of North Capitol Street directly behind Gino. Gino instantly spotted Mike Mike and Black leaning halfway out the passenger side windows, both holding what looked like semi-automatic handguns. "Nooooo!!!!!!!!!!!" Gino screamed out as shots rang out.

"POP . . . . POP . . . POP . . . POP . . . POP . . . POP . . . POP . . . POP . . . POP . . . POP . . . POP . . . POP . . . POP . . . POP . . . POP . . . POP!!!"

Gino and Kenny's bodies both jerked with the impact of the bullets. It looked as if they were having simultaneous seizures, as they both were pinned against the Benz.

The Mazda pulled off as a stunned crowd of wedding goers slowly rose from the ground and rushed to Gino and Kenny's side.

Unfortunately they both were dead. Another sad story of two young men trying to make it up out of these ghettos, but just can't. This game we play in the streets is real, and if you play by the sword, you'll die by the sword. The streets have its own separate rules and laws. Sometimes you're fortunate enough to make it out the game before it's too late, others aren't as fortunate. One rule that sticks out to me is rule #105 in street law: Some people forgive, but they never forget. Stay true to the streets. Death before dishonor!!!!

Printed in the United States
by Baker & Taylor Publisher Services